D1229983

A MEDIEVAL
STORYBOOK

a medieval storybook

selected and edited by Morris Bishop

drawings by Alison Mason Kingsbury

Cornell University Press/ ITHACA & LONDON

International Standard Book Number 0-8014-0562-9
Library of Congress Catalog Card Number 72-109334
Printed in the United States of America by Kingsport Press, Inc.

❧ Preface

MEDIEVAL MEN were great storytellers. In the long dark of winter evenings there was not much to do but tell stories and sing songs. At country markets professional narrators and ballad-singers profitably drew clusters of auditors, ready to pay with their farthings. The stories were mostly old and familiar, but each teller altered and localized his material to suit his hearers and his own taste. Thus a great body of oral literature existed. Most of it has disappeared, destroyed by printing and the enormous communications industry. Some remnants of the oral tradition are included in this volume.

At the same time a good number of original writers of fiction appeared, composing with conscious art. We can identify some of them, such as Marie de France, Huon Leroi, and of course Boccaccio and Chaucer. But most of them remain anonymous, and only by good luck have their works been preserved.

For this collection the compiler has picked examples of stories of various sorts. His essential requirement has been that the chosen tales should excel as *stories*, that they should progress from an initial state through altering incidents to a conclusion, logical but often unforeseen. While of course the tales illustrate medieval life and thought, the compiler's purpose has been to please the story-reader rather than the social or literary historian. The examples should stand alone as works of art, not illustrations of anything.

Most of the translations and modernizations were made in the

late nineteenth and early twentieth centuries. There flourished at that time a cult for the Middle Ages, in art and literature. Many medieval works were published or republished. The translators often assumed much freedom in their versions, preferring vividness to exactness. They were likely to adopt an archaizing style, sprinkling their contemporary language with *meseemeths* and *howbeits*. A later period of taste condemned this "Wardour-Street English." (Wardour Street was the London quarter of the imitation-antique-furniture trade.) Our times have chosen to render instead the medieval-colloquial into modern-colloquial. Well, one may argue on either side. The compiler likes a good imitation antique and Wardour-Street English, which looks and sounds medieval, while modern-colloquial does not. A medieval book, himthinketh, should be in medieval array bedight.

MORRIS BISHOP

Ithaca, New York
February 1970

Contents

I/ Romances of King Arthur's Court

The Story of Merlin 3
The Sword in the Stone, *by Sir Thomas Malory* 13
Launcelot, Elaine, and Guenever, *by Sir Thomas Malory* 23
Tristan's End 45

II/ Adventures and Escapades

The Story of Frithjof and Ingebjorg 65
Amleth's Revenge, *by Saxo Grammaticus* 92
A Knight Who Made a Bargain with a Merchant 103
A Story of beyond the Sea 109
The Cruelty of Francesco Orsini, *by Giovanni Fiorentino* 138
A Night in Naples, *by Giovanni Boccaccio* 142

III/ Lovers' Weal and Woe

The Dapple-Gray Palfrey, *by Huon Leroi* 157
The Lay of the Nightingale, *by Marie de France* 177
The Falcon, *by Giovanni Boccaccio* 181

IV/ Wonders and Prodigies

The Life of Saint Brandon, *by Jacobus de Voragine* 189
The Famous History of Friar Bacon 205

V/ Moral Tales

The Execrable Devices of Old Women 221

Of the Cunning of the Devil, and of the Secret Judgments of God 224

Of the Transgressions and Wounds of the Soul 227

Of Extreme Fear 230

The Marvelous Conversion of the Blessed Hildegund, Virgin, *by Caesarius of Heisterbach* 233

The Cleric Who Deflowered a Jewish Maiden, *by Caesarius of Heisterbach* 239

How the Novice Theobald Conquered His Pride, *by Caesarius of Heisterbach* 242

Friar Juniper 244

VI/ Merry Tales and Salty Fictions

Of the Churl Who Won Paradise 261

A Dean and a Magician, *by Juan Manuel* 264

King Ben Abit and Queen Romaquía, *by Juan Manuel* 270

A Profound Judgment 273

The Pear Tree 275

Fra Cipolla, *by Giovanni Boccaccio* 277

A Father's Wise Counsel, *by Franco Sacchetti* 286

The Rustic Ambassadors, *by Franco Sacchetti* 290

The Noble Crest, *by Franco Sacchetti* 294

Sacchetti and the Astrologer, *by Franco Sacchetti* 297

The Blind Man of Orvieto, *by Franco Sacchetti* 300

The Reeve's Tale, *by Geoffrey Chaucer* 305

»1«

ROMANCES OF
KING ARTHUR'S COURT

✥ The Story of Merlin

The story of Merlin goes back at least to the twelfth century. This version is a condensation and translation of a fifteenth-century French *Roman de Merlin*. It appears in Sir George W. Cox and Eustace Hinton Jones, *Popular Romances of the Middle Ages* (New York: Henry Holt, 1880).

WHEN CONSTAUNCE, King of Britain, who had freed the people from their enemies round about, was dead, his eldest son, Moyne the Monk, was taken from the cloister at Winchester to sit upon the throne. And seeing him to be an unwarlike prince, Angys the Dane gathered together an army of Danes and Saxons and sailed for Britain with many high-banked ships full of kings and earls. Then king Moyne looked that Sir Fortager, which was his father's steward and captain of the host, should lead the Britons out to fight against Angys. But Fortager feigned sickness and would not go out to battle. Wherefore King Moyne went himself, and being unskilled in fight, he was defeated with great slaughter; so that Angys took many British towns and castles, and fortified himself therein. Now twelve British kings which fought under King Moyne being much displeased at his losing this battle, said, "If Fortager had been our leader this had not been so"; and again, "As for this Moyne, a gabbling monk, he is no king for us"; so these went to Fortager to ask his counsel; but Fortager replied, "Seek counsel of your king; it is time enough to ask for mine when Moyne is king no longer." Wherefore the twelve went straight to King Moyne and slew him as he sat at meat within his hall. Then they returned and greeted Fortager and made him king. Yet there were many who loved still the race of old King Constaunce, and some faithful barons took the two young princes, brothers of King Moyne, Aurilisbrosias and Uther-Pendragon, and sent them into Brittany lest Fortager should slay them also.

Now Fortager gathered together all the British kings, and fought a great battle against Angys, and drave him to his ships, and would have killed him on the strand; but Angys sued for peace, and made a treaty with King Fortager to make war on him no more. So Angys sailed away with all the remnant of his host, and Fortager marched home in triumph. And while he made a feast there came to him the twelve kings which slew King Moyne, seeking reward, saying, "O King Fortager, behold we have placed thee on high and made thee king; wherefore give us now our meed." Fortager answered, "Being king, in sooth I will show how kings do punish treason": and he had wild horses brought and tare the traitors limb from limb upon his castle pavement and nailed their mangled bodies on his walls.

Howbeit Fortager thereby kindled against himself the wrath of all who had helped him to the throne, and these rose up and joined with them which spake of bringing back Aurilisbrosias and Uther-Pendragon, and very few held still to Fortager; so he was hunted through his kingdom, and ofttimes beaten sore, barely escaping with his life. Then he bethought to send to Angys into Denmark, and promised half the kingdom if he would come and help him in this strait. And Angys came over again with many men and ships, and helped Fortager to fight against the Britons till the people were subdued, kept down by force of sword and spear. So the war ceased, but peace never came. Fortager went in daily fear of his life from the Britons whom he had betrayed; nor could he now rid himself of Angys whom he feared almost as much lest with his great army he should seize the whole kingdom; and yet again he feared lest the Normans should come over and fight for Aurilisbrosias and Uther-Pendragon to bring them back to the throne of their father Constaunce.

Then Fortager thought with himself to build a huge castle made of well-hewn stone and timber,—a mighty fortress with a lofty tower and battlements, deep ditch and heavy drawbridge, —the like for strength and bigness the world had never seen: and he would build it on the bleak waste of Salisbury Plain, and so dwell safe among his enemies.

Three thousand men began the work at break of day, hewers of wood and carpenters and masons and such as wrought in carven stone. So they began to dig out the foundations and lay the mighty blocks of stone well clamped with iron bonds; and when night came they left the ponderous wall reared up breast high. Next morning, coming to their task, they marvelled much to find the great stones scattered up and down upon the ground, and all their work destroyed. They wrought another day and built the wall up as before, digging the foundations deeper still, and taking greater care to mix the mortar well and fit each stone and clamp it tight. But in the night the wall was overthrown, by what power none could tell.

So Fortager called ten wise and learned clerks and shut them in a chamber open to the sky, to read the stars and find why no man might build up this castle wall. And after nine days the wise men came to the king and said, "Sir, we have seen signs in the firmament how an elf-child has been born in Britain, knowing things past and things to come. Find the child and slay him on the plain, and mix the mortar with his blood; so shall the wall stand fast." Then Fortager sent men to journey three and three into all parts of the country, and seek the child. After wandering many days and weeks, one of these parties of messengers lighted on a town, where, in the market-place, some children at play were quarrelling in their game. "Thou black elf's son," the urchins said to one young playmate five years old, "we will not play with thee, for what thou art we cannot tell." The messengers hearing these words thought this must surely be the child they sought, but Merlin (for it was he) did not leave them long in doubt. "Welcome, O messengers," said he—"behold him whom you seek. Yet my blood will never make Fortager's castle wall stand firm for all the wise men say—blind fools, who grope among the stars for secrets and blunder past the portents at their feet." Hearing this the men wondered greatly, saying, "How wottest thou of our errand or of the king's intent?" Merlin answered, "Pictures pass before my mind of all the things that be and shall be. I will go with you to Fortager and show what

hinders building up his fortress on the plain." So he set out with the messengers, they on their horses, he upon a palfrey.

Now as they journeyed through a town they saw a man buy strong new shoes and clout leather wherewith to mend them when worn out: and Merlin laughed. "Why do you laugh?" the messengers asked. He answered, "Because the man will never wear the shoes." And sure enough he fell dead at his wicket gate. Next day they met a bier whereon was a child being carried to burial, and a priest sang at the head, and an old man followed behind and wept; and Merlin laughed again, for he said, "Did these but know whose son lies there, the priest would weep and the man would sing":—and this they found true, for the lad was not the mourner's son but the priest's. And on the third day as they rode, Merlin laughed again, and being asked why, he answered, "King Fortager in his palace is jealous of his wife's good-looking chamberlain and threatens to take his life; forsooth he wots not that this good-looking wight is but a woman in disguise." Then when they came to the palace they found it even as the child had said; and Merlin revealed the truth to the king, so the chamberlain was spared. Fortager marvelled much at the wisdom of this child of five years old, and talked with him about the mystery of his castle wall and why it was destroyed each night; and Merlin said, "The fiends deceived your wise men, showing false signs among the stars; for all my kindred in the air are wroth with me because I am baptized into Christendom, and so they fain would trick me out of life. They care not for your castle wall, but only for my death. But send men now to dig a yard beneath the wall's foundation; they shall find a swift running water, and, underneath, two mighty stones which keep two dragons down. Every night at sundown these two dragons wake and do battle underground, so that the earth quakes and trembles and the wall is shaken down."

Then straightway Fortager set his men to dig and find if this was true. And soon they came to the stream, which ran both deep and furiously; so they made a channel lined with masonry and led the water off by another way. And in the river bed were two

heavy slabs of stone which it took many men to rear up: and there beneath them lay the dragons. One was red as flame, with eyes that sparkled like the glint from off a brazen helm, his body a rood long and his tail very great and supple. The other one, milk-white and stern of look, had two fierce grisly heads which darted fire white as levin* forks. And as the dragons waked from slumber, all the men fled away quickly in a panic, save only Merlin. Then rising from their dens the two monsters closed in such a deadly combat that the air was full of the fire which they belched forth from their throats; and the very clouds lightened to the thunder of the battle, and the earth shook. Thus they fought all that long summer night with fang and claw and tail; they fell and rose again and rose and fell, nor flagged neither till the day dawned. Then the red dragon drave the white into a valley where for a little space he stood at bay, until recovering breath he made a fierce onset, hunting back the red dragon into the plain again, where fixing him by the gullet, he tare him down and with his white hot flames scorched the red dragon to a heap of ashes on the heath. Then the white dragon flew away through the air.

Now after this, Merlin grew in great favour with King Fortager, and was his counsellor in all things that he undertook. Moreover when the masons next began to build, the wall no longer fell down as before. So in due time they built the fortress on the plain, a mighty castle high and strong, of timber and of stone, ramparted about on every hand, a fair white castle the like whereof the world had never seen.

When it was done, men came to Fortager and prayed him ask of Merlin what the battle of the dragons should mean. So Fortager called Merlin, asking whether this strife betokened aught which should hereafter come to pass. But Merlin held his peace. Then waxing wroth King Fortager threatened to slay him. Merlin smiled in scorn, saying, "You will never see my death-day; nay, if you bound me fast and drew your sword to strike, you would only fight with air." Then Fortager entreated him, and

* Levin: lightning.—Ed.

sware upon the holy books that no harm should come to him, whatever the interpretation of the mystery might be. Then said Merlin, "Hearken to the reading of the portent. The red dragon so strong to fight betokens Fortager and all the power he has gained through killing Moyne the king; the white dragon with two heads, the rightful heirs Aurilisbrosias and Uther-Pendragon, whose kingdom you withhold from them. And as the white dragon, hunted to the valley, there regained his strength and drove the red dragon back to the plain, it means that these heirs whom you have driven to Brittany have there found help and succour, and even now sail hitherward with many thousand men, who will come and hunt you through the land till you are driven to your fortress on the plain, shut up therein, and with your wife and child there burnt to ashes. This is the reading of the portent."

Then Fortager had great sadness of heart, and prayed Merlin to tell him how to avoid the fate he had foretold, or at least how he might save his own life. But Merlin only answered sternly, "What will be, will be." And Fortager's anger being kindled, he started up and put forth his hand to seize the seer, but Merlin vanished suddenly from his sight. And while they sought him still within the palace, Merlin was far away in the cell of Blaise the holy hermit. There he remained long time, and wrote a book of prophecies of all the things to happen yet in Britain.

But as for Fortager it all fell out as Merlin had foretold, for Uther-Pendragon with his brother Aurilisbrosias landed with an army and marched to Winchester, and the citizens seeing the old banner of their own British kings, overpowered the Danish garrison and threw the gates wide open for the sons of King Constaunce. And when Fortager and Angys came against them with a host of Danes and Britons, the Britons of their army would not fight against their brethren, but rose into revolt. So Aurilisbrosias and Uther-Pendragon won an easy victory and pursued Fortager as far as Salisbury Plain, where he took refuge in the castle, and the Britons threw wildfire upon the walls and burned him there, together with his wife and child, and levelled the fortress with the ground.

But Angys fled into a citadel whither Uther-Pendragon followed, besieging him therein, but he could not take the place since it was strongly bulwarked on a hill. Then hearing some barons that had been with Fortager speak oftentimes of Merlin and his exceeding subtlety, Uther-Pendragon sent out men to search for him. And on a day these messengers being at dinner, an old beggar-man with a long white beard and ragged shoes, and a staff within his hand, came in and asked for alms. They jeered at him, bidding him begone. "Wise messengers are ye," the old man said, "that seek child Merlin, for he hath often met you by the road to-day, and yet you knew him not. Go home to Uther-Pendragon and say that Merlin waits him in the wood hard by; for truly ye will never find him." And as he spake these words the old man vanished suddenly. Scarce knowing if it were a dream, the messengers returned to Uther-Pendragon, who, hearing this, left Aurilisbrosias to maintain the siege while he went to the wood to seek for Merlin. And first a swineherd met him, next a chapman with his pack, each of whom spake of Merlin; and last there came a comely swain who bade him still wait on, since Merlin would be sure to keep the tryst, but he had first some work to do. So the prince waited until far into the night and then he saw the swain again, who greeted him, saying, "I am Merlin; I will go with you to the camp." When they got there Aurilisbrosias said, "Brother, there came a swain in the night and waked me, saying, 'Behold Angys is come out from his citadel and has stolen past your sentinels, seeking to take your life.' Then I leapt up, and seeing Angys at the tent door I fell on him and slew him easily, for while the swain stood by I seemed to have the strength of ten, and my sword cut through the brass and iron mail as though they were naught. As for the swain, I missed him when the fight was done." Uther-Pendragon answered, "Brother, the swain was Merlin, who is here with me." Then was Aurilisbrosias very glad, and both the princes thanked Merlin for his help. In the morning when they knew that their leader had been slain, the Danes and Saxons yielded up the citadel, asking only for their lives and for leave to sail away in peace to their own country. Thus the land

was free again, and all the people took the elder of the brothers, Uther-Pendragon, and made him king in Winchester, and held a seven nights' feast of coronation.

After this, Merlin told the brothers that one of them would fall in a battle with a very great host of Northmen that would come to avenge the death of Angys, yet would he not say which of them it should be. And in a little time the sea about the Bristol Channel was blackened with a multitude of crested ships, and Danes and Saxons swarmed upon the beach in numbers like the sand. Then Merlin divided the Britons into two companies, so that with one Uther-Pendragon might give battle from the front and draw them inland, whilst Aurilisbrosias with the other stole round between the Northmen and the sea and fought them in the rear. The fight was fierce and bloody before the Britons drove their foes to their ships. Of thirty thousand Danes and Saxons five thousand only went back, and Aurilisbrosias lay dead upon the sea-beach and with him fourteen thousand Britons, while on the battle-ground for a space three miles by two no man might walk without stepping upon the dead. Then Merlin made a tomb for Aurilisbrosias with huge stones which he brought from Ireland through the air by magic, and all the people mourned for him.*

For seven years after this Uther-Pendragon reigned and prospered, and conquered lands in Normandy and Brittany and Gaul, and Merlin counselled him in all things which he did. Merlin also made for him the famed Round Table whereat the best and bravest knights might sit in equal seat. One place alone was kept vacant, wherein none might sit till he came who should fulfil the marvel of the Holy Grail.

And all came to pass as the spirit of Merlin had foreseen, for, when Uther-Pendragon was dead, his son Arthur was chosen king when he had drawn the great sword which was fixed into the stone; and Merlin aided Arthur against all his enemies, and saved him from many perils which threatened his life. But at

* In other versions these are identified with the stones of Stonehenge.

length the time drew nigh when Merlin should no more sojourn among men.

And so it came to pass that Merlin made a wondrous tomb in the Church of St Stephen at Camelot over twelve kings which Arthur slew. He made twelve images of copper bronze overlaid with gold, and a figure of King Arthur raised above with his sword drawn in his hand. Each image bare a waxen taper which burned day and night. And Merlin told the king, "By these you shall be shown when I pass from the world of living men. That day the tapers will go out and never after be re-kindled. For you there remains a life of glory; the Sangreal* shall be achieved, and you shall pass almost within its presence, yet not see it with your eyes, since they have looked too much upon the blood and dust of war to read the marvel of that holy thing. Fightings will never cease in your day, but you shall gain the victory and be king of Christendom, and at last die nobly in battle as a king should die. For me, alas! I must be prisoned in the air alive, and wait through ages for the Judge, awake through weary years, whilst others sleep beneath the quiet ground."

Then Arthur counselled him, since he knew his fate, to guard himself against it by his subtile arts. But the seer answered, "That which shall be, is: unchangeable as that which was."

Now the spirits of the air, being very wroth at the discomfiture of all their plans, sought means, all through his life, to entrap Merlin, and snatch him from the world, but he being wistful of their schemes defeated them; nor could they in any wise have power on him until his work was done. But as he waxed in years he was beguiled by a beautiful damsel of the Lake, called Niniame, so that he fell into a dotage for love of her and would follow her whithersoever she went. But Niniame being passing weary of his love, made sport of him, and did but endure him for the wonders which he showed her. And it befell that one day as they sat together in a wood at Broceliande, she entreated Merlin

* Sangreal: the Holy Grail, Christ's communion cup.

to teach her a certain powerful spell, whereby a man might be shut up for ever in a narrow space about the earth, walled in by air, invisible to all for evermore. And this she begged with tears and promised him her love if he would show it her. And when she wearied him with asking, and beguiled him with many sweet words, he showed her all she asked. Then Niniame lulled him to sleep upon her lap, and rising softly, wrought the spell in the air; and so shut Merlin up for ever in a blackthorn tree within the lonesome wood at Broceliande, where his spirit, tangled in a hopeless maze among the weird black twigs, the more inweaves itself in trying to get free.

🦢 The Sword in the Stone
by Sir Thomas Malory

The rich cluster of stories of King Arthur and his knights have ever delighted the western world and in some part have imposed on us their ideals of gallantry and courtesy. Best known and best beloved of the English versions is the *Morte d'Arthur* of Sir Thomas Malory. Our selections are from the modernization by Sir Edmund Strachey, 1868, revised with some emendations by A. W. Pollard (London: Macmillan, 1900).

IT BEFELL in the days of Uther Pendragon, when he was king of all England and so reigned, that there was a mighty duke in Cornwall that held war against him long time. And the duke was named the duke of Tintagil. And so by means King Uther sent for this duke, charging him to bring his wife with him, for she was called a fair lady, and a passing wise, and her name was called Igraine. So when the duke and his wife were come unto the king, by the means of great lords they were accorded both. The king liked and loved this lady well, and he made them great cheer out of measure, and desired to have lain with her. But she was a passing good woman, and would not assent unto the king. And then she told the duke her husband, and said, I suppose that we were sent for that I should be bedded, wherefore, husband, I counsel you that we depart from hence suddenly, that we may ride all night to our own castle. And in like wise as she said so they departed, that neither the king nor none of his council were ware of their departing. All so soon as King Uther knew of their departing so suddenly, he was wonderly wroth.

Then he called to him his privy council, and told them of the sudden departing of the duke and his wife. Then they advised the king to send for the duke and his wife by a great charge; and if he

will not come at your summons, then may ye do your best, then have ye cause to make mighty war upon him. So that was done, and the messengers had their answers; and that was this shortly, that neither he nor his wife would not come at him.

Then was the king wonderly wroth. And then the king sent him plain word again, and bade him be ready and stuff him and garnish him, for within forty days he would fetch him out of the biggest castle that he hath.

When the duke had this warning, anon he went and furnished and garnished two strong castles of his, of the which the one hight Tintagil, and the other castle hight Terrabil. So his wife Dame Igraine he put in the castle of Tintagil, and himself he put in the castle of Terrabil, the which had many issues and posterns out. Then in all haste came Uther with a great host, and laid a siege about the castle of Terrabil. And there he pight many pavilions,* and there was great war made on both parties, and much people slain. Then for pure anger and for great love of fair Igraine the king Uther fell sick. So came to the King Uther Sir Ulfius, a noble knight, and asked the king why he was sick. I shall tell thee, said the king, I am sick for anger and for love of fair Igraine, that I may not be whole. Well, my lord, said Sir Ulfius, I shall seek Merlin, and he shall do you remedy, that your heart shall be pleased. So Ulfius departed, and by adventure he met Merlin in a beggar's array, and there Merlin asked Ulfius whom he sought. And he said he had little ado to tell him. Well, said Merlin, I know whom thou seekest, for thou seekest Merlin; therefore seek no farther, for I am he; and if King Uther will well reward me, and be sworn unto me to fulfill my desire, that shall be his honour and profit more than mine; for I shall cause him to have all his desire. All this will I undertake, said Ulfius, that there shall be nothing reasonable but thou shalt have thy desire. Well, said Merlin, he shall have his intent and desire. And therefore, said Merlin, ride on your way, for I will not be long behind.

* Pight many pavilions: pitched many tents, or shelters.—Ed.

Then Ulfius was glad, and rode on more than a pace till that he came to King Uther Pendragon, and told him he had met with Merlin. Where is he? said the king. Sir, said Ulfius, he will not dwell long. Therewithal Ulfius was ware where Merlin stood at the porch of the pavilion's door. And then Merlin was bound to come to the king. When King Uther saw him, he said he was welcome. Sir, said Merlin, I know all your heart every deal; so ye will be sworn unto me as ye be a true king anointed, to fulfill my desire, ye shall have your desire. Then the king was sworn upon the Four Evangelists. Sir, said Merlin, this is my desire: the first night that ye shall lie by Igraine ye shall get a child on her, and when that is born, that it shall be delivered to me for to nourish there as I will have it; for it shall be your worship, and the child's avail, as mickle as the child is worth. I will well, said the king, as thou wilt have it. Now make you ready, said Merlin, this night ye shall lie with Igraine in the castle of Tintagil; and ye shall be like the duke her husband, Ulfius shall be like Sir Brastias, a knight of the duke's, and I will be like a knight that hight Sir Jordanus, a knight of the duke's. But wait ye make not many questions with her nor her men, but say ye are diseased, and so hie you to bed, and rise not on the morn till I come to you, for the castle of Tintagil is but ten miles hence; so this was done as they devised. But the duke of Tintagil espied how the king rode from the siege of Terrabil, and therefore that night he issued out of the castle at a postern for to have distressed the king's host. And so, through his own issue, the duke himself was slain or ever the king came at the castle of Tintagil.

So after the death of the duke, King Uther lay with Igraine more than three hours after his death, and begat on her that night Arthur, and on day came Merlin to the king, and bade him make him ready, and so he kissed the lady Igraine and departed in all haste. But when the lady heard tell of the duke her husband, and by all record he was dead or ever King Uther came to her, then

she marvelled who that might be that lay with her in likeness of her lord; so she mourned privily and held her peace. Then all the barons by one assent prayed the king of accord betwixt the lady Igraine and him; the king gave them leave, for fain would he have been accorded with her. So the king put all the trust in Ulfius to entreat between them, so by the entreaty at the last the king and she met together. Now will we do well, said Ulfius, our king is a lusty knight and wifeless, and my lady Igraine is a passing fair lady; it were great joy unto us all, an it might please the king to make her his queen. Unto that they all well accorded and moved it to the king. And anon, like a lusty knight, he assented thereto with good will, and so in all haste they were married in a morning with great mirth and joy.

And King Lot of Lothian and of Orkney then wedded Margawse that was Gawaine's mother, and King Nentres of the land of Garlot wedded Elaine. All this was done at the request of King Uther. And the third sister Morgan le Fay was put to school in a nunnery, and there she learned so much that she was a great clerk of necromancy. And after she was wedded to King Uriens of the land of Gore, that was Sir Ewaine le Blanchemain's father.

Then Queen Igraine waxed daily greater and greater, so it befell after within half a year, as King Uther lay by his queen, he asked her, by the faith she owed to him, whose was the child within her body; then was she sore abashed to give answer. Dismay you not, said the king, but tell me the truth, and I shall love you the better, by the faith of my body. Sir, said she, I shall tell you the truth. The same night that my lord was dead, the hour of his death, as his knights record, there came into my castle of Tintagil a man like my lord in speech and in countenance, and two knights with him in likeness of his two knights Brastias and Jordanus, and so I went unto bed with him as I ought to do with my lord, and the same night, as I shall answer unto God, this child was begotten upon me. That is truth, said the king, as ye say; for it was I myself that came in the likeness, and therefore

dismay you not, for I am father of the child; and there he told her all the cause, how it was by Merlin's counsel. Then the queen made great joy when she knew who was the father of her child.

Soon came Merlin unto the king, and said, Sir, ye must purvey you for the nourishing of your child. As thou wilt, said the king, be it. Well, said Merlin, I know a lord of yours in this land, that is a passing true man and a faithful, and he shall have the nourishing of your child, and his name is Sir Ector, and he is a lord of fair livelihood in many parts in England and Wales; and this lord, Sir Ector, let him be sent for, for to come and speak with you, and desire him yourself, as he loveth you, that he will put his own child to nourishing to another woman, and that his wife nourish yours. And when the child is born let it be delivered to me at yonder privy postern unchristened. So like as Merlin devised it was done. And when Sir Ector was come he made fiaunce* to the king for to nourish the child like as the king desired; and there the king granted Sir Ector great rewards. Then when the lady was delivered, the king commanded two knights and two ladies to take the child, bound in a cloth of gold, and that ye deliver him to what poor man ye meet at the postern gate of the castle. So the child was delivered unto Merlin, and so he bare it forth unto Sir Ector, and made an holy man to christen him, and named him Arthur; and so Sir Ector's wife nourished him with her own pap.

Then within two years King Uther fell sick of a great malady. And in the meanwhile his enemies usurped upon him, and did a great battle upon his men, and slew many of his people. Sir, said Merlin, ye may not lie so as ye do, for ye must to the field though ye ride on an horse-litter: for ye shall never have the better of your enemies but if your person be there, and then shall ye have the victory. So it was done as Merlin had devised, and they carried the king forth in an horse-litter with a great host towards his enemies. And at St. Albans there met with the king a great

* Fiaunce: warrant.—Ed.

host of the North. And that day Sir Ulfius and Sir Brastias did great deeds of arms, and King Uther's men overcame the Northern battle and slew many people, and put the remnant to flight. And then the king returned unto London, and made great joy of his victory. And then he fell passing sore sick, so that three days and three nights he was speechless: wherefore all the barons made great sorrow, and asked Merlin what counsel were best. There is none other remedy, said Merlin, but God will have his will. But look ye all barons be before King Uther to-morn, and God and I shall make him to speak. So on the morn all the barons with Merlin came to-fore the king; then Merlin said aloud unto King Uther, Sir, shall your son Arthur be king after your days, of this realm with all the appurtenance? Then Uther Pendragon turned him, and said in hearing of them all, I give him God's blessing and mine, and bid him pray for my soul, and righteously and worshipfully that he claim the crown, upon forfeiture of my blessing; and therewith he yielded up the ghost, and then was he interred as longed* to a king. Wherefore the queen, fair Igraine, made great sorrow, and all the barons.

🌿

Then stood the realm in great jeopardy long while, for every lord that was mighty of men made him strong, and many weened to have been king. Then Merlin went to the Archbishop of Canterbury, and counselled him for to send for all the lords of the realm, and all the gentlemen of arms, that they should to London come by Christmas, upon pain of cursing; and for this cause, that Jesus, that was born on that night, that he would of his great mercy show some miracle, as he was come to be king of mankind, for to show some miracle who should be rightwise king of this realm. So the Archbishop, by the advice of Merlin, sent for all the lords and gentlemen of arms that they should come by Christmas even unto London. And many of them made them clean of their life, that their prayer might be the more acceptable

* Longed: belonged, was fitting.—Ed.

unto God. So in the greatest church of London, whether it were Paul's or not the French book maketh no mention, all the estates were long or* day in the church for to pray. And when matins and the first mass was done, there was seen in the churchyard, against the high altar, a great stone four square, like unto a marble stone; and in midst thereof was like an anvil of steel a foot on high, and therein stuck a fair sword naked by the point, and letters there were written in gold about the sword that said thus: —Whoso pulleth out this sword of this stone and anvil, is rightwise king born of all England. Then the people marvelled, and told it to the Archbishop. I command, said the Archbishop, that ye keep you within your church and pray unto God still, that no man touch the sword till the high mass be all done. So when all masses were done all the lords went to behold the stone and the sword. And when they saw the scripture some assayed, such as would have been king. But none might stir the sword nor move it. He is not here, said the Archbishop, that shall achieve the sword, but doubt not God will make him known. But this is my counsel, said the Archbishop, that we let purvey ten knights, men of good fame, and they to keep this sword. So it was ordained, and then there was made a cry, that every man should assay that would, for to win the sword. And upon New Year's Day the barons let make a jousts and a tournament, that all knights that would joust or tourney there might play, and all this was ordained for to keep the lords together and the commons, for the Archbishop trusted that God would make him known that should win the sword.

So upon New Year's Day, when the service was done, the barons rode unto the field, some to joust and some to tourney, and so it happened that Sir Ector, that had great livelihood about London, rode unto the jousts, and with him rode Sir Kay his son, and young Arthur that was his nourished brother; and Sir Kay was made knight at All Hallowmass afore. So as they rode to the jousts-ward, Sir Kay lost his sword, for he had left it at his

* Or: ere.—Ed.

father's lodging, and so he prayed young Arthur for to ride for his sword. I will well, said Arthur, and rode fast after the sword, and when he came home, the lady and all were out to see the jousting. Then was Arthur wroth, and said to himself, I will ride to the churchyard, and take the sword with me that sticketh in the stone, for my brother Sir Kay shall not be without a sword this day. So when he came to the churchyard, Sir Arthur alighted and tied his horse to the stile, and so he went to the tent, and found no knights there, for they were at the jousting. And so he handled the sword by the handles, and lightly and fiercely pulled it out of the stone, and took his horse and rode his way until he came to his brother Sir Kay, and delivered him the sword. And as soon as Sir Kay saw the sword, he wist well it was the sword of the stone, and so he rode to his father Sir Ector, and said: Sir, lo here is the sword of the stone, wherefore I must be king of this land. When Sir Ector beheld the sword, he returned again and came to the church, and there they alighted all three, and went into the church. And anon he made Sir Kay swear upon a book how he came to that sword. Sir, said Sir Kay, by my brother Arthur, for he brought it to me. How gat ye this sword? said Sir Ector to Arthur. Sir, I will tell you. When I came home for my brother's sword, I found nobody at home to deliver me his sword; and so I thought my brother Sir Kay should not be swordless, and so I came hither eagerly and pulled it out of the stone without any pain. Found ye any knights about this sword? said Sir Ector. Nay, said Arthur. Now, said Sir Ector to Arthur, I understand ye must be king of this land. Wherefore I, said Arthur, and for what cause? Sir, said Ector, for God will have it so; for there should never man have drawn out this sword, but he that shall be rightwise king of this land. Now let me see whether ye can put the sword there as it was, and pull it out again. That is no mastery, said Arthur, and so he put it in the stone; where-withal Sir Ector assayed to pull out the sword and failed.

☙

Now assay, said Sir Ector unto Sir Kay. And anon he pulled at the sword with all his might; but it would not be. Now shall ye

assay, said Sir Ector to Arthur. I will well, said Arthur, and pulled it out easily. And therewithal Sir Ector knelt down to the earth, and Sir Kay. Alas, said Arthur, my own dear father and brother, why kneel ye to me? Nay, nay, my lord Arthur, it is not so; I was never your father nor of your blood, but I wot well ye are of an higher blood than I weened ye were. And then Sir Ector told him all, how he was betaken him for to nourish him, and by whose commandment, and by Merlin's deliverance.

Then Arthur made great dole when he understood that Sir Ector was not his father. Sir, said Ector unto Arthur, will ye be my good and gracious lord when ye are king? Else were I to blame, said Arthur, for ye are the man in the world that I am most beholden to, and my good lady and mother your wife, that as well as her own hath fostered me and kept. And if ever it be God's will that I be king as ye say, ye shall desire of me what I may do, and I shall not fail you; God forbid I should fail you. Sir, said Sir Ector, I will ask no more of you, but that ye will make my son, your foster brother, Sir Kay, seneschal of all your lands. That shall be done, said Arthur, and more, by the faith of my body, that never man shall have that office but he, while he and I live. Therewithal they went unto the Archbishop, and told him how the sword was achieved, and by whom; and on Twelfth-day all the barons came thither, and to assay to take the sword, who that would assay. But there afore them all, there might none take it out but Arthur; wherefore there were many lords wroth, and said it was great shame unto them all and the realm, to be over-governed with a boy of no high blood born. And so they fell out at that time that it was put off till Candlemas, and then all the barons should meet there again; but always the ten knights were ordained to watch the sword day and night, and so they set a pavilion over the stone and the sword, and five always watched. So at Candlemas many more great lords came thither for to have won the sword, but there might none prevail. And right as Arthur did at Christmas, he did at Candlemas, and pulled out the sword easily, whereof the barons were sore aggrieved and put it off in delay till the high feast of Easter. And as Arthur sped before, so did he at Easter; yet there were some of the great lords

had indignation that Arthur should be king, and put it off in a delay till the feast of Pentecost.

Then the Archbishop of Canterbury by Merlin's providence let purvey then of the best knights that they might get, and such knights as Uther Pendragon loved best and most trusted in his days. And such knights were put about Arthur as Sir Baudwin of Britain, Sir Kay, Sir Ulfius, Sir Brastias. All these, with many other, were always about Arthur, day and night, till the feast of Pentecost.

And at the feast of Pentecost all manner of men assayed to pull at the sword that would assay; but none might prevail but Arthur, and pulled it out afore all the lords and commons that were there, wherefore all the commons cried at once, We will have Arthur unto our king, we will put him no more in delay, for we all see that it is God's will that he shall be our king, and who that holdeth against it, we will slay him. And therewithal they kneeled at once, both rich and poor, and cried Arthur mercy because they had delayed him so long, and Arthur forgave them, and took the sword between both his hands, and offered it upon the altar where the Archbishop was, and so was he made knight of the best man that was there. And so anon was the coronation made. And there was he sworn unto his lords and the commons for to be a true king, to stand with true justice from thenceforth the days of his life. . . .

❧ Launcelot, Elaine, and Guenever
by Sir Thomas Malory

> Like the previous story (*The Sword in the Stone*) this is
> an episode, somewhat modernized, from Malory's *Morte
> d'Arthur*.

NOW LEAVE we Sir Tristram de Liones, and speak we of
Sir Launcelot du Lake, and of Sir Galahad, Sir Launcelot's
son, how he was gotten, and in what manner, as the book of
French rehearseth. Afore the time that Sir Galahad was gotten or
born, there came in an hermit unto King Arthur upon Whitsun-
day, as the knights sat at the Table Round. And when the hermit
saw the Siege* Perilous, he asked the king and all the knights why
that siege was void. Sir Arthur and all the knights answered:
There shall never none sit in that siege but one, but if he be
destroyed. Then said the hermit: Wot ye what is he? Nay, said
Arthur and all the knights, we wot not who is he that shall sit
therein. Then wot I, said the hermit, for he that shall sit there is
unborn and ungotten, and this same year he shall be gotten that
shall sit there in that Siege Perilous, and he shall win the Sangreal.
When this hermit had made this mention he departed from the
court of King Arthur.

And then after this feast Sir Launcelot rode on his adventure,
till on a time by adventure he passed over the pont of Corbin; and
there he saw the fairest tower that ever he saw, and there-under
was a fair town full of people; and all the people, men and
women, cried at once: Welcome, Sir Launcelot du Lake, the
flower of all knighthood, for by thee all we shall be holpen out of
danger. What mean ye, said Sir Launcelot, that ye cry so upon

* Siege: seat.—Ed.

me? Ah, fair knight, said they all, here is within this tower a dolorous lady that hath been there in pains many winters and days, for ever she boileth in scalding water; and but late, said all the people, Sir Gawaine was here and he might not help her, and so he left her in pain. So may I, said Sir Launcelot, leave her in pain as well as Sir Gawaine did. Nay, said the people, we know well that it is Sir Launcelot that shall deliver her. Well, said Launcelot, then shew me what I shall do.

Then they brought Sir Launcelot into the tower; and when he came to the chamber thereas this lady was, the doors of iron unlocked and unbolted. And so Sir Launcelot went into the chamber that was as hot as any stew. And there Sir Launcelot took the fairest lady by the hand that ever he saw, and she was naked as a needle; and by enchantment Queen Morgan le Fay and the Queen of Northgalis had put her there in that pains, because she was called the fairest lady of that country; and there she had been five years, and never might she be delivered out of her great pains unto the time the best knight of the world had taken her by the hand. Then the people brought her clothes. And when she was arrayed, Sir Launcelot thought she was the fairest lady of the world, but if it were Queen Guenever.

Then this lady said to Sir Launcelot: Sir, if it please you will ye go with me hereby into a chapel that we may give loving and thanking unto God? Madam, said Sir Launcelot, come on with me, I will go with you. So when they came there and gave thankings to God all the people, both learned and lewd, gave thankings unto God and him, and said: Sir knight, since ye have delivered this lady, ye shall deliver us from a serpent there is here in a tomb. Then Sir Launcelot took his shield and said: Bring me thither, and what I may do unto the pleasure of God and you I will do. So when Sir Launcelot came thither he saw written upon the tomb letters of gold that said thus: Here shall come a leopard of king's blood, and he shall slay this serpent, and this leopard shall engender a lion in this foreign country, the which lion shall pass all other knights. So then Sir Launcelot lift up the tomb, and there came out an horrible and a fiendly dragon, spitting fire out

of his mouth. Then Sir Launcelot drew his sword and fought with the dragon long, and at the last with great pain Sir Launcelot slew that dragon. Therewithal came King Pelles, the good and noble knight, and saluted Sir Launcelot, and he him again. Fair knight, said the king, what is your name? I require you of your knighthood tell me!

Sir, said Launcelot, wit you well my name is Sir Launcelot du Lake. And my name is, said the king, Pelles, king of the foreign country, and cousin nigh unto Joseph of Armathie.* And then either of them made much of other, and so they went into the castle to take their repast. And anon there came in a dove at a window, and in her mouth there seemed a little censer of gold. And therewithal there was such a savour as all the spicery of the world had been there. And forthwithal there was upon the table all manner of meats and drinks that they could think upon. So came in a damosel passing fair and young, and she bare a vessel of gold betwixt her hands; and thereto the king kneeled devoutly, and said his prayers, and so did all that were there. O Jesu, said Sir Launcelot, what may this mean? This is, said the king, the richest thing that any man hath living. And when this thing goeth about, the Round Table shall be broken; and wit thou well, said the king, this is the holy Sangreal that ye have here seen. So the king and Sir Launcelot led their life the most part of that day. And fain would King Pelles have found the mean to have had Sir Launcelot to have lain by his daughter, fair Elaine. And for this intent: the king knew well that Sir Launcelot should get a child upon his daughter, the which should be named Sir Galahad the good knight, by whom all the foreign country should be brought out of danger, and by him the Holy Greal should be achieved.

Then came forth a lady that hight Dame Brisen, and she said unto the king: Sir, wit ye well Sir Launcelot loveth no lady in the

* Joseph of Armathie: Christ's disciple, reputed to have brought the Holy Grail to England.—Ed.

world but all only Queen Guenever; and therefore work ye by counsel, and I shall make him to lie with your daughter, and he shall not wit but that he lieth with Queen Guenever. O fair lady, Dame Brisen, said the king, hope ye to bring this about? Sir, said she, upon pain of my life let me deal; for this Brisen was one of the greatest enchantresses that was at that time in the world living. Then anon by Dame Brisen's wit she made one to come to Sir Launcelot that he knew well. And this man brought him a ring from Queen Guenever like as it had come from her, and such one as she was wont for the most part to wear; and when Sir Launcelot saw that token wit ye well he was never so fain. Where is my lady? said Sir Launcelot. In the Castle of Case, said the messenger, but five mile hence. Then Sir Launcelot thought to be there the same night. And then this Brisen by the command-ment of King Pelles let send Elaine to this castle with twenty-five knights unto the Castle of Case. Then Sir Launcelot against night rode unto that castle, and there anon he was received worship-fully with such people, to his seeming, as were about Queen Guenever secret.

So when Sir Launcelot was alighted, he asked where the queen was. So Dame Brisen said she was in her bed; and then the people were avoided, and Sir Launcelot was led unto his chamber. And then Dame Brisen brought Sir Launcelot a cup full of wine; and anon as he had drunken that wine he was so assotted and mad that he might make no delay, but withouten any let he went to bed; and he weened that maiden Elaine had been Queen Guenever. Wit you well that Sir Launcelot was glad, and so was that lady Elaine that she had gotten Sir Launcelot in her arms. For well she knew that same night should be gotten upon her Galahad that should prove the best knight of the world; and so they lay together until underne of the morn;* and all the windows and holes of that chamber were stopped that no manner of day might be seen. And then Sir Launcelot remembered him, and he arose up and went to the window.

* Underne of the morn: 9:00 A.M.—Ed.

And anon as he had unshut the window the enchantment was gone; then he knew himself that he had done amiss. Alas, he said, that I have lived so long; now I am shamed. So then he gat his sword in his hand and said: Thou traitress, what art thou that I have lain by all this night? thou shalt die right here of my hands. Then this fair lady Elaine skipped out of her bed all naked, and kneeled down afore Sir Launcelot, and said: Fair courteous knight, come of king's blood, I require you have mercy upon me, and as thou art renowned the most noble knight of the world, slay me not, for I have in my womb him by thee that shall be the most noblest knight of the world. Ah, false traitress, said Sir Launcelot, why hast thou betrayed me? anon tell me what thou art. Sir, she said, I am Elaine, the daughter of King Pelles. Well, said Sir Launcelot, I will forgive you this deed; and therewith he took her up in his arms, and kissed her, for she was as fair a lady, and thereto lusty and young, and as wise, as any was that time living. So God me help, said Sir Launcelot, I may not wite* this to you; but her that made this enchantment upon me as between you and me, an I may find her, that same Lady Brisen, she shall lose her head for witchcrafts, for there was never knight deceived so as I am this night. And so Sir Launcelot arrayed him, and armed him, and took his leave mildly of that lady young Elaine, and so he departed. Then she said: My lord Sir Launcelot, I beseech you see me as soon as ye may, for I have obeyed me unto the prophecy that my father told me. And by his commandment to fulfil this prophecy I have given the greatest riches and the fairest flower that ever I had, and that is my maidenhood that I shall never have again; and therefore, gentle knight, owe me your goodwill.

And so Sir Launcelot arrayed him and was armed, and took his leave mildly of that young lady Elaine; and so he departed, and rode till he came to the Castle of Corbin, where her father was.

* Wite: blame.—Ed.

And as fast as her time came she was delivered of a fair child, and they christened him Galahad; and wit ye well that child was well kept and well nourished, and he was named Galahad because Sir Launcelot was so named at the fountain stone; and after that the Lady of the Lake confirmed him Sir Launcelot du Lake.

Then after this lady was delivered and churched, there came a knight unto her, his name was Sir Bromel la Pleche, the which was a great lord; and he had loved that lady long, and he evermore desired her to wed her; and so by no mean she could put him off, till on a day she said to Sir Bromel: Wit thou well, sir knight, I will not love you, for my love is set upon the best knight of the world. Who is he? said Sir Bromel. Sir, she said, it is Sir Launcelot du Lake that I love and none other, and therefore woo me no longer. Ye say well, said Sir Bromel, and sithen ye have told me so much, ye shall have but little joy of Sir Launcelot, for I shall slay him wheresomever I meet him. Sir, said the Lady Elaine, do to him no treason. Wit ye well, my lady, said Bromel, and I promise you this twelvemonth I shall keep the pont* of Corbin for Sir Launcelot's sake, that he shall neither come nor go unto you, but I shall meet with him.

❧

Then as it fell by fortune and adventure, Sir Bors de Ganis, that was nephew unto Sir Launcelot, came over that bridge; and there Sir Bromel and Sir Bors jousted, and Sir Bors smote Sir Bromel such a buffet that he bare him over his horse's croup. And then Sir Bromel, as an hardy knight, pulled out his sword, and dressed his shield to do battle with Sir Bors. And then Sir Bors alighted and avoided his horse, and there they dashed together many sad strokes; and long thus they fought, till at the last Sir Bromel was laid to the earth, and there Sir Bors began to unlace his helm to slay him. Then Sir Bromel cried Sir Bors mercy, and yielded him. Upon this covenant thou shalt have thy life, said Sir Bors, so thou go unto Sir Launcelot upon Whitsunday that next

* Pont: bridge.—Ed.

cometh, and yield thee unto him as knight recreant. I will do it, said Sir Bromel, and that he sware upon the cross of the sword. And so he let him depart, and Sir Bors rode unto King Pelles, that was within Corbin.

And when the king and Elaine his daughter wist that Sir Bors was nephew unto Sir Launcelot, they made him great cheer. Then said Dame Elaine: We marvel where Sir Launcelot is, for he came never here but once. Marvel not, said Sir Bors, for this half year he hath been in prison with Queen Morgan le Fay, King Arthur's sister. Alas, said Dame Elaine, that me repenteth. And ever Sir Bors beheld that child in her arms, and ever him seemed it was passing like Sir Launcelot. Truly, said Elaine, wit ye well this child he gat upon me. Then Sir Bors wept for joy, and he prayed to God it might prove as good a knight as his father was. And so came in a white dove, and she bare a little censer of gold in her mouth, and there was all manner of meats and drinks; and a maiden bare that Sangreal, and she said openly: Wit you well, Sir Bors, that this child is Galahad, that shall sit in the Siege Perilous, and achieve the Sangreal, and he shall be much better than ever was Sir Launcelot du Lake, that is his own father. And then they kneeled down and made their devotions, and there was such a savour as all the spicery in the world had been there. And when the dove took her flight, the maiden vanished with the Sangreal as she came.

Sir, said Sir Bors unto King Pelles, this castle may be named the Castle Adventurous, for here be many strange adventures. . . .

Anon withal there came an old man into the hall, and he sat him down in a fair chair, and there seemed to be two adders about his neck; and then the old man had an harp, and there he sang an old song how Joseph of Armathie came into this land. Then when he had sung, the old man bade Sir Bors go from thence. For here shall ye have no more adventures; and full worshipfully have ye done, and better shall ye do hereafter. And then Sir Bors seemed that there came the whitest dove with a little golden censer in her mouth. And anon therewithal the tempest ceased and passed, that afore was marvellous to hear. So

was all that court full of good savours. Then Sir Bors saw four children bearing four fair tapers, and an old man in the midst of the children with a censer in his own hand, and a spear in his other hand, and that spear was called the Spear of Vengeance.

🐦

Now, said that old man to Sir Bors, go ye to your cousin, Sir Launcelot, and tell him of this adventure the which had been most convenient for him of all earthly knights; but sin is so foul in him he may not achieve such holy deeds, for had not been his sin he had passed all the knights that ever were in his days; and tell thou Sir Launcelot, of all worldly adventures he passeth in manhood and prowess all other, but in these spiritual matters he shall have many his better. And then Sir Bors saw four gentlewomen come by him, purely beseen: and he saw where that they entered into a chamber where was great light as it were a summer light; and the women kneeled down afore an altar of silver with four pillars, and as it had been a bishop kneeled down afore that table of silver. And as Sir Bors looked over his head he saw a sword like silver, naked, hoving* over his head, and the clearness thereof smote so in his eyes that as at that time Sir Bors was blind; and there he heard a voice that said: Go hence, thou Sir Bors, for as yet thou art not worthy for to be in this place. And then he yede† backward to his bed till on the morn. And on the morn King Pelles made great joy of Sir Bors; and then he departed and rode to Camelot, and there he found Sir Launcelot du Lake, and told him of the adventures that he had seen with King Pelles at Corbin.

So the noise sprang in Arthur's court that Launcelot had gotten a child upon Elaine, the daughter of King Pelles, wherefore Queen Guenever was wroth, and gave many rebukes to Sir Launcelot, and called him false knight. And then Sir Launcelot told the queen all, and how he was made to lie by her by enchantment in likeness of the queen. So the queen held Sir

* Hoving: hovering.—Ed. † Yede: went.—Ed.

Launcelot excused. And as the book saith, King Arthur had been in France, and had made war upon the mighty King Claudas, and had won much of his lands. And when the king was come again he let cry a great feast, that all lords and ladies of all England should be there, but if it were such as were rebellious against him.

And when Dame Elaine, the daughter of King Pelles, heard of this feast she went to her father and required him that he would give her leave to ride to that feast. The king answered: I will well ye go thither, but in any wise as ye love me and will have my blessing, that ye be well beseen in the richest wise; and look that ye spare not for no cost; ask and ye shall have all that you needeth. Then by the advice of Dame Brisen, her maiden, all thing was apparelled unto the purpose, that there was never no lady more richlier beseen. So she rode with twenty knights, and ten ladies, and gentlewomen, to the number of a hundred horses. And when she came to Camelot, King Arthur and Queen Guenever said, and all the knights, that Dame Elaine was the fairest and the best beseen lady that ever was seen in that court. And anon as King Arthur wist that she was come he met her and saluted her, and so did the most part of all the knights of the Round Table, both Sir Tristram, Sir Bleoberis, and Sir Gawaine, and many more that I will not rehearse. But when Sir Launcelot saw her he was so ashamed, and that because he drew his sword on the morn when he had lain by her, that he would not salute her nor speak to her; and yet Sir Launcelot thought she was the fairest woman that ever he saw in his life-days.

But when Dame Elaine saw Sir Launcelot that would not speak unto her she was so heavy that she weened her heart would have to-brast; for wit you well, out of measure she loved him. And then Elaine said unto her woman, Dame Brisen: The unkindness of Sir Launcelot slayeth me near. Ah, peace, madam, said Dame Brisen, I will undertake that this night he shall lie with you, an ye would hold you still. That were me liefer, said Dame Elaine, than all the gold that is above the earth. Let me deal, said Dame Brisen.

So when Elaine was brought unto Queen Guenever either made other good cheer by countenance, but nothing with hearts. But all men and women spake of the beauty of Dame Elaine, and of her great riches.

Then, at night, the queen commanded that Dame Elaine should sleep in a chamber nigh her chamber, and all under one roof; and so it was done as the queen commanded. Then the queen sent for Sir Launcelot and bade him come to her chamber that night: Or else I am sure, said the queen, that ye will go to your lady's bed, Dame Elaine, by whom ye gat Galahad. Ah, madam, said Sir Launcelot, never say ye so, for that I did was against my will. Then, said the queen, look that ye come to me when I send for you. Madam, said Launcelot, I shall not fail you, but I shall be ready at your commandment. This bargain was soon done and made between them, but Dame Brisen knew it by her crafts, and told it to her lady, Dame Elaine. Alas, said she, how shall I do? Let me deal, said Dame Brisen, for I shall bring him by the hand even to your bed, and he shall ween that I am Queen Guenever's messenger. Now well is me, said Dame Elaine, for all the world I love not so much as I do Sir Launcelot.

So when time came that all folks were abed, Dame Brisen came to Sir Launcelot's bed's side and said: Sir Launcelot du Lake, sleep you? My lady, Queen Guenever, lieth and awaiteth upon you. O my fair lady, said Sir Launcelot, I am ready to go with you where ye will have me. So Sir Launcelot threw upon him a long gown, and his sword in his hand; and then Dame Brisen took him by the finger and led him to her lady's bed, Dame Elaine; and then she departed and left them in bed together. Wit you well the lady was glad, and so was Sir Launcelot, for he weened that he had another in his arms.

Now leave we them kissing and clipping, as was kindly thing; and now speak we of Queen Guenever that sent one of her women unto Sir Launcelot's bed; and when she came there she found the bed cold, and he was away; so she came to the queen

and told her all. Alas, said the queen, where is that false knight become? Then the queen was nigh out of her wit, and then she writhed and weltered as a mad woman, and might not sleep a four or five hours. Then Sir Launcelot had a condition that he used of custom, he would clatter in his sleep, and speak oft of his lady, Queen Guenever. So as Sir Launcelot had waked as long as it had pleased him, then by course of kind he slept, and Dame Elaine both. And in his sleep he talked and clattered as a jay, of the love that had been betwixt Queen Guenever and him. And so as he talked so loud the queen heard him thereas she lay in her chamber; and when she heard him so clatter she was nigh wood* and out of her mind, and for anger and pain wist not what to do. And then she coughed so loud that Sir Launcelot awaked, and he knew her hemming. And then he knew well that he lay not by the queen; and therewith he leapt out of his bed as he had been a wood man, in his shirt, and the queen met him in the floor; and thus she said: False traitor knight that thou art, look thou never abide in my court, and avoid my chamber, and not so hardy, thou false traitor knight that thou art, that ever thou come in my sight. Alas, said Sir Launcelot; and therewith he took such an heartly sorrow at her words that he fell down to the floor in a swoon. And therewithal Queen Guenever departed. And when Sir Launcelot awoke of his swoon, he leapt out at a bay window into a garden, and there with thorns he was all to-scratched in his visage and his body; and so he ran forth he wist not whither, and was wild wood as ever was man; and so he ran two year, and never man might have grace to know him.

Now turn we unto Queen Guenever and to the fair Lady Elaine, that when Dame Elaine heard the queen so to rebuke Sir Launcelot, and also she saw how he swooned, and how he leaped out at a bay window, then she said unto Queen Guenever: Madam, ye are greatly to blame for Sir Launcelot, for now have

* Wood: mad.—Ed.

ye lost him, for I saw and heard by his countenance that he is mad for ever. Alas, madam, ye do great sin, and to yourself great dishonour, for ye have a lord of your own, and therefore it is your part to love him; for there is no queen in this world hath such another king as ye have. And, if ye were not, I might have the love of my lord Sir Launcelot; and cause I have to love him for he had my maidenhood, and by him I have borne a fair son, and his name is Galahad, and he shall be in his time the best knight of the world. Dame Elaine, said the queen, when it is daylight I charge you and command you to avoid my court; and for the love ye owe unto Sir Launcelot discover not his counsel, for an ye do, it will be his death. As for that, said Dame Elaine, I dare undertake he is marred for ever, and that have ye made; for ye, nor I, are like to rejoice him; for he made the most piteous groans when he leapt out at yonder bay window that ever I heard man make. Alas, said fair Elaine, and alas, said the Queen Guenever, for now I wot well we have lost him for ever.

So on the morn Dame Elaine took her leave to depart, and she would no longer abide. Then King Arthur brought her on her way with mo than an hundred knights through a forest. And by the way she told Sir Bors de Ganis all how it betid that same night, and how Sir Launcelot leapt out at a window, araged out of his wit. Alas, said Sir Bors, where is my lord, Sir Launcelot, become? Sir, said Elaine, I wot ne'er. Alas, said Sir Bors, betwixt you both ye have destroyed that good knight. As for me, said Dame Elaine, I said never nor did never thing that should in any wise displease him, but with the rebuke that Queen Guenever gave him I saw him swoon to the earth; and when he awoke he took his sword in his hand, naked save his shirt, and leapt out at a window with the grisliest groan that ever I heard man make. Now farewell, Dame Elaine, said Sir Bors, and hold my lord Arthur with a tale as long as ye can, for I will turn again to Queen Guenever and give her a heat; and I require you, as ever ye will have my service, make good watch and espy if ever ye may see my lord Sir Launcelot. Truly, said fair Elaine, I shall do all that I may do, for as fain would I know and wit where he is become, as you, or any of his kin, or Queen Guenever; and cause

great enough have I thereto as well as any other. And wit ye well, said fair Elaine to Sir Bors, I would lose my life for him rather than he should be hurt; but alas, I cast me never for to see him, and the chief causer of this is Dame Guenever. Madam, said Dame Brisen, the which had made the enchantment before betwixt Sir Launcelot and her, I pray you heartily, let Sir Bors depart, and hie him with all his might as fast as he may to seek Sir Launcelot, for I warn you he is clean out of his mind; and yet he shall be well holpen an but by miracle.

Then wept Dame Elaine, and so did Sir Bors de Ganis; and so they departed, and Sir Bors rode straight unto Queen Guenever. And when she saw Sir Bors she wept as she were wood. Fie on your weeping, said Sir Bors de Ganis, for ye weep never but when there is no bote.* Alas, said Sir Bors, that ever Sir Launce-lot's kin saw you, for now have ye lost the best knight of our blood, and he that was all our leader and our succour; and I dare say and make it good that all kings, christian nor heathen, may not find such a knight, for to speak of his nobleness and courtesy, with his beauty and his gentleness. Alas, said Sir Bors, what shall we do that be of his blood? Alas, said Sir Ector de Maris. Alas, said Lionel.

And when the queen heard them say so she fell to the earth in a dead swoon. And then Sir Bors took her up, and dawed† her; and when she was awaked she kneeled afore the three knights, and held up both her hands, and besought them to seek him. And spare not for no goods but that he be found, for I wot he is out of his mind. And Sir Bors, Sir Ector, and Sir Lionel departed from the queen, for they might not abide no longer for sorrow. And then the queen sent them treasure enough for their expenses, and so they took their horses and their armour, and departed. And then they rode from country to country, in forests, and in wilderness, and in wastes; and ever they laid watch both at forests

* Bote: remedy.—Ed.
† Dawed: roused.—Ed.

and at all manner of men as they rode, to hearken and spere* after him, as he that was a naked man, in his shirt, with a sword in his hand. And thus they rode nigh a quarter of a year, endlong and overthwart,† in many places, forests and wilderness, and oft-times were evil lodged for his sake; and yet for all their labour and seeking could they never hear word of him. And wit you well these three knights were passing sorry.

Then at the last Sir Bors and his fellows met with a knight that hight Sir Melion de Tartare. Now fair knight, said Sir Bors, whither be ye away? for they knew either other afore time. Sir, said Melion, I am in the way toward the court of King Arthur. Then we pray you, said Sir Bors, that ye will tell my lord Arthur, and my lady, Queen Guenever, and all the fellowship of the Round Table, that we cannot in no wise hear tell where Sir Launcelot is become. Then Sir Melion departed from them, and said that he would tell the king, and the queen, and all the fellowship of the Round Table, as they had desired him. So when Sir Melion came to the court of King Arthur he told the king, and the queen, and all the fellowship of the Round Table, what Sir Bors had said of Sir Launcelot. Then Sir Gawaine, Sir Uwaine, Sir Sagramore le Desirous, Sir Aglovale, and Sir Percivale de Galis took upon them by the great desire of King Arthur, and in especial by the queen, to seek throughout all England, Wales, and Scotland, to find Sir Launcelot, and with them rode eighteen knights mo to bear them fellowship; and wit ye well, they lacked no manner of spending; and so were they three and twenty knights. . . .

And now speak we of Sir Launcelot that suffered and endured many sharp showers, that ever ran wild wood from place to place, and lived by fruit and such as he might get, and drank water two year; and other clothing had he but little but his shirt

* Spere: question.—Ed.
† Endlong and overthwart: lengthwise and crosswise.—Ed.

and his breech. Thus as Sir Launcelot wandered here and there he came in a fair meadow where he found a paviilon; and there by, upon a tree, there hung a white shield, and two swords hung thereby, and two spears leaned there by a tree. And when Sir Launcelot saw the swords, anon he leapt to the one sword, and took it in his hand, and drew it out. And then he lashed at the shield, that all the meadow rang of the dints, that he gave such a noise as ten knights had foughten together.

Then came forth a dwarf, and leapt unto Sir Launcelot, and would have had the sword out of his hand. And then Sir Launcelot took him by the both shoulders and threw him to the ground upon his neck, that he had almost broken his neck; and therewithal the dwarf cried help. Then came forth a likely knight, and well apparelled in scarlet furred with minever. And anon as he saw Sir Launcelot he deemed that he should be out of his wit. And then he said with fair speech: Good man, lay down that sword, for as meseemeth thou hadst more need of sleep and of warm clothes than to wield that sword. As for that, said Sir Launcelot, come not too nigh, for an thou do, wit thou well I will slay thee.

And when the knight of the pavilion saw that, he stert backward within the pavilion. And then the dwarf armed him lightly; and so the knight thought by force and might to take the sword from Sir Launcelot, and so he came stepping out; and when Sir Launcelot saw him come so all armed with his sword in his hand, then Sir Launcelot flew to him with such a might, and hit him upon the helm such a buffet, that the stroke troubled his brains, and therewith the sword brake in three. And the knight fell to the earth as he had been dead, the blood brasting out of his mouth, the nose, and the ears. And then Sir Launcelot ran into the pavilion, and rushed even into the warm bed; and there was a lady in that bed, and she gat her smock, and ran out of the pavilion. And when she saw her lord lie at the ground like to be dead, then she cried and wept as she had been mad. Then with her noise the knight awaked out of his swoon, and looked up weakly with his eyes; and then he asked her, where was that mad

man that had given him such a buffet: For such a buffet had I never of man's hand. Sir, said the dwarf, it is not worship to hurt him, for he is a man out of his wit; and doubt ye not he hath been a man of great worship, and for some heartly sorrow that he hath taken, he is fallen mad; and me beseemeth, said the dwarf, he resembleth much unto Sir Launcelot, for him I saw at the great tournament beside Lonazep. Jesu defend, said that knight, that ever that noble knight, Sir Launcelot, should be in such a plight; but whatsomever he be, said that knight, harm will I none do him: and this knight's name was Bliant. Then he said unto the dwarf: Go thou fast on horseback, unto my brother Sir Selivant, that is at the Castle Blank, and tell him of mine adventure, and bid him bring with him an horse litter, and then will we bear this knight unto my castle.

So the dwarf rode fast, and he came again and brought Sir Selivant with him, and six men with an horse litter; and so they took up the feather bed with Sir Launcelot, and so carried all away with them unto the Castle Blank, and he never awaked till he was within the castle. And then they bound his hands and his feet, and gave him good meats and good drinks, and brought him again to his strength and his fairness; but in his wit they could not bring him again, nor to know himself. Thus was Sir Launcelot there more than a year and a half, honestly arrayed and fair faren withal.

Then upon a day this lord of that castle, Sir Bliant, took his arms, on horseback, with a spear, to seek adventures. And as he rode in a forest there met with him two knights adventurous, the one was Breuse Saunce Pité, and his brother, Sir Bertelot; and these two ran both at once upon Sir Bliant, and brake their spears upon his body. And then they drew out swords and made great battle, and fought long together. But at the last Sir Bliant was sore wounded, and felt himself faint; and then he fled on horseback toward his castle. And as they came hurling under the castle whereas Sir Launcelot lay in a window, [he] saw how two

knights laid upon Sir Bliant with their swords. And when Sir
Launcelot saw that, yet as wood as he was he was sorry for his
lord, Sir Bliant. And then Sir Launcelot brake the chains from his
legs and off his arms, and in the breaking he hurt his hands sore;
and so Sir Launcelot ran out at a postern, and there he met with
the two knights that chased Sir Bliant; and there he pulled down
Sir Bertelot with his bare hands from his horse, and therewithal
he wrothe his sword out of his hand; and so he leapt unto Sir
Breuse, and gave him such a buffet upon the head that he tumbled
backward over his horse's croup. And when Sir Bertelot saw
there his brother have such a fall, he gat a spear in his hand, and
would have run Sir Launcelot through: that saw Sir Bliant, and
struck off the hand of Sir Bertelot. And then Sir Breuse and Sir
Bertelot gat their horses and fled away.

When Sir Selivant came and saw what Sir Launcelot had done
for his brother, then he thanked God, and so did his brother, that
ever they did him any good. But when Sir Bliant saw that Sir
Launcelot was hurt with the breaking of his irons, then was he
heavy that ever he bound him. Bind him no more, said Sir
Selivant, for he is happy and gracious. Then they made great joy
of Sir Launcelot, and they bound him no more; and so he abode
there an half year and more. And on the morn early Sir Launcelot
was ware where came a great boar with many hounds nigh him.
But the boar was so big there might no hounds tear him; and the
hunters came after, blowing their horns, both upon horseback and
some upon foot; and then Sir Launcelot was ware where one
alighted and tied his horse to a tree, and leaned his spear against
the tree.

So came Sir Launcelot and found the horse bounden till a tree,
and a spear leaning against a tree, and a sword tied to the saddle
bow; and then Sir Launcelot leapt into the saddle and gat that
spear in his hand, and then he rode after the boar; and then Sir
Launcelot was ware where the boar set his arse to a tree fast by an
hermitage. Then Sir Launcelot ran at the boar with his spear, and

therewith the boar turned him nimbly, and rove out the lungs and the heart of the horse, so that Launcelot fell to the earth; and, or ever Sir Launcelot might get from the horse, the boar rove him on the brawn of the thigh up to the hough bone. And then Sir Launcelot was wroth, and up he gat upon his feet, and drew his sword, and he smote off the boar's head at one stroke. And therewithal came out the hermit, and saw him have such a wound. Then the hermit came to Sir Launcelot and bemoaned him, and would have had him home unto his hermitage; but when Sir Launcelot heard him speak, he was so wroth with his wound that he ran upon the hermit to have slain him, and the hermit ran away. And when Sir Launcelot might not overget him, he threw his sword after him, for Sir Launcelot might go no further for bleeding; then the hermit turned again, and asked Sir Launcelot how he was hurt. Fellow, said Sir Launcelot, this boar hath bitten me sore. Then come with me, said the hermit, and I shall heal you. Go thy way, said Sir Launcelot, and deal not with me.

Then the hermit ran his way, and there he met with a good knight with many men. Sir, said the hermit, here is fast by my place the goodliest man that ever I saw, and he is sore wounded with a boar, and yet he hath slain the boar. But well I wot, said the hermit, and he be not holpen, that goodly man shall die of that wound, and that were great pity. Then that knight at the desire of the hermit gat a cart, and in that cart that knight put the boar and Sir Launcelot, for Sir Launcelot was so feeble that they might right easily deal with him; and so Sir Launcelot was brought into the hermitage, and there the hermit healed him of his wound. But the hermit might not find Sir Launcelot's sustenance, and so he impaired and waxed feeble, both of his body and of his wit: for the default of his sustenance he waxed more wooder than he was aforehand.

And then upon a day Sir Launcelot ran his way into the forest; and by adventure he came to the city of Corbin, where Dame Elaine was, that bare Galahad, Sir Launcelot's son. And so when he was entered into the town he ran through the town to the castle; and then all the young men of that city ran after Sir

Launcelot, and there they threw turves at him, and gave him many sad strokes. And ever as Sir Launcelot might overreach any of them, he threw them so that they would never come in his hands no more; for of some he brake the legs and the arms, and so fled into the castle; and then came out knights and squires and rescued Sir Launcelot. And when they beheld him and looked upon his person, they thought they saw never so goodly a man. And when they saw so many wounds upon him, all they deemed that he had been a man of worship. And then they ordained him clothes to his body, and straw underneath him, and a little house. And then every day they would throw him meat, and set him drink, but there was but few would bring him meat to his hands.

So it befell that King Pelles had a nephew, his name was Castor; and so he desired of the king to be made knight, and so at the request of this Castor the king made him knight at the feast of Candlemas. And when Sir Castor was made knight, that same day he gave many gowns. And then Sir Castor sent for the fool—that was Sir Launcelot. And when he was come afore Sir Castor, he gave Sir Launcelot a robe of scarlet and all that longed unto him. And when Sir Launcelot was so arrayed like a knight, he was the seemliest man in all the court, and none so well made. So when he saw his time he went into the garden, and there Sir Launcelot laid him down by a well and slept. And so at-after noon Dame Elaine and her maidens came into the garden to play them; and as they roamed up and down one of Dame Elaine's maidens espied where lay a goodly man by the well sleeping, and anon showed him to Dame Elaine. Peace, said Dame Elaine, and say no word: and then she brought Dame Elaine where he lay. And when that she beheld him, anon she fell in remembrance of him, and knew him verily for Sir Launcelot; and therewithal she fell a-weeping so heartily that she sank even to the earth; and when she had thus wept a great while, then she arose and called her maidens and said she was sick.

And so she yede out of the garden, and she went straight to her father, and there she took him apart by herself; and then she said: O father, now have I need of your help, and but if that ye help me farewell my good days for ever. What is that, daughter? said King Pelles. Sir, she said, thus is it: in your garden I went for to sport, and there, by the well, I found Sir Launcelot du Lake sleeping. I may not believe that, said King Pelles. Sir, she said, truly he is there, and meseemeth he should be distract out of his wit. Then hold you still, said the king, and let me deal. Then the king called to him such as he most trusted, a four persons, and Dame Elaine, his daughter. And when they came to the well and beheld Sir Launcelot, anon Dame Brisen knew him. Sir, said Dame Brisen, we must be wise how we deal with him, for this knight is out of his mind, and if we awake him rudely what he will do we all know not; but ye shall abide, and I shall throw such an enchantment upon him that he shall not awake within the space of an hour; and so she did.

Then within a little while after, the king commanded that all people should avoid, that none should be in that way thereas the king would come. And so when this was done, these four men and these ladies laid hand on Sir Launcelot, and so they bare him into a tower, and so into a chamber where was the holy vessel of the Sangreal, and by force Sir Launcelot was laid by that holy vessel; and there came an holy man and unhilled* that vessel, and so by miracle and by virtue of that holy vessel Sir Launcelot was healed and recovered. And when that he was awaked he groaned and sighed, and complained greatly that he was passing sore.

And when Sir Launcelot saw King Pelles and Elaine, he waxed ashamed and said thus: O Lord Jesu, how came I here? for God's sake, my lord, let me wit how I came here. Sir, said Dame Elaine, into this country ye came like a madman, clean out of your wit, and here have ye been kept as a fool; and no creature here knew

* Unhilled: uncovered.—Ed.

what ye were, until by fortune a maiden of mine brought me unto you whereas ye lay sleeping by a well, and anon as I verily beheld you I knew you. And then I told my father, and so were ye brought afore this holy vessel, and by the virtue of it thus were ye healed. O Jesu, mercy, said Sir Launcelot; if this be sooth, how many there be that know of my woodness! So God me help, said Elaine, no more but my father, and I, and Dame Brisen. Now for Christ's love, said Sir Launcelot, keep it in counsel, and let no man know it in the world, for I am sore ashamed that I have been thus miscarried; for I am banished out of the country of Logris for ever, that is for to say the country of England.

And so Sir Launcelot lay more than a fortnight or ever that he might stir for soreness. And then upon a day he said unto Dame Elaine these words: Lady Elaine, for your sake I have had much travail, care, and anguish, it needeth not to rehearse it, ye know how. Notwithstanding I know well I have done foul to you when that I drew my sword to you, to have slain you, upon the morn when I had lain with you. And all was the cause, that ye and Dame Brisen made me for to lie by you maugre mine head;* and as ye say, that night Galahad your son was begotten. That is truth, said Dame Elaine. Now will ye for my love, said Sir Launcelot, go unto your father and get me a place of him wherein I may dwell? for in the court of King Arthur may I never come. Sir, said Dame Elaine, I will live and die with you, and only for your sake; and if my life might not avail you and my death might avail you, wit you well I would die for your sake. And I will go to my father, and I am sure there is nothing that I can desire of him but I shall have it. And where ye be, my lord Sir Launcelot, doubt ye not but I will be with you with all the service that I may do. So forthwithal she went to her father and said, Sir, my lord, Sir Launcelot, desireth to be here by you in some castle of yours. Well daughter, said the king, sith it is his desire to abide in these marches he shall be in the Castle of Bliant, and there shall ye be

* Maugre mine head: without my intending it.—Ed.

with him, and twenty of the fairest ladies that be in the country, and they shall all be of the great blood, and ye shall have ten knights with you; for, daughter, I will that ye wit we all be honoured by the blood of Sir Launcelot.

Then went Dame Elaine unto Sir Launcelot, and told him all how her father had devised for him and her. Then came the knight Sir Castor, that was nephew unto King Pelles, unto Sir Launcelot, and asked him what was his name. Sir, said Sir Launcelot, my name is Le Chevaler Mal Fet, that is to say the knight that hath trespassed. Sir, said Sir Castor, it may well be so, but ever meseemeth your name should be Sir Launcelot du Lake, for or now I have seen you. Sir, said Launcelot, ye are not as a gentle knight: I put case my name were Sir Launcelot, and that it list me not to discover my name, what should it grieve you here to keep my counsel, and ye be not hurt thereby? but wit thou well an ever it lie in my power I shall grieve you, and that I promise you truly. Then Sir Castor kneeled down and besought Sir Launcelot of mercy: For I shall never utter what ye be, while that ye be in these parts. Then Sir Launcelot pardoned him.

And then, after this, King Pelles with ten knights, and Dame Elaine, and twenty ladies, rode unto the Castle of Bliant that stood in an island beclosed in iron, with a fair water deep and large. And when they were there Sir Launcelot let call it the Joyous Isle; and there was he called none otherwise but Le Chevaler Mal Fet, the knight that hath trespassed. Then Sir Launcelot let make him a shield all of sable, and a queen crowned in the midst, all of silver, and a knight clean armed kneeling afore her. And every day once, for any mirths that all the ladies might make him, he would once every day look toward the realm of Logris, where King Arthur and Queen Guenever was. And then would he fall upon a weeping as his heart should to-brast.

In the twelfth-century Celtic tale, Tristan is irrevocably bound to Iseult the Fair, wife of King Mark of Cornwall, by a love-philtre drunk by the two unawares. In a vain effort to conjure away his destiny, Tristan marries Iseult of the White Hands, daughter of Duke Hoël of Carhaix in Brittany. Drawn back to Tintagel in Cornwall, he is rebuffed by Iseult the Fair and returns to Carhaix.

This concluding passage of the story is taken from an amalgamation of several early versions by Joseph Bédier, published in French in 1900 and translated by Hilaire Belloc as *The Romance of Tristan and Iseult* (London: G. A. Allen, 1903); it is reprinted by permission of the publisher and the estate of Hilaire Belloc.

TRISTAN SAW Brittany again, Carhaix, Duke Hoël, and his wife Iseult of the White Hands. All welcomed him, but Iseult the Fair had driven him away: nothing else mattered. Long he languished, far from her, till on a day he knew he must see her again, even if she had him basely beaten by her men-at-arms and valets. Far from her, death came surely; and he had rather die at once than day by day. Who lives in sorrow is like a man dead. And he desired some death, but that the Queen might know it was for love of her he had died; then would death come easily.

So he left Carhaix secretly, telling no man, neither his kindred nor even Kaherdin, his brother in arms. He went in rags afoot (for no one marks the beggar on the high road) till he came to the shore of the sea.

He found in a haven a great ship ready, the sail was up and the anchor-chain short at the bow.

"God save you, my lords," he said, "and send you a good journey. To what land sail you now?"

"To Tintagel," they said.

Then he cried out:

"Oh, my lords! take me with you thither!"

And he went aboard, and a fair wind filled the sail, and she ran five days and nights for Cornwall, till, on the sixth day, they dropped anchor in Tintagel Haven. The castle stood above, fenced all around. There was but the one armed gate, and two knights watched it night and day. So Tristan went ashore and sat upon the beach, and a man told him that Mark was there and had just held his court.

"But where," said he, "is Iseult, the Queen, and her fair maid, Brangien?"

"In Tintagel too," said the other, "and I saw them lately; the Queen sad, as she always is."

At the hearing of the name, Tristan suffered, and he thought that neither by guile nor courage could he see that friend, for Mark would kill him.

And he thought "Let him kill me and let me die for her, since every day I die. But you, Iseult, even if you knew me here, would you not drive me out?" And he thought "I will try guile. I will seem mad, but with a madness that shall be great wisdom. And many shall think me a fool that have less wit than I."

Just then a fisherman passed in a rough cloak and cape, and Tristan seeing him, took him aside, and said:

"Friend, will you not change clothes?"

And as the fisherman found it a very good bargain, he said in answer:

"Yes friend, gladly."

And he changed and ran off at once for fear of losing his gain. Then Tristan shaved his wonderful hair; he shaved it close to his head and left a cross all bald, and he rubbed his face with magic herbs distilled in his own country, and it changed in colour and skin so that none could know him, and he made him a club from a young tree torn from a hedge-row and hung it to his neck, and went bare-foot towards the castle.

The porter made sure that he had to do with a fool and said:

"Good morrow, fool, where have you been this long while?"

And he answered:

"At the abbot of St. Michael's wedding, and he wed an abbess, large and veiled. And from the Alps to Mount St. Michael how they came, the priests and abbots, monks and regulars, all dancing on the green with croziers and with staves under the high trees' shade. But I left them all to come hither, for I serve at the King's board to-day."

Then the porter said:

"Come in, lord fool; the Hairy Urgan's son, I know, and like your father."

And when he was within the courts the serving men ran after him and cried:

"The fool! the fool!"

But he made play with them though they cast stones and struck him as they laughed, and in the midst of laughter and their cries, as the rout followed him, he came to that hall where, at the Queen's side, King Mark sat under his canopy.

And as he neared the door with his club at his neck, the King said:

"Here is a merry fellow, let him in."

And they brought him in, his club at his neck. And the King said:

"Friend, well come; what seek you here?"

Tristan replied in a strangely distorted voice:

"Sire, good and noble King among all, I knew that at the sight of you, my heart would melt in tenderness. God save you, fair King."

"Friend, what seek you in these parts?"

"Iseult," said he, "whom I love so well; I bring my sister with me, Brunehild, the beautiful. Come, take her, you are weary of the Queen. Take you my sister and give me here Iseult, and I will hold her and serve you for her love."

The King said laughing:

"Fool, if I gave you the Queen, where would you take her, pray?"

"Oh! very high," he said, "between the clouds and heaven, into a fair chamber glazed. The beams of the sun shine through it, yet

the winds do not trouble it at all. There would I bear the Queen into that crystal chamber of mine all compact of roses and the morning."

The King and his barons laughed and said:

"Here is a good fool at no loss for words."

But the fool as he sat at their feet gazed at Iseult most fixedly.

"Friend," said King Mark, "what warrant have you that the Queen would heed so foul a fool as you?"

"O! Sire," he answered gravely, "many deeds have I done for her, and my madness is from her alone."

"What is your name?" they said, and laughed.

"Tristan," said he, "that loved the Queen so well, and still till death will love her."

But at the name the Queen angered and weakened together, and said: "Get hence for an evil fool!"

But the fool, marking her anger, went on:

"Queen Iseult, do you mind the day, when, poisoned by the Morholt's spear, I took my harp to sea and fell upon your shore? Your mother healed me with strange drugs. Have you no memory, Queen?"

But Iseult answered:

"Out, fool, out! Your folly and you have passed the bounds!"

But the fool, still playing, pushed the barons out, crying:

"Out! madmen, out! Leave me to counsel with Iseult, since I come here for the love of her!"

And as the King laughed, Iseult blushed and said:

"King, drive me forth this fool!"

But the fool still laughed and cried:

"Queen, do you mind you of the dragon I slew in your land? I hid its tongue in my hose, and, burnt of its venom, I fell by the roadside. Ah! what a knight was I then, and it was you that succoured me."

Iseult replied: "Silence! You wrong all knighthood by your words, for you are a fool from birth. Cursed be the seamen that brought you hither; rather should they have cast you into the sea!"

The fool burst out laughing.

"Queen Iseult," he still said on, "do you mind you of your haste when you would have slain me with my own sword? And of the hair of gold? And of how I stood up to the seneschal?"

"Silence!" she said, "you drunkard. You were drunk last night, and so you dreamt these dreams."

"Drunk, and still so am I," said he, "but of such a draught that never can the influence fade. Queen Iseult, do you mind you of that hot and open day on the high seas? We thirsted and we drank together from the same cup, and since that day have I been drunk with an awful wine."

When the Queen heard these words which she alone could understand, she rose and would have gone.

But the King held her by her ermine cloak, and made her to sit down again.

"Wait a while, Iseult, let us hear these ravings to the end. Fool, have you any skills?"

"I have served Kings and Counts."

"Honestly, do you know how to hunt with dogs, with falcons?"

"Indeed, when it pleases me to hunt in the forest, I know how to seize with my hounds the cranes which fly through the clouds; with my beagles, the swans, the white or coloured geese, the wood-doves; with my bow, the loons and bitterns."

All laughed merrily and the King asked:

"And what do you catch, brother, when you hunt big game?"

"I catch everything I find; with my traps I take timber-wolves and brown bears; with my gerfalcons, I take stags; roebucks and does with my sparrow-hawks; foxes with my pilgrim-hawks; hares with my merlins. And when I return to the house that harbours me, I know how to play the game of quarter-staves, deal out blows among the squires, tune my harp and sing pieces of music, love the queens and throw neat shavings into the brooks. In truth, am I not a good minstrel? This very day you have seen how I can spar with my stick."

He struck about him with his staff.

"Be off from here, Cornish lords," cried he. "Why do you tarry? Have you not already eaten your fill? Are you not stuffed?"

The King, having had his fun with the fool, called for his charger and his hawks and went to hunt with his knights and squires. Iseult said to him:

"Sire, I am weak and sad; let me go rest in my room; I am tired of these follies."

And she went to her room in thought and sat upon her bed, calling herself a slave and saying:

"Why was I born? Brangien, dear sister, life is so hard to me that death were better! There is a fool without, shaven crisscross, and come in an evil hour, and he is warlock, for he knows in every part myself and my whole life; he knows what you and I and Tristan only know."

Then Brangien said: "It may be Tristan."

But—"No," said the Queen, "for he was the first of knights, but this fool is foul and made awry. May God curse him, and cursed be the hour in which he was born, and cursed the ship which brought him hither instead of sinking him out there in the depths."

"My lady!" said Brangien, "soothe you. You curse and excommunicate overmuch these days! Where indeed have you learned such ways? May be he comes from Tristan?"

"I cannot tell. I know him not. But go find him, friend, and see if you know him."

So Brangien went to the hall where the fool still sat alone. Tristan knew her and let fall his club and said:

"Brangien, dear Brangien, before God! have pity on me!"

"Foul fool," she answered, "what devil taught you my name?"

"Lady," he said, "I have known it long. By my head, that once was fair, if I am mad the blame is yours, for it was yours to watch over the wine we drank on the high seas. The cup was of silver and I held it to Iseult and she drank. Do you remember, lady?"

"No," she said, and as she trembled and left he called out: "Pity me!"

He followed and saw Iseult. He stretched out his arms, but in her shame, sweating agony she drew back, and seeing that she shunned him, Tristan trembled for shame and anger, stepped back towards the wall by the door, and said in his distorted voice:

"I have lived too long, for I have seen the day that Iseult repulses me, refuses her love, holds me in contempt. Iseult, how hard love dies! Iseult, a welling water that floods and runs large is a mighty thing; on the day that it fails it is nothing; so love that turns."

But she said: "Brother, I look at you and doubt and tremble, and I know you not for Tristan."

"Queen Iseult, I am Tristan indeed that do love you; mind you for the last time of the dwarf, and of the flour, and of the blood I shed in my leap and of the gift I sent you, the dog Pticru with the fairy-bell? Do you not remember the bits of shaven wood which I cast into the brook?"

Iseult looked at him, sighed, knew not what to say or believe, saw that he knew all things, yet it would have been madness to acknowledge that he was Tristan; and Tristan said to her:

"My lady Queen, I know well you have withdrawn yourself from me and I accuse you of treason. Nevertheless I have known days, my fair one, in which you loved me well. It was in the forest depths, under the hut of branches. Do you not remember the day when I gave you my good dog Hodain? Ah, he at least has always loved me, and for my sake he would leave Iseult the Fair. Where is he? What have you done with him? He at least would recognize me."

"He recognize you? You speak madness; for since Tristan left, he has stayed below, crouched in his kennel, and bites every man who comes near him. Brangien, bring him here."

Brangien brought him.

"Come here, Hodain," said Tristan, "you were mine and I take you back."

No sooner had Hodain heard his voice than he yanked his leash out of Brangien's hands, sprang to his master, rolled at his feet, licked his hands and barked for joy.

"Hodain," cried the fool, "blessed be the pains I took in rearing

you! You have bidden me better welcome than she whom I so loved. She will not recognize me: will she at least recognize this ring which she gave me, long since, with tears and kisses, on the day we parted? This little ring of jasper has never left me: often in my torment I have asked advice of it, often have I moistened its green jasper with my hot tears."

Iseult saw the ring. She opened wide her arms:

"Come! Take me, Tristan!"

Then Tristan ceased to distort his voice:

"Friend, how could you so long have failed to recognize me, longer than this very dog? What mattered this ring? Do you not feel how far sweeter it would have been to have been recognized at the very mention of our former love? What mattered the sound of my voice? You should have overheard the sound of my heart."

"Friend," said Iseult, "perhaps I did hear it sooner than you thought; but we are surrounded by treachery: should I, like this dog, have followed my wishes at the risk of having you caught and killed under my eyes? I saved you and myself. Neither the mention of your past life, nor the sound of your voice, not even this very ring, proved anything to me, for all these might have been the evil tricks of a sorcerer. Nevertheless I yield myself at the sight of this ring: did I not swear, as soon as I should see it again, at the risk of my life to always do what you bade me, be it wisdom or folly? Wisdom or folly, come; take me, Tristan!"

And her eyes darkened and she fell; but when the light returned she was held by him who kissed her eyes and her face. He drew her behind the arras. In his arms he held the Queen.

To have their fun with the fool, the valets let him sleep under the stairs to the hall, like a dog in his kennel. Patiently he endured their banter and their blows, for again and again, taking on his own form and beauty, he passed from his dirty hole to the chamber of the Queen.

So passed they three full days. But, on the third, two maids that watched them told the traitor Andret, and he put spies well-

armed before the women's rooms. And when Tristan would enter
they cried:

"Back, fool! Go lie on your truss of straw!"

But he brandished his club laughing, and said:

"What! May I not kiss the Queen who loves me and awaits me
now?"

And they feared him for a mad fool, and he passed in through
the door.

Then, being with the Queen for the last time, he held her in his
arms and said:

"Friend, I must fly, for they are wondering. I must fly, and
perhaps shall never see you more. My death is near, and far from
you my death will come of desire."

"Oh friend," she said, "fold your arms round me close and
strain me so that our hearts may break and our souls go free at
last. Take me to that happy place of which you told me long ago.
The fields whence none return, but where great singers sing their
songs for ever. Take me now."

"I will take you to the Happy Palace of the living, Queen! The
time is near. We have drunk all joy and sorrow. The time is near.
When it is finished, if I call you, will you come, my friend?"

"Friend," said she, "call me and you know that I shall come."

"Friend," said he, "God send you His reward."

As he went out the spies would have held him; but he laughed
aloud, and flourished his club, and cried:

"Peace, gentlemen, I go and will not stay. My lady sends me to
prepare that shining house I vowed her, of crystal, and of rose
shot through with morning."

And as they cursed and drave him, the fool went leaping on his
way.

When he was come back to Brittany, to Carhaix, it happened
that Tristan, riding to the aid of Kaherdin his brother in arms,
made war on a baron named Bedalis. He fell into an ambush laid
by Bedalis and his brothers. Tristan slew the seven brothers. But

he himself was wounded by a blow from a spear, and this spear was poisoned.

Painfully he returned to the castle of Carhaix and had his wounds dressed. Many doctors came but none could cure him of the poison, for they did not even find it. They fixed no plaster to draw the poison forth, and vainly pounded and ground their roots, culled their herbs, boiled their potions. And Tristan weakened, the poison spread throughout his body, he paled and his bones showed.

Then he knew that his life was going, and that he must die, and he had a desire to see once more Iseult the Fair, but he could not seek her, for the sea would have killed him in his weakness, and how could Iseult come to him? And sad, and suffering the poison, he awaited death.

He called Kaherdin secretly to tell him his pain, for they loved each other with a loyal love; and as he would have no one in the room save Kaherdin, nor even in the neighbouring rooms, Iseult of the White Hands began to wonder. She was afraid and wished to hear, and she came back and listened at the wall by Tristan's bed; and as she listened one of her maids kept watch for her.

Now, within, Tristan had gathered up his strength, and had half risen, leaning against the wall, and Kaherdin wept beside him. They wept their good comradeship, broken so soon, and their friendship.

"Fair friend and gentle," said Tristan, "I am in a foreign land where I have neither friend nor cousin, save you; and you alone in this place have given me comfort. My life is going, and I wish to see once more Iseult the Fair. Ah, did I but know of a messenger who would go to her! For now I know that she will come to me—Kaherdin, my brother in arms, by our friendship, by the nobility of your heart, by our comradeship, I entreat you: undertake this errand for me, and if you carry my word, I will become your liege, and I will cherish you beyond all other men."

And as Kaherdin saw Tristan broken down, his heart reproached him and he said:

"Fair comrade, do not weep; I will do what you desire, even if it were risk of death I would do it for you. Nor no distress nor anguish will let me from doing it according to my power. Give me the word you send, and I will make ready."

And Tristan answered:

"Thank you, friend; this is my prayer: take this ring, it is a sign between her and me; and when you come to her land pass yourself at court for a merchant, and show her silk and stuffs, but make so that she sees the ring, for then she will find some ruse by which to speak to you in secret. Then tell her that my heart salutes her; tell her that she alone can bring me comfort; tell her that if she does not come I shall die. Tell her to remember our past time, and our great sorrows, and all the joy there was in our loyal and tender love. And tell her to remember that draught we drank together on the high seas. For we drank our death together. Tell her to remember the oath I swore to serve a single love, for I have kept that oath."

But behind the wall, Iseult of the White Hands heard all these things; and she almost swooned. Tristan continued:

"Hasten, my friend, and come back quickly, or you will not see me again. Take forty days for your term, but come back with Iseult the Fair. And tell your sister nothing, or tell her that you seek some doctor. Take my fine ship, and two sails with you, one white, one black. And as you return, if you bring Iseult, hoist the white sail; but if you bring her not, the black. Now I have nothing more to say, but God guide you and bring you back safe."

He sighed, wept and bewailed his fate, and Kaherdin also wept, embraced Tristan and took leave.

With the first fair wind Kaherdin took the open, weighed anchor and hoisted sail, and ran with a light air and broke the seas. They bore rich merchandise with them, dyed silks of rare colours, enamel of Touraine, wines of Poitou, and gerfalcons from Spain, for by this ruse Kaherdin thought to reach Iseult. Eight days and nights they ran full sail to Cornwall.

Now a woman's wrath is a fearful thing, and all men fear it, for

according to her love, so will her vengeance be; and their love and their hate come quickly, but their hate lives longer than their love; and they will make play with love, but not with hate. Standing by the wall, Iseult of the White Hands had overheard everything. How much she had loved Tristan! . . . At last she learned of his love for another. She kept every word in mind: if only some day she could, how she would avenge herself on her whom he loved most in the world. But she hid it all; and when the doors were open again she came to Tristan's bed and served him with food as a lover should, and spoke him gently and kissed him on the lips, and asked him if Kaherdin would soon return with one to cure him . . . but all day long she thought upon her vengeance.

And Kaherdin sailed and sailed till he dropped anchor in the haven of Tintagel. He landed, placed a great gerfalcon on his wrist, took with him a cloth of rare dye and a cup well chiselled and worked, and made a present of them to King Mark, and courteously begged of him his peace and safeguard that he might traffick in his land; and the King gave him his peace before all the men of his palace.

Then Kaherdin offered the Queen a buckle of fine gold; and "Queen," said he, "the gold is good."

Then taking from his finger Tristan's ring, he put it side by side with the jewel and said:

"See, O Queen, the gold of the buckle is the finer gold; yet that ring also has its worth."

When Iseult saw what ring that was, her heart trembled and her colour changed, and fearing what might next be said she drew Kaherdin apart near a window, as if to see and bargain the better; and Kaherdin said to her, low down:

"Lady, Tristan is wounded of a poisoned spear and is about to die. He sends you word that you alone can bring him comfort, and recalls to you the sorrows that you bore together. Keep you the ring—it is yours."

But Iseult answered, nearly swooning:

"Friend, I will follow you; get ready your ship tomorrow at dawn."

And on the morrow at dawn the Queen announced that she wished to hunt with falcons and had her dogs and birds made ready. But Duke Andret, ever on the watch, accompanied her. When they reached the fields not far from the shore of the sea, a pheasant whirred up. Andret unleashed a falcon to seize it; but the day was clear and fine: the falcon soared aloft and disappeared.

"See, Sir Andret," said the Queen, "the falcon has perched itself on the mast of a ship which I do not know. Whose is it?"

"Mistress," said Andret, "it is the ship of that Breton merchant who yesterday made you a present of a gold clasp. Let us go there to recapture our falcon."

Kaherdin had stretched a plank as a gangway from his ship to the shore. He came to meet the Queen:

"Lady, if it please you, enter my ship and I will show you my rich wares."

"Willingly, Sir," said the Queen.

She dismounted, stepped to the plank, crossed it, and stepped into the ship. Andret sought to follow her and was on the plank when Kaherdin from the deck struck him with his oar: Andret staggered and fell into the sea. He tried to swim; Kaherdin struck him blow after blow and held him under the waves and cried:

"Die, traitor! These are your wages for the evil you have done to Tristan and to the Queen Iseult."

Thus God avenged the lovers on the felons who had so hated them. All four were dead: Guenelon, Gondoïne, Denoalen, Andret.

They raised anchor, stepped mast and hoisted sail. The fresh wind of morning whistled in the rigging and swelled the sails. Out of the harbour, towards the high seas, white and flashing under the rays of the sun, sailed the ship.

But at Carhaix Tristan lay and longed for Iseult's coming. Nothing now filled him any more, and if he lived it was only as

awaiting her; and day by day he sent watchers to the shore to see if some ship came, and to learn the colour of her sail. There was no other thing left in his heart.

He had himself carried to the cliff of the Penmarks, where it overlooks the sea, and all the daylight long he gazed far off over the water.

Hear now a tale most sad and pitiful to all who love. Already was Iseult near; already the cliff of the Penmarks showed far away, and the ship ran heartily, when a storm wind rose on a sudden and grew, and struck the sail, and turned the ship all round about, and the sailors bore away and sore against their will they ran before the wind. The wind raged and big seas ran, and the air grew thick with darkness, and the ocean itself turned dark, and the rain drove in gusts. The yard snapped, and the sheet; they struck their sail, and ran with wind and water. In an evil hour they had forgotten to haul their pinnace aboard; it leapt in their wake, and a great sea broke it away.

Then Iseult cried out: "God does not will that I should live to see him, my love, once—even one time more. God wills my drowning in this sea. O, Tristan, had I spoken to you but once again, it is little I should have cared for a death come afterwards. But now, my love, if I do not come to you, it is because God does not will it, and this is my deepest grief. My death is as nothing to me: since God wishes it, I accept it; but, friend, when you learn of it, you will die, well I know. Our love is such that you cannot die without me nor I without you. I see your death before me at the same time as my own. Alas, friend, I have failed of my wish: it was to die in your arms, to be buried in your tomb; but we both have failed. I shall die alone, and without you, disappear in the sea. Perhaps you will not hear of my death, you will live, ever hoping that I come. If God wishes, you may even grow well again. . . . Ah, maybe afterwards you will love another woman, you will love Iseult of the White Hands. I do not know how it will be with you: for my part, if I knew you dead, I would not live on. May God bring us together, friend, or may I heal you, or may we both die of the same wound."

And thus the Queen complained so long as the storm endured; but after five days it died down. Kaherdin hoisted the sail, the white sail, right up to the very masthead with great joy; the white sail, that Tristan might know its colour from afar: and already Kaherdin saw Brittany far off like a cloud. Hardly were these things seen and done when a calm came, and the sea lay even and untroubled. The sail bellied no longer, and the sailors held the ship now up, now down the tide, beating backwards and forwards in vain. They saw the shore afar off, but the storm had carried their boat away and they could not land. On the third night Iseult dreamt this dream: that she held in her lap a boar's head which befouled her skirts with blood; then she knew that she would never see her lover again alive.

Tristan was now too weak to keep his watch from the cliff of the Penmarks, and for many long days, within walls, far from the shore, he had mourned for Iseult because she did not come. Dolorous and alone, he mourned and sighed in restlessness: he was near death from desire.

At last the wind freshened and the white sail showed. Then it was that Iseult of the White Hands took her vengeance.

She came to where Tristan lay, and she said:

"Friend, Kaherdin is here. I have seen his ship upon the sea. She comes up hardly—yet I know her; may he bring that which shall heal thee, friend."

And Tristan trembled and said:

"Beautiful friend, you are sure that the ship is his indeed? Then tell me what is the manner of the sail?"

"I saw it plain and well. They have shaken it out and hoisted it very high, for they have little wind. For its colour, why, it is black."

And Tristan turned him to the wall, and said:

"I cannot keep this life of mine any longer." He said three times: "Iseult, my friend." And in saying it the fourth time, he died.

Then throughout the house, the knights and the comrades of

Tristan wept out loud, and they took him from his bed and laid him on a rich cloth, and they covered his body with a shroud. But at sea the wind had risen; it struck the sail fair and full and drove the ship to shore, and Iseult the Fair set foot upon the land. She heard loud mourning in the streets, and the tolling of bells in the minsters and the chapel towers; she asked the people the meaning of the knell and of their tears. An old man said to her:

"Lady, we suffer a great grief. Tristan that was so loyal and so right, is dead. He was open to the poor; he ministered to the suffering. It is the chief evil that has ever fallen on this land."

But Iseult, hearing them, could not answer them a word. She went up to the palace, following the way, and her cloak was random and wild. The Bretons marvelled as she went; nor had they ever seen woman of such a beauty, and they said:

"Who is she, or whence does she come?"

Near Tristan, Iseult of the White Hands crouched, maddened at the evil she had done, and calling and lamenting over the dead man. The other Iseult came in and said to her:

"Lady, rise and let me come by him; I have more right to mourn him than have you—believe me. I loved him more."

And when she had turned to the east and prayed God, she moved the body a little and lay down by the dead man, beside her friend. She kissed his mouth and his face, and clasped him closely; and so gave up her soul, and died beside him of grief for her lover.

When King Mark heard of the death of these lovers, he crossed the sea and came into Brittany; and he had two coffins hewn, for Tristan and Iseult, one of chalcedony for Iseult, and one of beryl for Tristan. And he took their beloved bodies away with him upon his ship to Tintagel, and by a chantry to the left and right of the apse he had their tombs built round. But in one night there sprang from the tomb of Tristan a green and leafy briar, strong in its branches and in the scent of its flowers. It climbed the chantry and fell to root again by Iseult's tomb. Thrice did the peasants cut it down, but thrice it grew again as flowered and as strong. They

told the marvel to King Mark, and he forbade them to cut the briar any more.

The good singers of old time, Beroul and Thomas of Built, Gilbert and Gottfried told this tale for lovers and none other, and, by my pen, they beg you for your prayers. They greet those who are cast down, and those in heart, those troubled and those filled with desire, those who are overjoyed and those disconsolate, all lovers. May all herein find strength against inconstancy, against unfairness and despite and loss and pain and all the bitterness of loving.

»II«

ADVENTURES

AND ESCAPADES

⁂ The Story of Frithjof and Ingebjorg

The story, though laid in Norway, belongs to the cycle of
Icelandic sagas. It was probably composed in the late thir-
teenth or the early fourteenth century. The action is pre-
sumed to take place in the early ninth century, but it is
doubtful if it has any basis in fact. The translation, by Eustace
Hinton Jones, is taken from Sir George W. Cox and E. H.
Jones, *Popular Romances of the Middle Ages* (New York:
Henry Holt, 1880).

KING BELÉ of Norroway had a little daughter named
Ingebjorg. The boy Frithjof was her playfellow in her
father's palace. No king's son nor royal prince was Frithjof: he
was only Thane Thorsten's boy. But the king and the thane were
friends; and because friendship makes all men equal, there was no
more constraint betwixt king and thane than betwixt their two
children which played together in the palace.

When Ingebjorg was six years old it came into King Belé's
mind to send her to the sage Hilding, to learn the wisdom of men
and the knowledge of the gods; but liking not to part the chil-
dren, he asked leave of Thorsten and sent Frithjof also, to be
brought up with her in all the learning of the time.

Hilding dwelt by the sea. Above the windy cliffs, far up a
bleak down-side, was a garden in the hollow of the hills, sheltered
by wood and mountain; a garden where one might always hear
the breaking of the waters on the beach. There Hilding dwelt;
there he taught Ingebjorg and Frithjof many years. You have
seen the bud that swells and pinkens till the glory of the rose
unfolds? So fair grew Ingebjorg. You have seen the sapling oak
grow up and lift its arms to brave the storm? So strong grew
Frithjof. Hilding taught Frithjof the Runes because he was the
elder; but Ingebjorg learned them of her playmate. In the open

air she learned them, from his lips, wandering with him across breezy hills, or through forests of murmurous pine, or sitting at his feet by the sea-shore, watching the white-fringed waves curl in. The first spring flowers of the year, the first summer fruit, Ingebjorg took from Frithjof's hands. For her he climbed the tallest trees to bring down birds' nests; for her he clambered up the steep black crag upon the promontory, and robbed the eagle's eyrie. Sometimes in a little boat the boy would venture with her far out upon the heaving sea; but if the wind blew and heeled the boat a-list, or drave the spray in sheets upon them, Ingebjorg would only clap her hands for joy: she had no fear where Frithjof was.

As their childhood wore away Ingebjorg stayed oftener at home, learning embroidery and womanly work; Frithjof grew up a great hunter. Yet ever he brought his spoils to Ingebjorg—no longer flowers and fruit, but heads of wild boar, skins of bear.

In the long winter evenings, sitting round the hearth, Hilding would tell them stories of the gods. Sometimes he spake of Freyja and her golden hair which is praised in all lands; but Frithjof would smooth Ingebjorg's shining tresses, and think, "Freyja's hair is less beautiful and golden than this." Sometimes he talked of Frigga, and how she had the most lovely eyes in all the world; but Frithjof looked into Ingebjorg's sweet blue eyes, and believed it not.*

. . . Hilding taught them of the Death of Summer time. When it thundered he would say, "Hark, that is the rumbling of Thor's chariot wheels over the clouds!" And when it lightened, "See how his hammer flashes across the sky! He is flinging at the Trolls." So Hilding joined earth and heaven in their minds, and showed them the parables of trees and hills and clouds.

What wonder that, as they grew in years, great love sprang up between the two? What wonder if they saw the beauty of the gods within each other's eyes? Frithjof was Ingebjorg's Baldur; she, his soft-eyed Nanna. And when Frithjof would tell Inge-

* An interpolated story is here omitted.—Ed.

bjorg that she would be his wife some day, it made her glad: in truth she wished no better lot.

But Hilding when he knew of this was sorry and said: "O Frithjof, root out this love from thy heart before it grow up and bear thorns. Thou art a bondsman's son. Ingebjorg is daughter of King Belé, whose generation springeth from the gods."

Frithjof answered, "Hast thou not taught me that before the gods a man is what he is, not what his fathers were? Do not the gods deny their own offspring if they prove unworthy, and take instead to sit with them in Valhalla the noble-minded and the fierce in war?"

But Hilding only bade him think no more of his love, for that evil would certainly come of it.

King Belé waxed old and feeble. One day as he sat in his palace he leaned on the hand of his friend, the grey old thane Thorsten. And the king said, "Good friend, our life-day is far spent, and the night draws on. The steel helmet presses heavily on my weary head; the mead has lost its flavour. It is time to rest. But through the darkness we will muse upon the brightness of the gods—so shall our thoughts be like stars to cheer the night, until the day break on the golden splendour of Valhalla. Summon hither my sons, and with them thy son Frithjof, that I may bless them while I have strength, and bid them hold together as we have done."

Thither came the king's sons, Helgi and Halfdan, to the palace; Frithjof was with them. Dark and gloomy was the countenance of Helgi: he came from communion with the priests; blood fresh upon his hands from the noontide sacrifice. Halfdan, the younger, bright as sunshine, had the face and form of some fair wilful girl who had girt on sword and ringmail for a merry jest. Frithjof stood a head above them both, and nobler, as the noon is twixt the night and day.

King Belé said: "When I am gone I would have you three dwell in one mind. As the spear-ring bindeth the spear-shaft together, so fellowship shall make you strong. Let the sword-point guard your borders, but cover ye the kingdom with the

shield. In the people is the strength of a king. He is a fool that oppresseth them; the tree withers when the roots lack nourishment. There be four pillars which do carry the heavens, but only one pillar supporteth the throne of a king. Law is its name; and that king which doeth his own will instead of the law, pulleth down the seat whereon he sitteth. Son Helgi, be strong, but forget not mercy. Mercy adorneth might as a flower is an ornament to a brazen shield. The mighty should be tender; the best blade bendeth most. Trust not to auguries; the signs in the altar-victim may deceive, but never the Runes that Odin writes upon an honest heart. Get trusty friends; they are to a man like bark to a tree, to shelter the heart in the evil day of winter storm. Boast never of thy sires. What profiteth a mighty bow to him that cannot bend it to send forth the arrow? Every river rolleth to the sea on his own waves. Halfdan, thou art bright and pleasant; but the sweetest honey without hops will make no mead. Let thy sword-hilt glisten with gems, if so thou hast the mind, but when thou drawest it let all man know that the blade is steel. Get knowledge; fools are many, wise men few. Remember folk will come to thy feasts because thou art a king's son; they will eat thy dainty meats and drink thy mead; but if a fool sitteth at the head of the table, they will turn and listen to a wise man in a lowly seat. Choose not too many friends; only an empty house is open to everybody."

Thorsten likewise spake to Frithjof: "My son, honour the gods. Though their dwelling-place is in Disirsaal, they see everywhere, even into the hearts of men. As the flowers are gladdened when they look up to the sun, so is a man's heart when he thinketh of the gods. Honour the king: it is needful that there should be one master in a kingdom; the bright day hath one sun, but the darksome night hath many stars. The people is the kingdom's sword against the enemy: one man may take the sword by the hilt, but many grasping it by the blade shall wound themselves. Son, thou art strong, and strength is the gift of the gods. Nevertheless, be not proud of thy strength: for a bear hath the strength of twelve men, yet one man taketh him. Many a one that stilteth himself up with pride, cometh down to walk on crutches. Death

is sure to every man: his might faileth and his strength dieth with him, but his fame liveth after he is gone, and sweet is the savour of good deeds."

Then after the two old friends, king and thane, had counselled their children, they gave commandment to be laid side by side in two mounds on the seashore, where the murmur of the waves might hush them in their sleep. And it came to pass soon after that they closed their eyes and died. Never, all his life, had King Belé faced fight without the trusty Thorsten at his right hand; and even in death the thane went with him down to Hel's dark kingdom.

They which go by the mounds to this day hear oftentimes strange murmurings like far-off voices. Some say that it is nothing but the wash of the sea upon the beach, or the wind blowing through the crisp brown grasses on the cliffs; others lift a finger and say, "Listen, King Belé and his faithful thane are whispering in their sleep!"

Then Helgi and Halfdan began to reign in Norroway, ruling the kingdom between them.

But Frithjof went away to take possession of his inheritance of Framnäs:* three miles of farm and pasture bordered by the sea. Birchwoods crowned the heights: on the slopes waved yellow barley and rye, tall as a man; sleek herds browsed in the lush green meadows; on the plains the woolly sheep slow drifted, white as the cloud-flocks in the sky; the lakes were full of fish, the forests of broad-antlered elk. Twelve pair of chargers, bridled storm-winds, champed impatient in their stalls; their manes knotted with scarlet, their hoofs bright with iron. The mead-hall, built of pine, would seat six hundred men. Holm oak benches and tables were ranged round against the walls. A black, glossy bearskin, with a mouth of scarlet, and silver claws, lay thrown across the chief seat at the end, where Thorsten had been wont to sit; and on either side were carven in elm the images of Odin, All-ruler, and Frig the god of rain and sunshine. In the midst of

* Framnäs: on the Sognefjord, about fifty miles north of Bergen.—Ed.

the hall was a hearth of polished stone, whereon was always a merry blaze, sweet-scented of the resinous pine-wood, and above it a great chimney, so wide that at night one might look up and see the stars twinkle. Against the walls hung suits of mail and arms enough to furnish a host of men; well filled were the cellars with good ale and mead, and the chests in the store-rooms were heavy with booty.

But greater riches had Frithjof than these, for he inherited three far-famed treasures.

The first was Angurvadel, bright as the northern light, the wondrous sword made by the dwarfs, the hilt whereof was gold, and on whose blade were written mystic Runes which none might read. In time of peace the Runes grew dull and pale, but in the battle-day they blazed forth red as blood and fierce as fire.

Next was a golden arm-ring, wrought about the hoop with pictures of the gods, and in the midst a glittering ruby. Lame Wayland the smith made it for the first of Thorsten's race. But a Viking named Soté stole it from Thorsten, and taking ship hasted to Britain. Thither Thorsten pursued him, King Belé also bearing him company. On the rocky shore they found a cavern wherein was a mighty tomb. Thorsten and Belé looked in and saw a fearful vision of the black ship of the Viking, that moved and shimmered like to flame. Upon the vessel's mast, in a robe of fire, sat a skeleton scouring a sword-blade to get the blood-stains out, but all in vain; and on his arm of bone there shone the bracelet. Then they knew that Soté was dead, and that this was his spirit: and King Belé said, "Let us both go in"; but Thorsten answered, "Nay, shame it were for two to fight with one." Then went he in. King Belé listened and heard the clash of swords, and horrible wailings which cannot be uttered. Then came a long and fearful cry; then silence. Thorsten came running out, white as a stone, with cold dews upon his face: but the ring was on his arm. What had happened King Belé never knew, and Thorsten would not tell. Once only the thane spake of it, and said; "Would rather I had died than bought the ring so dear."

The third great treasure was the ship Ellide. It was in likeness

of a dragon, with golden head and open jaws at the prow; the belly thereof was scaled with blue and gold; and it ended at the stern with a twisted tail of silver. The planks of the ship were not joined by the shipwright, but had grown together. It had black sails, bordered curiously with red, like to a dragon's wings; and when they were outspread the ship flew over the calmest sea as though before a storm. One of Thorsten's forefathers, when out at sea, picked off a sinking wreck an old man with green tangled locks like seaweed, and brought him home, warmed him at his fire, and gave him mead. Not knowing who he was, he would have sheltered him through the night; but the old man said that it was time to be away at sea, and vanished, none knew whither. That was the great god Ægir, the sea-ruler: he sent the ship for a present for befriending him.

Those were the treasures of Frithjof.

Frithjof came to the mead-hall to the funeral feast. Twelve champions sate round his board. At his right hand was the fair-haired Björn, bright as a flower among withered leaves. There in the wine-cup, Frithjof and Björn sware fellowship for life. Then silently all drained the mead-horn to the memory of good Thane Thorsten. The Skalds came in and sang the praises of the dead.

Helgi and Halfdan sate in judgment by the gravemound of their father. To them came Frithjof, sailing across the sea in Ellide his dragon-ship, Björn and his companions with him. Lightly stepped Frithjof from the ship, and coming into the circle of men thus spake: "King Helgi and King Halfdan, are we friends, even as our fathers were? I crave a boon of you. I am not of kingly race as ye are, and might have waited till with my strong hand I had won a kingdom for myself, made myself your equal, and then, with a crown of red gold on my head, come and proffered my request. But love of the land and the throne is strong in me, and I would rather stay and fight for Norroway, to keep her kings in safety on the throne, and her peasants secure within their homesteads. Wherefore I pray you give me Inge-bjorg to wife. Have we not grown together from childhood, till love has made us part and parcel of each other? Surely King Belé

willed it so in training us together. Here, by his mound I ask it: beneath the earth he hears me: let it be according as he willed."

Helgi's face grew dark, and with a sneer he answered: "The thane's son, bred upon my father's alms, would seek to mate with Odin's line! Bounty is wasted on a bondsman. Raise a peasant from the dunghill, and he will want to elbow thee from off the throne. Kind it is of thee to offer to guard my people and my land. Know that the king is the people's shield. Cease from presumption, and perchance, for my father's sake and the odd liking he bare to thine, I may find room for thee among my hired servants."

Frithjof laughed bitterly, and to his sword cried, "Wake, Angurvadel!" The good blade leaped from the scabbard, blood-red its runes. But Frithjof said, "Helgi, I cannot smite thy black heart from its bone-house; thou art son of my father's friend." Then went he to a tree where Helgi's shield of gold and brass hung upon a bough, and at one blow of his sword cleft it in twain. "That was well struck, good Angurvadel: back to thy scabbard and dream of war till I awake thee next." Then whilst Helgi and his men stood silent, cowering for fear, Frithjof cried scornfully, "Birth! Lineage! He says we are not equal! Look at the sons of Odin's line, trembling before the thane!" Angry he gat him to his dragon-ship, and crossed the sea-ways home.

Far away north dwelt old King Ring, gentle as Baldur, wise as Mimir. His people loved his silver hairs; his ear was ever open to their cry; the wronged he righted, the distressed he comforted. No war-ships anchored in his bays, but merchant ships came thither from all lands to barter. No war-steeds trampled down the standing corn on the peasant's land. Ring dwelt in peace, the father of his people. From every home prayers went up continually to Odin for his welfare. But King Ring's wife was dead, and he had mourned her long, till, being desolate, and his folk urging him, he looked to find a mother for his dead wife's child, and a queen for the comfort of his people. And hearing the fame of Ingebjorg, who men said was gentle as she was fair, the king sent messengers with costly presents to woo her from her brothers.

But King Helgi spake austerely to the messengers, and bade them wait three days for an answer, whilst he sought auguries from the entrails of falcons and horses new-killed upon the altar-stone. On the fourth day Helgi returned from communing with the priests, and said to the messengers, "Many victims have we slain to learn the will of the gods, and the augury of them all is, Nay. King Ring must be a man of evil heart: he is displeasing to the gods: I have no will but theirs." Halfdan said merrily, "Tell old Greybeard to come himself, and see how quickly we will help him on his horse again." And with that they turned and left the messengers without so much as a farewell or a courtesy.

So the messengers returned to their king and told him how they were treated. King Ring pushed back his golden seat and stood upright. He said, "Old Greybeard *will* go himself." Then strode he to the courtyard, and smote upon the great brazen war-shield of the land that rusted there upon a lime-tree. Quick gathered he his warriors, and filled the bay with war-ships, numberless and terrible.

Helgi was afraid and knew not what to do when he learned that King Ring was coming to fight him. But he took Ingebjorg and shut her up in the temple of Baldur for safety; for Baldur's temple is safe against unhallowed feet amongst all Northmen. Moreover, Helgi prevailed upon old Hilding to go and intercede for him with Frithjof and to persuade him to come and help them against King Ring.

Hilding found Frithjof playing chess with Björn, at a board with gold and silver squares. Frithjof greeted his old tutor gladly, but would not listen to his message: he poured out a horn of mead and bade him refresh himself whilst they finished the game.

Then Hilding said, "O Frithjof, cease to be angry with Helgi and Halfdan. Haste to help them, for King Ring cometh with all his men to fight against us."

Frithjof made as though he heard not. "Björn, here is check to the king. Will you save it with the pawn? But what is a pawn, a paltry pawn, that it should save the king?"

Hilding, well knowing for whom the speech was meant, said, "My son, be not high-minded: Helgi and Halfdan may be weak against King Ring, but against thee they are strong enough to lay waste thy house and take thy land."

Frithjof laughed: "So Björn, you would have my castle? Well, I have guarded it with my knights; so try your worst."

Hilding said, "Leave the game, Frithjof, for the game of war. Behold Ingebjorg weeps day and night in Baldur's grove. Let her tears intercede with you."

Frithjof cried, "Björn! Björn! would you take my queen away? But the queen shall be saved!"

Frithjof left his game and stood up, and took Hilding by the hand. "You have heard my answer. Go, tell Helgi, 'The king is the people's shield,' and I will not be his thane."

Hilding answered, "Son, I have done my duty; but I blame thee not."

At sunset Frithjof led Björn to the beach where Ellide, his dragon-ship, pulled impatient at her cable. They got into the ship. "Whither goest thou?" asked Björn. "To Ingebjorg," he said.

"What! To profane the grove of Baldur?"

Frithjof answered, "I care not, and I dare. I must see Ingebjorg. I will see Ingebjorg. Friend Björn, the gods see everywhere. Baldur knows that my heart is clean of ill-intent. An honest heart defiles no temple. I will go."

Baldur's grove was bounded by a wall which reached the sea. No man might enter that holy place on pain of death, save after sacrifice and purification by the priests. Frithjof heeded not: he climbed the steep wall by the sea, and came to Ingebjorg, who trembled for fear because he had profaned the grove. "Fear not, dear Ingebjorg, but come, let us seek Baldur's pardon, and Baldur's blessing on our love." Together they walked through the silent grove, and came into the temple and bowed themselves before the altar of the god. When they arose a calm fell upon Frithjof's mind. Ingebjorg said, "Dear Frithjof, they who worship here, being sanctified, may listen to the promptings of their hearts, for Baldur from his altar sheddeth peace. What wouldst

thou do?" Frithjof answered, "My anger against thy brethren is turned away. I will do all to make the peace save give thee up. I will go to Helgi in presence of all the people, will give my hand to him in friendship, and ask him to forget the past, to give thee to me, and to take the faithful service of my life." Ingebjorg kissed him, saying, "Go; they are Baldur's words and mine." So he went upon the errand.

Three days passed by; then Frithjof climbed the wall again, and came into the grove to Ingebjorg. Pale and cast-down he came. She saw the answer in his face, yet asked him, "It has failed?"

He answered, "It has failed. Hear what I have borne with a patient and a steadfast mind. I came to them as they sate by the mounds; thousands were with them, taking counsel about the war. Meekly I said to Helgi, 'O king, I have been hasty and impatient, and maybe have presumed too much. Let all the past be past. The enemy is near. Let us be friends. What do I seek? I ask thee to make thy sister happy and our land strong against the foe. Give me Ingebjorg, and bid me fight against this Ring or any man. By Thor! you shall see how strong my arm is.' All the people urged him, saying, 'Give him thy sister, for there is no better mate for her in all the Northland.' Then spake old Hilding long and wisely, urging him, and even Halfdan thy brother, sitting at his side, turned round and likewise spake for me. But Helgi sat listening to their words and mine as a stone upon the altar listens to the pleadings of a victim. He would not take my hand, nor yet refuse it, but sat still as an image. There was silence. He cannot speak without a sneer: he said, 'I am well-nigh minded to make friends. Forced by sore need to buy my friendship dear, I would be fain to give my sister to a thrall's son; but never to him that has profaned the sanctuary. Perchance it is not true; yet I have heard how one brake into Baldur's temple, and defiled his holy grove. Is this so? Answer me—was it thou?' Up rose the people's cry, 'It is not true! Frithjof has not done this abominable thing!' My Ingebjorg, it was hard to answer; to turn the people's clamour in my cause to hate; to lose thee, almost won. But I never

thought to lie. I answered, 'Unbidden I climbed into Baldur's grove, since Ingebjorg was there. Where she is I will go, in Asgard or in Hel, and neither man nor god shall keep me back. Yet hearken; I defiled not the temple of the god; judge ye, for lo I entered it burning with hate—peace fell on me there, and thence, straightway, I came to thee with gentle words which Baldur put into my mind.' Then I became accursed in men's sight, and folk drew back and shunned me like a leper. No longer any raised his voice for me. Helgi said, 'Death is the penalty, but my judgment shall be as gentle as the god whose temple you have polluted. Away in the western islands dwelleth Yarl Angantyr, who paid us tribute till King Belé died; now he holdeth fast his gold. Men say he sleeps upon it as the dragon Fafnir did upon the treasure. Go, wrest the tribute from him. If you bring it, well; if not, return no more.' Such, Ingebjorg, is my sentence. Men think it just and merciful. Ellide swims at anchor yonder, and I go."

"And leave me, Frithjof?"

"Nay, sweet one, nay, I will take thee with me. Come, where none shall point the finger at thy mate, and say, 'Profane!' and shudder and turn aside. See, Ellide spreads her wings all eager for the sea. Come to Yarl Angantyr's islands. He was my father's friend, though Helgi knows it not, and he will welcome us."

"And wouldst thou break thy word and not bring back the tribute?"

"Never fear but we will send Helgi back his dross, and be for ever free of him. Come!"

"O Frithjof, I was to blame. My heart goes with thee, but I cannot come. Helgi is in my father's place. I dare not disobey him. It is theft to steal the happiness forbidden; not less so when it hangs within our reach, but only harder to refrain from plucking it."

"Hast thou no other word for me?"

"Go, Frithjof, alone. I will not have men say of thee, he lurked about and stole his wife and fled lest he should face her brother."

Heavily turned Frithjof away. "Proud daughter of a king, I go alone: farewell."

"Proud? Aye proud; but only proud of thee, dear Frithjof." She came and leaned upon his breast and covered him with kisses. "Do I not love thee, Frithjof, that thou wouldst go away without a kiss, whilst I shall sit and weep till thy return? Go, with a brave, strong heart, and trust in me."

Then Frithjof felt that she was right, and he kissed her and drew forth the armlet of Soté and set it for a pledge upon her arm. So they parted; and he gat him to his dragon-ship and sailed away.

When Frithjof had been many days at sea, the wind blew cold, the hoar-frost whitened deck and spars, the rigging grew stiff with ice, and the oarsmen's hands were numbed with cold. The clouds piled black and brooded down; the sea, moved from its depths, rolled in great tossing hills, and seethed and roared. Furious the storm-waves leaped upon Ellide to swamp her. The good ship quivered with the blows, and lurching, shook herself, then fearless swooped down the yawning water-valleys, and darted up the green sea-hills. Afar they saw the storm-fiends riding on a whale; one like a white bear, the other the great storm-eagle, fanning the tempest with her huge black wings. They are the sea-witches Heyd and Ham; and it was Helgi who sent them to raise this storm to swallow up his enemy. Then Frithjof took the tiller in hand and steered straight on the fiends. "Help me, brave Ellide; show thyself the sea-god's gift. On, on, with all thy speed." And when the good ship heard her master's voice, all her deck-planks creaked as she flew on and smote the whale with her bow so mightily that he sank into the depths; and the storm-fiends were left tossing on the water, till the sea-weed tangled them and the storm went down. The sun shone out, the sea grew calm and blue, and Frithjof anchored off the island where Angantyr dwelt.

Yarl Angantyr was feasting in his castle. He looked out of his window and said, "That is Thane Thorsten's dragon-ship Ellide." Then arose Atli, fiercest of his Vikings, and said, "If this be Frithjof, I will know if there be a spell in his sword as men have said." The battle-madness came on Atli as he went forth to fight.

Frithjof had landed with twelve of his men. They had brought food and kindled a fire, and being very tired, sate them down on the beach to eat their meal. Atli came haughtily, and called with a loud voice, "Choose! Fight, flee, or yield!"

Frithjof answered, "We are men already wearied with fighting the sea; but we will neither flee nor yield." With that they fell to and fought, till Frithjof, with Angurvadel, cut Atli's sword in twain.

"There is witchery in thy sword," cried Atli.

Frithjof said, "Try my hands then," and flung away his sword and wrestled with the Viking. Back he bent the big man like a reed, and held him arched upon a balance, till he overcame his quivering sinews and flung Atli heavily upon his shoulders.

Kneeling on his enemy's breast, Frithjof said, "Had I now my sword I would still that tongue of thine, that it should no more boast itself against tired men."

"Fetch it. I will not stir. Valhalla for the brave! for you to-morrow, for me to-day." So spake the Viking.

Frithjof fetched his sword, but Atli quailed not. He drew the blade, and the fierce runes shone red; the Viking stirred not, but with a quiet eye awaited death. Frithjof put back his sword into its sheath, and taking Atli by the hand, said, "Man, arise; thou art too brave to die: let us be friends." So they went together to Angantyr's castle.

Frithjof marvelled at the richness of the mead-hall. The walls were hung with gilded leather curiously wrought with flowers. The hearth was marble. White tapers in silver candlesticks shone everywhere like stars. There was glass in the windows of many colours: the doors had locks. In the chief seat, on a chair of silver, sat Yarl Angantyr, clad in armour of gold and steel. From his shoulders fell a purple robe sprinkled with silver stars. The meats were served in silver dishes. Many warriors sate round the board, and when Frithjof entered all rose and hailed him, and having drained the mead-horn to his honour, led him to a seat on Yarl Angantyr's right hand.

The Yarl said, "Son of Thorsten my old friend, thou art

welcome." Then Frithjof told his story, and wherefore he had come; told of his love for Ingebjorg, and the sentence laid on him by Helgi.

Angantyr answered, "Never yet paid I tribute to any man, but I gave King Belé of Norroway many gifts for friendship's sake. As to his sons, I know them not; and for tribute, bid them first unlock my coffers with their swords. But I will give a gift to thee for Thorsten's sake. I loved him, and his son is dear to me." Then he called for a purse, and his daughter fetched one which she had broidered with needlework and precious stones. On it was the likeness of a castle in a forest, with golden beasts among the trees, and it was fringed with pearls. Angantyr filled the purse to the brim with gold, and gave it to Frithjof, saying, "Take it: it is thine: a gift of welcome to my friend. Do with it as thou wilt. Only abide with us for a while." So the good-hearted Yarl persuaded him to tarry on from day to day, till whilst he lingered winter passed and springtime came. Then, longing for his home and Ingebjorg, Frithjof pushed Ellide into the sea and stood for the Northland.

Seven days he sailed the sea; then looking out afar he saw the land; a long blue line of cliff and hill, soft as a cloud betwixt the earth and sky. His heart beat fast, for he was nearing home; and as the blue waxed grey he strove to make out Framnäs, the dwelling of his fathers—looked for its birch-crowned heights, its mellow fields dotted with flocks and herds. But as he looked the view faded; a mist came over the sun and dwelt on sea and land. So he ran Ellide to shore, and coasted till he reached the well-known creek and heard the waterfall leap down the hills of his home to the sea. He beached the ship, and with a glad heart set foot on the misty shore, and took the path up by the cliffs.

His homestead gate was gone. His home was gone. There was a wild and a waste where Framnäs was. He trode on ashes every-where. Black ashes heaped on scorched grass: trees cindered into black stumps of arms where they stood: ruin and blackness—that was Framnäs. And in the midst a heap of charred timber, and stone cracked and powdered white with fire—that was his mead-

hall. His favourite hound, half starved, crept up and licked his hand. His horse came neighing for some corn and thrust his nose against his master's fingers.

That was Frithjof's welcome home.

There had been a great battle with King Ring. Halfdan fought bravely, but was beaten; Helgi took flight, and as he fled fired Framnäs betwixt him and his pursuers to keep them back. Then Belé's sons had begged for peace. Ring bade them choose whether they would give up the land or give him Ingebjorg to wife. They had given up their sister. King Ring had wedded her and taken her away.

Old Hilding told him: Hilding that would not lie. He said, "I saw her wed. They set her on a black horse; she, white as a ghost upon a thunder cloud; and led her to Baldur's temple. There she fell down and made her prayer to Baldur so pitifully, that all which heard her wept. She alone wept not. But I—I know. Often by night when she has deemed herself alone, I have heard her walk and weep, and call upon thy name, and wrestle with her grief. The stricken sea-mew dives that none may see her bleed. She said, 'Baldur hath brought all this to pass because we profaned his temple.' 'Heaven pity *him,*' she said; 'for he will live, but I shall fade and die.' Yes. I saw them wed; and when the Skalds had done their songs, Helgi caught sight of your armlet on her cold white arm. With an oath he snatched it from her and set it on the arm of Baldur's statue. Straightway I drew my sword: fury made me strong; I could have cut him down in the temple where he stood. But she laid a finger on my hand, and whispered, 'Good friend, forbear: Allfather sees and knows; leave judgment unto him.' "

Frithjof said fiercely, "Allfather judgeth by the hand of man. The gods put vengeance in our hearts to do their will. Beware of me; I am harmful to friend and foe: henceforth I am a firebrand on the earth." So the berserk madness fell on Frithjof.

In Baldur's temple they kept the feast of the longest day. Though it was midnight, the sun lay dusky-red upon the moun-

tains. A ruddy twilight glimmered through the grove; within the temple the pine-fire crackled on the hearth. Priests in white bearskin robes stirred the wood-pile, and made the sparks fly up. King Helgi in his royal robes stood sacrificing before the altar. Suddenly there was a noise at the temple-gate, and a sound of voices.

"Björn, keep the door; let no man pass alive!"

Frithjof and his men pushed their way through priests and people to the altar.

Then cried Frithjof, "Helgi, I have done your bidding: I have brought the tribute; but I will first be requited of you. You have robbed me of home and wife; and now, before Allfather, you shall answer for it. Nay, seek not to skulk away; I have tracked the rat to his hiding place and stopped his hole. Here, by the light of Baldur's flames, uncovered by shield, we will fight together with sword, or knife, or hand-gripe."

In terror at his fierceness Helgi slank down against the altar and cowered upon the altar-steps.

Frithjof cried, "Pitiful coward, my sword despises thee!" He took the heavy purse of tribute money, flung it full in Helgi's face, and stunned him there, saying, "Take thy tribute!" and spurned him with his foot. Then to the threatening priests, "Put up your sacrificial knives, you wool-clad mob; lest our thirsty swords mistake you for the victims, us for priests."

Then perceived he the armlet upon Baldur's arm, and he said, "By your good leave, dear god, lame Wayland forged it not for thee. That ring is Ingebjorg's and I will have it!" Fast was the ring upon the arm; but Frithjof pulled and plucked until he tare it off; when lo! with his violence the statue fell into the fire. The fire leaped up and lapped it in its arms; the flames rose high and licked the rafters of the roof, until the temple was ablaze and the gold plates of the ceiling melted and dripped gold upon the floor. In vain they made a chain of men to the sea, and passed buckets of water hand to hand to Frithjof mounted on the roof. The flames would not be quenched. A wind arose and the grove took fire; dry with the summer heat, bough kindled bough, and when

the morning brake, grove and temple were a smouldering heap of ashes.

Frithjof in horror gat him to his ship, and put to sea. He saw the smoke go up to Odin to accuse him, and he said, "There is no hope for me, and no forgiveness for my sin. A wanderer will I be. The sea is free. There will I dwell. I have no home; but thou, my grim dragon, henceforth shalt be my Framnäs; no wife—be thou, my black-winged Ellide, my bride."

Then came Björn and touched him while he mused. "See yonder! Helgi with ten war-ships gives us chase." Quick he forgat his sorrow, and put the ship about, and made ready his men for fight. But Björn was very cool; while the rest shouted the battle-cry and clanged their weapons, he sat still upon the oar-bank watching. Presently the ten ships sank like stones, and all on board were drowned save Helgi, who contrived to swim ashore. And when Frithjof and his men marvelled greatly, Björn laughed aloud; he said, "I bored holes in them last night. Ho! Ho!"

Thenceforth Frithjof and his men became Vikings and roved the seas. Very strict were the laws which he made for his champions. No man might take shelter from storm or sun, by night or day. The deck was the Viking's bed, a shield his pillow, the sky his coverlid. His sword must be short to bring him near his enemy. The Viking never furls sail in a storm: the hurricane carries him the way he would go; the force of the storm helps the arms of the rower. He shall protect merchant ships, but they shall pay him tribute; the merchantmen is a slave to gain, but the Viking's steel is worth as much as his gold. Booty shall be shared by lot without murmuring; all shall share it alike, save their chief; for him the glory alone sufficeth. The Viking shall board the enemy's ship to fight; and he that yieldeth so much as a hair's breadth shall be thrust out of the company. The plea for mercy shall be heeded: he that giveth up his weapon is no more an enemy. No man shall dress his wounds until the fight be done; battle-scars are the ornaments of the Viking.

Three years fought Frithjof, unconquered through all seas, till

victory cloyed on him and he grew sick of spoiling. A lonely man, the longing grew and strengthened in his mind—"If I might look upon her face again!" Fierce fighting lulled it for the time, but ever it came back strong and stronger. So at last he turned the good ship's head to Northland, and like an eagle, Ellide stretched her black wings and sped as though before a storm.

King Ring kept Yule-feast in his hall. The winter of old age had snowed his hairs, yet noble was his countenance. Beside him at the board sat Ingebjorg his queen, pale and drooping as a lily-flower. There was clamour in the hall from noisy warriors merry over the mead-cup, mingled with the sound of pipe and harp.

On the beggars' bench against the door there came and sat an old man bent with age, wrapped from head to foot in a tattered bearskin. He laid aside his staff and rested on the bench. A bluff old warrior, the bully of the board, now blustering in his cups, came up to jeer the beggarman for the others' sport. The beggarman's eye kindled, and in a moment he took the warrior by the middle betwixt his hands, twirled him head over heels, and set him on his feet again.

Then said King Ring, "By all the Gods, that is a strong old man! Come hither, O stranger! Who art thou? Whence comest thou? What is thy name, thy country, and thine errand here?"

The old man answered, "Sorrow nurtured me; want is mine inheritance; my last lodging was a wolf's den. Once I rode a winged dragon. For years I have ploughed green fields, yet left no furrow, reaped no crop but salt. Now in mine age I have journeyed far to hear thy wisdom, which is famed throughout the North."

The king said, "Thy grasp is strong; thy voice is clear. Thou art not old. Wherefore, throw off thy disguise that we may know our guest."

Then Frithjof threw off his bearskin, and behold a young man, bright like Baldur, strong of limb like Thor, golden his hair as sunshine. From his shoulder a blue mantle fell; his coat was girded

with a silver belt whereto a sword was slung; and on his arm were many rings of gold.

Did anyone know him? In the queen's cheeks the colour came and went like the red north-light flushing the snow-fields. But King Ring gave no sign.

There was a blast of horns, and serving-men bare in upon a lordly dish the wild boar on bended knees, served whole, and decked with garlands in Freyr's honour. And when the dish was set upon the table, King Ring laid his finger upon the boar's head and thus spake: "Helgi and Halfdan have I conquered, and hereby I vow by Freyr, whose is this feast and offering, that Frithjof likewise I will overcome."

Frithjof upstarted, wrathful and fierce. "The man you speak of is my friend. I swear I will protect him with all I have and am!"

The king smiled gravely. "Stranger, whoever thou art, I like the bold of speech. Be our guest through the winter. Nay, deny me not." Then spake he to the queen to fill the cup of honour and bear to him.

Trembling she poured the yellow wine into the gold-ringed horn. Scarce could she bear the cup, her hand was shaking so that the mead was spilled upon the floor. Her eyes fastened on the pavement as she bare it, so the stranger should not see her face; but he saw the blushes coursing on her fair white arm. He took the cup and drained it at a draught. Long sate the warriors at their carouse, to the sound of merry music and the brave songs of the Skalds.

While Frithjof tarried with King Ring the sea froze hard; and the king commanded swift horses to be yoked to his sledge, for he would go upon the ice-plain.

"Go not," said Frithjof; "for treacherous is the ice-bound sea; Ran, wife of the sea-god, lurks beneath the brittle ice to drag men down."

Ring answered not, but cried to his steeds, "Away, and show yourselves of Sleipnir's breed!" So saying, he shook loose the reins, and away went the coursers athwart the ringing crust of ice. Then quickly Frithjof fastened his skates upon his feet and

overtook the king's sledge and skated circles round about it, whilst for all the horses might do they could not so much as pass him. Suddenly brake the ice: sledge, steeds, and king went down into the sea. But Frithjof came to the hole, planted his skates firmly in the ice, and gripping the horses by the manes, dragged sledge and all upon the ice again.

"Stranger, that was a brave hand-grip," said the king; "Frithjof himself could not have done better." Frithjof laughed, for he deemed that the king knew him not.

While yet he tarried, springtime came. The birds made music in the new-leafed trees; loosed from their frost-bonds the brooks sang merrily down the valley-sides; and pink as Freya's cheek the rose brake from its coverlid. And as it befell, the king and queen would go a hunting. With them went a multitude of their people to join the sport. Frithjof went also. Like a star upon a fleecy cloud the queen seemed on the proud white horse that bare her. Her hunting-gown was green and gold, and in her hat blue feathers waved. Frigga, earth goddess—Rota, the bright-eyed battle-maid—was scarce more fair than she.

Now, in the midst of the hunting the king grew weary, and fell back from the rest with Frithjof only for company. Afar they heard the baying of the hounds, and the frightened game break-ing through the wood; saw the falcons soar and dart for prey, and the herons swoop in their circles. And lagging still they came into a lonesome place, shut in three sides by trees, but on the fourth was a yawning chasm rent in the cliff—above, a mighty rock-side, and far down the narrow cleft uprose a steam and the faint noise of water plashing in the abyss.

For a while neither spake; but at the last King Ring gat off his horse and said, "O stranger, I am weary; I would rest awhile."

Quick answered Frithjof, "Nay, rest not here. There is danger in this lonely place; I cannot stay with thee. We will hasten to the castle. There shalt thou rest."

The King said, "Not so; slumber cometh at the will of the gods, unlooked for, but when sought avoideth us." So he pre-vailed on him, and Frithjof came down from off his horse, and

sate under a beech-tree against the trunk; he spread his mantle on the ground, and the old king lay down. On Frithjof's lap he laid his head, and closed his eyes; gentle was his rest, as a child's upon his mother's knee, fearing no evil.

Frithjof looked on his quiet face and sat a thinking. This was the man that stood betwixt him and Ingebjorg. His fingers wandered scarce knowing to his sword-hilt, but feeling it they shrank away again.

There came two birds and sate in the tree, the one coal-black, the other white as snow. The black bird sang:—

> Quick! 'twill never be known nor seen.
> Kill the King and win the Queen;
> For she is thine with plighted kiss,
> And a man may take his own, I wis.

But the white bird sang:—

> Allfather sees, and he will know
> The man that slays a sleeping foe;
> Odin can make thy winning vain,
> Or turn thy patience into gain.

Then, fingering at his sword with trembling hand, he drew it forth and shuddering flung it from him. It turned glittering in the air, and dropped far off among the dark trees of the wood. Immediately the black bird fled down to Nastrond, the night kingdom; but lightly the snow-white bird unfolded her wings and soared up into the blue sky, making music in her flight, sweet as the sound of harpstrings.

And the old king awakened upon Frithjof's lap and said, "Sweetly, O my friend, have I slumbered; for a pleasant thing it is to enter the shadow of sleep guarded by a brave man's blade. But where is thy sword? Where is Angurvadel, the lightning's brother?"

Frithjof answered, "It availeth little; there are other swords in the Northland. But it is not well to commune always with

Angurvadel. Sharp is its tongue; it thirsteth evermore for blood, for a dark spirit from Niflheim dwelleth in the steel. It hath no respect for slumber nor grey hairs."

Then said the King, "Frithjof, I know thee. When first thou didst cross my threshold I knew thee; yet I made as though I knew thee not, for I had heard of Frithjof, called of men the Wolf, Frithjof which defiled the sanctuary, the strong-handed one that brake up shield and ship and temple when he willed. And I said I will know this man and prove him. Frithjof, I slept not; I put my life into thy hand to try thee. I know what came into thy mind. Friend, I have tried thee and thou art true. Yet one thing passeth my knowledge—how, being thus true and brave, thou couldst have stolen into my house in beggar's guise to rob me of my wife."

Frithjof said, "The gods well know I never came to rob thee of her—only to look upon her face. Had I the mind to have taken her, who should have hindered me? But I have my punishment to bear. Thou hast not wronged me. She pledged herself to me; she was mine; but Baldur took her from me for my sin and gave her to thee. For this same cause men shun me—call me Wolf of the sanctuary; the very children shrink away when I draw near; Baldur, the gentle god that loveth all things, hateth me, and hideth his face before the blackness of my sin. So I became a wanderer and ploughed the dreary sea. But the longing came on me to see her yet once more; I strove against it, yet I came—a beggar, to look on her sweet face—disguised so that none, not even she, might know me—then without word or sign to go back to the waste wide sea unto my banishment. Thou madest me throw off my beggar dress, and day by day didst urge me to remain, till, deeming myself unknown to all but her, and since my wish was stronger than my will, I yielded. I wronged thee not in word nor thought. But I have stayed too long. To-morrow I will go away, and thou shalt never see me more. Good Ellide! thou hast rested all too long. To-morrow thou shalt spread thy wings to the breeze, and bathe thy dusky bosom in the welcome sea.

The thunderstorm, the roaring hurricane, and the battle-din shall be to me, henceforth, instead of any sweet voice of wife or child, until I die in fight and go up to Valhalla."

Tearfully answered the grey old king: "Dear friend, I blame thee not for loving her. Who that hath seen her can help loving her? I call to mind the fires of my youth, even though in my age the embers have grown cold. Go not away. Stay with us yet. I am old; my days are few; bear with me for a little while until I die; then shalt thou take the queen and all my kingdom for her dower."

King Ring sat on the morrow upon his royal throne; Ingebjorg, all white and trembling sat at his side, knowing what had come to pass. His warriors stood round about.

Haggard and worn came Frithjof into the hall. He had not slept.

He said, "The livelong night I have thought and thought. It must not be. I cannot stay; I cannot look on her and love her not. I dare not stay; I dare not stay to break her peace. But I have brought the arm-ring back. When I am gone I pray thee put it on her arm—'tis hers; 'twill comfort me to know that she is wearing it. One other word, and then farewell. Go not with Ingebjorg to the sea-shore, lest after all I cannot tear myself away, and Angur-vadel drink my life upon the sand; or lest, dying on the sea, my very bones drift back to whiten on your beach."

He turned to go.

The king cried, "Stay! It behoveth never a warrior to be bowed down like a woman. What is death for a king to fear, save only lest he meanly languish out his days and die on straw! To me, alas, it was never given to rise to Valhalla from the battle-plain. The unkind Valkyries chose me not. But Frithjof—I am old and thou art young. To me Death's message cometh, O my friend —to me!"

So saying, he thrust his sword into his breast, and whilst his life-blood spouted to the ground he signed to Frithjof to come near, and placed Ingebjorg's hand in his. Then lifted he the mead-horn high, and with a cheerful countenance cried, "I drink

to my land, to the old Northland. Hail ye gods! Hail warriors of Valhalla! I greet you; and I come!"

So died King Ring of the Northland. The people made his grave-mound, and the bards sang of his wisdom and his gentleness.

After this the folk gathered to the Thing-stone to choose a king; and with one voice the people said, "Yarl Frithjof shall be our king, for Ring's boy is too young." But Frithjof took the little gold-haired child and set him on his shield, and lifted him aloft in sight of all the multitude, saying, "This is your king! Howbeit, until he be grown I will protect the land, and hold the throne for him. Here swear I never to seek my own, but his in all things; and if I am false may Baldur smite me with a yet more heavy punishment!"

The child sprang fearless from the shield to the ground and took Frithjof's hand; and the people shouted: "The boy is king! Yarl Frithjof keeps the throne for him, and he shall wed with Ingebjorg."

But Frithjof went away alone and said within himself—"How can I wed with one so sweet and fair, when I am yet accursed in the sight of the gods and before the people of my land?" Then he took his journey and came to his father's grave-mound by the sea-beach. There he sat all one weary night praying Baldur to take the curse away. And Baldur showed him a sign in the darkness; for lo! he saw a temple in the air, which shone out from the gloom, rose up, and waned away. So Frithjof hasted back, and came to King Ring's palace; and he sent for artificers in wood and stone, and smiths that could work in gold and silver, and he began to build a temple to Baldur after the pattern which he had seen in the vision. All the while it was building he took no pleasure in hunt, or feast, or sound of harp. And when it was done, behold a grove of trees which no man planted sprang up round about, and shut it in on three sides; on the fourth the sea washed the rock whereon it stood, and pictured the temple on its shining face.

The temple was the wonder of the land. It had a gate of brass inwrought with curious work. Huge pillars upbore the roof—a

mighty golden shield. The altar was one hewn stone of North-
land marble, bright-polished, and carved with Runic words of
power. Above it stood the image of Baldur wrought in pure,
shining silver.

When all things were ready, Frithjof went up to the dedication
of the temple to make atonement. As he came into the hall twelve
youthful priestesses in white robes walked two and two about the
altar, singing a sweet hymn to Baldur. Frithjof listened, leaning
on his sword, and as they sang, his soul grew restful; his burden
seemed to pass; and from above the altar the god shone mildly as
the moon upon the peaceful night.

With stately tread came forth the grey high-priest, hoar in the
service of the god; a man of lofty stature, whom age had not
bent; noble his visage, stern of line, yet from his eyes was shed a
kindly light.

Thus he spake:—"Son, welcome to the holy place. The strong
man cometh tired home.

"Baldur has set a parable in the heart of man. To every child
Hel gives back Baldur; but as the child grows, Hoder the blind
god comes; then steals Loki into his heart, making Hoder's hand
to swerve, and Baldur is slain, to dwell thereafter only as a
shadow in his grown-up mind. A man must fight with Loki even
as the gods must do. What careth Baldur that thou heap up stone
on stone? Thrust Loki from thee, if peradventure the bright god
may dimly shine within thy heart again as in thy childhood's
days. He careth not for sacrifice, save only sacrifice of that which
keepeth him from thee.

"Wherefore lay neither horse nor falcon on the altar, but lay
thereon thy pride, thine anger, and thine hate of Belé's sons. Why
dost thou hate them? For their pride of birth? Thou art prouder
of thy strength; yet it is not thine. The gods gave to thee thy
strength, and to them their lineage. Have they wronged thee?
Forgiveness is very sweet to Baldur. But thou hast been high-
minded and high-handed with them. They have suffered; suffered
wasting of their kingdom; their women mourn for warriors sleep-
ing in the great war-mounds; their sister was carried away; Helgi
died wretchedly——."

Frithjof stopped him. "Helgi dead—nay, nay, kind priest! O say not he is dead, and I forgave him not!"

"Helgi is dead. Whilst yet this temple was a-building he warred with the Finns, and laid waste their land. On a cliff there stood an ancient temple to Yumala. No man had entered it for years, because of a saying among the people, 'He that first goeth in shall meet the god upon the threshold.' Helgi cared not. Rashly he sought to spoil the temple of them which he called heathen—men which worship God beneath another shape. The rusty key would not turn in the lock. He tore away the pillars, and shaking down the door, ran in. The heavy idol tumbled from its rotten seat, and fell on him, and crushed him in the temple's dust.

"Frithjof, forgive the dead. Lay by all bitterness and malice against the living. Make peace with Halfdan. Be at peace with all; so peace shall come into thy heart. Baldur hath spoken through me his priest."

Then Frithjof beheld and saw Halfdan standing timidly upon the brazen threshold, fearing to come in. Quick loosed he the sword from his side; and he took the sword and his golden shield and laid them for an offering on Baldur's altar. And he ran to where Halfdan stood, and put his hand in his. The men spake not. Their cheeks reddened; and as they looked into each other's eyes, neither man saw, for that which gathered in his own.

So they were made friends; and the high-priest took off the curse from Frithjof.

Then was heard a sound of music, and from behind the altar, lo there came a band of maidens clad in bridal white, and foremost among them walked Ingebjorg in an ermine robe. She came to Halfdan, meekly to do his bidding in her father's place. He took her hand and said, "My sister!" and he took Frithjof's hand and said, "My brother!" then placed them hand in hand. The old priest lifted up his hands and blessed Frithjof and Ingebjorg in Baldur's name, and the temple was lightened all about with the shining of the god.

❧ Amleth's Revenge
by Saxo Grammaticus

> Saxo Grammaticus, a Danish cleric, wrote, about 1200, the
> *Gesta Danorum,* a chronicle of his countrymen's high deeds.
> He supplies the earliest surviving record of the Hamlet story,
> but it is certainly based on earlier traditions. This translation
> from Danish by Reginald Spink is in a complimentary book
> published by the Press and Information Department of the
> Ministry of Foreign Affairs of Denmark in 1961.

FENG HAS MURDERED HIS BROTHER, THE KING OF DENMARK AND
AMLETH'S FATHER, AND HAS MARRIED THE QUEEN. AMLETH, THE
HEIR TO THE THRONE, FEELS THAT HIS LIFE IS THREATENED.

SEEING THIS, but not wanting to arouse his uncle's suspicions by intelligent action, Amleth behaved like a witless fool, pretending to have taken leave of his senses; by which ruse he not only concealed his intelligence but also saved his life. Day in and day out he sat listless at his mother's hearth, covered in dust and dirt, or he flung himself on the floor and rolled in all the grime and filth. With befouled face and smeared visage he resembled a grotesque and ridiculous fool. His every word was utter nonsense, and all his actions denoted profound folly. In short, one would scarcely have thought him a man at all, but an absurd abortion of some perverse fate. Sometimes he would sit by the hearth, poking the embers with his fingers, and twisting branches into crooks which he would harden in the fire and furnish with barbs to make them hold tighter. When asked what he was about, he would say that he was making spearheads for his father's revenge. This reply evoked no little amusement, all men deriding such an absurd and idle pursuit; but afterwards this very work helped him to carry out his purpose. At the same time, it was his

diligence and care which first aroused suspicion that it was all a ruse on his part; for his very persistence in such a pastime revealed the hidden skill of the craftsman, and no one could believe that a simpleton would be so nimble-fingered and ingenious. Lastly, he would lay the hardened stakes in a pile and most carefully hide them.

For this reason, there were some who pronounced him sane enough, and said that he only concealed his intelligence under a show of simplicity, and cunningly hid his real mind beneath a feigned manner. The surest way of detecting his ruse (they said) would be to bring to him at some secluded place a fair woman who might tempt him to lust; for the natural desire for a woman's embrace was so intense that it could not be held back by cunning, the instinct too powerful to be subdued by guile. If then the apathy were feigned, he would forthwith seize the opportunity and yield to his strong desire. So men were commissioned who would ride deep into the forest with the young man, and there tempt him in this manner. Now among them it so happened that there was a foster-brother of Amleth, who had not forgotten how they had been brought up together, and who rated the memory of their past fellowship higher than the present command. Thus in joining the other appointed companions it was his intention to warn Amleth rather than to entrap him; for he had little doubt that certain death awaited him if he betrayed but the slightest sign of sanity, and especially if he embraced the woman in their sight: an outcome of which Amleth himself was well aware. When they bade him mount his horse he therefore deliberately seated himself the wrong way round, turning his back to its head and his face towards its tail, and laying the reins round its tail, as if to check the horse's wild career from there. By this ingenious device he made a mockery of his uncle's trick and frustrated his evil design. Ludicrous it was indeed to see the horse run off unreined, with the rider holding on by its tail.

On the way Amleth encountered a wolf in the thicket; and when his companions said it was a young colt, he retorted that Feng had few of that kind in his army, thereby alluding wittily

and with subtlety to his uncle's failing.* Then when the others exclaimed that this was wisely answered, he assured them that he had spoken deliberately, that he might in no way be thought of as one who told falsehoods; for he was anxious to appear free from duplicity and guile, and so mingled truth with craft in such a manner that his words could not be called untruthful, yet without betraying his intelligence by revealing his true meaning. When, later, he came down to the beach and his companions found there the rudder of a ship which had been wrecked, saying what a huge knife it was they had come upon, he replied: "Ah, but that is for carving the biggest ham with," whereby he of course meant the wild ocean which the rudder matched. When they also passed the sandhills, and would have him believe that the sand was flour, he answered that it had surely been ground by the beating of the surf. When his companions praised his reply, he retorted that he had indeed spoken shrewdly.

They now left him to himself, that he might more easily gain courage for the satisfaction of his lust, and the woman whom his uncle had intended for him came forward to meet him, as if accidentally, at a secluded spot. He would also have enjoyed her, had not his foster-brother secretly revealed to him their schemes. While pondering the best manner of privily warning the young man, and so restraining his dangerous desire, he observed a passing gadfly, and picking up a straw from the ground he fastened it to its tail and drove the fly in the direction where he supposed Amleth to be; whereby he rendered the unsuspecting young man a great service. The sign was interpreted as shrewdly as it had been given; for observing the gadfly, and perceiving on closer inspection that it had a straw in its tail, Amleth at once understood that this was a secret warning to beware of treachery.† He

* Amleth seems to allude to Feng's cowardice: to the fact that when campaigning he never supplied food for the wolves (note by translator).

† Here there is doubtless an allusion to the word *Agnbak* (Straw-back), a nickname given to one who stole sheaves of corn from the fields, and betrayed himself by the straw which clung to his clothes. It was a crime for which there were heavy penalties. By thus reminding him of this word, Amleth's friend was warning him against self-betrayal (note by translator).

was at once alarmed and suspected mischief, and in order to accomplish his desire safely, he took the woman in his arms and carried her off to a remote and impassable fen. There he lay with her, and begged her earnestly to reveal it to no one; and the young woman was as avid to promise silence as Amleth to plead for it, since they had been friendly of old, having been fostered together and brought up in the same charge.

They now accompanied him home again; and when all jestingly inquired if he had controlled his desire, he announced that he had enjoyed the maid. When they next asked him where he had had the sport, and what had been his bridal sheet, he replied that he had lain on horses' hooves, cocks' combs, and on roof gutters; for, when starting out to be tempted, he had taken some of all of these with him, to avoid having to dissemble.* This remark evoked merriment from the bystanders, though his joke was within a hair's breadth of the truth. They also questioned the maid, but she declared that he had done no such thing, and they accepted her denial, especially as the attendants were unaware of what had occurred. Then the companion who had marked the gadfly in order to warn Amleth spoke up and said, so that Amleth would know that it was to *his* ingenuity that he owed his life, that he had lately done him a special service. Amleth's reply was apt; in order that his wellwisher should not think him unmindful of his warning, he exclaimed: "Yes, I did see something fly past with a straw in its tail." At these words the others burst into laughter; but Amleth's friend rejoiced at the cleverness of the reply.

Now all being confounded, and none capable of opening the secret lock of the young man's wisdom, a friend of Feng, one more gifted with assurance than with sagacity, spoke up and said that such unfathomable cunning could not be made to betray itself by ordinary stratagem; the man was too obstinate to be mastered by a common plot, nor would craftiness so versatile be caught in so simple a trap. Therefore, on deeper reflection he had

* Saxo misunderstands the legend: "horses' hooves," "cocks' combs," and "roof gutters" are plants—butterbur, cockscomb, and reed-grass (note by translator).

thought of a more subtle means, one which would not be difficult to apply, and which would surely discover all they desired to know. Feng was deliberately to absent himself on the pretext of an important errand, and Amleth was to be closeted alone with his mother; but first a man should be stationed in some concealed place unknown to either of them, that he might listen closely to what they talked of. For if the son had any wits at all, he would speak freely and openly in his mother's hearing, and would not fear to confide in her. He declared himself ready to do the spying himself, in case he be judged quick to advise but slow to perform. Pleased with his advice, Feng departed, pretending to go on a long journey.

Now the man who had given the counsel went secretly to the closet where Amleth was admitted to his mother, and hid in the straw on the floor. Amleth, however, was equal to the plot; suspecting the presence of an eavesdropper, he at first had recourse to his usual folly: crowing like a cock, beating his arms as if flapping wings, treading on the straw, and jumping on it to find out if anyone was hiding there beneath it. Feeling something firm under his feet, he thrust his sword into the spot, struck the eavesdropper who lay hidden there, and dragging him from his concealment slew him. Then, cutting his body to pieces, he boiled them in hot water, and flung them into the gutter for the pigs to eat, the miserable limbs being fouled in stinking mire.

Having thus frustrated his designs, he returned to the closet; and when his mother set up a loud wailing, and began to lament her son's madness, he cried: "How dare you, infamous woman, make such false complaints, which are no more than a cloak for your own grievous offence? Wanton like a harlot, you consented to a wicked and abominable marriage, incestuously embracing your husband's murderer, and kissing and caressing the man who slew the father of your child: So does the mare join with the stallion that triumphs; only brute beasts couple indiscriminately, but now, like them, you have wiped out the memory of your former mate. It is not without reason that I now behave like a fool; for I have little doubt that he who took his brother's life

will proceed just as cruelly with his kindred. Better, therefore, to behave foolishly than to display one's wits, and so to save one's life by posing madness and frenzy. It remains my steadfast purpose to avenge my father; but I await a favourable opportunity and will bide my time. There is a time for all things; against a dark and pitiless heart one must use intelligence and ingenuity. For your part, you have no need to bewail my madness, but ought rather to grieve for your own shame. You certainly have cause to weep, not for others, but because you have suffered harm to your own soul. Now see that you hold your peace!" Thus scornfully did he chide his mother, recalling her to the path of virtue, and urging her to set past love above her present lust.

When Feng returned, he could nowhere find the crafty eavesdropper, though he searched long and diligently for him; no one had seen aught of him anywhere. When Amleth, too, was asked jestingly if he had seen any trace of him, he replied that he had gone to the privy, and, falling through the hole, been smothered in the filth, and so had been devoured by the pigs which went there. This statement contained only the bare truth, yet seemed to those who heard it so foolish that they ridiculed it.

Now Feng grew suspicious of his stepson, and being convinced of his guile resolved to make away with him, but dared not for fear of his uncle Rorik, as well as his own wife; for which reason he found it expedient to request the king of Britain to slay him, so feigning innocence himself while another did the deed. Anxious to conceal his own cruelty, he thus chose to sully his friend's reputation rather than to bring disgrace on himself. Amleth, on departing from his mother, secretly charged her to hang the hall with woven tapestries, and in a year falsely to mourn his death, promising that he would return at that time. Two of Feng's retainers went with him, bearing a rod that was engraved with runes (such being in olden days the manner of writing letters) which enjoined the king of Britain to slay the youth who had been sent to him. But while the others lay asleep, Amleth searched their belongings, found there the letter, read the instructions, and erasing the runes that were engraved on the rod carved

other symbols in their place, altering the wording of the message so as to transfer the death sentence from himself to his companions. Besides averting his own doom and destruction, and plunging others into the misery intended for himself, he also falsely added, in the name of Feng, a petition to the king of Britain that he should give his daughter in marriage to the intelligent young man he was sending him.

Arrived in Britain, the envoys waited on the king and presented to him their letter which they believed would encompass another's death, but which contained their own death warrant. Betraying no sign of his intentions, the king hospitably invited them to a banquet. Here Amleth thrust aside everything which was on the king's table, as if the food offered to him had been poor, to everyone's surprise abstaining from the rich feast, and touching neither food nor drink. All were amazed by this foreign young man who disdained the sumptuous dishes on the king's table, and refused all the delicacies as if they had been poor peasant fare.

When the banquet was over, and the king took leave of his companions for the night, he instructed one of them to steal into the bedchamber and secretly listen to the conversation of the foreign guests in the night. Now Amleth, when asked by his companions how it was that the evening before he had left all the feast untouched, as if it had been poison, replied that the bread had been saturated with blood, that the liquor tasted of iron, and that the meat reeked of corpses and had the rotten stench of the grave. Furthermore, he said that the king had the eyes of a slave, and the queen had exhibited three acts of a thrall. Thus it was not so much the banquet as the hosts that he had found fault with. His companions now held his old weakness against him, and taunted him with all manner of abuse for blaming what should be praised, speaking ill of what was good, affronting an excellent king and a gentle lady with shameless talk, and making a laughing-stock of those who merited praise.

The king, when he heard this from his retainer, declared that whoever spoke thus must be either the wisest or the most foolish

of mortals, when in so few words he could display such perfect acumen. Then summoning his steward, he asked where he had got the bread. The steward replying that his own baker had made it, the king asked where the corn had grown from which the flour had been made, and whether there was any sign that anyone had been slain there. He replied that near to the king's palace was a field, strewn with the bones of slaughtered men, and bearing clear traces of former carnage; and that, expecting a specially good harvest from this, compared with the rest, he had sown it in the spring in hopes of a rich crop. Therefore, it might well be that the bread had caught a taint from the congealed blood. Hearing this, and believing that Amleth had spoken the truth, the king next inquired whence the pork had come. The steward replied that by neglect his pigs had escaped from their sty and had eaten the rotten corpse of a robber, and that this might be the reason why the meat had been tainted. Perceiving the truth of Amleth's words in this matter also, the king then asked what he had mixed in the mead. When he heard that it had been brewed from honey and water, he demanded to be shown the spring, and ordered men to dig there, and they found several rusty swords, which could have tainted the water. (Others say that Amleth had criticized the liquor because on tasting it he had detected that the bees had fed on the entrails of a dead man and thereby had infected the combs, the taint being afterwards imparted to the mead.)

Realizing now that Amleth had given good reasons for his fastidiousness, and supposing that in scorning him for the meanness of his eyes he had been alluding to his ignoble birth, the king went secretly to his mother and questioned her about his father. She replied that she had known no man save the king; but on threatening to draw the truth from her by torture, he learnt that he was the son of a thrall. By this enforced confession his doubts and the fault in his birth alluded to by Amleth were confirmed. Ashamed at his own fate, but agreeably surprised by the young man's intelligence, he inquired of Amleth why he had imputed to the queen the habits of a slave. Annoyed though he indeed was

because his guest, in the night's conversation, had found fault with his wife's courtly behaviour, he was now forced to hear that she had been born a thrall. For Amleth said that he had observed three actions of a bondwoman in her: first, she had, like a servant, drawn her mantle over her head; secondly, she had lifted up her gown when she walked; and thirdly, she had picked her teeth with a splinter and chewed the scraps of food she dug out. He also said that her mother had been a thrall taken in war; from which fact he might tell that she was as much a slave by birth as she was from habit.

The king esteemed Amleth's intelligence like the wisdom of heaven; he gave him his daughter in marriage and honoured his words as evidence from above. He hanged his companions the next day, in order to carry out his friend's bidding to the full. This service Amleth interpreted as a wrong done to himself, and pretended to be angered by it; whereupon for blood money the king gave him gold, which he melted down in the fire and secretly poured into two hollow sticks.

Amleth dwelt with the king for a year, but then begged leave of absence and returned home, taking of the rich treasures of the king only the two sticks with the gold in them. Going ashore in Jutland, he laid aside his present conduct and resumed all his former habits, deliberately giving a ridiculous air to his manner in place of his present normal behaviour. Besmirched with filth, he entered the banquet hall, where his funeral celebration was just then taking place, and all present were astonished, as it had been falsely reported that he was dead. Fear turned gradually to mirth, as the guests ridiculed one another because the man whose funeral they were celebrating had suddenly appeared in the flesh amidst them. They then inquired about his companions; and showing them the two sticks he had brought with him, he said: "They are both here." This observation was as witty as it was true; for though most of them thought his words foolish, he spoke the truth, except that, in place of the hanged men, he showed them the blood money he had received for them. Later he joined the other cup-bearers at table and plied the guests with liquor in

order to increase the merriment; and so that his long dress should not hamper his movements, he fastened it round his loins with his sword belt. From time to time he deliberately drew his sword from its scabbard, wounding himself at the finger-tips; whereupon the bystanders had a steel pin driven through the sword and scabbard. In order to carry out his plot in greater safety, he diligently filled the noblemen's cups, making them heavy and stupid with drink, and so lulling them into such a drowsy intoxication that they could not stand on their legs, but staggered about until they fell to rest in the king's hall, making their beds in the banquet room. Finding them now in the state which suited his purpose, and so seeing his chance to obtain his revenge, he gathered up the crooks which he had previously made in his robe, and going with them into the banquet hall, where the nobles lay sprawling on the floor, vomiting in their intoxication, cut off the supports of the tapestries which his mother had made, and which hung on the inner walls of the hall. Then, having cut down the hanging and laid it over the sleepers, he took out the crooked stakes, and fixed it so thoroughly and tightly that none of those who lay beneath it had the strength to get up, struggle as he might. He then set fire to the house; and the fire spread far and wide, the flames leaping hither and thither and enveloping the whole house, so that the royal palace was reduced to ashes and all within perished, whether they lay fast asleep or made fruitless attempts to rise. Next he went to Feng's closet—he had some time before been conducted by his men to bed—and taking his sword which hung by his bedside, hung up his own in its place. Then, rousing his uncle, he told him that his nobles were perishing in the flames, and that Amleth was there with his old crooks, intending to exact due vengeance for his father's murder. At these words, Feng sprang from his bed, but failing to find his own sword was cut down as he vainly endeavoured to draw the other from its scabbard.

Valiant and of immortal memory was the hero who shrewdly behaved like a fool, and under a guise of madness with wondrous art concealed superior intelligence; for by his stratagem he not

only saved himself but also succeeded in avenging his father. Cunningly he defended himself and manfully he avenged his parent, so that it is hard to say which was the greater: his courage or his wits.

A Knight Who Made a Bargain with a Merchant

This, the earliest extant version of the Portia story, is taken from a Latin manuscript of the late thirteenth or early fourteenth century. Shakespeare certainly did not know it in this form. It was first printed in Thomas Wright, *A Selection of Latin Stories* (London: The Percy Society, 1842). The translation, from this version, is by Morris Bishop.

CELESTINUS, Roman Emperor, a very careful and prudent man, had a beautiful daughter. And a certain knight was much enamored of the girl. He reflected: "There is no doubt that the Emperor will never give me his daughter to wife, since I am not of fit rank. Yet if by some means I could capture the young lady's love, that would be enough for me."

Often he held converse with her, and questioned her closely about her desire. But she replied: "You are wasting your time. Do you think you can gull me with your cajoling words? You will never persuade me."

Said the knight: "Well then, since I cannot have you to wife, what can I give you to win you to a night of love?"

"If you give me a hundred-mark of florins, you can lie with me all night."

"Done!" said the knight. Forthwith he gathered the money and brought it to the girl.

When night fell, the knight entered the maiden's bed; but immediately he fell asleep. She removed her clothing and crept into bed beside him. And all night long the knight slept.

In the morning the girl arose, dressed, and washed her hands. And the knight arose, in a great taking. He said to her: "Come here and let me have my will of you!" But she replied: "I swear on my father's life I will not. I do you no wrong, my good friend.

Did you not stipulate that you should lie with me for a night, and did I not do so? But you slept the whole night through, and brought me no solace. So blame yourself, not me."

When the knight heard this he was very unhappy. He said: "What can I give you, that I may sleep with you another night?"

"The same sum as before; not a penny less."

"Good! I accept!"

He then sold all his movable goods, and gave her the same amount of florins as before. But remarkable to state, the same fate befell him as on the first night. The knight was unbelievably cast down; he was shaken to the core. He said to himself: "I have wasted all my wealth, and have taken nothing! But though I die, I will have a different issue!" He said to the girl: "How much shall I give you for a third night?" Said she: "The same as before; not a penny less." And he: "Very well; let your will be done."

The knight then set forth and journeyed until he came to a big city abounding in merchants and all sorts of philosophers, among them Master Virgil. And the knight had converse with a rich merchant. He said: "My good friend, I am short of money. If you will accommodate me with a hundred marks until a certain day, I will pledge all my lands to you. And if I let pass the agreed date, all my lands will be yours in perpetuity."

Said the merchant: "I think but little of your lands. But if you will make a certain pact with me you shall have all you desire."

"Whatever you say I shall agree to, if only you satisfy my need."

"When you accept my condition," said the merchant, "I shall advance the money. This will be our agreement: you will write me a note in your own blood, stating that if you don't pay on the appointed day, I shall have the right, without condition, to cut off all the flesh of your body with a sharp sword. If you consent to this, I am ready to fulfill your desire."

The knight was so madly in love with the girl that he granted all, wrote the letter with his own blood, and signed it. The merchant then handed over the money he sought.

Taking the cash, the knight reflected: "If I don't have my will

by means of this money, I am done for. But no, this must not happen." And since he had heard of Virgil's reputation, he visited that philosopher and said to him: "Good master, I ask a secret interview with you, and I beg you to afford me your good counsel."

"Say what you will," said Virgil, "and I shall answer your desire according to my best judgment."

"I love the Emperor's daughter with an unbelievable love. I made a pact with her for a great sum of money, and for two nights I was cheated. And now for a third night I have written a bond with a merchant, that if I don't keep the appointed date he shall have the right to separate my flesh from the bones with a sword. But he can't do this without killing me. Thus I have come to you to obtain your help, and also the love of my lady."

Virgil replied: "You made a very silly bargain with the merchant, for the Emperor's law lays down that whatever a man undertakes of his own free will must be fulfilled unconditionally. Therefore you would do well to keep the appointed date. As for the girl, I will tell you the fact: between her bed-covers is concealed a writing of such virtue that whoever enters her bed immediately falls asleep, nor will he wake till he is thrust forth from the bed. So when you come to the bedside and before you enter, look between the sheet and coverlet, and when you find the writing, throw it far away from the bed. Then boldly get into bed; and you won't sleep unless you want to. And thus you may do what you please with the girl, and you will gain much honor and glory."

When the knight heard this he was overjoyed; he thanked Virgil for his good counsel. He immediately hastened to the lady, bringing her the money. And when night fell, he entered her chamber, and secretly put his hand between sheet and coverlet. He found the writing and threw it far away. Then he got into bed and pretended to sleep. The girl, thinking him asleep as before, undressed and entered the bed. Straightway the knight grasped her. Amazed, she said: "Take pity on me! Don't rob me of my virginity! I will double all the money you have given me!"

"There's no use your talking! I am going to obtain what I have labored for so long!" Thus he knew the girl carnally.

Afterwards he captured her love, and was held marvellously bound, beyond the fortnight agreed upon between him and the merchant. So deep was his love that from day to day he forgot the assigned date. But one night, lying in bed, he recalled his bond. Stirred and shaken, he said to the girl: "Alas that ever I saw you! Now I am a dead man! For love of you I made a deal with a merchant, borrowing money with the condition that if I should let pass the due date he would have by contract full and absolute power to strip all the flesh from my body. But the due date has passed; I forgot about it till now, because I loved you so much."

Said she: "Don't grieve overmuch. Go to the merchant and double the money due. If he refuses, let him ask what he will and I will pay it."

The knight was much comforted by this. He went to the merchant's city, and meeting him in the street, greeted him very humbly. Said the merchant: "I do not return your salutation."

"My dear friend," said the knight, "since I have faulted our agreement I shall double my payment."

"This was not nominated in the bond! I want my due, according to the pact."

"Ask of me as much as you wish for my lapse, and I shall pay it."

"Don't waste your words," said the merchant. "If you should give me all the wealth of the city I shouldn't accept it; nothing but what has been agreed, signed, and sealed."

He immediately had the soldier arrested and clapped into the castle prison, until a judge should come to the city and hold court.

When the judge arrived the knight was haled out among other litigants. The merchant stood forth, and introduced the letter written with the knight's blood under his seal. When the judge saw the executed instrument, he said: "It is manifest to all the empire that the law rules that if any man undertakes an obligation of his own free will, that obligation must be scrupulously ful-

filled. I therefore rule that the merchant shall proceed according to the agreement with the knight, that the law may be observed."

Meanwhile the lady, the knight's beloved, had sent agents to find how the law was dealing with her lover. When she learned that he was in danger of death, she cut her hair and dressed in a man's sumptuous clothing. She mounted her palfrey and rode to the palace in which her lover was appearing before the court. She entered the palace and saluted the judge with great deference. Everyone thought she was a knight. The judge asked her whence she came and what was her business.

Said she: "I am a knight from a distant region. I happened to be riding through your city, and I heard rumors that a certain knight here present has been condemned to death on account of an obligation toward a merchant; and I have come to save the knight from death."

Said the judge: "The imperial law rules that as a man makes a pact of his own free will, so the pact must be executed. However, if, by your intervention, the merchant, party to the pact, would take mercy upon him, I should rejoice."

The young lady turned to the merchant and said: "My dear friend, what does it profit you if this knight, standing ready to receive judgment, should be killed? It is better for you to take the money than that the knight should die."

"Don't waste your words!" said the merchant. "I shall assuredly claim the law's justice, since he bound himself of his own free will. I shall have the fulfillment of the contract, made of my own free will, as the law dictates. And I shall grant him no pardon. He came to me, not I to him."

"I ask you," said the lady, "to hear my proposal. I shall double your money as my gift; and if you do not accept my offer, ask me how much you want, and I shall give it to you."

"Didn't I tell you that I want the fulfillment of my contract without any paltering? You may believe what I say."

The lady then turned to the court and said: "Your honor, make a just ruling on what I am about to say. You have heard how much I offered the merchant for the knight's life, and he refused

outright, asking the strict application of the law. Very well; I agree. So hear me, men of authority! You know that the knight never bound himself in writing to anything except that the merchant should have the right to strip the flesh from his bones. But not a word was set down regarding the shedding of blood. If then he can cut the flesh without effusion of blood, let him set about it forthwith. But if he should shed a drop of blood, the king will bring action against him."

When the merchant heard this, he said: "Give me my money, and I will drop the case."

"Amen!" said the girl. "But you won't have a penny, for in face of all present I offered you all I could, and you refused, saying openly: 'I want the fulfillment of my contract!' So lay your hands upon him but take care that you spill no blood!"

The merchant, confounded, retreated. Thus the knight's life was saved, and he paid not a penny.

The girl returned home, doffed her male costume, and resumed that of a woman. The knight sought his own home. The girl joined him there, and asked him how he had escaped his peril and how his case had gone. Said he: "My dearest lady, beloved above all, today I came close to losing my life. But when I was about to be condemned to death, a knight entered suddenly, a very handsome young man, indeed I never before saw such a handsome knight. And not only did he save me from death by his wit, but also he saved me from any payment of money."

"You were very ungrateful," said she, "since you did not invite to dinner the knight who saved your life."

"He came in all of a sudden, and all of a sudden he left."

"If you should see him again, would you recognize him?"

"Indeed I should."

Thereupon the girl went into the bedroom and dressed herself as she had been before, and again came forth. When the knight saw her he recognized her and embraced her, weeping with joy, and crying: "Blessed be the hour in which I met you!"

Shortly after this he married the girl, and they offered their sanctified souls to God.

This is a superior example of a thirteenth-century French adventure story. It shows the influence of the Crusades; one will note the respectful, even comradely, treatment of the Moslem rulers. The story is taken from Louis Moland and Charles d'Héricault, *Nouvelles françoises en prose du XIII^e siècle* (Paris: Janet, 1856), where it is titled *Istoire d'outre mer: La Comtesse de Ponthieu*. This translation, by Eugene Mason, is from his book *French Mediaeval Romances*, Everyman's Library Edition (New York: E. P. Dutton, 1911); it is reprinted by permission of E. P. Dutton & Co., Inc., and J. M. Dent & Sons Ltd.

IN TIMES gone by there lived a Count of Ponthieu, who loved chivalry and the pleasures of the world beyond measure, and moreover was a stout knight and a gallant gentleman. In the self-same day there lived a Count of St. Pol, who was lord of much land, and a right worthy man. One grief he had, that there was no heir of his body; but a sister was his, a prudent woman and a passing good gentlewoman, who was dame of Dommare in Ponthieu. This lady had a son, Thibault by name, who was heir to this County of St. Pol, but he was a poor man so long as his uncle lived. He was a prudent knight, valiant and skilled with the spear, noble and fair. Greatly was he loved and honoured of all honest people, for he was of high race and gentle birth.

The Count of Ponthieu, of whom the tale hath spoken, had to wife a very worthy lady. He and his dame had but one child, a daughter, very good and gracious, who increased with her days in favour and in virtues; and the maid was of some sixteen years. The third year after her birth her mother died, whereof she was sorely troubled and right heavy. The Count, her father, took to himself another wife with no long tarrying, a dame of gentle race and breeding. Of this lady he got him quickly a son; very near was the boy to his father's heart. The lad grew with his years in

stature and in valour, and gave promise to increase in all good qualities.

The Count of Ponthieu marked my lord Thibault of Dommare. He summoned the knight to his castle, and made him of his house for guerdon. When Sir Thibault was of his fellowship he rejoiced greatly, for the Count prospered in goods and in praise by reason of his servant's deeds. As they came from a tournament on a day, the Count and my lord Thibault together, the Count required of his companion and said,

"Thibault, by the aid of God tell me truly which jewel of my crown shines the fairest in your eyes!"

"Sir," replied Messire Thibault, "I am only a beggar, but so help me God, of all the jewels in your crown I love and covet none, save only my demoiselle, your daughter."

When he heard this thing the Count had great content. He laughed in his heart and said,

"Thibault, I will grant her to the beggar, if it be to her mind."

"Sir," answered he, "thanks and gramercy. May God make it up to you."

Then went the Count to his daughter, and said,

"Fair daughter, I have promised you in marriage, so it go not against your heart."

"Sir," inquired the maid, "to whom?"

"In the name of God, to a loyal man, and a true man, of whom much is hoped; to a knight of my own household, Thibault of Dommare."

"Dear sir," answered the maiden sweetly, "if your county were a kingdom, and I were the king's only child, I would choose him as my husband, and gladly give him all that I had."

"Daughter," said the Count, "blessed be your pretty person, and the hour that you were born."

Thus was this marriage made. The Count of Ponthieu and the Count of St. Pol were at the feast, and many another honourable man besides. Great was the joy in which they met, fair was the worship, and marvellous the delight. The bride and groom lived together in all happiness for five years. This was their only

sorrow, that it pleased not our Lord Jesus Christ that they should have an heir to their flesh.

On a night Sir Thibault lay in his bed. He considered within himself and said,

"Lord, whence cometh it that I love this dame so fondly, and she me, yet we may have no heir of our bodies to serve God and to do a little good in the world?"

Then he remembered my lord St. James, the Apostle of Spain, who gives to the fervent supplicant that which rightly he desires. Earnestly, to his own heart, he promised that he would walk a pilgrim in his way. His wife lay sleeping at his side, but when she came from out her sleep, he took her softly in his arms, and required of her that she would bestow on him a gift.

"Sir," said the lady, "what gift would you have?"

"Wife," he made answer, "that you shall know when it is mine."

"Husband," said she, "if it be mine to grant, I will give it you, whatever the price."

"Wife," he said, "I pray you to grant me leave to seek my lord St. James the Apostle, that he may intercede with our Lord Jesus Christ to bestow on us an heir of our flesh, whereby God may be served in this world and Holy Church glorified."

"Sir," cried the lady, "sweet and dear it is that you should crave such bounty, and I grant the permission you desire right willingly."

Deep and long was the tenderness that fell betwixt these twain. Thus passed a day, and another day, and yet a third. On this third day it chanced that they lay together in their bed, and it was night. Then said the dame,

"Husband, I pray and require of you a gift."

"Wife," he replied, "ask, and I will give it you, if by any means I can."

"Husband," she said, "I require leave to come with you on this errand and journey."

When Messire Thibault heard this thing he was right sorrowful, and said,

"Wife, grievous would be the journey to your body, for the way is very long, and the land right strange and perilous."

Said she,

"Husband, be not in doubt because of me. You shall be more hindered of your squire than of your wife."

"Dame," said he, "as God wills and as you wish."

The days went, and these tidings were so noised abroad that the Count of Ponthieu heard thereof. He commanded my lord Sir Thibault to his house, and said,

"Thibault, you are a vowed pilgrim, as I hear, and my daughter too!"

"Sir," answered he, "that is verily and truly so."

"Thibault," replied the Count, "as to yourself what pleases you is to my mind also, but concerning my daughter that is another matter."

"Sir," made answer Sir Thibault, "go she must, and I cannot deny her."

"Since this is so," said the Count, "part when you will. Make ready for the road your steeds, your palfreys, and the pack horses, and I will give you riches and gear enough for the journey."

"Sir," said Messire Thibault, "thanks and gramercy."

Thus these pilgrims arrayed them, and sought that shrine with marvellous joy. They fared so speedily upon the way, that at length they came near to my lord St. James, by less than two days faring. That night they drew to a goodly town. After they had eaten in the hostel, Sir Thibault called for the host and inquired of him the road for the morrow, how it ran, and whether it were smooth.

"Fair sir," replied the innkeeper to the knight, "at the gate of this town you will find a little wood. Beyond the wood a strong smooth road runs for the whole day's journey."

Hearing this they asked no more questions, but the beds being laid down, they went to their rest. The morrow broke full sweetly. The pilgrims rose lightly from their beds as soon as it

was day, and made much stir and merriment. Sir Thibault rose
also, since he might not sleep, but his head was heavy. He
therefore called his chamberlain, and said,

"Rise quickly, and bid the company to pack the horses and go
their way. Thou shalt remain with me, and make ready our
harness, for I am a little heavy and disquieted."

The chamberlain made known to the sergeants the pleasure of
their lord, so that presently they took the road. In no great while
Messire Thibault and his dame got them from the bed, and
arraying their persons, followed after their household. The cham-
berlain folded the bed linen, and it was yet but dawn, though
warm and fair. The three went forth through the gate of the city,
those three together, with no other companion save God alone,
and drew near to the forest. When they came close they found
two roads, the one good, the other ill; so that Sir Thibault said to
his chamberlain,

"Put spurs to your horse, and ride swiftly after our people. Bid
them await our coming, for foul it is for lady and knight to pass
through this wood with so little company."

The servitor went speedily, and Messire Thibault entered the
forest. He drew rein beside the two roads, for he knew not which
to follow.

"Wife," he said, "which way is ours?"

"Please God, the good," she answered.

Now in this wood were robbers, who spoiled the fair way, and
made wide and smooth the false, so that pilgrims should mistake
and wander from the path. Messire Thibault lighted from his
horse. He looked from one to the other, and finding the wrong
way broader and more smooth than the true, he cried,

"Wife, come now; in the name of God, this."

They had proceeded along this road for some quarter of a mile
when the path grew strict and narrow, and boughs made dark the
way.

"Wife," said the knight, "I fear that we fare but ill."

When he had thus spoken he looked before him, and marked

four armed thieves, seated on four strong horses, and each bore lance in hand. Thereupon he glanced behind him, and, lo, four other robbers, armed and set in ambush, so he said,

"Dame, be not affrighted of aught that you may see from now."

Right courteously Sir Thibault saluted the robbers in his path, but they gave no answer to his greeting. Afterwards he sought of them what was in their mind, and one replied that he should know anon. The thief, who had thus spoken, drew towards my lord Thibault, with outstretched sword, thinking to smite him in the middle. Messire Thibault saw the blow about to fall, and it was no marvel if he feared greatly. He sprang forward nimbly, as best he might, so that the glaive smote the air. Then as the robber staggered by, Sir Thibault seized him fiercely, and wrested the sword from his hand. The knight advanced stoutly against those three from whom the thief had come. He struck the foremost amidst the bowels, so that he perished miserably. Then he turned and went again to that one who had first come against him with the sword, and slew him also. Now it was decreed of God that after the knight had slain three of this company of robbers, that the five who were left, encompassed him round about, and killed his palfrey. Sir Thibault tumbled flat upon his back, although he was not wounded to his hurt. Since he had neither sword nor other harness he could do no more. The thieves therefore stripped him to his very shirt, his boots and hosen, and binding him hand and foot with a baldrick, cast him into a thorn bush, right thick and sharp. When they had done this they hastened to the lady. From her they took her palfrey and her vesture, even to the shift. Passing fair was the lady; she wept full piteously, and never was dame more sorrowful than she. Now one of these bold robbers stared upon the lady, and saw that she was very fair. He spoke to his companions in this fashion,

"Comrades, I have lost my brother in this broil. I will take this woman for his blood money."

But the others made answer,

"I, too, have lost my kin. I claim as much as you, and my right is good as yours."

So said a third, and a fourth, and a fifth. Then spake yet another,

"In keeping of the lady will be found neither peace nor profit. Rather let us lead her from here within the forest, there do our pleasure upon her, and then put her again upon the path, so that she may go her way."

Thus they did as they had devised together, and left her on the road.

Right sick at heart was Messire Thibault when he saw her so entreated, but nothing could he do. He bore no malice against his wife by reason of that which had befallen, for well he knew that it was by force, and not according to her will. When he saw her again, weeping bitterly and altogether shamed, he called to her, and said,

"Wife, for God's love unloose me from these bonds, and deliver me from the torment that I suffer, for these thorns are sharper than I can endure."

The lady hastened to the place where Sir Thibault lay, and marked a sword flung behind the bush, belonging to one of those felons that were slain. She took the glaive, and went towards her lord, filled full of wrath and evil thoughts because of what had chanced to her. She feared greatly lest her husband should bear malice for that which he had seen, reproaching her upon a day, and taunting her for what was past. She said,

"Sir, you are out of your pain already."

She raised the sword, and came towards her husband, thinking to strike him midmost the body. When he marked the falling glaive he deemed that his day had come, for he was a naked man, clad in nought but his shirt and hosen. He trembled so sorely that his bonds were loosed, and the lady struck so feebly that she wounded him but little, severing that baldrick with which his hands were made fast. Thereat the knight brake the cords about his legs, and leaping upon his feet, cried,

"Dame, by the grace of God it is not to-day that you shall slay me with the sword."

Then she made answer,

"Truly, sir, the sorer grief is mine."

Sir Thibault took the sword, and set it again in the sheath, afterwards he put his hand upon the lady's shoulder, and brought her back by the path they had fared. At the fringe of the woodland he found a large part of his fellowship, who were come to meet him. When these saw their lord and lady so spoiled and disarrayed they inquired of them,

"Sir, who hath put you in this case?"

He set them by, saying that they had fallen amongst felons who had done them much mischief.

Mightily the sergeants lamented; but presently they fetched raiment from the packs, and arrayed them, for enough they had and to spare. So they climbed into the saddle, and continued their journey.

They rode that day, nor for aught that had chanced did Messire Thibault show sourer countenance to the lady. At night-fall they came to a goodly town, and there took shelter in an inn. Messire Thibault sought of his host if there was any convent of nuns in those parts where a lady might repose her. The host made answer to him,

"Sir, you are served to your wish. Just beyond the walls is a right fair religious house, with many holy women."

On the morrow Messire Thibault went to this house, and heard Mass. Afterwards he spoke to the Abbess and her chapter, praying that he might leave his lady in their charge, until his return; and this they accorded very willingly. Messire Thibault bestowed the lady in this convent, with certain of his house to do her service, and went his way to bring his pilgrimage to a fair end. When he had knelt before the shrine, and honoured the Saint, he came again to the convent and the lady. He gave freely of his wealth to the house, and taking to himself his wife, returned with her to their own land, in the same joy and honour as he had brought her forth, save only that they lay not together.

Great was the gladness of the folk of that realm when Sir Thibault returned to his home. The Count of Ponthieu, the father of his wife was there, and there, too, was his uncle the Count of St. Pol. Many worthy and valiant gentlemen came for his welcome, and a fair company of dames and maidens likewise honoured the lady. That day the Count of Ponthieu sat at meat with my lord Thibault, and ate from the same dish, the two together. Then it happed that the Count spake to him,

"Thibault, fair son, he who journeys far hears many a strange matter and sees many strange sights, which are hidden from those who sit over the fire. Tell me therefore, of your favour, something of all you have seen and heard since you went from amongst us."

Messire Thibault answered shortly that he knew no tale worth the telling. The Count would take no denial, but plagued him so sorely, begging him of his courtesy to tell over some adventure, that at the last he was overborne.

"Sir, I will narrate a story, since talk I must; but at least let it be in your private ear, if you please, and not for the mirth of all."

The Count replied that his pleasure was the same. After meat, when men had eaten their fill, the Count rose in his chair, and taking my lord Thibault by the hand, entreated,

"Tell me now, I pray, that which it pleases you to tell, for there are few of the household left in hall."

Then Messire Thibault began to relate that which chanced to a knight and a dame, even as it has been rehearsed before you in this tale; only he named not the persons to whom this lot was appointed. The Count, who was wise and sober of counsel, inquired what the knight had done with the lady. Thibault made answer that the knight had brought the lady back by the way she went, with the same joy and worship as he led her forth, save only that they slept not together.

"Thibault," said the Count, "your knight walked another road than I had trod. By my faith in God and my love for you, I had hanged this dame by her tresses to a tree. The laces of her gown would suffice if I could find no other cord."

"Sir," said Messire Thibault, "you have but my word. The truth can only be assured if the lady might bear witness and testify with her own mouth."

"Thibault," said the Count, "know you the name of this knight?"

"Sir," cried Messire Thibault, "I beg you again to exempt me from naming the knight to whom this sorrow befell. Know of a truth that his name will bring no profit."

"Thibault," said the Count, "it is my pleasure that his name should not be hid."

"Sir," answered Thibault, "tell I must, as you will not acquit me; but I take you to witness that I speak only under compulsion, since gladly I would have kept silence, had this been your pleasure, for in the telling there is neither worship nor honour."

"Thibault," replied the Count, "without more words I would know forthwith who was the knight to whom this adventure chanced. By the faith that you owe to your God and to me, I conjure you to tell me his name, since it is in your mind."

"Sir," replied Messire Thibault, "I will answer by the faith I owe my God and you, since you lay this charge upon me. Know well, and be persuaded, that I am the knight on whom this sorrow lighted. Hold it for truth that I was sorely troubled and sick of heart. Be assured that never before have I spoken to any living man about the business, and moreover that gladly would I have held my peace, had such been your will."

When the Count heard this adventure he was sore astonied, and altogether cast down. He kept silence for a great space, speaking never a word. At the last he said,

"Thibault, was it indeed my child who did this thing?"

"Sir, it is verily and truly so."

"Thibault," said the Count, "sweet shall be your vengeance, since you have given her again to my hand."

Because of his exceeding wrath the Count sent straightway for his daughter, and demanded of her if those things were true of which Messire Thibault had spoken. She inquired of the accusation, and her father answered,

"That you would have slain him with the sword, even as he has told me?"

"Sir, of a surety."

"And wherefore would you slay your husband?"

"Sir, for reason that I am yet heavy that he is not dead."

When the Count heard the lady speak in this fashion, he answered her nothing, but suffered in silence until the guests had departed. After these were gone, the Count came on a day to Rue-sur-Mer, and Messire Thibault with him, and the Count's son. With them also went the lady. Then the Count caused a ship to be got ready, very stout and speedy, and he made the dame to enter in the boat. He set also on the ship an untouched barrel, very high and strong. These three lords climbed into the nave,* with no other company, save those sailors who should labour at the oar. The Count commanded the mariners to put the ship to sea, and all marvelled greatly as to what he purposed, but there was none so bold as to ask him any questions. When they had rowed a great way from the land, the Count bade them to strike the head from out the barrel. He took that dame, his own child, who was so dainty and so fair, and thrust her in the tun, whether she would or whether she would not. This being done he caused the cask to be made fast again with staves and wood, so that the water might in no manner enter therein. Afterwards he dragged the barrel to the edge of the deck, and with his own hand cast it into the sea, saying,

"I commend thee to the wind and waves."

Passing heavy was Messire Thibault at this, and the lady's brother also, and all who saw. They fell at the Count's feet, praying him of his grace that she might be delivered from the barrel. So hot was his wrath that he would not grant their prayer, for aught that they might do or say. They therefore left him to his rage, and turning to the Heavenly Father, besought our Lord Jesus Christ that of His most sweet pity He would have mercy on her soul, and give her pardon for her sins.

* Nave: ship.—Ed.

The ship came again to land, leaving the lady in sore peril and trouble, even as the tale has told you. But our Lord Jesus Christ, who is Lord and Father of all, and desireth not the death of a sinner, but rather that he should turn from his wickedness and live—as each day He showeth us openly by deed, by example and by miracle—sent succour to this lady, even as you shall hear. For a ship from Flanders, laden with merchandise, marked this barrel drifting at the mercy of winds and waters, before ever the Count and his companions were come ashore. One of the merchants said to his comrades,

"Friends, behold a barrel drifting in our course. If we may reach it, perchance we may find it to our gain."

This ship was wont to traffic with the Saracens in their country, so the sailors rowed towards the barrel, and partly by cunning and partly by strength, at the last got it safely upon the deck. The merchants looked long at the cask. They wondered greatly what it could be, and wondering, they saw that the head of the barrel was newly closed. They opened the cask, and found therein a woman at the point of death, for air had failed her. Her body was gross, her visage swollen, and the eyes started horribly from her head. When she breathed the fresh air and felt the wind blow upon her, she sighed a little, so that the merchants standing by, spoke comfortably to her, but she might not answer them a word. In the end, heart and speech came again to her. She spoke to the chapmen and the sailors who pressed about her, and much she marvelled how she found herself amongst them. When she perceived that she was with merchants and Christian men she was the more easy, and fervently she praised Jesus Christ in her heart, thanking Him for the lovingkindness which had kept her from death. For this lady was altogether contrite in heart, and earnestly desired to amend her life towards God, repenting the trespass she had done to others, and fearing the judgment that was rightly her due. The merchants inquired of the lady whence she came, and she told them the truth, saying that she was a miserable wretch and a poor sinner, as they could see for themselves. She related the cruel adventure which had chanced to her, and prayed them

to take pity on a most unhappy lady, and they answered that mercy they would show. So with meat and drink her former beauty came to her again.

Now this merchant ship fared so far that she came to the land of the Paynims, and cast anchor in the port of Aumarie.* Galleys of these Saracens came to know their business, and they answered that they were traffickers in divers merchandise in many a realm. They showed them also the safe conduct they carried of princes and mighty lords that they might pass in safety through their countries to buy and sell their goods. The merchants got them to land in this port, taking the lady with them. They sought counsel one of the other to know what it were best to do with her. One was for selling her as a slave, but his companion proposed to give her as a sop to the rich Soudan of Aumarie, that their business should be the less hindered. To this they all agreed. They arrayed the lady freshly in broidered raiment, and carried her before the Soudan, who was a lusty young man. He accepted their gift, receiving the lady with a right glad heart, for she was passing fair. The Soudan inquired of them as to who she was.

"Sire," answered the merchants, "we know no more than you, but marvellous was the fashion in which she came to our hands."

The gift was so greatly to the Soudan's mind that he served the chapmen to the utmost of his power. He loved the lady very tenderly, and entreated her in all honour. He held and tended her so well, that her sweet colour came again to her, and her beauty increased beyond measure. The Soudan sought to know by those who had the gift of tongues as to the lady's home and race, but these she would not reveal to any. He was the more thoughtful therefore, because he might see that she was a dame of birth and lineage. He inquired of her as to whether she were a Christian woman, promising that if she would deny her faith, he would take her as his wife, since he was yet unwed. The lady saw clearly that it were better to be converted by love than perforce; so she answered that her religion was to do her master's pleasure. When

* Aumarie: perhaps Morocco.—Ed.

she had renounced her faith, and rejected the Christian law, the Soudan made her his dame according to the use and wont of this country of the Paynim. He held her very dear, cherishing her in all honour, for his love waxed deeper as the days wore on.

In due time it was with this lady after the manner of women, and she came to bed of a son. The Soudan rejoiced greatly, being altogether merry and content. The lady, for her part, lived in fair fellowship with the folk of her husband's realm. Very courteous was she, and very serviceable, so that presently she was instructed in the Saracen tongue. In no long while after the birth of her son she conceived of a maid, who in the years that befell grew passing sweet and fair, and richly was she nurtured as became the daughter of so high a prince. Thus for two years and a half the lady dwelt with the Paynim in much softness and delight.

Now the story keeps silence as to the lady and the Soudan, her husband, till later, as you may hear, and returns to the Count of Ponthieu, the son of the Count, and to my lord Thibault of Dommare, who were left grieving for the dame who was flung into the sea, as you have heard, nor knew aught of her tidings, but deemed that she were rather dead than alive. Now tells the story—and the truth bears witness to itself and is its own confirmation—that the Count was in Ponthieu, together with his son, and Messire Thibault. Very heavy was the Count, for in no wise could he get his daughter from his mind, and grievously he lamented the wrong that he had done her. Messire Thibault dared not take to himself another wife, because of the anguish of his friend. The son of the Count might not wed also; neither durst he to become knight, though he was come to an age when such things are greatly to a young man's mind.

On a day the Count considered deeply the sin that he had committed against his own flesh. He sought the Archbishop of Rheims in confession, and opened out his grief, telling in his ear the crime that he had wrought. He determined to seek those holy fields beyond the sea, and sewed the Cross upon his mantle. When Messire Thibault knew that his lord, the Count, had taken the Cross, he confessed him, and did likewise. And when the Count's

son was assured of the purpose of his sire and of Messire Thi-
bault, whom he loved dearly, he took the Cross with them.
Passing heavy was the Count to mark the Sign upon his son's
raiment.

"Fair son, what is this you have done; for now the land remains
without a lord!"

The son answered, and said,

"Father, I wear the Sign first and foremost for the love of God;
afterwards for the saving of my soul, and by reason that I would
serve and honour Him to the utmost of my power, so long as I
have life in my body."

The Count put his realm in ward full wisely. He used diligence
in making all things ready, and bade farewell to his friends.
Messire Thibault and the son of the Count ordered their business,
and the three set forth together, with a fair company. They came
to that holy land beyond the sea, safe of person and of gear. There
they made devout pilgrimage to every place where they were
persuaded it was meet to go, and God might be served. When the
Count had done all that he was able, he deemed that there was yet
one thing to do. He gave himself and his fellowship to the service
of the Temple for one year; and at the end of this term he
purposed to seek his country and his home. He went to Acre, and
made ready a ship against his voyage. He took his leave of the
Knights Templar, and other lords of that land, and greatly they
praised him for the worship that he had brought them. When the
Count and his company were come to Acre they entered in the
ship, and departed from the haven with a fair wind. But little was
their solace. For when they drew to the open sea a strong and
horrible tempest sprang suddenly upon them, so that the sailors
knew not where they went, and feared each hour that all would
be drowned. So piteous was their plight that, with ropes, they
bound themselves one to another, the son to the father, the uncle
to the nephew, according as they stood. The Count, his son, and
Messire Thibault for their part, fastened themselves together, so
that the same end should chance to all. In no long time after this
was done they saw land, and inquired of the shipmen whither

they were come. The mariners answered that this realm belonged
to the Paynim, and was called the Land of Aumarie. They asked
of the Count,

"Sire, what is your will that we do? If we seek the shore,
doubtless we shall be made captives, and fall into the hands of the
Saracen."

The Count made answer,

"Not my will, but the will of Jesus Christ be done. Let the ship
go as He thinks best. We will commit our bodies and our lives to
His good keeping, for a fouler and an uglier death we cannot die,
than to perish in this sea."

They drove with the wind along the coast of Aumarie, and the
galleys and warships of the Saracens put out to meet them. Be
assured that this was no fair meeting, for the Paynims took them
and led them before the Soudan, who was lord of that realm.
There they gave him the goods and the bodies of these Christians
as a gift. The Soudan sundered this fair fellowship, setting them
in many places and in divers prisons; but since the Count, his son,
and Messire Thibault were so securely bound together, he com-
manded that they should be cast into a dungeon by themselves,
and fed upon the bread of affliction and the water of affliction. So
it was done, even as he commanded. In this prison they lay for a
space, till such time as the Count's son fell sick. His sickness was
so grievous that the Count and Messire Thibault feared greatly
that this sorrow was to death.

Now it came to pass that the Soudan held high Court because
of the day of his birth, for such was the custom of the Saracens.
After they had well eaten, the Saracens stood before the Soudan,
and said,

"Sire, we require of you our right."

He inquired of what right they were speaking, and they an-
swered,

"Sire, a Christian captive to set as a mark for our arrows."

When the Soudan heard this he gave no thought to such a
trifle, but made reply,

"Get you to the prison, and take out that captive who has the least of life in him."

The Paynim hastened to the dungeon, and brought forth the Count, bearded, unkempt and foredone. The Soudan marked his melancholy case, so he said to them,

"This man has not long to live; take him hence, and do your will on him."

The wife of the Soudan, of whom you have heard, the daughter of this very Count, was in the hall, when they brought forth her father to slay him. Immediately that her eyes fell upon him the blood in her veins turned to water; not so much that she knew him as her sire, but rather that Nature tugged at her heart strings. Then spake the dame to the Soudan,

"Husband, I, too, am French, and would gladly speak with this poor wretch ere he die, if so I may."

"Wife," answered the Soudan, "truly, yes; it pleases me well."

The lady came to the Count. She took him apart, and bidding the Saracens fall back, she inquired of him whence he was.

"Lady, I am from the kingdom of France, of a county that men call Ponthieu."

When the lady heard this her bowels were moved. Earnestly she demanded his name and race.

"Of a truth, lady, I have long forgotten my father's house, for I have suffered such pain and anguish since I departed, that I would rather die than live. But this you may know, that I—even the man who speaks to you—was once the Count of Ponthieu."

The lady hearkened to this, but yet she made no sign. She went from the Count, and coming to the Soudan, said,

"Husband, give me this captive as a gift, if such be your pleasure. He knows chess and draughts and many fair tales to bring solace to the hearer. He shall play before you, and we will make our pastime of his skill."

"Wife," answered the Soudan, "I grant him to you very willingly; do with him as you wish."

The lady took the captive, and bestowed him in her chamber.

The gaolers sought another in his stead, and brought forth my lord Thibault, the husband to the dame. He came out in tatters, for he was clothed rather in his long hair and great beard, than in raiment. His body was lean and bony, and he seemed as one who had endured pain and sorrow enough, and to spare. When the lady saw him she said to the Soudan,

"Husband, with this one also would I gladly speak, if so I may."

"Wife," answered the Soudan, "it pleases me well."

The lady came to my lord Thibault, and inquired of him whence he was.

"Lady, I am of the realm of that ancient gentleman who was taken from prison before me. I had his daughter to wife, and am his knight."

The lady knew well her lord, so she returned to the Soudan, and said to him,

"Husband, great kindness will you show me, if you give me this captive also."

"Wife," said the Soudan, "I grant him to you very willingly."

She thanked him sweetly, and bestowed the gift in her chamber, with the other.

The archers hastened together, and drawing before the Soudan said,

"Sire, you do us wrong, for the day is far spent."

They went straight to the prison, and brought forth the son of the Count, shagged and filthy, as one who had not known of water for many a day. He was a young man, so young that his beard had not come on him, but for all his youth he was so thin and sick and weak, that he scarce could stand upon his feet. When the lady saw him she had compassion upon him. She came to him asking whose son he was and of his home, and he replied that he was son to that gentleman, who was first brought out of the dungeon. She knew well that this was her brother, but she made herself strange unto him.

"Husband," said she to the Soudan, "verily you will shew

kindness to your wife beyond measure if you grant me this captive. He knows chess and draughts and other delights passing fair to see and hear."

And the Soudan made answer,

"Wife, by our holy law if they were a hundred I would give them all to you gladly."

The lady thanked him tenderly, and bestowed the captive swiftly in her chamber. The Saracens went again to the prison and fetched out another, but the lady left him to his fate, when she looked upon his face. So he won a martyr's crown, and our Lord Jesus Christ received his soul. As for the dame, she hid herself from the sight, for it gave her little joy, this slaying of the Christian by the Paynims.

The lady came to her chamber, and at her coming the captives would have got them to their feet, but she made signs that they should remain seated. Drawing close she made gestures of friendship. The Count, who was very shrewd, asked at this,

"Lady, when will they slay us?"

She answered that their time had not yet come.

"Lady," said he, "the sorer grief is ours, for we are so anhungered, that for a little our souls would leave our bodies."

The lady went out, and bade meat to be made ready. This she carried in, giving to each a little, and to each a little drink. When they had eaten, they had yet greater hunger than before. In this manner she fed them, little by little, ten times a day, for she deemed that should they eat to their desire, they would die of repletion. For this reason she caused them to break their fast temperately. Thus the good lady dealt with them for the first seven days, and at nights, by her grace, they lay softly at their ease. She did away with their rags, and clad them in seemly apparel. When the week was done she set before them meat and drink to their heart's desire, so that their strength returned to them again. They had chess and draughts, and played these games to their great content. The Soudan was often with them. He watched the play, and took pleasure in their gladness. But the

lady refrained, so that none might conceive, either by speech or fashion, that she had known them before.

Now a short while after this matter of the captives, the story tells that the Soudan had business enough of his own, for a mighty Sultan laid waste his realm, and sought to do him much mischief. To avenge his wrong the Soudan commanded his vassals from every place, and assembled a great host. When the lady knew this, she entered the chamber where the captives lay, and sitting amidst them lifted her hand, and said,

"Sirs, you have told me somewhat of your business; now will I be assured whether you are true men or not. You told me that in your own land you were once the Count of Ponthieu, that this man was wedded to your daughter, and that this other was your son. Know that I am a Saracen, having the science of astrology; so I tell you plainly that you were never so near to a shameful death, as you are now, if you hide from me the truth. What chanced to your daughter, the wife of this knight?"

"Lady," replied the Count, "I deem her to be dead."

"How came she to her death?"

"Certes, lady," said the Count, "because for once she received her deserts."

"Tell me of these deservings," said the dame.

Then the Count began to tell, with tears, of how she was wedded, but was yet a barren wife; how the good knight vowed pilgrimage to my lord St. James in Galicia, and how the lady prayed that she might go with him, which prayer he granted willingly. He told how they went their way with joy, till alone, in the deep wood, they met with sturdy felons who set upon them. The good knight might do nothing against so many, for he was a naked man; but despite of all, he slew three, and five were left, who killed his palfrey, and spoiling him to the very shirt, bound him hands and feet, and flung him into a thorn bush. They spoiled the lady also and stole her palfrey from her. When they looked upon her, and saw that she was fair, each would have taken her. Afterwards they accorded that she should be to all, and

having had their will in her despite, they departed and left her weeping bitterly. This the good knight saw, so he besought her courteously to unloose his hands, that they might get them from the wood. But the lady marked a sword belonging to one of these felons that were slain. She seized upon it, and hastening where he lay, cried in furious fashion, "You are unbound already." Then she raised the naked sword, and struck at his body. But by the loving kindness of God, and the vigour of the knight, she but sundered the bonds that bound him, so that he sprang forth, and wounded as he was, cried,

"Dame, by the grace of God it is not to-day that you shall kill me with the sword."

At this word that fair lady, the wife of the Soudan, spoke suddenly, and said,

"Ah, sir, you have told the tale honestly, and very clear it is why she would have slain him."

"For what reason, lady?"

"Certes," answered she, "for reason of the great shame which had befallen her."

When Messire Thibault heard this he wept right tenderly, and said,

"Alas, what part had she in this wickedness! May God keep shut the doors of my prison if I had shown her the sourer face therefore, seeing that her will was not in the deed."

"Sir," said the lady, "she feared your reproach. But tell me which is the more likely, that she be alive or dead?"

"Lady," said Thibault, "we know not what to think."

"Well I know," cried the Count, "of the great anguish we have suffered, by reason of the sin I sinned against her."

"If it pleased God that she were yet living," inquired the lady, "and tidings were brought which you could not doubt, what would you have to say?"

"Lady," said the Count, "I should be happier than if I were taken from this prison, or were granted more wealth than ever I have had in my life."

"Lady," said Messire Thibault, "so God give me no joy of my heart's dearest wish, if I had not more solace than if men crowned me King of France."

"Certes, lady," said the dansellon,* who was her brother, "none could give or promise me aught so sweet, as the life of that sister, who was so fair and good."

When the lady hearkened to these words her heart yearned with tenderness. She praised God, rendering Him thanks, and said to them,

"Be sure that you speak with unfeigned lips."

And they answered and said that they spoke with unfeigned lips. Then the lady began to weep with happy tears, and said to them,

"Sir, now may you truly say that you are my father, for I am that daughter on whom you wrought such bitter justice. And you, Messire Thibault, are my lord and husband; and you, sir dansellon, are my brother."

Then she rehearsed to them in what manner she was found of the chapmen, and how they bestowed her as a gift on the Soudan. They were very glad, and rejoiced mightily, humbling themselves before her, but she forbade them to show their mirth, saying,

"I am a Saracen, and have renounced the faith; otherwise I should not be here, but were dead already. Therefore I pray and beseech you as you love your lives and would prolong your days, whatever you may see or hear, not to show me any affection, but keep yourselves strange to me, and leave me to unravel the coil. Now I will tell why I have revealed myself to you. My husband, the Soudan, rides presently to battle. I know well, Messire Thibault, that you are a hardy knight, and I will pray the Soudan to take you with him. If ever you were brave, now is the time to make it plain. See to it that you do him such service that he have no grievance against you."

* Dansellon: young gentleman.—Ed.

The lady departed forthwith, and coming before the Soudan, said,

"Husband, one of my captives desires greatly to go with you, if such be your pleasure."

"Wife," answered he, "I dare not put myself in his hand, for fear that he may do me a mischief."

"Husband, he will not dare to be false, since I hold his companions as hostages."

"Wife," said he, "I will take him with me, because of your counsel, and I will deliver him a good horse and harness, and all that warrior may require."

The lady returned straightway to the chamber. She said to Messire Thibault,

"I have persuaded the Soudan to bring you to the battle. Act therefore manfully."

At this her brother knelt at her knee, praying her to plead with the Soudan that he might go also.

"That I may not do," said she, "or the thing will be too clear."

The Soudan ordered his business, and went forth, Messire Thibault being with him, and came upon the enemy. According to his word, the Soudan had given to the knight both horse and harness. By the will of Jesus Christ, who faileth never such as have faith and affiance in Him, Messire Thibault did such things in arms that in a short space the enemies of the Soudan were put under his feet. The Soudan rejoiced greatly at his knight's deeds and his victory, and returned bringing many captives with him. He went straight to the dame, and said,

"Wife, by my law I have naught but good to tell of your prisoner, for he has done me faithful service. So he deny his faith, and receive our holy religion, I will grant him broad lands, and find him a rich heiress in marriage."

"Husband, I know not, but I doubt if he will do this thing."

No more was spoken of the matter; but the lady set her house in order, as best she was able, and coming to her captives said,

"Sirs, go warily, so that the Saracens see nothing of what is in

our mind; for, please God, we shall yet win to France and the county of Ponthieu."

On a day the lady came before the Soudan. She went in torment, and lamented very grievously.

"Husband, it is with me as it was before. Well I know it, for I have fallen into sore sickness, and my food has no relish in my mouth, no, not since you went to the battle."

"Wife, I am right glad to hear that you are with child, although your infirmity is very grievous unto me. Consider and tell me those things that you deem will be to your healing, and I will seek and procure them whatever the cost."

When the lady heard this, her heart beat lightly in her breast. She showed no semblance of joy, save this only, that she said,

"Husband, my old captive tells me that unless I breathe for awhile such air as that of my native land, and that quickly, I am but dead, for in nowise have I long to live."

"Wife," said the Soudan, "your death shall not be on my conscience. Consider and show me where you would go, and there I will cause you to be taken."

"Husband, it is all one to me, so I be out of this city."

Then the Soudan made ready a ship, both fair and strong, and garnished her plenteously with wines and meats.

"Husband," said the lady to the Soudan, "I will take of my captives the agèd and the young, that they may play chess and draughts at my bidding, and I will carry with me my son for my delight."

"Wife," answered he, "your will is my pleasure. But what shall be done with the third captive?"

"Husband, deal with him after your desire."

"Wife, I desire that you take him on the ship; for he is a brave man, and will keep you well, both on land and sea, if you have need of his sword."

The lady took leave of the Soudan, bidding him farewell, and urgently he prayed her to return so soon as she was healed of her sickness. The stores being put upon the ship and all things made ready, they entered therein and set sail from the haven. With a

fair wind they went very swiftly, so that the shipmen sought the lady, saying,

"Madam, this wind is driving the boat to Brindisi. Is it your pleasure to take refuge there, or to go elsewhere?"

"Let the ship keep boldly on her course," answered the lady to them, "for I speak French featly and other tongues also, so I will bring you to a good end."

They made such swift passage by day and by night, that according to the will of Our Lord they came quickly to Brindisi. The ship cast anchor safely in the harbour, and they lighted on the shore, being welcomed gladly by the folk of that country. The lady, who was very shrewd, drew her captives apart, and said,

"Sirs, I desire you to call to mind the pledge and the covenant you have made. I must now be certain that you are true men, remembering your oaths and plighted words. I pray you to let me know, by all that you deem of God, whether you will abide or not by our covenant together; for it is yet not too late to return to my home."

They answered,

"Lady, know beyond question that the bargain we have made we will carry out loyally. By our faith in God and as christened men we will abide by this covenant; so be in no doubt of our assurance."

"I trust you wholly," replied the lady; "but, sirs, see here my son, whom I had of the Soudan, what shall we do with him?"

"Lady, the boy is right welcome, and to great honour shall he come in our own land."

"Sirs," said the dame, "I have dealt mischievously with the Soudan, for I have stolen my person from him, and the son who was so dear to his heart."

The lady went again to the shipmen, and lifting her hand, said to them,

"Sirs, return to the Soudan whence you came, and greet him with this message. Tell him that I have taken from him my body and the son he loved so well, that I might deliver my father, my lord, and my brother from the prison where they were captive."

When the sailors heard this they were very dolent, but there was naught that they might do. They set sail for their own country, sad and very heavy by reason of the lady, of the young lad, whom they loved greatly, and of the captives who were escaped altogether from their hand.

For his part the Count arrayed himself meetly by grace of merchants and Templars, who lent him gladly of their wealth. He abode in the town, together with his fellowship, for their solace, till they made them ready for the journey, and took the road to Rome. The Count sought the Pontiff, and his company with him. Each confessed him of the secrets of his heart, and when the Bishop heard thereof, he accepted their devotion, and comforted them right tenderly. He baptised the child, who was named William. He reconciled the lady with Holy Church, and confirmed the lady and Messire Thibault her lord, in their marriage bond, reknitting them together, giving penance to each, and absolution for their sins. After this they made no long sojourn in Rome, but took their leave of the Apostle who had honoured them so greatly. He granted them his benison, and commended them to God. So they went their way in great solace and delight, praising God and His Mother, and all the calendar of saints, and rendering thanks for the mercies which had been vouchsafed to them. Journeying thus they came at last to the country of their birth, and were met by a fair procession of bishops and abbots, monks and priests, who had desired them fervently. But of all these welcomes they welcomed most gladly her who was recovered from death, and had delivered her sire, her lord, and her brother from the hands of the Paynim, even as you have heard. There we leave them for awhile, and will tell you of the shipmen and Saracens who had fared with them across the sea.

The sailors and Saracens who had carried them to Brindisi, returned as quickly as they were able, and with a fair wind cast anchor before Aumarie. They got them to land, very sad and heavy, and told their tidings to the Soudan.

Right sorrowful was the Soudan, and neither for time nor

reason could he forget his grief. Because of this mischief he loved that daughter the less who tarried with him, and showed her the less courtesy. Nevertheless the maiden increased in virtue and in wisdom, so that the Paynim held her in love and honour, praising her for the good that was known of her. But now the story is silent as to that Soudan who was so tormented by reason of the flight of his dame and captives; and comes again to the Count of Ponthieu, who was welcomed to his realm with such pomp and worship, as became a lord of his degree.

In no long while after his return the son of the Count was dubbed knight, and rich was the feast. He became a knight both chivalrous and brave. Greatly he loved all honourable men, and gladly he bestowed fair gifts on the poor knights and poor gentlewomen of the country. Much was he esteemed of lord and hind, for he was a worthy knight, generous, valiant and debonair, proud only to his foes. Yet his days on earth were but a span, which was the sorer pity, for he died lamented of all.

Now it befell that the Count held high Court, and many a knight and lord sat with him at the feast. Amongst these came a very noble man and knight, of great place in Normandy, named my lord Raoul des Preaux. This Raoul had a daughter, passing sweet and fair. The Count spoke so urgently to Raoul and to the maiden's kin that a marriage was accorded between William, his grandson, the son of the Soudan of Aumarie, and the daughter of my lord Raoul, the heiress to all his wealth. William wedded the damsel with every rich observance, and in right of his wife this William became Lord of Preaux.

For a long while the realm had peace from its foes. Messire Thibault dwelt with the lady, and had of her two sons, who in later days were worthy gentlemen of great worship. The son of the Count of Ponthieu, of whom we have spoken much and naught but good, died shortly after, to the grief of all the land. The Count of St. Pol was yet alive; therefore the two sons of my lord Thibault were heirs to both these realms, and attained thereto in the end. That devout lady, their mother, because of her

contrite heart, gave largely to the poor; and Messire Thibault, like the honourable gentleman he was, abounded in good works so long as he was quick.

Now it chanced that the daughter of the lady, who abode with the Soudan her father, increased greatly in favour and in virtue. She was called the Fair Captive, by reason that her mother had left her in the Soudan's keeping, as you have heard. A certain brave Turk in the service of the Soudan—Malakin of Baudas by name—saw this damsel, so fair and gracious, and desired her dearly in his heart, because of the good men told of her. He came before his master, and said to him,

"Sire, in return for his labour your servant craves a gift."

"Malakin," returned the Soudan, "what gift would you have?"

"Sire, I would dare to tell it to your face, if only she were not so high above my reach."

The Sultan who was both shrewd and quick witted made reply,

"Say out boldly what is in your mind, for I hold you dear, and remember what you have done. If there is aught it beseems me to grant—saving only my honour—be assured that it is yours."

"Sire, well I know that your honour is without spot, nor would I seek anything against it. I pray you to bestow on your servant —if so it be your pleasure—my lady your daughter, for she is the gift I covet most in all the world."

The Soudan kept silence, and considered for a space. He knew well that Malakin was both valiant and wise, and might easily come to great honour and degree. Since the servant was worthy of his high desire, the Soudan said,

"By my law you have required of me a great thing, for I love my daughter dearly, and have no other heir. You know well, and it is the simple truth, that she comes of the best and bravest blood in France, for her mother is the child of the Count of Ponthieu. But since you too are valiant, and have done me loyal service, for my part I will give her to you willingly, save only that it be to the maiden's mind."

"Sire," said Malakin, "I would not take her against her wish."

The Soudan bade the girl be summoned. When she came, he said,

"Fair daughter, I have granted you in marriage, if it pleases you."

"Sir," answered the maiden, "my pleasure is in your will."

The Soudan took her by the hand, saying,

"Take her, Malakin, the maid is yours."

Malakin received her with a glad heart, and wedded her according to the Paynim rite, bringing her to his house right joyously, with the countenance of all his friends. Afterwards he returned with her to his own land. The Soudan escorted them upon their way, with such a fair company of his household as seemed good to him. Then he bade farewell to his child and her lord, and returned to his home. But a great part of his fellowship he commanded to go with her for their service.

Malakin came back to his own land, where he was welcomed right gladly of his friends, and served and honoured by all the folk of his realm. He lived long and tenderly with his wife, neither were they childless, as this story testifies. For of this lady, who was called the Fair Captive, was born the mother of that courteous Turk, the Sultan Saladin, an honourable, a wise, and a conquering lord.

The Cruelty of Francesco Orsini
by Giovanni Fiorentino

The author, Giovanni Fiorentino, flourished dimly at the end of the fourteenth century. He set down a collection of old traditional tales called, for some reason, *Il Pecorone*, or *The Big Sheep*. From this Shakespeare took the Shylock story. Ser Giovanni here recounts a notable revenge of the thirteenth century. The phrase "Bring on the fruit" became proverbial as a signal for massacre. Our version is from *The Pecorone of Ser Giovanni*, translated by W. G. Waters (Boston: The Burton Ethnological Society, c. 1900).

NOT LONG ago there lived in Rome a gentleman named Messer Francesco Orsino da Monte Giordano, who had to wife a certain Donna Lisabetta, a lady fair and prudent and of very seemly manners. She had lived with him some time, and had borne him two sons. But it chanced that a youth fell in love with this lady, and she with him; and, as they were not wise enough to keep hidden their love, Messer Francesco was told divers times of the same; but he refused to believe the report, seeing that the youth was neither comely, nor well-born, nor rich, and also because he had shown himself a friend and follower of the house. At last the steward saw it with his own eyes, and informed Messer Francesco, who said to him, "Go and place yourself where you can espy him as he comes in, and then let me know, for I wish to see for myself; otherwise I shall never believe," which thing the steward promised to do.

One day Messer Francesco made pretence to go to a country house of his, and took horse with several companions, but at nightfall he returned to Rome and lay hid till the steward came and fetched him. Then Messer Francesco beheld the youth wantoning with his wife in the bedchamber, and saying, what time he kissed it, "Whose little mouth is this?" and the lady replied, "It is

thine." "And these roguish eyes?" "They are thine." "And these cheeks?" "They are thine." "And this lovely throat?" "It is thine." "And this fair bosom?" "It is thine." And thus, as he touched all the parts of her, she answered that they were his, except her hinder part, which she gave to her husband. And over this jest they raised a great laugh. When Messer Francesco saw and heard what they were doing and saying, he spake to himself, "Praised be God that some part of her is allowed to me!" and, as soon as he had seen all and more than enough, he went away stealthily back to his country house, where he remained as long as it pleased him. When he returned home he caused to be fashioned for his wife a dress of coarse cloth, but with the hinder part thereof made of samite trimmed with ermine, and likewise let prepare at his country house a very rich banquet, to which he invited the youth aforesaid and his two brothers, and divers of his kinsmen and associates. Having settled to give the feast on a certain Sunday morning, Messer Francesco made his wife put on the dress he had prepared, and took her through the streets of Rome. Then he directed her to repair to his country house, and join his guests at table, which thing she did in due course. When they were all assembled at the banquet, Messer Francesco placed his wife beside the youth, who was called Rinaldo, and then ranged in order all their kinsfolk and friends, setting before them a fair and sumptuous banquet.

When the guests beheld in what manner the lady was attired, they were astonished, and especially those who were akin to her and to Rinaldo, and said to themselves, "Surely there is some great matter in hand," while Rinaldo was mightily afeared. Then, when they had finished their repast, Messer Francesco said, "Now I will set before you some fruit"; and, having risen, he first gave to every one of them at the table a stick, and then withdrew into a room where he had in readiness eight of his servants—the same as the number of the guests—also armed with sticks. He made these surround the table, and then said to those who sat thereat, "Defend yourselves"; and, having turned to his servants who stood there sticks in hand, he cried, "Now bring out the fruit."

Whereupon the servants, as they had been commanded, over-threw the table and began to belabour with their sticks the guests who had been sitting there. With each party laying about a sharp fray arose, forasmuch as those at the table, finding themselves beaten with a will, were minded to give a proper return to their assailants. In short, the servants were so far superior in strength that they beat down all the guests, and laid them dead on the floor of the room. Then Messer Francesco made them take the corpse of the young man Rinaldo and fasten it with arms outspread on a crucifix, and convey it to a room in his house, while all the other bodies were taken back to their several homes.

This deed caused great complaint in Rome, on account of the death of so many worthy citizens, but no man dare open his mouth thereanent because the worker of the deed was a man of power in the city. Every night Messer Francesco took his wife and bound her to the corpse of Rinaldo, and made her remain all night in his embraces, and rise therefrom at daybreak. Every day he gave her naught else but two slices of bread and a beaker of water, so that her life might be all the more wretched. And in this wise she lived several days, sending constantly to beg mercy of Messer Francesco, but he was deaf to her prayers.

Then she, perceiving that she was to die, and that there was no remedy, prayed that she might see her children before her death; whereupon they brought her two sons to her. She took them in her arms, and weeping plentifully spake to them these words: "Dearest sons of mine, I leave you with God's blessing and my own. You are indeed the sons of Messer Francesco, born in lawful wedlock, but the enmity of one of my servants has brought me to this pass. And albeit this excuse of mine be not a valid one, nevertheless I leave to God and to you, as my sons, the duty of avenging the fate of your wretched and unfortunate mother." And she could not kiss them enough, for the anxiety that possessed her. Then, after blessing them, she gave them up to their nurse with these words: "Take these children whom I leave you, and, by God's faith and by your own soul, see that, when they shall be grown up, you recall my death to their memory, and

especially to this the younger one," and this little boy in sooth wept grievously and would not let himself be taken from her neck. When she had delivered them over, and assured them that they were lawfully born and not bastards, she commended her soul to God, and spake no more in this life, but died after the lapse of a few days.

They took her body and her lover's and bore them away, and the cruel deed was praised by some and blamed by others; and it came to pass that the nurse, when the time was ripe, told the children the story of their mother's death; and the consequence of this revelation was that Messer Francesco lost his wits, and for a long time went wandering distraught about the world, being in the most bitter enmity with his sons, and especially with the younger. Messer Francesco abode in the woods, sleeping there as if he had been a savage, working all the crazy antics which madmen are wont to practise. And thus they say the lady's fate was avenged.

A Night in Naples
by Giovanni Boccaccio

> Giovanni Boccaccio (1313–1375) is, of course, one of the world's great story-tellers. His *Decameron*, a collection of stories presumed to be told by a group of Florentine ladies and gentlemen taking refuge from the Great Plague (of 1348), gives us a vivid picture of fourteenth-century life. Our selections are taken from *The Decameron*, a translation by John Payne (London: privately printed, 1895).

THERE WAS once in Perugia, as I have heard tell aforetime, a young man, a horse-dealer, by name Andreuccio di Pietro, who, hearing that horses were good cheap at Naples, put five hundred gold florins in his purse and betook himself thither with other merchants, having never before been away from home. He arrived there one Sunday evening, towards vespers, and having taken counsel with his host, sallied forth next morning to the market, where he saw great plenty of horses. Many of them pleased him and he cheapened one and another, but could not come to an accord concerning any. Meanwhile, to show that he was for buying, he now and again, like a raw unwary clown as he was, pulled out the purse of florins he had with him, in the presence of those who came and went. As he was thus engaged, with his purse displayed, it chanced that a Sicilian damsel, who was very handsome, but disposed for a small matter to do any man's pleasure, passed near him, without his seeing her, and catching sight of the purse, said straightway in herself, "Who would fare better than I, if yonder money were mine!" And passed on.

Now there was with her an old woman, likewise a Sicilian, who, seeing Andreuccio, let her companion pass on and running to him, embraced him affectionately, which when the damsel saw, she stepped aside to wait for her, without saying aught. Andreuc-

cio, turning to the old woman and recognizing her, gave her a hearty greeting and she, having promised to visit him at his inn, took leave, without holding over-long parley there, whilst he fell again to chaffering, but bought nothing that morning. The damsel, who had noted first Andreuccio's purse and after her old woman's acquaintance with him, began cautiously to enquire of the latter, by way of casting about for a means of coming at the whole or part of the money, who and whence he was and what he did there and how she came to know him. The old woman told her every particular of Andreuccio's affairs well nigh as fully as he himself could have done, having long abidden with his father, first in Sicily and after at Perugia, and acquainted her, to boot, where he lodged and wherefore he was come thither.

The damsel, being thus fully informed both of his name and parentage, thereby with subtle craft laid her plans for giving effect to her desire and returning home, set the old woman awork for the rest of the day, so she might not avail to return to Andreuccio. Then, calling a maid of hers, whom she had right well lessoned unto such offices, she despatched her, towards evensong, to the inn where Andreuccio lodged. As chance would have it, she found him alone at the door and enquired at him of himself. He answered that he was the man she sought, whereupon she drew him aside and said to him, "Sir, an it please you, a gentlewoman of this city would fain speak with you." Andreuccio, hearing this, considered himself from head to foot and himseeming he was a handsome varlet of his person, he concluded (as if there were no other well-looking young fellow to be found in Naples), that the lady in question must have fallen in love with him. Accordingly, he answered without further deliberation that he was ready and asked the girl when and where the lady would speak with him; whereto she answered, "Sir, whenas it pleaseth you to come, she awaiteth you in her house"; and Andreuccio forthwith rejoined, without saying aught to the people of the inn, "Go thou on before; I will come after thee."

Thereupon the girl carried him to the house of her mistress,

who dwelt in a street called Malpertugio,* the very name whereof denoteth how reputable a quarter it is. But he, unknowing neither suspecting aught thereof and thinking to go to a most honorable place and to a lady of quality, entered the house without hesitation,—preceded by the serving-maid, who called her mistress and said, "Here is Andreuccio,"—and mounting the stair, saw the damsel come to the stairhead to receive him. Now she was yet in the prime of youth, tall of person, with a very fair face and very handsomely dressed and adorned. As he drew near her, she came down three steps to meet him with open arms and clasping him round the neck, abode awhile without speaking, as if hindered by excess of tenderness; then kissed him on the forehead, weeping, and said, in a somewhat broken voice, "O my Andreuccio, thou art indeed welcome."

He was amazed at such tender caresses and answered, all confounded, "Madam, you are well met." Thereupon, taking him by the hand, she carried him up into her saloon and thence, without saying another word to him, she brought him into her chamber, which was all redolent of roses and orange flowers and other perfumes. Here he saw a very fine bed, hung round with curtains, and store of dresses upon the pegs and other very goodly and rich gear, after the usance of those parts; by reason whereof, like a freshman as he was, he firmly believed her to be no less than a great lady. She made him sit with her on a chest that stood at the foot of the bed and bespoke him thus, "Andreuccio, I am very certain thou marvellest at these caresses that I bestow on thee and at my tears, as he may well do who knoweth me not and hath maybe never heard speak of me; but I have that to tell thee which is like to amaze thee yet more, namely, that I am thy sister; and I tell thee that, since God hath vouchsafed me to look upon one of my brothers, (though fain would I see you all), before my death, henceforth I shall not die disconsolate; and as perchance thou hast never heard of this, I will tell it thee.

"Pietro, my father and thine, as I doubt not thou knowest,

* I.e., ill hole.

abode long in Palermo and there for his good humor and pleasant composition was and yet is greatly beloved of those who knew him; but, among all his lovers, my mother, who was a lady of gentle birth and then a widow, was she who most affected him, insomuch that, laying aside the fear of her father and brethren, as well as the care of her own honor, she became so private with him that I was born thereof and grew up as thou seest me. Presently, having occasion to depart Palermo and return to Perugia, he left me a little maid with my mother, nor ever after, for all that I could hear, remembered him of me or of her; whereof, were he not my father, I should blame him sore, having regard to the ingratitude shown by him to my mother (to say nothing of the love it behoved him bear me, as his daughter, born of no serving-wench nor woman of mean extraction) who had, moved by very faithful love, without anywise knowing who he might be, committed into his hands her possessions and herself no less. But what skilleth it? Things ill done and long time passed are easier blamed than mended; algates,* so it was.

"He left me a little child in Palermo, where being grown well nigh as I am now, my mother, who was a rich lady, gave me to wife to a worthy gentleman of Girgenti, who, for her love and mine, came to abide at Palermo and there, being a great Guelph,† he entered into treaty with our King Charles,‡ which, being discovered by King Frederick,§ ere effect could be given to it, was the occasion of our being enforced to flee from Sicily, whenas I looked to be the greatest lady was ever in the island; wherefore, taking such few things as we might (I say few, in respect of the many we had) and leaving our lands and palaces, we took refuge in this city, where we found King Charles so mindful of our services that he hath in part made good to us the losses we had sustained for him, bestowing on us both lands and houses, and still maketh my husband, thy kinsman that is, a

* Algates: anyway.—Ed.
† I.e., a member of the Papal party, as against the Ghibellines or partisans of the Emperor. ‡ Charles d'Anjou, afterwards King of Sicily.
§ Emperor Frederick II.

goodly provision, as thou shalt hereafter see. On this wise come I
in this city, where, Godamercy and no thanks to thee, sweet my
brother, I now behold thee." So saying, she embraced him over
again and kissed him on the forehead, still weeping for tenderness.

Andreuccio, hearing this fable so orderly, so artfully delivered
by the damsel, without ever stammering or faltering for a word,
and remembering it to be true that his father had been in Pa-
lermo, knowing, moreover, by himself the fashions of young men
and how lightly they fall in love in their youth and seeing the
affectionate tears and embraces and the chaste kisses that she
lavished on him, held all she told him for more than true; where-
fore, as soon as she was silent, he answered her, saying, "Madam,
it should seem to you no very great matter if I marvel, for that in
truth, whether it be that my father, for whatsoever reason, never
spoke of your mother nor of yourself, or that if he did, it came
not to my notice, I had no more knowledge of you than if you
had never been, and so much the dearer is it to me to find you my
sister here, as I am alone in this city and the less expected this.
Indeed, I know no man of so high a condition that you should not
be dear to him, to say nothing of myself, who am but a petty
trader. But I pray you make me clear of one thing; how knew
you that I was here?" Whereto she made answer, "A poor
woman, who much frequenteth me, gave me this morning to
know of thy coming, for that, as she telleth me, she abode long
with our father both at Palermo and at Perugia; and but that
meseemed it was a more reputable thing that thou shouldst visit
me in my own house than I thee in that of another, I had come to
thee this great while agone." After this, she proceeded to enquire
more particularly of all his kinsfolk by name, and he answered
her of all, giving the more credence, by reason of this, to that
which it the less behoved him to believe.

The talk being long and the heat great, she called for Greek
wine and confections and let give Andreuccio to drink, after
which he would have taken leave, for that it was supper-time; but
she would on no wise suffer it and making a show of being sore
vexed, embraced him and said, "Ah, woe is me! I see but too

clearly how little dear I am to thee! Who would believe that thou
couldst be with a sister of thine, whom thou hast never yet seen
and in whose house thou shouldst have lighted down, whenas
thou camest hither, and offer to leave her, to go sup at the inn?
Indeed, thou shalt sup with me, and albeit my husband is abroad,
which grieveth me mightily, I shall know well how to do thee
some little honor, such as a woman may." To which Andreuccio,
unknowing what else he should say, answered, "I hold you as
dear as a sister should be held; but, an I go not, I shall be expected
to supper all the evening and shall do an unmannerliness."
"Praised be God!" cried she. "One would think I had no one in
the house to send to tell them not to expect thee; albeit thou
wouldst do much greater courtesy and indeed but thy duty an
thou sentest to bid thy companions come hither to supper; and
after, an thou must e'en begone, you might all go away together."

Andreuccio replied that he had no desire for his companions
that evening; but that, since it was agreeable to her, she might do
her pleasure of him. Accordingly, she made a show of sending to
the inn to say that he was not to be expected to supper, and after
much other discourse, they sat down to supper and were sump-
tuously served with various meats, whilst she adroitly contrived
to prolong the repast till it was dark night. Then, when they rose
from table and Andreuccio would have taken his leave, she
declared that she would on no wise suffer this, for that Naples
was no place to go about in by night, especially for a stranger,
and that, whenas she sent to the inn to say that he was not to be
expected to supper, she had at the same time given notice that he
would lie abroad. Andreuccio, believing this and taking pleasure
in being with her, beguiled as he was by false credence, abode
where he was, and after supper they held much and long dis-
course, not without reason,* till a part of the night was past,
when she withdrew with her women into another room, leaving

* The reason was that she wished to keep him in play till late into the
night, when all the folk should be asleep and she might the lightlier deal
with him (translator's note).

Andreuccio in her own chamber, with a little lad to wait upon him, if he should lack aught.

The heat being great, Andreuccio, as soon as he found himself alone, stripped to his doublet and putting off his hosen, laid them at the bedhead; after which, natural use soliciting him to rid himself of the overmuch burden of his stomach, he asked the boy where this might be done, who showed him a door in one corner of the room and said, "Go in there." Accordingly he opened the door and passing through in all assurance, chanced to set foot on a plank, which, being broken loose from the joist at the opposite end, flew up, and down they went, plank and man together. God so favored him that he did himself no hurt in the fall, albeit he fell from some height; but he was all bemired with the ordure whereof the place was full; and in order that you may the better apprehend both that which hath been said and that which en- sueth, I will show you how the place lay. There were in a narrow alley, such as we often see between two houses, a pair of rafters laid from one house to another, and thereon sundry boards nailed and the place of session set up; of which boards that which gave way with Andreuccio was one.

Finding himself, then, at the bottom of the alley and sore chagrined at the mishap, he fell a-bawling for the boy; but the latter, as soon as he heard him fall, had run to tell his mistress, who hastened to his chamber and searching hurriedly if his clothes were there, found them and with them the money, which, in his mistrust, he still foolishly carried about him. Having now gotten that for which, feigning herself of Palermo and sister to a Perugian, she had set her snare, she took no more reck of him, but hastened to shut the door whereby he had gone out when he fell.

Andreuccio, getting no answer from the boy, proceeded to call loudlier, but to no purpose; whereupon, his suspicions being now aroused, he began too late to smoke the cheat. Accordingly, he scrambled over a low wall that shut off the alley from the street, and letting himself down into the road, went up to the door of the house, which he knew very well, and there called long and loud and shook and beat upon it amain, but all in vain. Where-

fore, bewailing himself, as one who was now fully aware of his mischance, "Ah, woe is me!" cried he. "In how little time have I lost five hundred florins and a sister!" Then, after many other words, he fell again to battering the door and crying out and this he did so long and so lustily that many of the neighbors, being awakened and unable to brook the annoy, arose and one of the courtezan's waiting-women, coming to the window, apparently all sleepy-eyed, said peevishly, "Who knocketh below there?"

"What?" cried Andreuccio. "Dost thou not know me? I am Andreuccio, brother to Madam Fiordaliso." Whereto quoth she, "Good man, an thou have drunken overmuch, go sleep and come back to-morrow morning. I know no Andreuccio nor what be these idle tales thou tellest. Begone in peace and let us sleep, so it please thee." "How?" replied Andreuccio. "Thou knowest not what I mean? Certes, thou knowest; but, if Sicilian kinships be of such a fashion that they are forgotten in so short a time, at least give me back my clothes and I will begone with all my heart." "Good man," rejoined she, as if laughing, "methinketh thou dreamest"; and to say this and to draw in her head and shut the window were one and the same thing. Whereat Andreuccio, now fully certified of his loss, was like for chagrin to turn his exceeding anger into madness and bethought himself to seek to recover by violence that which he might not have again with words; wherefore, taking up a great stone, he began anew to batter the door more furiously than ever.

At this many of the neighbors, who had already been awakened and had arisen, deeming him some pestilent fellow who had trumped up this story to spite the woman of the house and provoked at the knocking he kept up, came to the windows and began to say, no otherwise than as all the dogs of a quarter bark after a strange dog, " 'Tis a villainous shame to come at this hour to decent women's houses and tell these cock-and-bull stories. For God's sake, good man, please you begone in peace and let us sleep. An thou have aught to mell with her, come back to-morrow and spare us this annoy to-night." Taking assurance, perchance, by these words, there came to the window one who was

within the house, a bully of the gentlewoman's, whom Andreuccio had as yet neither heard nor seen, and said, in a terrible big rough voice, "Who is below there?"

Andreuccio, hearing this, raised his eyes and saw at the window one who, by what little he could make out, himseemed should be a very masterful fellow, with a bushy black beard on his face, and who yawned and rubbed his eyes, as he had arisen from bed or deep sleep; whereupon, not without fear, he answered, "I am a brother of the lady of the house." The other waited not for him to make an end of his reply, but said, more fiercely than before, "I know not what hindereth me from coming down and cudgelling thee what while I see thee stir, for a pestilent drunken ass as thou must be, who will not let us sleep this night." Then, drawing back into the house, he shut the window; whereupon certain of the neighbors, who were better acquainted with the fellow's quality, said softly to Andreuccio, "For God's sake, good man, begone in peace and abide not there to-night to be slain; get thee gone for thine own good."

Andreuccio, terrified at the fellow's voice and aspect and moved by the exhortations of the neighbors, who seemed to him to speak out of charity, set out to return to his inn, in the direction of the quarter whence he had followed the maid, without knowing whither to go, despairing of his money and woebegone as ever man was. Being loathsome to himself, for the stench that came from him, and thinking to repair to the sea to wash himself, he turned to the left and followed a street called Ruga Catalana, that led towards the upper part of the city. Presently, he espied two men coming towards him with a lantern and fearing they might be officers of the watch or other ill-disposed folk, he stealthily took refuge, to avoid them, in a hovel, that he saw hard by. But they, as of malice aforethought, made straight for the same place and entering in, began to examine certain irons which one of them laid from off his shoulder, discoursing various things thereof the while.

Presently, "What meaneth this?" quoth one. "I smell the worst stench meseemeth I ever smelt." So saying, he raised the lantern

and seeing the wretched Andreuccio, enquired, in amazement, "Who is there?" Andreuccio made no answer, but they came up to him with the light and asked him what he did there in such a pickle; whereupon he related to them all that had befallen him, and they, conceiving where this might have happened, said, one to the other, "Verily, this must have been in the house of Scarabone Buttafuoco." Then, turning to him, "Good man," quoth one, "albeit thou hast lost thy money, thou hast much reason to praise God that this mischance betided thee, so that thou fellest nor couldst after avail to enter the house again; for, hadst thou not fallen, thou mayst be assured that, when once thou wast fallen asleep, thou hadst been knocked on the head and hadst lost thy life as well as thy money. But what booteth it now to repine? Thou mayst as well look to have the stars out of the sky as to recover a farthing of thy money; nay thou art like to be murdered, should yonder fellow hear that thou makest any words thereof." Then they consulted together awhile and presently said to him, "Look you, we are moved to pity for thee; wherefore, an thou wilt join with us in somewhat we go about to do, it seemeth to us certain that there will fall to thee for thy share much more than the value of that which thou hast lost." Whereupon Andreuccio, in his desperation, answered that he was ready.

Now there had been that day buried an archbishop of Naples, by name Messer Filippo Minutolo, and he had been interred in his richest ornaments and with a ruby on his finger worth more than five hundred florins of gold. Him they were minded to despoil and this their intent they discovered to Andreuccio, who, more covetous than well-advised, set out with them for the cathedral. As they went, Andreuccio still stinking amain, one of the thieves said, "Can we not find means for this fellow to wash himself a little, be it where it may, so he may not stink so terribly?" "Ay can we," answered the other. "We are here near a well, where there useth to be a rope and pulley and a great bucket; let us go thither and we will wash him in a trice." Accordingly they made for the well in question and found the rope there, but the bucket had been taken away; wherefore they took counsel together to tie

him to the rope and let him down into the well, so he might wash himself there, charging him shake the rope as soon as he was clean, and they would pull him up.

Hardly had they let him down when, as chance would have it, certain of the watch, being athirst for the heat and with running after some rogue or another, came to the well to drink, and the two rogues, setting eyes on them, made off incontinent, before the officers saw them. Presently, Andreuccio, having washed himself at the bottom of the well, shook the rope, and the thirsty officers, laying by their targets and arms and surcoats, began to haul upon the rope, thinking the bucket full of water at the other end. As soon as Andreuccio found himself near the top, he let go the rope and laid hold of the marge with both hands; which when the officers saw, overcome with sudden affright, they dropped the rope, without saying a word, and took to their heels as quickliest they might. At this Andreuccio marvelled sore, and but that he had fast hold of the marge, would have fallen to the bottom, to his no little hurt or maybe death. However, he made his way out and finding the arms, which he knew were none of his companions' bringing, he was yet more amazed; but, knowing not what to make of it and misdoubting some snare, he determined to begone without touching aught and accordingly made off he knew not whither, bewailing his ill-luck.

As he went, he met his two comrades, who came to draw him forth of the well; and when they saw him, they marvelled exceedingly and asked him who had drawn him up. Andreuccio replied that he knew not and told them orderly how it had happened and what he had found by the well-side, whereupon the others, perceiving how the case stood, told him, laughing, why they had fled and who these were that had pulled him up. Then, without farther parley, it being now middle night, they repaired to the cathedral and making their way thereinto lightly enough, went straight to the archbishop's tomb, which was of marble and very large. With their irons they raised the lid, which was very heavy, and propped it up so as a man might enter; which being done, quoth one, "Who shall go in?" "Not I,"

answered the other. "Nor I," rejoined his fellow; "let Andreuccio enter." "That will I not," said the latter; whereupon the two rogues turned upon him and said, "How! Thou wilt not? Cock's faith, an thou enter not, we will clout thee over the costard with one of these iron bars till thou fall dead."

Andreuccio, affrighted, crept into the tomb, saying in himself the while, "These fellows will have me go in here so they may cheat me, for that, when I shall have given them everything, they will begone about their business, whilst I am laboring to win out of the tomb, and I shall abide empty-handed." Accordingly, he determined to make sure of his share beforehand; wherefore, as soon as he came to the bottom, calling to mind the precious ring whereof he had heard them speak, he drew it from the archbishop's finger and set it on his own. Then he passed them the crozier and mitre and gloves and, stripping the dead man to his shirt, gave them everything, saying that there was nothing more. The others declared that the ring must be there and bade him seek everywhere; but he replied that he found it not and, making a show of seeking it, kept them in play awhile. At last, the two rogues, who were no less wily than himself, bidding him seek well the while, took occasion to pull away the prop that held up the lid and made off, leaving him shut in the tomb.

What became of Andreuccio, when he found himself in this plight, you may all imagine for yourselves. He strove again and again to heave up the lid with his head and shoulders, but only wearied himself in vain; wherefore, overcome with chagrin and despair, he fell down in a swoon upon the archbishop's dead body; and whoso saw him there had hardly known which was the deader, the prelate or he. Presently, coming to himself, he fell into a passion of weeping, seeing he must there without fail come to one of two ends, to wit, either he must, if none came thither to open the tomb again, die of hunger and stench, among the worms of the dead body, or, if any came and found him there, he would certainly be hanged for a thief.

As he abode in this mind, exceeding woebegone, he heard folk stirring in the church and many persons speaking and presently

perceived that they came to do that which he and his comrades had already done; whereat fear redoubled upon him. But, after the newcomers had forced open the tomb and propped up the lid, they fell into dispute of who should go in, and none was willing to do it. However, after long parley, a priest said, "What fear ye? Think you he will eat you? The dead eat not men. I will go in myself." So saying, he set his breast to the marge of the tomb and turning his head outward, put in his legs, thinking to let himself drop. Andreuccio, seeing this, started up and catching the priest by one of his legs, made a show of offering to pull him down into the tomb. The other, feeling this, gave a terrible screech and flung precipitately out of the tomb; whereupon all the others fled in terror, as they were pursued by an hundred thousand devils, leaving the tomb open.

Andreuccio, seeing this, scrambled hastily out of the tomb, rejoiced beyond all hope, and made off out of the church by the way he had entered in. The day now drawing near, he fared on at a venture, with the ring on his finger, till he came to the seashore and thence made his way back to his inn, where he found his comrades and the host, who had been in concern for him all that night. He told them what had betided them and themseemed, by the host's counsel, that he were best depart Naples incontinent. Accordingly, he set out forthright and returned to Perugia, having invested his money in a ring, whereas he came to buy horses.

»III«

LOVERS' WEAL
AND WOE

The Dapple-Gray Palfrey
by Huon Leroi

This is a *fabliau*, or realistic French story of the twelfth or thirteenth century, in verse, designed to be sung by a minstrel, and addressed to a bourgeois rather than to a noble audience. It is included, as *Le Vair palefroi*, in the *Recueil des fabliaux*, edited by A. de Montaiglon and G. Raynaud (Paris: Librairie des Bibliophiles, 1872–1890). Our prose version is from Isabel Butler, *Tales from the Old French* (Boston: Houghton Mifflin, 1910). Some slight changes in wording have been made.

THIS TALE is set in writing to portray and call to remembrance the worth, gentleness and honour that can be drawn from women; for well should we hold in mind the virtues that may be seen in them. Right sorry am I, and much it irketh me that they are not exalted and praised of all men to the height of their deserts. God! if but their hearts were sound and steadfast, strong and true, there were in all the world no treasure like unto them. It is great loss and great pity that they take not more heed to themselves; at the lightest breath a woman will change and shift and vary; her heart seemeth a very weather cock, for oft it chances that in a little space her spirit changeth more quickly than the storm wind.

Now in that I have been commanded to that I have set my hand, I will not leave it for dread of faithless cowards who envy those whose hearts are brave and valiant, nor fail to run my race out, to make me known and win me fame. In the lay of the Dapple-Gray Palfrey, hear now the wisdom of Huon Leroi wisely come down to you; and inasmuch as he knoweth how to listen to reason, he would fain display his sayings,—right well he turns them, methinketh.

Now know ye that a valiant knight, courteous and right chival-

rous, high of heart but poor in havings, dwelt in the land of Champagne. Full meet it is I portray his worth and the valour wherewith he was kindled; in many a place he proved his prowess, for he had wisdom and honour and a heart of great valiancy. Had he but been as rich in gear as he was in desire for good—provided always he did not worsen by reason of his wealth—he would have known no peer, equal or fellow. And now I make me ready for the story, for meet it is the deeds of a man of prowess be told from end to end, that we may take therefrom a fair and goodly example. Now this knight was praised of all folk.

Wheresoever he went his valour was confessed, for those who knew him not yet loved the fame of him by reason of the good that sprang from him. When he had helm on head and rode into the tourney, no thought had he for the wooing of ladies, nor did he linger on the outskirts. There where the press was greatest he smote right hardily. Armed and ahorseback he was full fair to see; ever he went gaily clad, even in midwinter; and of some he was blamed for his gaiety of heart. Little wealth of land he had; at the most it yielded him no more than two hundred pounds a year; but ever he rode far and wide in search of honour.

In those days in Champagne the woodland was wilder than it is today and likewise the open. Now it came to pass this knight fell to dreaming of a love fair and valiant,—a damsel, to wit, daughter to one of the foremost men of that land, one no wise wanting in riches, rather was he well supplied with goods and gear, and dwelt within strong walls. A full thousand pounds each year his land brought him; and often men came to him to seek his daughter in marriage, in that all folk were won by her great beauty. No other children he had, nor any wife living, and his time was almost spent. His dwelling stood in a wood, and all round about it the forest was great and thick.

Now the young knight of whom I told you made bold to seek the damsel, but her father gainsaid him, no desire had he that the youth should love her, or win him honour by means of her. The young knight's name was Messire Guillaume of a sooth, and he

abode in that same forest wherein the old vavasour* had his stronghold, with its riches and its wide lands. The one manor was two leagues distant from the other; but on both sides love could not fail to spring up, and on nought else was their thought set save its maintenance. And when the knight wished to go to her he loved, he made a path through the deep forest that was great and thick thereabouts, a way traversed by no living man save him only. By it he rode secretly to the damsel many a time, he and his palfrey, all still and quietly. Sore vexed was he that he could not speak to her face to face, but the court was right strongly enclosed, and high was the barrier; the damsel dared not issue out, but her comfort was that she spoke to him many a time through the timbers of the wall. Without, the fosse was wide, and the hedge thick and strong, so they could not come close to one another. The house stood upon a rock, and was full strongly enclosed. At the entrance was a drawbridge; moreover, the old knight who was in all ways crafty, and who had well nigh run out his time, seldom stirred out of the house, for he could no longer ride abroad, but sat at home in peace. He had his daughter well watched; and for his delight he made her sit with him, which ofttimes irked her in that thereby she lost that joy to which her heart was rooted. But the young knight who was wise and valiant did not forget the way to her; he asketh only to see her.

Inasmuch as he saw that matters could not be otherwise, ofttimes he returned to her dwelling, but never could he enter in, and never could he see her, who was so close a prisoner, as nigh at hand as his heart desired. Oft he came to see her, yet never could he look upon her, for she could not so stand that he could see her face all clearly. And the heart of each was sore stricken.

The knight, whom it beseemed to love the maid who was of such marvelous worth her like was not known, had—so the tale telleth us—a palfrey of great price; a *vair*† it was, of wondrous

* Vavasour: a noble landholder, ranking below a baron.—Ed.
† *Vair:* Dapple-gray.—Ed.

colour, that no man might conceive of any colour, or the semblance of any flower so perfect in its beauty; know ye that in no kingdom was there its like in those days for goodliness, and none that went so soft an amble. The knight loved it much, and certes, he would not part with it for any treasure; long had the folk of that land seen it in his possession. Now ofttimes on this palfrey he rode to seek the damsel through the fair and solitary forest where he had worn a path, known to none save to him and to the palfrey. Little noise he made as he rode to seek his love; right great care must he take that he be not seen of her father, for full bitter was her life to her.

Thus then they spent their days, each longing for the other, for they could never comfort themselves with kiss or embrace, and I tell you of a sooth that if ever the lips of the one might have touched those of the other, right sweet had it seemed to the fellowship of those twain. Full fierce was the fire they could in no wise quench, for if they might have drawn each other close, and kissed and embraced full sweetly as they had great will and desire to do, then could no man have wrought them annoy, but their joy had been perfect. Now right great was their pain in that they might in no wise touch or solace one another.

Little joy could they have in one another save that of speech and hearing, and rarely they saw one another, for too cruel was the interdict between these two lovers. She was in fear of her father, for were he to know of the intercourse between those twain, he would more quickly give her in marriage elsewhere; and the knight on his part desired to do nought that might undo the love that was between them, and would not risk a quarrel, for much he feared that old man who was rich out of all measure.

Now the knight bethought himself, and day after day pondered the life he led, for ever he held it in mind. And at length the thought came to his heart that let it be for good or for ill, he would go speak to the old vavasour, and ask him for his daughter to wife, let what so will come of it, for he knoweth not what his present life will bring to him. Every day of the week he is denied that which he coveteth, for over narrow is the path.

So one day he made him ready and went to hold speech with the old man in his own house, there where his daughter was. Right well was he received, for full well was he known to the old man and to his household. And the knight who was brave and courteous, and ready of speech like a man of worth in whom naught lacketh, spoke, saying: "Sir, I am come hither, and of your grace I pray you hearken to my words. I have come into your house to ask a boon, may God let you grant it me." The old man looked upon him, and thereafter asked: "What may it be? By my faith, I will help you herein, if I may, saving my honour." "Yea, sir, this much I know of your matters that right well ye may do it; now may God grant you concede it." "I will if it liketh me, but if it liketh me not, right well shall I know how to give denial; and if it is not my will to vouchsafe it, I will not deceive you by either token or promise." "Sir," he saith, "I will tell you now the gift I would ask of you. You know somewhat of my estate; well knew ye my father, my house and dwelling, and right well know ye the time and manner wherein I take my delight; and now in guerdon of this, sir, I would ask of you your daughter, if it be your will. Now may God grant that no thought so trouble your heart that by reason of the presumption of my request ye refuse me this gift. And I would that you know I was never of her acquaintance; right glad and joyous had I been if I might have spoken with her, and seen for myself the goodliness for which she is famed. Greatly is she beloved in this land by reason of her virtues; meseemeth she hath not her like in all the world. So tell me all those who know her, though but to few is she known, in that she lives imprisoned herewithin. An overbold thought was mine when I dared ask her of you, but if I have your consent, and ye deign to give me the gift of her by way of service and guerdon, right glad and joyful shall I be thereof. Now have I made my prayer and do you answer me at your pleasure."

Then forthright and without staying for any counsel the old man saith to him: "Right well do I understand all ye have said, for all is plain therein. My daughter is young and fair and wise and a damsel of high lineage; and I am a rich vavasour, sprung of

a noble house, and my land yieldeth a good thousand pounds each year. Now I am not so out of my wit that I would give my daughter to a knight who lives by what he may chance to win; for I have no other children save her only, nor has she failed my love, and after my time all will be hers, wherefore I desire to marry her well. I know of no prince in this kingdom, nor from here even to Lorraine, who howsoever wise and valiant he may be would not do well in having her to wife. Awhile agone, scarce a month since, one asked her of me in marriage whose land yieldeth a good five hundred pounds a year, which would now be made over to me, if I would give assent to his offer. But my daughter can well wait a little, for I am so rich in goods and gear that she will not lose her price or her value in marriage. The man of highest lineage in all this land or from here to Alemaigne, save only king or count, may well be hers."

Now when the knight heard this he was sorely abashed, nor did he make any tarrying but took leave and went away. But he knew not what to do in that he was so swayed and constrained by love, wherefore he made bitter lament.

When the damsel knew of the dismissal, and what her father had said, she was full sorrowful, for she was not light of love but had given her heart wholly to the knight, more so than words can tell. Before he who was wrathful with grief returned home again, they held speech together without the wall, and both spoke their thought. The knight told her all he had said to her father and of their falling out. "O lady, frank and free," saith the knight, "now what shall I do? Meseemeth I must leave this land and ride at errantry, for all I desired is vanished. You I may not win, and I know not what will become of me. On an ill day I came to know the great riches whereon your father so prides himself; liefer would I have you poorer, for had your father not been so rich he would have looked with favour on what I may win." "Certes," saith she, "and I might have my way, gladly would I have less than I am to have. Ah, sir, if my father would but give thought to your valour and worth, by my faith, he would not gainsay your wooing me, and making a covenant with him; if he but weighed

your riches over against your valiancy surely he would grant the compact. But his heart is overladen with prudence; he does not desire what I desire, nor sorrow at my sorrow. If he were at one with my thought, right soon were the thing granted. But the heart that beats in old age giveth no thought to youth nor to the desire of youth, for the heart of the old is not as that of the young, methinketh. Yet if you will do according to my counsel you cannot fail of winning me."

"Yes, by my faith, even so will I do, damsel; now without fail tell me your will." "I have bethought me," she saith, "of a thing on which my mind hath often dwelt. You know right well you have an uncle who is of great wealth, and a strong manor he hath within his defences. Even so rich as my father is he, and he hath neither wife nor child nor brother, nor any heir nearer than you yourself. 'Tis well and fully known that after his death all will be yours, and his money and rents are well worth sixty marks of fine gold. Now go to him straightway, old he is and frail, as ye know right well; tell him that you have had such words with my father that never can you be of accord with him unless he aid you in the matter. Let him promise you as much land as will bring in three hundred pounds yearly, and let him come to ask this thing of my father, who greatly loves him. Your uncle looks on my father as a sage, and each deems the other a man of worth; both are old and full of years, each wholly trusts the other; and if your uncle will graciously do so much for your love that you can induce him to promise you so much of his havings that he can say to my father: 'My nephew shall have three hundred pounds of my land in return for your daughter whom he seeketh,' then the marriage will indeed come to pass, for I truly believe my father would yea-say it, if your uncle spoke in this wise. And when you shall have married me, you will return to him again all the land which he will have promised to you on these terms; and I have so given myself over to your love that I shall be well content of the bargain." "Fair one," he saith, "now know ye of a sooth that never did I desire anything so much, and straightway will I speak with my uncle."

So he took his leave and returned home again; but his thoughts were sad and sombrous because of the refusal he had met with. Thus he rideth through the forest upon his gray palfrey; in sore wrath is he, and yet right glad at heart by reason of the wise and good counsel the damsel had given him. So he rode without let or hindrance to Medet where his uncle dwelleth. Straightway he came before him and maketh to him sore complaint and lament. Thereafter they went into an upper chamber, and there he told his uncle plainly all his plight and his covenant. "Uncle, if you will do so much," saith he, "that you will speak to him of the matter, and tell him that you have given over to me three hundred pounds of your land, I will without condition pledge you, and my hand in your hand, herewith promise you, that when I shall have married the damsel who is now denied me you shall have your land again all quit, as guerdon and reward; now do as I beseech you." "Nephew," saith his uncle, "right willingly, for I am well pleased and content with the project. By my head, you would marry the best in the land, and I think I can bring it to pass." "Uncle," saith he, "prithee hasten my suit, and so press it that he consent to the marriage, for I would fain no longer waste my time; and meantime, I will go to the tournament at Galardon; I shall be full richly accoutred, and may God grant me as guerdon that I do so well that my suit may thereby be bettered. And do you bethink you to so contrive that the wedding may be on my return." "Right willingly, fair nephew," saith he, "I am right glad of your tidings, in that the maid is frank and free." Then Messire Guillaume rode away forthwith; and he made great joy in that his uncle had said that he should of a sooth have to wife her whom he so desired,—of no other joy is he fain. So all alight with happiness he rode to the tourney as one who is well wont thereto.

The next morning at dawn of day, his uncle got him to horseback, and six more with him, and before the hour of prime came to the spot where dwelt the old vavasour, who maintained a full rich household, and who was father to her whose beauty

knew no fault. He was received with full great state, for he was much beloved of the old man whose fellow he was in years, in that he was his neighbour and mightily rich. So the old man made great cheer and joy, in that this other who was of high estate had come to see him, and forgot not to say: "Right welcome are you, fair sir." And a goodly feast was spread, for the old man was frank and free, and knew well how to honour him whom he would.

When the tables were removed there were tales told,—old meetings of lance and sword and shield; and of old deeds was many a fair word said. But the uncle of the good knight did not over long forget himself, but laid bare his thought, and all openly he saith to the old man: "Where am I wandering? As God may aid me, I love you right well, as you shall now hear. I am come to you to seek help in a matter; may God so incline your heart that my prayer be heard in such wise and manner that I may attain it." And the old vavasour maketh answer: "By my head, I have so taken you into my heart, that even though it be to my hurt, nothing sought by you shall be refused, but rather shall the boon be granted you." "Sir, thanks and guerdon will I gladly give you," saith the old man, who delayeth no longer to speak his thought: "Fair sir, I have come to ask for your daughter who is wise and discreet; fain would I take her to wife, and before I marry her, she shall receive a dower from my own store, for I am passing rich. Ye know I have no heir of my own flesh and blood, which sore grieveth me, and to her I will be of good faith inasmuch as you are right dear to me. When I shall have taken your daughter to wife, I shall not be fain to leave you, or to dispart my wealth from yours, rather all shall be one; and together we will hold in common that which God hath given us." Then he who was prudent and wise was right glad, and said: "Sir, without any nay-saying I will give her to you, and right willingly, inasmuch as you are a man of worth and honesty. Full glad am I that you have asked her of me; had I been given the best castle in all Friesland I would not have known such joy; to none

would I give her in marriage so gladly as to you, for I have found you discreet and a man of wisdom in all points wherein I have known aught of your affairs."

Thereupon he promised and affianced to him the damsel who had no desire for him, but thought surely to have another. Now when the damsel knew the truth she was in sore grief and dismay. Ofttimes she maketh oath to Saint Mary that she would never be married to that old man; all woful she was, and weeping, ofttimes she made lament: "Alas, unhappy that I am, how am I undone. What treason hath this old man wrought! Surely he deserves death. How he hath deceived his nephew, that brave and gentle knight who is all compact of goodness. And now, lo you, I am given to this old man, all only because of his riches. May God give him his reward for it. Surely he hath wrought great folly; never will he know gladness, and on the day he weddeth me he will win a mortal enemy. Alas, that I should ever see the day. Nay, may God not grant me life so long that I do see it. Now hath my friend sorrow and great anguish; never have I heard of such treason. If I were not so imprisoned right soon would I end this matter; but I can do nought, nor even issue out of this house. I must needs abide here and endure my father's will; but the pain is over cruel. Ah, God, what can I do, and when will he who hath been so cruelly betrayed return again? If he knew how his uncle had dealt by him, and had sinned towards me, I know full well that all joyless I would die and cease to be; and if he knew this, by my head, I think he would come to his end; and my great woes would cease. God, how my heart is torn; better would I love death than life. What envy and what treason! How did that old man dare think this thing? None can dispute with him for me, for my father loveth covetousness which doth overmuch tempt and allure him. Fie upon old age, fie upon wealth! Shall no man ever win a wife rich and of high lineage unless he have great possessions? Certes, I ought to hate him who separateth me from the one in whom I claim a part, and who thought of a surety to have me, but now meseemeth, I shall fail him."

Thus the damsel made lament in her sore distress, for her heart

was so bound in love to the young knight that scarce can she conceal her thought from any; and contrarywise, she hateth him to whom her father hath given her. She thinketh herself evilly bestowed, for he is old and of great age, his face is all wrinkled and his eyes red and hateful. From Chalons even unto Beauvais was no knight older than he seemed in all points, nor even unto Sens any of greater riches, so men say. But the folk of that land held him for coward and felon, whereas she so shone with beauty and valiancy that in all the kingdom of France was no woman so fair, or so frank and courteous. Full diverse was the portioning, on one side bright, on the other dark; nor was there any shadow in the light, or any glimmer in the darkness. Fain would the damsel whom love so grieved and tormented have changed her plight. But he who had betrothed her and had great joy of her well devised his affair, and set term for the wedding, even as one who had no suspicions, and knew nought of the debate and grief in her whom love held captive, even as ye have heard me relate.

Now I must not fail to tell you of the conclusion of the marriage. He who was wise and a man of worth made himself ready fully richly. And before the third day dawned the old vavasour had bidden all the hoary old heads sprung of that land and countryside, those he deemed men of most wisdom, to be present at the high marriage of his daughter,—she who had set her heart elsewhere. She had given her love and desire to the brave and far-famed knight, but now 't is seen how without hope she is tricked and betrayed. The two old knights have assembled a goodly company, for they were well known to all the men of years and worth in that land, and the more part came thither, a good thirty in number; not one of them but had revenue and safeguard from the old vavasour, and now they are come together in his house.

So the word is gone forth that the damsel shall be married at dawn of day. And the maidens who attend her are bidden to make her ready; but they give thought to the day and the hour, which sorely displeases them, and assume looks of great dismay. The old knight asketh them on whom his command is laid if his

daughter is fully prepared, and if she is in doubt about aught, and if anything lacketh whereof she hath need. "No, fair sir, nought that I can see," so made answer one of the damsels, "if but we had palfreys and saddles to carry us all to the minster; for there will be, methinketh, great company of ladies, cousins and kindred who dwell nigh at hand." "There need be no fear for palfreys," quoth he, "methinketh there will be enough and to spare." And there was not a baron in the land from whom he did not command one; and he to whom the message was given went straightway to the dwelling of him whose heart was all fulfilled with valour,—he who shone with prowess.

Now Messire Guillaume, the brave and wise, knew not that the marriage had been plotted to this point, but love which goaded his heart had hastened his return. Of nought could he think save that which tormented him; and his love waxed and flourished. Yet he had come back from the tourney as one no wise unglad, for he still thought to have for his own her he has now lost,—unless it please God and some adventure betide. Each day he expected fair and pleasant tidings, and that his uncle would send word to him that he might marry the damsel. So he went singing through the house, and he made a minstrel play new songs upon the viol; full of joy and mirth he was, for furthermore, he had won every prize at the tourney. But ever he looks towards the door to see if anyone cometh with news.

Much he wonders when they will send to him, and at the last he stops his singing, for love forbids him to set his thought on aught beside. And now, lo you, without more tarrying, a varlet enters the court. When Messire Guillaume saw him his heart leaped and trembled with joy; and the varlet saith to him: "God save you, sir; the old vavasour who has long been your friend, as ye well know, hath in great need sent me to you. You have a palfrey of great price, no other in the world goeth so soft an amble; now my lord prayeth and commandeth that you loan it to him of your love, and send it to him this same night." "And wherefore, friend?" saith he. "Sir, to bear his daughter to the minster, our lady gracious and fair." "And to what end goeth she

thither?" "Fair sir, there she is to marry your uncle to whom she is affianced; and tomorrow morning at dawn she is to be escorted to the disused chapel that lieth on the edge of the forest. But ye delay too long, sir, prithee haste; lend now to your uncle and my liege lord your palfrey, the best in the kingdom as I well know, for oft has it been so proven."

Messire Guillaume heareth him. "God," saith he, "hath my uncle whom I so trusted, and besought so fairly that he help me in my need, now betrayed me? May the Lord God never forgive him his misdeed and his treason! Scarce can I believe he has done this; methinketh you speak not truly." "You may know it of a truth tomorrow," saith he, "before the hour of prime; and already great is the assembly at his house of ancient knights of the land." "Alas," saith he, "how I have been tricked and deceived and betrayed." And for sorrow he well nigh fell to the ground in a swoon; in sooth, had he not feared blame from the folk of the household he would have done otherwise than he did. All hot he was with wrath and sorrow, and knew not what to do or say. Unceasingly he made lament; but despite his sore distress, the messenger urgeth him and changeth his thought: "Sir, let your good palfrey be saddled straightway, and my lady will ride upon him to the minster, for softly he goeth." And he who was easily moved still maketh sorrow, even while he masters his grief in bethinking what he will do, namely, to know of a truth if he will indeed send his gray palfrey to him he needs must hate above all others. "Yes," saith he straightway, "she who is of such high excellence, and whom I have now lost, hath no blame herein,— much it irketh me. My palfrey will go to serve her, and requite the high honour I have always found in her, for I have proven her at all points; but never more will she be mine, this I may know of a truth.

"Now I have not spoken wisely, rather have I lost my wit and fallen short of the mark, when I thought to send my palfrey for the joy and delight of him who has betrayed me and brought me to nought. Hath he not forced me to turn away from her whom I thought to have for mine own? No man should love one who

seeketh his betrayal. Over bold is he who asketh for my palfrey; nothing of mine will I send to him of whom I have nought. Hath he not disinherited me of the sweetness, beauty and great courtesy for which my lady is praised?

"Long time I served her in vain; well had I deserved the sovereign honour of her; but now no joy of her shall I have henceforth. How send him who maketh me so sorrowful anything whereof he will be glad? But none the less, though it cost me somewhat that she who is of such goodness should ride upon my palfrey, well I know that when she looks on him, he will recall me to her remembrance. I have loved her in good faith, I do love her and shall love her always, but her love costs me too dear. All solitary I will be her lover, yet I know not if she put her heart into the old intimacy that hath made my heart so heavy and sorrowful; methinketh it was not dear to her; Cain the brother of Abel did no greater treason. Now is my heart in sore torment by reason of her of whom I have no comfort." Thus he made lament unceasingly; but he let saddle the palfrey and called the squire; to his enemy he sent the gray palfrey, and the messenger set out straightway.

Messire Guillaume had no respite from his sorrow, he shut himself into his chamber all wrathful and sorrowful, and said to all his sergeants that were any so bold as to attempt to make merry, he would have him hung or put to the sword. No heart had he for joy, rather he was fain to lead a life without cheer, for he could no wise drive out the heaviness, the grief and the pain from his heart. Meantime, he to whom he had given the palfrey led it away, and returned forthwith to the house of his master, who made great joy.

The night was clear and still, and within the house was a great company of ancient knights. When they had eaten plenteously, the old man bade the watch, and said to all and commanded them, that an hour before daylight they be all awake and ready, and horses and palfreys be saddled and accoutred without noise or disorder; and thereafter they all went to rest and sleep. But she whom love caused to sigh and tremble with dread had no thought

of sleep, not once that night did she slumber; all others slept, she watched. Nor was her heart asleep but all intent on making moan; and if it might have been, she would never have waited for the stirring of the men or the coming of the dawn, but would have fled away forthwith.

After midnight, the moon arose, and lighted all the heavens and the air; and when the watch, who had drunk deep, saw the great light round about him, he thought the dawn was breaking. "The high company of knights should have been astir before now," he thought; and he sounded the dawn, and called aloud and cried: "Up lordings, the day breaketh." So cried he who was all bemuddled from the wine he had drunk over night. And they who had scarce rested or slept arose all bewildered, and hastily the squires saddled the horses, for they thought the day had come. But before ever the dawn shall break they may well ride and travel a good five leagues.

The palfreys were saddled, and all the old men who were to escort the damsel to the waste chapel on the edge of the forest had mounted, and the maiden was committed to the care of the most discreet. The gray palfrey had been saddled, and when it was led forth, she made greater sorrow than ever she had made before. But the wise old men guessed nothing, nor knew her thought, rather they deemed she wept because she was leaving her father's house; nought they understood of her tears or the sorrow that she made; all wofully she got her to horseback.

So they rode forth together, and turned straight towards the forest, methinketh. They found the path so narrow that no two could ride abreast; now they who accompanied the damsel were in the rear, and the others went on before; and he who was her escort, in that he saw the path was narrow, made her go before him, while he rode behind by reason of the straitness of the way.

Long was the cavalcade, but inasmuch as they had slept little they were wearied and worn, and somewhat dispirited; also they rode the more heavily in that they old were and ancient, and by reason it was long before day they were the more given over to

slumber. So drowsing upon the necks of their horses they rode up hill and down dale; and he who had been chosen as the most discreet escorted the damsel; but passing little rest had he had in his bed that night, and sleep tricked him into forgetfulness, for great was his desire of slumber.

Now as for the damsel she was distressed by nought save her love and her grief. And while she was in this narrow path whereof I have spoken, the great company of knights and barons passed on; the more part were bent low over their saddles, some few watched, but their thoughts were on other matters than the escort of the damsel; and ever they rode on swiftly through the deep forest. The damsel was in deep distress, even as one who would fain be elsewhere, in London or Winchester.

The gray palfrey well knew this old and narrow way, for many a time had he traversed it. Anon they rode down a steep hillside where the forest grew so thick that the light of the moon was hidden; full dusky there was the wood, for right deep was the valley. Loud was the noise of the horses, and the more part of the barons rode before her. Some bent low in sleep over their comrades, some waked and talked; and so they all fared on together. Now the gray palfrey which the damsel rode, following in the rear of the company, did not know the way of the highroad that ran straight before them, but chose a by-path to the right which led directly to the house of Messire Guillaume. The palfrey seeth the path, full oft had he traversed it, and straightway left the road and the cavalcade of horses. As for the knight who accompanied the damsel, he was so overtaken with sleep that ever and again he let his palfrey stop short in the roadway. And now no one guides the damsel, save God only; she gives her palfrey the rein and he turns into the tangled by-way. Not one of the knights discover that the damsel is no longer following them, more than a league they ride before they take note thereof; little care hath her guide and leader given her. And she did not wittingly take flight, but rather rode on as one who knoweth not the way nor to what land the road leadeth.

The palfrey follows the path nor goeth astray, for often, both

summer and winter, had he been there before. The damsel all
woful ofttimes looketh about her, but sees neither knight nor
baron. Full perilous seemed the forest, sombre and darksome; and
she was right fearful in that she was without companions. No
great marvel is it that she was afraid, and much she wondered
what had become of the knights who had borne her company.
Full glad she was of the mischance, yet woful that she had no
guide, save God alone, for herself and the palfrey who had often
passed that way before. But she committed her to God, and the
palfrey bore her away. She who was sore discomforted gave him
the rein, nor did she utter a single cry, for she had no wish that
those others should hear her, or return to her again. Rather would
she die in the wild wood than make such a marriage.

Thus she rode deep in thought, and the palfrey, which knew
the path well and was eager to get him home again, went at so
swift a pace that he speedily traversed that great forest. On a
hillside was a stream which ran swift and dark; the palfrey went
straight thither, for he knew the ford, which was not very deep
or wide, and he passed over it as fast as might be. Scarce had they
left it behind when the damsel heard the sound of a horn from
the side whither the gray palfrey was bearing her. The watch was
above the gate, and played upon his horn to herald the day, and
thither rode the damsel. Straight to the house she came, all
abashed and astray, even as one who knoweth neither the road
nor the pass nor how to ask the way. Thus the palfrey left the
path, and came out upon the bridge which led across a deep water
that enclosed all the manor.

And the watch on guard sounding his horn heard the noise and
clatter of the palfrey upon the bridge, which had crossed there
many a time before. He stopped his horn blowing for a little and
cometh down from his place, and asketh forthright: "Who is it
rides so hard over the bridge at this hour?" And the damsel
maketh answer: "Surely the most unhappy lady ever born of
woman. In God's name let me within until the day dawneth, for I
know not whither I should go." "Certes, damsel," he maketh
answer, "that I dare not do, nor to bring anyone into this house,

save by the leave of my lord; and never hath any man been in greater grief than he now is; right sorrowful is he in that he hath been cruelly betrayed."

Now even as he spoke in this wise, he put his face and eyes to an opening in the postern; neither torch nor lantern had he, for the moon shone clear, and he seeth the gray palfrey; right well he knew it,—often had he looked on it aforetime. Much he wondered whence it came; and long he looked upon the damsel who held it by the rein, and who was richly dight in new and goodly raiment. Speedily the watch goeth to his master, who lay upon his bed all joyless. "Sir," saith he, "a damsel is come hither out of the wood, all uncounselled is she, and young of look and seeming; rich is her array, full rich her garments; meseemeth, she is wrapped about in a mantle richly furred, and her gown, methinketh, is of fine scarlet. Sad and downcast she rideth upon your gray palfrey; no whit unpleasing is her speech, but fair and gracious: I would not willingly lie to you, sir, but I believe in all this land is no maid so fair and winsome. Methinketh she is a fay that God hath brought hither to you, to make good the loss that hath rendered you so heavy hearted; fair amends will she make you for her ye have lost."

Messire Guillaume heareth him, and forthwith springeth to his feet; with a surcoat upon his back and nought beside he cometh to the door, and bade it be speedily opened. The damsel crieth out to him, sighing: "Ah, gentle sir, sore travail hath been mine this night. Sir, in God's name, be not angry, but let me enter now your house,—I ask not to abide there. I am in sore distress by reason of a company of knights who are now in great dismay inasmuch as they have lost me. For safeguard I have come to you, even as chance has led me; right sorrowful am I and all astray."

Messire Guillaume heard her and had great joy thereof. He knew the palfrey that had long been his own, and he looketh hard upon the damsel,—a more joyful man there might not be. So he leadeth her into his house; he hath set her down from her palfrey, and taking her by the hand hath kissed her more than twenty times. And she made no denial, for right well she knew him. One

looked upon the other, and right great joy made they between them; and in one another they forgot all their griefs. He took from her her mantle, and joyfully they sat them down upon a cushion of rich silk bordered with gold. Each maketh the sign of the cross a good twenty times, for scarcely can they believe it is not a dream they look upon. And when the serving-men were gone, much they solaced themselves with kisses, but no other misdoing was there between them.

Freely the damsel told him all her plight; now she saith blessed was the hour of her birth, in that God that led her thither, and hath, as fortune willed it, delivered her from that other who thought to make her his own in return for his chattels and gear. Now in the morning at dawn of day, Messire Guillaume arrays himself, and lets bring the damsel into his court and chapel, and without delay he lets summon his chaplain. Speedily the knight had himself married and bound in holy wedlock; not lightly may the twain be disparted. And when the mass was sung, maids and serving-men and squires made great joy within the house.

But great annoy was theirs who had heedlessly lost her. They were come together at the deserted chapel, and right weary were they from riding the night long, not one of them but was the worse for it. Then the old man demanded his daughter of him who had guarded her so ill; he knew not what to say, but speedily he made answer; "Sir, she rode before me, I was behind, for right narrow was the path and the forest great and thick. I know not if she turned aside, for I drowsed in my saddle; now and again I awoke and ever I deemed her near me, but certes, she is not here now, and I know not what hath become of her; right ill have we guarded her."

The old man looked for her up and down, and asked and inquired of all where she was, and if they had seen her; sorely were they all abashed thereat, and had no word to say. And he who was to wed the damsel was yet more woful. He was not slow to seek her, but nought avails him his search, for the right scent was lost. Now even amid their dismay a squire rode spurting down the path, and anon he cometh before the old man. "Sir,"

said he, "Messire Guillaume sendeth you his goodliest fellowship. Very early this morning in the first dawn he married your daughter; wherefore right glad and joyful is he. Come ye to him, sir; and likewise he biddeth his uncle who did so falsely by him, but now he pardoneth him the offence, inasmuch as he hath the gift of your daughter."

The old man gave ear to the marvel, never had he heard its like. He calleth and assembleth all his barons, and when they were come together he taketh counsel that he will go, and take with him that other to whom he had pledged his daughter; the marriage he seeth to be a sooth, no undoing may there be of that. So he who was right wise rode thither quickly and all his barons with him. When they came to the house they were received full richly, and Messire Guillaume made great joy, even as one who is glad at heart by reason of his guerdon. The father must needs grant the marriage whether he would or no, and the old man of the twisted moustaches took what comfort he might therein. Even so, lordings, the Lord God willed that this marriage which seemed good to him be established.

Messire Guillaume was brave, courteous and right valorous, and no whit did his prowess abate, but rather he strove the more, and was well looked on by counts and princes. Now before the third year, as the tale telleth us, the old man died, this is sooth, and he gave and granted all his wealth to the knight, who thereafter held all his lands which were rich and plenteous. A good thousand pounds a year the land yielded him. . . . And he held it quit of all claim.

So the adventure I have related endeth in this wise, as truth telleth you.

The Lay of the Nightingale
by Marie de France

Marie de France is the first identifiable woman writer in northern French. A cultivated noblewoman, she was domiciled at the court of Henry II of England in the later years of the twelfth century. This version of her well-known narrative poem is taken from the book *French Mediaeval Romances*, translated by Eugene Mason, Everyman's Library Edition (New York: E. P. Dutton, 1911); it is reprinted by permission of E. P. Dutton & Co., Inc., and J. M. Dent & Sons Ltd.

NOW WILL I tell you a story, whereof the Breton harper already has made a Lay. Laustic, I deem, men name it in that country, which, being interpreted, means rossignol in French, and nightingale in good plain English.

In the realm of Brittany stands a certain rich and mighty city, called Saint Malo. There were citizens of this township two knights, so well spoken and reputed of all, that the city drew therefrom great profit and fame. The houses of these lords were very near the one to the other. One of the two knights had to wife a passing fair lady, right gracious of manner and sweet of tongue. Wondrous pleasure found this dame to array herself richly, after the wont and fashion of her time. The other knight was yet a bachelor. He was well accounted of amongst his fellows as a hardy knight and as an honourable man. He gave hospitality gladly. Largely he gained, largely he spent, and willingly bestowed gifts of all that he had.

This bachelor set his love upon his neighbour's wife. By reason of his urgent prayers, his long suit and service, and by reason that all men spake naught of him but praise—perchance, also, for reason that he was never far from her eye—presently this lady came to set her heart on him again. Though these two friends loved right tenderly, yet were they so private and careful in their

loves that none perceived what was in their hearts. No man pried on them, or disturbed their goings and comings. These were the more easy to devise since the bachelor and the lady were such near neighbours. Their two houses stood side by side, hall and cellar and combles.* Only between the gardens was built a high and ancient wall, of worn gray stone. When the lady sat within her bower, by leaning from the casement she and her friend might speak together, he to her, and she to him. They could also throw messages in writing, and divers pretty gifts, the one to the other. Little enough had they to displease them, and greatly were they at their ease, save only that they might not take their pleasure together, so often as their hearts had wished. For the dame was guarded very straitly when her husband was abroad. Yet not so strictly but that they might have word and speech, the now by night and now by day. At least, however close the watch and ward, none might hinder that at times these fair lovers stood within their casements, and looked fondly on the other's face.

Now after these friends had loved for a great space it chanced that the season became warm and sweet. It was the time when meadow and copse are green; when orchards grow white with bloom, and birds break into song as thickly as the bush to flower. It is the season when he who loves would win to his desire. Truly I tell you that the knight would have done all in his power to attain his wish, and the lady, for her part, yearned for sight and speech of her friend. At night, when the moon shone clearly in the sky, and her lord lay sleeping at her side, often the dame slipped softly from her bed, and hastening to the casement, leaned forth to have sight of him who watched. The greater part of the dark they kept vigil together, for very pleasant it is to look upon your friend, when sweeter things are denied. This chanced so often, and the lady rose so frequently from her bed, that her lord was altogether wrathful, and many a time inquired the reason of her unrest.

"Husband," replied the dame, "there is no dearer joy in this

* Combles: attics.—Ed.

world, than to hear the nightingale sing. It is to hearken to the song that rises so sweetly on the night, that I lean forth from the casement. What tune of harp or viol is half so fair! Because of my delight in his song, and of my desire to hear, I may not shut my eyes till it be morn."

When the husband heard the lady's words he laughed within himself for wrath and malice. He purposed that very soon the nightingale should sing within a net. So he bade the servants of his house to devise fillets and snares, and to set their cunning traps about the orchard. Not a chestnut tree nor hazel within the garth but was limed and netted for the caging of this bird. It was not long therefore ere the nightingale was taken, and the servants made haste to give him to the pleasure of their lord. Wondrous merry was the knight when he held him living in his hand. He went straightway to the chamber of his dame, and entering, said,

"Wife, are you within? Come near, for I must speak with you. Here is the nightingale, all limed and taken, who made vigil of your sleeping hours. Take now your rest in peace, for he will never disturb you more."

When the lady understood these words she was marvellously sorrowful and heavy. She prayed her lord to grant her the nightingale for a gift. But for all answer he wrung his neck with both hands so fiercely that the head was torn from the body. Then, right foully, he flung the bird upon the knees of the dame, in such fashion that her breast was sprinkled with the blood. So he departed, incontinent, from the chamber in a rage.

The lady took the little body in her hands, and wept his evil fate. She railed on those who with nets and snares had betrayed the nightingale to his death; for anger and hate beyond measure had gained hold on her heart.

"Alas," cried she, "evil is come upon me. Never again may I rise from my bed in the night, and watch from the casement, so that I may see my friend. One thing I know full well, that he will deem my love is no more set upon him. Woe to her who has none to give her counsel. This I will do. I will bestow the nightingale

upon him, and send him tidings of the chance that has befallen."

So this doleful lady took a fair piece of white samite, broidered with gold, and wrought thereon the whole story of this adventure. In this silken cloth she wrapped the body of the little bird, and calling to her a trusty servant of her house, charged him with the message, and bade him bear it to her friend. The varlet went his way to the knight, and having saluted him on the part of the lady, he told over to him the story, and bestowed the nightingale upon him. When all had been rehearsed and shown to him, and he had well considered the matter, the knight was very dolent; yet in no wise would he avenge himself wrongfully. So he caused a certain coffret to be fashioned, made not of iron or steel, but of fine gold and fair stones, most rich and precious, right strongly clasped and bound. In this little chest he set the body of the nightingale, and having sealed the shrine, carried it upon him whenever his business took him abroad.

This adventure could not long be hid. Very swiftly it was noised about the country, and the Breton folk made a Lay thereon, which they called the Lay of the Laustic, in their own tongue.

❧ The Falcon
by Giovanni Boccaccio

This sentimental story, included in *The Decameron*, gained
a great vogue in the western world. The translation is by
John Payne (London: privately printed, 1895).

YOU MUST know that Coppo di Borghese Domenichi, who
was of our days and maybe is yet a man of great worship and
authority in our city and illustrious and worthy of eternal re-
nown, much more for his fashions and his merit than of the
nobility of his blood, being grown full of years, delighted often-
times to discourse with his neighbors and others of things past,
the which he knew how to do better and more orderly and with
more memory and elegance of speech than any other man.
Amongst other fine things of his, he was used to tell that there
was once in Florence a young man called Federigo, son of Messer
Filippo Alberighi and renowned for deeds of arms and courtesy
over every other bachelor in Tuscany, who, as betideth most
gentlemen, became enamored of a gentlewoman named Madam
Giovanna, in her day held one of the fairest and sprightliest
ladies that were in Florence; and to win her love, he held jousts
and tourneyings and made entertainments and gave gifts and
spent his substance without any stint; but she, being no less
virtuous than fair, recked nought of these things done for her nor
of him who did them. Federigo spending thus far beyond his
means and gaining nought, his wealth, as lightly happeneth, in
course of time came to an end and he abode poor, nor was aught
left him but a poor little farm, on whose returns he lived very
meagrely, and to boot a falcon he had, one of the best in the
world. Wherefore, being more in love than ever and himseeming
he might no longer make such a figure in the city as he would
fain do, he took up his abode at Campi, where his farm was, and

there bore his poverty with patience, hawking whenas he might and asking of no one.

Federigo being thus come to extremity, it befell one day that Madam Giovanna's husband fell sick and seeing himself nigh upon death, made his will, wherein, being very rich, he left a son of his, now well grown, his heir, after which, having much loved Madam Giovanna, he substituted her to his heir, in case his son should die without lawful issue, and died. Madam Giovanna, being thus left a widow, betook herself that summer, as in the usance of our ladies, into the country with her son to an estate of hers very near that of Federigo; wherefore it befell that the lad made acquaintance with the latter and began to take delight in hawks and hounds, and having many a time seen his falcon flown and being strangely taken therewith, longed sore to have it, but dared not ask it of him, seeing it so dear to him. The thing standing thus, it came to pass that the lad fell sick, whereat his mother was sore concerned, as one who had none but him and loved him with all her might, and abode about him all day, comforting him without cease; and many a time she asked him if there were aught he desired, beseeching him tell it her, for that, an it might be gotten, she would contrive that he should have it. The lad, having heard these offers many times repeated, said, "Mother mine, an you could procure me to have Federigo's falcon, methinketh I should soon be whole."

The lady, hearing this, bethought herself awhile and began to consider how she should do. She knew that Federigo had long loved her and had never gotten of her so much as a glance of the eye; wherefore quoth she in herself, "How shall I send or go to him to seek of him this falcon, which is, by all I hear, the best that ever flew and which, to boot, maintaineth him in the world? And how can I be so graceless as to offer to take this from a gentleman who hath none other pleasure left?" Perplexed with this thought and knowing not what to say, for all she was very certain of getting the bird, if she asked for it, she made no reply to her son, but abode silent. However, at last, the love of her son so got the better of her that she resolved in herself to satisfy him, come

what might, and not to send, but to go herself for the falcon and fetch it to him. Accordingly she said to him, "My son, take comfort and bethink thyself to grow well again, for I promise thee that the first thing I do to-morrow morning I will go for it and fetch it to thee." The boy was rejoiced at this and showed some amendment that same day.

Next morning, the lady, taking another lady to bear her company, repaired, by way of diversion, to Federigo's little house and enquired for the latter, who, for that it was no weather for hawking nor had been for some days past, was then in a garden he had, overlooking the doing of certain little matters of his, and hearing that Madam Giovanna asked for him at the door, ran thither, rejoicing and marvelling exceedingly. She, seeing him come, rose and going with womanly graciousness to meet him, answered his respectful salutation with "Give you good day, Federigo!" then went on to say, "I am come to make thee amends for that which thou hast suffered through me, in loving me more than should have behoved thee; and the amends in question is this that I propose to dine with thee this morning familiarly, I and this lady my companion." "Madam," answered Federigo humbly, "I remember me not to have ever received any ill at your hands, but on the contrary so much good that, if ever I was worth aught, it came about through your worth and the love I bore you; and assuredly, albeit you have come to a poor host, this your gracious visit is far more precious to me than it would be an it were given me to spend over again as much as that which I have spent aforetime." So saying, he shamefastly received her into his house and thence brought her into his garden, where, having none else to bear her company, he said to her, "Madam, since there is none else here, this good woman, wife of yonder husbandman, will bear you company, whilst I go see the table laid."

Never till that moment, extreme as was his poverty, had he been so dolorously sensible of the straits to which he had brought himself for the lack of those riches he had spent on such disorderly wise. But that morning, finding he had nothing wherewithal he might honorably entertain the lady, for love of whom he had

aforetime entertained folk without number, he was made perforce aware of his default and ran hither and thither, perplexed beyond measure, like a man beside himself, inwardly cursing his ill fortune, but found neither money nor aught he might pawn. It was now growing late and he having a great desire to entertain the gentle lady with somewhat, yet choosing not to have recourse to his own laborer, much less any one else, his eye fell on his good falcon, which he saw on his perch in his little saloon; whereupon, having no other resource, he took the bird and finding him fat, deemed him a dish worthy of such a lady. Accordingly, without more ado, he wrung the hawk's neck and hastily caused a little maid of his pluck it and truss it and after put it on the spit and roast it diligently. Then, the table laid and covered with very white cloths, whereof he had yet some store, he returned with a blithe countenance to the lady in the garden and told her that dinner was ready, such as it was in his power to provide. Accordingly, the lady and her friend, arising, betook themselves to table and in company with Federigo, who served them with the utmost diligence, ate the good falcon, unknowing what they did.

Presently, after they had risen from table and had abidden with him awhile in cheerful discourse, the lady, thinking it time to tell that wherefor she was come, turned to Federigo and courteously bespoke him, saying, "Federigo, I doubt not a jot but that, when thou hearest that which is the especial occasion of my coming hither, thou wilt marvel at my presumption, remembering thee of thy past life and of my virtue, which latter belike thou reputedst cruelty and hardness of heart; but, if thou hadst or hadst had children, by whom thou mightest know how potent is the love one beareth them, meseemeth certain that thou wouldst in part hold me excused. But, although thou hast none, I, who have one child, cannot therefore escape the common laws to which other mothers are subject and whose enforcements it behoving me ensue, need must I, against my will and contrary to all right and seemliness, ask of thee a boon, which I know is supremely dear to thee (and that with good reason, for that thy sorry fortune hath left thee none other delight, none other diversion, none other

solace), to wit, thy falcon, whereof my boy is so sore enamored that, an I carry it not to him, I fear me his present disorder will be so aggravated that there may presently ensue thereof somewhat whereby I shall lose him. Wherefore I conjure thee,—not by the love thou bearest me and whereto thou art nowise beholden, but by thine own nobility, which in doing courtesy hath approved itself greater than in any other,—that it please thee give it to me, so by the gift I may say I have kept my son alive and thus made him for ever thy debtor."

Federigo, hearing what the lady asked and knowing that he could not oblige her, for that he had given her the falcon to eat, fell a-weeping in her presence, ere he could answer a word. The lady at first believed that his tears arose from grief at having to part from his good falcon and was like to say that she would not have it. However, she contained herself and awaited what Federigo should reply, who, after weeping awhile, made answer thus: "Madam, since it pleased God that I should set my love on you, I have in many things reputed fortune contrary to me and have complained of her; but all the ill turns she hath done me have been a light matter in comparison with that which she doth me at this present and for which I can never more be reconciled to her, considering that you are come hither to my poor house, whereas you deigned not to come what while I was rich, and seek of me a little boon, the which she hath so wrought that I cannot grant you; and why this cannot be I will tell you briefly. When I heard that you, of your favor, were minded to dine with me, I deemed it a right thing and a seemly, having regard to your worth and the nobility of your station, to honor you, as far as in me lay, with some choicer victual than that which is commonly set before other folk; wherefore, remembering me of the falcon which you ask of me and of his excellence, I judged him a dish worthy of you. This very morning, then, you have had him roasted upon the trencher, and indeed I had accounted him excellently well bestowed; but now, seeing that you would fain have had him on other wise, it is so great a grief to me that I cannot oblige you therein that methinketh I shall never forgive myself therefor." So

saying, in witness of this, he let cast before her the falcon's feathers and feet and beak.

The lady, seeing and hearing this, first blamed him for having, to give a woman to eat, slain such a falcon, and after inwardly much commended the greatness of his soul, which poverty had not availed nor might anywise avail to abate. Then, being put out of all hope of having the falcon and fallen therefore in doubt of her son's recovery, she took her leave and returned, all disconsolate, to the latter, who, before many days had passed, whether for chagrin that he could not have the bird or for that his disorder was e'en fated to bring him to that pass, departed this life, to the inexpressible grief of his mother. After she had abidden awhile full of tears and affliction, being left very rich and yet young, she was more than once urged by her brothers to marry again, and albeit she would fain not have done so, yet, finding herself importuned and calling to mind Federigo's worth and his last magnificence, to wit, the having slain such a falcon for her entertainment, she said to them, "I would gladly, an it liked you, abide as I am; but, since it is your pleasure that I take a [second] husband, certes I will never take any other, an I have not Federigo degli Alberighi." Whereupon her brothers, making mock of her, said, "Silly woman that thou art, what is this thou sayest? How canst thou choose him, seeing he hath nothing in the world?" "Brothers mine," answered she, "I know very well that it is as you say; but I would liefer have a man that lacketh of riches than riches that lack of a man." Her brethren, hearing her mind and knowing Federigo for a man of great merit, poor though he was, gave her, with all her wealth, to him, even as she would; and he, seeing himself married to a lady of such worth and one whom he had loved so dear and exceeding rich, to boot, became a better husband of his substance and ended his days with her in joy and solace.

»IV«

WONDERS AND PRODIGIES

The Life of Saint Brandon
by Jacobus de Voragine

The Golden Legend, a collection of lives of the saints, was compiled by Jacobus de Voragine, a Genoese bishop, about 1275, and was translated into English and published, in 1483, by William Caxton, the scholar-printer. The *Life of Saint Brandon* records an old tale, dating back at least to the eleventh century, of adventures and discoveries in the wild western ocean. There has been much dispute whether or not the story preserves memories of pre-Columbian ventures. Our presentation is from Caxton's text, modernized by F. S. Ellis (London: J. M. Dent, 1900).

S. BRANDON, the holy man, was a monk, and born in Ireland, and there he was abbot of a house wherein were a thousand monks, and there he had a full strait and holy life in great penance and abstinence, and he governed his monks full virtuously. And then within short time after, there came to him a holy abbot that hight Birinus to visit him, and each of them was joyful of other. And then S. Brandon began to tell to the abbot Birinus of many wonders that he had seen in divers lands, and when Birinus heard that of S. Brandon, he began to sigh and sore weep, and S. Brandon comforted him the best wise he could, saying: Ye come hither for to be joyful with me, and therefore for God's love leave your mourning and tell me what marvels ye have seen in the great sea-ocean that compasseth all the world about, and all other waters come out of him which runneth in all parts of the earth. And then Birinus began to tell to S. Brandon and to his monks the marvels that he had seen, full sore weeping, and said: I have a son, his name is Mervok, and he was a monk of great fame, which had great desire to seek about by ship in divers countries to find a solitary place wherein he might dwell secretly, out of the business of the world, for to serve God quietly with

more devotion, and I counselled him to sail into an island far in the sea, beside the mountain of stones which is full well known, and then he made him ready and sailed thither with his monks. And when he came thither he liked that place full well, where he and his monks served our Lord full devoutly.

And then Birinus saw in a vision that this monk Mervok was sailed right far eastward in the sea, more than three days' sailing, and suddenly to his seeming there came a dark cloud and over-covered them, that a great part of the day they saw no light, and as our Lord would, the cloud passed away and they saw a full fair island, and thitherward they drew. In that island was joy and mirth enough, and the earth of that island shined as bright as the sun, and there were the fairest trees and herbs that ever any man saw, and there were many precious stones shining bright, and every herb there was full of flowers, and every tree full of fruit, so that it was a glorious sight and a heavenly joy to abide there. And there, there came to them a fair young man, and full courteously he welcomed them all, and called every monk by his name, and said that they were much bound to praise the name of our Lord Jesu, that would of his grace show to them that glorious place where is ever day and never night, and this place is called Paradise terrestrial. By this island is another island wherein no man may come, and this young man said to them: Ye have been here half a year without meat, drink, or sleep, and they supposed that they had not been there the space of half an hour, so merry and joyful they were there. And the young man told them that this is the place that Adam and Eve dwelt in first and ever should have dwelled here, if that they had not broken the commandment of God. And then the young man brought them to their ship again, and said they might no longer abide there, and when they were all shipped, suddenly this young man vanished away out of their sight. And then within short time after, by the purveyance of our Lord Jesu Christ, they came to the abbey where S. Brandon dwelled, and then he with his brethren received them goodly and demanded them where they had been so long, and they said: We have been in the land of Behest tofore the gates of Paradise,

whereas is ever day and never night, and they said all that the place is full delectable, for yet all their clothes smelled of that sweet and joyful place.

And then S. Brandon purposed soon after for to seek that place by God's help, and anon began to purvey for a good ship and a strong, and victualled it for seven years. And then he took his leave of all his brethren and took twelve monks with him, but ere they entered into the ship they fasted forty days and lived devoutly, and each of them received the sacrament. And when S. Brandon with his twelve monks were entered in to the ship, there came other two of his monks and prayed him that they might sail with him, and then he said: Ye may sail with me, but one of you shall go to hell ere ye come again, but not for that they would go with him. And then S. Brandon bade the shipmen to wind up the sail and forth they sailed in God's name, so that on the morrow they were out of sight of any land. And forty days and forty nights after they sailed east, and then they saw an island far from them, and they sailed thitherward as fast as they could, and they saw a great rock of stone appear above all the water, and three days they sailed about it ere they could get into the place, but at the last by the purveyance of God they found a little haven and there went aland every each one. And then suddenly came a fair hound, and fell down at the feet of S. Brandon and made him good cheer in his manner, and then he bade his brethren be of good cheer, for our Lord hath sent to us his messenger to lead us into some good place. And the hound brought them into a fair hall where they found the tables spread, ready set full of good meat and drink. And then S. Brandon said graces, and then he and his brethren sat down and ate and drank of such as they found, and there were beds ready for them, wherein they took their rest after their long labour.

And on the morn they returned again to their ship, and sailed a long time in the sea after, ere they could find any land, till at last by the purveyance of God, they saw far from them a full fair island, full of green pasture, wherein were the whitest and greatest sheep that ever they saw. For every sheep was as great as an

ox, and soon after came to them a goodly old man, which welcomed them and made them good cheer, and said: This is the island of sheep, and here is never cold weather, but ever summer, and that causeth the sheep to be so great and white; they eat of the best grass and herbs that is anywhere. And then this old man took his leave of them and bade them sail forth right east, and within short time by God's grace, they should come in to a place like Paradise, wherein they should keep their Eastertide.

And then they sailed forth, and came soon after to that land, but because of little depth in some places, and in some places were great rocks, but at the last they went upon an island weening to them that they had been safe, and made thereon a fire for to dress their dinner, but S. Brandon abode still in the ship, and when the fire was right hot and the meat nigh sodden,* then this island began to move, whereof the monks were afeard, and fled anon to ship and left the fire and meat behind them, and marvelled sore of the moving. And S. Brandon comforted them and said that it was a great fish named Jasconye, which laboureth night and day to put his tail in his mouth, but for greatness he may not. And then anon they sailed west three days and three nights ere they saw any land, wherefore they were right heavy, but soon after, as God would, they saw a fair island full of flowers, herbs, and trees, whereof they thanked God of his good grace, and anon they went on land, and when they had gone long in this they found a full fair well, and thereby stood a fair tree full of boughs, and on every bough sat a fair bird, and they sat so thick on the tree that unnethe† any leaf of the tree might be seen. The number of them was so great, and they sang so merrily that it was a heavenly noise to hear, wherefore S. Brandon kneeled down on his knees and wept for joy, and made his prayers devoutly to our Lord God to know what these birds meant.

And then anon one of the birds fled from the tree to S. Brandon, and he with flickering of his wings made a full merry noise like a fiddle, that him seemed he heard never so joyful a

* Sodden: boiled.—Ed. † Unnethe: hardly.—Ed.

melody. And then S. Brandon commanded the bird to tell him the cause why they sat so thick on the tree and sang so merrily; and then the bird said: Sometime we were angels in heaven, but when our master Lucifer fell down into hell for his high pride, we fell with him for our offences, some higher and some lower after the quality of the trespass, and because our trespass is but little, therefore our Lord hath set us here out of all pain, in full great joy and mirth after his pleasing, here to serve him on this tree in the best manner we can. The Sunday is a day of rest from all worldly occupation, and therefore that day all we be made as white as any snow for to praise our Lord in the best wise we may. And then this bird said to S. Brandon: That it is twelve months passed that ye departed from your abbey, and in the seventh year hereafter, ye shall see the place that ye desire to come to, and all these seven years ye shall keep your Easter here with us every year, and in the end of the seventh year ye shall come into the land of Behest. And this was on Easter day that the bird said these words to S. Brandon, and then this fowl flew again to his fellows that sat on the tree, and then all the birds began to sing evensong so merrily that it was a heavenly noise to hear. And after supper S. Brandon and his fellows went to bed and slept well, and on the morn they arose betimes, and then these birds began matins, prime, and hours, and all such service as christian men use to sing. And S. Brandon with his fellows abode there eight weeks, till Trinity Sunday was passed, and they sailed again to the island of sheep and there they victualled them well, and sith took their leave of that old man, and returned again to ship. And then the bird of the tree came again to S. Brandon and said: I am come to tell you that ye shall sail from hence into an island wherein is an abbey of twenty-four monks, which is from this place many a mile, and there ye shall hold your Christmas, and your Easter with us, like as I told you; and then this bird flew to his fellows again.

And then S. Brandon and his fellows sailed forth in the ocean, and soon after fell a great tempest on them in which they were greatly troubled long time, and sore forlaboured, and after that

they found by the purveyance of God an island which was far from them, and then they full meekly prayed our Lord to send them thither in safety, but it was forty days after ere they came thither, wherefore all the monks were so weary of that trouble that they set little price by their lives, and cried continually to our Lord to have mercy on them, and bring them to that island in safety. And by the purveyance of God they came at the last into a little haven, but it was so strait that unnethe the ship might come in, and after they came to an anchor, and anon the monks went to land. And when they had long walked about, at the last they found two fair wells, that one was fair and clear water, and that other was somewhat troubly and thick. And then they thanked our Lord full humbly that had brought them thither in safety, and they would fain have drunk of that water, but S. Brandon charged them they should not take without licence. For if we abstain us a while our Lord will purvey for us in the best wise.

And anon after came to them a fair old man with hoar hair, and welcomed them full meekly and kissed S. Brandon, and led them by many a fair well till they came to a fair abbey, where they were received with great honour and solemn procession with twenty-four monks, all in royal copes of cloth of gold and a royal cross was before them. And then the abbot welcomed S. Brandon and his fellowship, and kissed them full meekly, and took S. Brandon by the hand and led him with his monks into a fair hall, and set them down arow upon the bench, and the abbot of the place washed all their feet with fair water of the well that they saw before, and after, led them into the fraitour* and there set them among his convent. And anon there came one by the purveyance of God which served them well of meat and drink, for every monk had set before him a fair white loaf, and white roots and herbs, which was right delicious, but they wist not what roots they were. And they drank of the water of the fair clear well that they saw before when they came first aland, which

* Fraitour: dining hall.—Ed.

S. Brandon forbade them. And then the abbot came and cheered S. Brandon and his monks, and prayed them eat and drink for charity; for every day our Lord sendeth a goodly old man that covereth this table and setteth our meat and drink tofore us, but we know not how it cometh, ne we ordain never no meat ne drink for us, and yet we have been eighty years here, and ever our Lord, worshipped may he be, feedeth us. We be twenty-four monks in number, and every ferial* day of the week he sendeth to us twelve loaves, and every Sunday and feast-day twenty-four loaves, and the bread that we leave at dinner we eat at supper, and now at your coming our Lord hath sent to us forty-eight loaves, for to make you and us merry together as brethren. And always twelve of us go to dinner whiles other twelve keep the quire, and thus have we done these eighty years, for so long have we dwelled here in this abbey. And we came hither out of the abbey of S. Patrick in Ireland, and thus as ye see our Lord hath purveyed for us, but none of us knoweth how it cometh, but God alone, to whom be given honour and laud world without end. And here in this land is ever fair weather, and none of us hath been sick sith we came hither. And when we go to mass, or to any other service of our Lord in the church, anon seven tapers of wax be set in the quire and be lighted at every time without man's hand, and so burn day and night at every hour of service, and never waste ne minish as long as we have been here, which is eighty years. And then S. Brandon went to the church with the abbot of the place, and there they said evensong together full devoutly, and then S. Brandon looked upward toward the crucifix, and saw our Lord hanging on the cross, which was made of fine crystal and curiously wrought. And in the quire were twenty-four seats for twenty-four monks, and the seven tapers burning, and the abbot's seat was made in the midst of the quire, and then S. Brandon demanded of the abbot how long they had kept that silence, that none of them spake to other, and he said: These twenty-four years we spake never one to another. And

* Ferial: ordinary.—Ed.

then S. Brandon wept for joy of their holy conversation. And then S. Brandon desired of the abbot that he and his monks might dwell there still with him. To whom the abbot said: Sir, that may ye not do in no wise, for our Lord hath showed to you in what manner ye shall be guided till the seven years be fulfilled, and after that term thou shalt with thy monks return into Ireland in safety, but one of the two monks that came last to you shall dwell in the island of ankers,* and that other shall go quick† to hell. And as S. Brandon kneeled in the church he saw a bright shining angel come in at the window, and lighted all the lights in the church, and then he flew out again at the window unto heaven, and then S. Brandon marvelled greatly how the light burned so fair and wasted not. And then the abbot said that it is written that Moses saw a bush all on afire and yet it burned not, and therefore marvel not hereof for the might of our Lord is now as great as it ever was.

And when S. Brandon had dwelled there from Christmas even till the twelfth day was passed, then he took his leave of the abbot and convent and returned with his monks to his ship, and sailed from thence with his monks toward the abbey of S. Illaries,‡ but they had great tempests in the sea from that time till Palm-Sunday, and then they came to the island of sheep, and there were received of the old man, which brought them to a fair hall and served them. And on Shere-Thursday§ after supper he washed their feet and kissed them, like as our Lord did to his disciples, and there abode till Saturday, Easter-even, and they departed and sailed to the place where the great fish lay, and anon they saw their caldron upon the fishes back, which they had left there twelve months tofore, and there they kept the service of the resurrection on the fishes back, and after, they sailed that same day by the morning to the island whereas the tree of birds was, and then the said bird welcomed S. Brandon and all his fellowship, and went again to the tree and sang full merrily, and there

* Ankers: anchorites.—Ed. † Quick: alive.—Ed.
‡ Illaries: Hilary's.—Ed.
§ Shere-Thursday: Thursday before Easter.—Ed.

he and his monks dwelled from Easter till Trinity Sunday as they did the year before, in full great joy and mirth. And daily they heard the merry service of the birds sitting on the tree. And then the bird told to S. Brandon that he should return again at Christmas to the abbey of monks, and at Easter thither again, and the other deal of the year labour in the ocean in full great perils, and from year to year till the seven years be accomplished. And then shall ye come to the joyful place of Paradise and dwell there forty days in full great joy and mirth, and after, ye shall return home into your own abbey in safety, and there end your life, and come to the bliss of heaven, to which our Lord bought you with his precious blood. And then the angel of our Lord ordained all thing that was needful to S. Brandon and to his monks in victuals and all other things necessary, and then they thanked our Lord of his great goodness that he had showed to them oft in their great need, and then sailed forth into the great sea ocean, abiding the mercy of our Lord in great trouble and tempests.

And soon after came to them an horrible fish which followed the ship long time, casting so much water out of his mouth into the ship that they supposed to have been drowned, wherefore they devoutly prayed God to deliver them of that great peril. And anon after, came another fish greater than he, out of the west sea, and fought with him, and at the last clave him into three pieces, and then returned again. And then they thanked meekly our Lord of their deliverance from this great peril, but they were in great heaviness because their victuals were nigh spent; but by the ordinance of our Lord there came a bird and brought to them a great branch of a vine full of red grapes, by which they lived fourteen days, and then they came to a little island, wherein were many vines full of grapes, and they there landed and thanked God, and gathered as many grapes as they lived by forty days after, always sailing in the sea in many storms and tempests, and as they thus sailed, suddenly came flying towards them a great grip* which assailed them and was like to have destroyed them.

* Grip: griffin.—Ed.

Wherefore they devoutly prayed for help and aid of our Lord Jesu Christ. And then the bird of the tree of the island where they had holden their Easter tofore, came to the grip and smote out both his eyes, and after slew him, whereof they thanked our Lord, and then sailed forth continually till S. Peter's day, and then sang they solemnly their service in the honour of the feast. And in that place the water was so clear that they might see all the fishes that were about them, whereof they were full sore aghast, and the monks counselled S. Brandon to sing no more, for all the fishes lay then as they had slept. And then S. Brandon said: Dread ye not, for ye have kept by two Easters the feast of the Resurrection upon the great fishes back, and therefore dread ye not of these little fishes. And then S. Brandon made him ready and went to mass, and bade his monks to sing the best way they could, and then anon all the fishes awoke, and came about the ship so thick that unnethe they might see the water for the fishes, and when the mass was done all the fishes departed so as they were no more seen. And seven days they sailed always in that clear water.

And then there came a south wind and drove the ship northward, whereas they saw an island full dark and full of stench and smoke, and there they heard great blowing and blasting of bellows, but they might see nothing, but heard great thundering, whereof they were sore afeard, and blessed them oft. And soon after there came one starting out all burning in fire, and stared full ghastly on them with great staring eyes, of whom the monks were aghast, and at his departing from them he made the horriblest cry that might be heard, and soon there came a great number of fiends and assailed them with hooks and burning iron malles,* which ran on the water, following their ship fast, in such wise that it seemed all the sea to be on fire. But by the pleasure of our Lord they had no power to hurt ne grieve them ne their ship, wherefore the fiends began to roar and cry, and threw their hooks and malles at them. And they then were sore afraid, and

* Malles: mauls, hammers.—Ed.

prayed to God for comfort and help, for they saw the fiends all about the ship, and them seemed then all the island and the sea to be on fire. And with a sorrowful cry all those fiends departed from them and returned to the place that they came from. And then S. Brandon told to them that this was a part of hell, and therefore he charged them to be steadfast in the faith, for they should yet see many a dreadful place ere they came home again. And then came the south wind, and drove them farther into the north, where they saw a hill all of fire, and a foul smoke and stench coming from thence, and the fire stood on each side of the hill like a wall all burning. And then one of his monks began to cry and weep full sore, and said that his end was come, and that he might abide no longer in the ship, and anon he leapt out of the ship into the sea, and then he cried and roared full piteously, cursing the time that he was born, and also father and mother that begat him, because they saw no better to his correction in his young age, for now I must go to perpetual pain. And then the saying of S. Brandon was verified that he said to him when he entered; therefore it is good a man to do penance and forsake sin, for the hour of death is uncertain.

And then anon the wind turned into the north and drove the ship into the south, which sailed seven days continually, and they came to a great rock standing in the sea, and thereon sat a naked man in full great misery and pain, for the waves of the sea had so beaten his body that all the flesh was gone off, and nothing left but sinews and bare bones. And when the waves were gone, there was a canvas that hung over his head which beat his body full sore with the blowing of the wind, and also there were two ox-tongues and a great stone that he sat on, which did him full great ease. And then S. Brandon charged him to tell him what he was, and he said: My name is Judas that sold our Lord Jesu Christ for thirty pence, which sitteth here thus wretchedly, howbeit I am worthy to be in the greatest pain that is, but our Lord is so merciful that he hath rewarded me better than I have deserved, for of right my place is in the burning hell, but I am here but certain times of the year, that is, from Christmas to twelfth day,

and from Easter till Whitsuntide be past, and every feastful day of our Lady, and every Saturday noon till Sunday, that evensong be done, but all other times I lie still in hell in full burning fire, with Pilate, Herod, and Caiaphas, therefore accursed be the time that ever I knew them. And then Judas prayed S. Brandon to abide still there all that night, and that he would keep him there still, that the fiends should not fetch him to hell. And he said: With God's help thou shalt abide here all this night; and then he asked Judas what cloth that was that hung over his head, and he said it was a cloth that he gave to a leper, which was bought with the money that he stole from our Lord when I bare his purse, wherefore it doth to me full great pain now, in beating my face with the blowing of the wind, and these two ox-tongues that hang here above me I gave them sometime to two priests to pray for me, them I bought with mine own money, and therefore they ease me because the fishes of the sea gnaw on them and spare me, and this stone that I sit on, lay sometime in a desolate place where it eased no man, and I took it thence and laid it in a foul way where it did much ease to them that went by that way, and therefore it easeth me now, for every good deed shall be rewarded and every evil deed shall be punished. And the Sunday, against even, there came a great multitude of fiends, blasting and roaring and bade S. Brandon go thence that they might have their servant Judas, for we dare not come into the presence of our master but if we bring him to hell with us. And then said S. Brandon: I let* not you to do your master's commandment, but by the power of our Lord Jesu Christ I charge you to leave him this night till to-morrow. They said: how darest thou help him that so sold his master for thirty pence to the Jews, and caused him also to die the most shameful death upon the cross? And then S. Brandon charged the fiends by his passion that they should not noy him that night. And then the fiends went their way roaring and crying towards hell, to their master the great devil, and then Judas thanked S. Brandon so ruthfully, that it was pity to see, and

* Let: prevent.—Ed.

on the morn the fiends came with a horrible noise, saying that they had that night suffered great pain because they brought not Judas and said that he should suffer double pain the six days following, and they took then Judas, trembling for fear, with them to pain.

And after, S. Brandon sailed southward three days and three nights, and on the Friday they saw an island, and then S. Brandon began to sigh, and said: I see the island wherein S. Paul the hermit dwelleth, and hath dwelled there forty years without meat and drink ordained by man's hand. And when they came to the land, S. Paul came and welcomed them humbly. He was old and foregrown, so that no man might see his body, of whom S. Brandon said weeping: Now I see a man that liveth more like an angel than a man, wherefore we wretches may be ashamed that we live not better. Then S. Paul said to S. Brandon: Thou art better than I, for our Lord hath showed to thee more of his privities than he hath done to me, wherefore thou oughtest to be more praised than I. To whom S. Brandon said: We be monks, and must labour for our meat, but God hath provided for thee such meat as thou holdest thee pleased, wherefore thou art much better than I. To whom S. Paul said: Sometime I was a monk of S. Patrick's Abbey in Ireland, and was warden of the place whereas men enter into S. Patrick's purgatory, and on a day there came one to me, and I asked him what he was, and he said: I am your abbot Patrick, and charge thee that thou depart from hence to-morn early to the seaside, and there thou shalt find a ship into which thou must enter, which God hath ordained for thee, whose will thou must accomplish. And so the next day I arose and went forth and found the ship, in which I entered, and by the purvey-ance of God was I brought into this island the seventh day after. And then I left the ship and went to land, and there I walked up and down a good while, and then, by the purveyance of God, there came an otter, going on his hinder feet, and brought me a flint stone and an iron to smite fire with, in his two foreclaws of his feet, and also he had about his neck great plenty of fish, which he cast down before me and went his way. And I smote fire, and

made a fire of sticks, and did seethe the fish by which I lived three days, and then the otter came again and brought to me fish for other three days, and thus he hath done these fifty-one years, through the grace of God. And there was a great stone, out of which our Lord made to spring fair water, clear and sweet, whereof I drink daily, and thus have I lived one and fifty years. And I was forty years old when I came hither, and am now one hundred and eleven years old, and abide till it please our Lord to send for me, and if it pleased him I would fain be discharged of this wretched life. And then he bade S. Brandon to take of the water of the well, and to carry into his ship: For it is time that thou depart, for thou hast a great journey to do, for thou shalt sail to an island which is forty days sailing hence, where thou shalt hold thine Easter like as thou hast done tofore, whereas the tree of birds is, and from thence thou shalt sail into the land of Behest, and shalt abide there forty days, and after return home into thy country in safety.

And then these holy men took leave each of other, and they wept both full sore, and kissed each other; and then S. Brandon entered into his ship and sailed forty days even south in full great tempest, and on Easter even came to their procurator, which made to them good cheer as he had beforetime, and from thence they came to the great fish, whereon they said matins and mass on Easter day, and when the mass was done the fish began to move and swam forth fast into the sea, whereof the monks were sore aghast which stood upon him, for it was a great marvel to see such a fish, so great as all a country, for to swim so fast in the water, but by the will of our Lord this fish set all the monks aland in the paradise of birds, all whole and sound, and then returned to the place he came from. And then S. Brandon and his monks thanked our Lord of their deliverance of the great fish, and kept their Easter-tide till Trinity Sunday, like as they had done beforetime, and after this they took their ship and sailed east forty days.

And at the forty days end it began to hail right fast, and therewith came a dark mist which lasted long after, which feared

S. Brandon and his monks, and they prayed to our Lord to keep and help them. And then anon came their procurator and bade them to be of good cheer, for they were come into the land of Behest. And soon after that mist passed away, and anon they saw the fairest country eastward that any man might see, and it was so clear and bright that it was a heavenly sight to behold, and all the trees were charged with ripe fruit, and herb* full of flowers. In which land they walked forty days, but they could see none end of that land, and there was always day and never night, and the land temperate, ne too hot ne too cold. And at the last they came to a fair river, but they durst not go over, and there came to them a fair young man and welcomed them courteously, and called each of them by his name, and did great reverence to S. Brandon, and said to them: Be ye now joyful, for this is the land that ye have sought, but our Lord will that ye depart hence hastily and he will show to you more of his secrets when ye come again into the sea, and our Lord will that you lade your ship with the fruit of this land, and hie you hence for ye may no longer abide here, but thou shalt sail again into thine own country, and soon after thou comest home thou shalt die. And this water that thou seest here departeth the world asunder, for on that other side of this water may no man come that is in this life, and the fruit that ye see here is always thus ripe every time of the year, and always it is here light as ye now see, and he that keepeth our Lord's hests at all times shall see this land ere he pass out of this world. And then S. Brandon and his monks took of that fruit as much as they would, and also took with them great plenty of precious stones, and then took their leave, and went to ship weeping sore because they might no longer abide there. And then they took their ship and came home into Ireland in safety, whom their brethren received with great joy, giving thankings to our Lord which had kept them all those seven years from many a peril and brought them home in safety, to whom be given honour and glory, world without end. Amen. And soon after, this holy man S. Brandon

* I.e., the grass.—Ed.

waxed feeble and sick, and had but little joy of this world, but ever after his joy and mind was in the joys of heaven. And in a short time after he being full of virtues, departed out of this life to everlasting life, and was worshipfully buried in a fair abbey which he himself founded, where our Lord showeth for this holy saint many fair miracles. Wherefore let us devoutly pray to this holy saint that he pray for us to our Lord that he have mercy on us, to whom be given land and honour and empire, world without end. Amen.

❧ The Famous History
of Friar Bacon

> Roger Bacon, a pioneer of modern science, was born in
> 1214 and died some eighty years later. A Franciscan, domi-
> ciled in Oxford, he pursued his scientific purpose against
> every difficulty. Rejecting tradition and untested authority,
> he codified and practiced an experimental method, especially
> in physics and optics. Hence he was suspected of dealing in
> magic. All sorts of wild tales clustered about his name and
> those of his associate, Friar Bungay, and his servant, Miles.
> Our history of Friar Bacon assembles many of the current
> stories, primitive science-fiction. It is revised from Henry
> Morley, *Early Prose Romances* (London: George Routledge,
> 1889).

IN MOST men's opinions he was born in the west part of
England and was son to a wealthy farmer, who put him to
school to the parson of the town where he was born—not with
intent that he should turn friar (as he did), but to get so much
understanding that he might manage the better that wealth he was
to leave him. But young Bacon took his learning so fast that the
priest could not teach him any more; which made him desire his
master that he would speak to his father to put him to Oxford,
that he might not lose that little learning that he had gained. His
master was very willing so to do, and one day meeting his father,
told him that he had received a great blessing of God, in that he
had given him so wise and hopeful a child as his son Roger Bacon
was (for so he was named), and wished him withal to do his duty
and to bring up so his child that he might show his thankfulness
to God, which could not better be done than in making of him a
scholar; for he found by his sudden taking of his learning that he
was a child likely to prove a very great clerk. Hereat old Bacon
was not well pleased (for he desired to bring him up to plough

and to the cart, as he himself was brought). Yet he for reverence'
sake to the priest showed not his anger, but kindly thanked him
for his pains and counsel, yet desired him not to speak any more
concerning that matter, for he knew best what best pleased him-
self, and that he would do. So broke they off their talk, and
parted.

So soon as the old man came home he called to his son for his
books, which when he had he locked them up, and gave the boy a
cart whip in place of them, saying: "Boy, I will have you no
priest; you shall not be better learned than I. You can tell now by
the almanack when it is best sowing wheat, when barley, peas,
and beans, and when the best libbing* is. When to sell grain and
cattle I will teach thee, for I have all fairs and markets as perfect
in my memory as Sir John our priest has masses without book.
Take me this whip; I will teach thee the use of it, it will be more
profitable to thee than this harsh Latin. Make no reply, but follow
my counsel, or else by the mass thou shalt feel the smart hand of
my anger."

Young Bacon thought this but hard dealing, yet would he not
reply, but within six or eight days he gave his father the slip and
went to a cloister some twenty miles off, where he was enter-
tained. And so continued he his learning, and in small time came
to be so famous that he was sent for to the University of Oxford,
where he long time studied, and grew so excellent in the studies
of art and nature that not England only but all Christendom
admired him.

The king being in Oxfordshire at a nobleman's house was very
desirous to see this famous friar, for he had heard many times of
his wondrous things that he had done by his art. Therefore he
sent one for him to desire him to come to the court. Friar Bacon
kindly thanked the king by the messenger and said that he was at
the king's service and would suddenly attend him. "But, sir," saith
he to the gentleman, "I pray you make haste, or else I shall be two
hours before you at the court."

* Libbing: gelding.—Ed.

"For all your learning," answered the gentleman, "I can hardly believe this; for scholars, old men, and travelers may lie by authority."

"To strengthen your belief," said Friar Bacon, "I could presently show you the last wench that you kissed, but I will not at this time."

"One is as true as the other," said the gentleman, "and I would laugh to see either."

"You shall see them both within these four hours," quoth the friar, "and therefore make what haste you can."

"I will prevent that by my speed!" said the gentleman, and with that rid his way. But he rid out of his way, as it should seem; for he had but five miles to ride, and yet was he better than three hours a-riding them. So that Friar Bacon by his art was with the king before he came.

The king welcomed him and said that he long time had desired to see him. Friar Bacon answered him that fame had belied him, and given him that report that his poor studies had never deserved, for he believed that art had many sons more excellent than himself was. The king commended him for his modesty, and told him that nothing could become a wise man less than boasting; but yet withal he requested him now to be no niggard of his knowledge, but to show his queen and him some of his skill.

"I were worthy of neither art nor knowledge," quod Friar Bacon, "should I deny Your Majesty this small request. I pray you seat yourselves, and you shall see presently what my poor skill can perform."

The king, queen, and nobles sat them all down. They having so done, the friar waved his wand, and presently was heard such excellent music that they were all amazed, for they all said they had never heard the like.

"This is," said the friar, "to delight the sense of hearing. I will delight all your other senses ere you depart hence." So waving his wand again, there was louder music heard, and presently five dancers entered, the first like a court-laundress, the second like a footman, the third like an usurer, the fourth like a prodigal, the

fifth like a fool. These did divers excellent changes, so that they gave content to all the beholders. And having done their dance, they all vanished away in their order as they came in. Thus feasted he two of their senses. Then waved he his wand again, and there was another kind of music heard, and while it was playing, there was suddenly before them a table richly covered with all sorts of delicates. Then desired he the king and queen to taste of some certain rare fruits that were on the table; which they and the nobles there present did, and were very highly pleased with the taste. They being satisfied, all vanished away on the sudden.

Then waved he his wand again, and suddenly there was such a smell as if all the rich perfumes in the whole world had been there prepared in the best manner that art could set them out. Whilst he feasted thus their smelling, he waved his wand again, and there came divers nations in sundry habits (as Russians, Polanders, Indians, Armenians), all bringing sundry kinds of furs, such as their countries yielded, all which they presented to the king and queen. These furs were so soft in the touch that they highly pleased all those that handled them. Then after some odd fantastic dances, after their country manner, they vanished away.

Then asked Friar Bacon the king's Majesty if that he desired any more of his skill. The king answered that he was fully satisfied for that time, and that he only now thought of something that he might bestow on him that might partly satisfy the kindness that he had received. Friar Bacon said that he desired nothing so much as his Majesty's love, and if that he might be assured of that he would think himself happy in it. "For that," said the king, "be thou ever sure of it; in token of which receive this jewel," and withal gave him a costly jewel from his neck.

The friar did with great reverence thank his Majesty, and said: "As Your Majesty's vassal you shall ever find me ready to do you service; your time of need shall find it both beneficial and delightful. But amongst all these gentlemen I see not the man that Your Grace did send for me by. Sure he hath lost his way, or else met with some sport that detains him so long. I promised to be here before him, and all this noble assembly can witness I am as good

as my word. I hear him coming!" With that entered the gentle-man all bedirted, for he had rid through ditches, quagmires, plashes, and waters, that he was in a most pitiful case. He seeing the friar there looked full angerly, and bid a plague on all his devils, for they had led him out of his way and almost drowned him.

"Be not angry, sir," said Friar Bacon. "Here is an old friend of yours that hath more cause, for she has tarried these three hours for you." With that he pulled up the hangings, and behind them stood a kitchen-maid with a basting-ladle in her hand. "Now am I as good as my word with you, for I promised to help you to your sweetheart. How do you like this?"

"So ill," answered the gentleman, "that I will be revenged of you."

"Threaten not," said Friar Bacon, "lest I do you more shame; and do you take heed how you give scholars the lie again. But because I know not how well you are stored with money at this time I will bear her charges home." With that she vanished away. The king, queen, and all the company laughed to see with what shame this gentleman endured the sight of his greasy sweet-heart; but the gentleman went away discontented. This done, Friar Bacon took his leave of the king and queen, and received from them divers gifts, as well as thanks, for his art he showed them. . . .

Friar Bacon reading one day of the many conquests of England bethought himself how he might keep it hereafter from the like conquests, and so make himself famous hereafter to all posterities. This, after great study, he found could be no way so well done as one, which was to make a head of brass, and if he could make this head to speak, and hear it when it speaks, then might he be able to wall all England about with brass. To this purpose he got one Friar Bungay to assist him, who was a great scholar and a magi-cian (but not to be compared to Friar Bacon). These two with great study and pains so framed a head of brass that in the inward parts thereof there was all things like as in a natural man's head. This being done, they were as far from perfection of the work as

they were before, for they knew not how to give those parts that they had made motion, without which it was impossible that it should speak. Many books they read, but yet could not find out any hope of what they sought, that at the last they concluded to raise a spirit, and to know of him that which they could not attain to by their own studies. To do this they prepared all things ready and went one evening to a wood thereby, and after many ceremonies used they spake the words of conjuration, which the Devil straight obeyed and appeared unto them, asking what they would.

"Know," said Friar Bacon, "that we have made an artificial head of brass, which we would have to speak, to the furtherance of which we have raised thee; and being raised, we will here keep thee, unless thou tell to us the way and manner to make this head to speak." The Devil told him that he had not the power of himself. "Beginner of lies!" said Friar Bacon, "I know that thou dost dissemble, and therefore tell it us quickly, or else we will here bind thee to remain during our pleasures!"

At these threatenings the Devil consented to do it, and told them that with a continual fume of the six hottest simples it should have motion, and in one month space speak; the time of the month or day he knew not. Also he told them that if they heard it not before it had done speaking all their labor would be lost. They, being satisfied, licensed the spirit to depart.

Then went these two learned friars home again, and prepared the simples ready, and made the fume, and with continual watching attended when this brazen head would speak. Thus watched they for three weeks without any rest, so that they were so weary and sleepy that they could not any longer refrain from rest. Then called Friar Bacon his man Miles, and told him that it was not unknown to him what pains Friar Bungay and himself had taken for three weeks' space, only to make and to hear the brazen head speak; which if they did not, then had they lost all their labor, and England had a great loss thereby. Therefore he entreated Miles that he would watch whilst that they slept, and call them if the head speak. "Fear not, good master," said Miles.

"I will not sleep, but hearken and attend upon the head; and if it do chance to speak, I will call you. Therefore I pray take you both your rests and let me alone for watching this head."

After Friar Bacon had given him a great charge the second time, Friar Bungay and he went to sleep, and Miles, alone to watch the brazen head. Miles, to keep himself from sleeping, got a tabor and pipe, and being merry disposed, sung this song to a northern tune, of "Cam'st Thou Not from Newcastle?":

> To couple is a custom,
> all things thereto agree;
> Why should not I then love,
> since love to all is free?
>
> But I'll have one that's pretty,
> her cheeks of scarlet dye
> For to breed my delight,
> when that I am her by.
>
> Though virtue be a dowry,
> yet I'll choose money store;
> If my love prove untrue,
> with that I can get more.
>
> The fair is oft inconstant,
> the black is often proud.
> I'll choose a lovely brown—
> come fiddler, scrape thy crowd.*
>
> Come fiddler, scrape thy crowd,
> for Peggy the brown is she
> Must be my bride; God guide
> that Peggy and I agree.

With his own music and such songs as these spent he his time, and kept from sleeping at last. After some noise the head spake these two words: TIME IS. Miles hearing it speak no more, thought his master would be angry if he waked him for that, and therefore he let them both sleep, and began to mock the head in

* Crowd: fiddle.—Ed.

this manner: "Thou brazen-faced head, hath my master took all this pains about thee, and now dost thou requite him with two words: TIME IS? Had he watched with a lawyer as long as he hath watched with thee, he would have given him more and better words than thou hast yet. If thou canst speak no wiser they shall sleep till doomsday for me. TIME IS! I know TIME IS, and that you shall hear, goodman Brazenface (to the tune of 'Dainty Come Thou with Me'):

> Time is for some to plant,
> Time is for some to sow;
> Time is for some to graft
> The horn as some do know.
>
> Time is for some to eat,
> Time is for some to sleep,
> Time is for some to laugh,
> Time is for some to weep.
>
> Time is for some to sing,
> Time is for some to pray,
> Time is for some to creep
> That have drunk all the day.

"Do you tell us, copper-nose, when TIME IS? I hope we scholars know our times, when to drink drunk, when to kiss our hostess, when to go on her score and when to pay it—that time comes seldom."

After half an hour had passed, the head did speak again—two words, which were these: TIME WAS. Miles respected these words as little as he did the former, and would not wake them, but still scoffed at the brazen head, that it had learned no better words, and have such a tutor as his master; and in scorn of it sung this song (to the tune of "A Rich Merchant Man"):

> Time was when thou, a kettle,
> wert fill'd with better matter;
> But Friar Bacon did thee spoil,
> when he thy sides did batter.

Time was when conscience dwelled
 with men of occupation;
Time was when lawyers did not thrive
 so well by men's vexation.

Time was when kings and beggars
 of one poor stuff had being;
Time was when office kept no knaves—
 that time it was worth seeing.

Time was a bowl of water
 did give the face reflection;
Time was when women knew no paint,
 which now they call complexion.

"Time was! I know that, Brazenface, without your telling. I know Time was, and I know what things there was when Time was, and if you speak no wiser, no master shall be waked for me!"

Thus Miles talked and sung till another half hour was gone. Then the brazen head spake again these words: Time is past, and therewith fell down. And presently followed a terrible noise, with strange flashes of fire, so that Miles was half dead with fear. At this noise the two friars awaked, and wondered to see the whole room so full of smoke. But that being vanished they might perceive this brazen head broken and lying on the ground. At this sight they grieved, and called Miles to know how this came. Miles, half dead with fear, said that it fell down of itself, and that with the noise and fire that followed he was almost frighted out of his wits. Friar Bacon asked him if he did not speak. "Yes," quoth Miles, "it spake, but to no purpose. I'll have a parrot speak better in that time that you have been teaching this brazen head."

"Out on thee, villain!" said Friar Bacon. "Thou has undone us both! Hadst thou but called us when it did speak, all England had been walled round about with brass, to its glory and our eternal fames! What were the words it spake?"

"Very few," said Miles, "and those were none of the wisest that I have heard neither. First he said: 'Time is.' "

"Hadst thou called us then," said Friar Bacon, "we had been made forever."

"Then," said Miles, "half an hour after it spake again and said: 'TIME WAS.' "

"And wouldst thou not call us then?" said Bungay.

"Alas," said Miles, "I thought he would have told me some long tale, and then I purposed to have called you; then half an hour after he cried: 'TIME IS PAST,' and made such a noise that he hath waked you himself, methinks." At this Friar Bacon was in such a rage that he would have beaten his man, but he was restrained by Bungay. But nevertheless for his punishment he with his art struck him dumb for one whole month's space. Thus the great work of these learned friars was overthrown, to their great griefs, by this simple follow. . . .

In those times when Friar Bacon did all his strange tricks, the Kings of England had a great part of France, which they held a long time, till civil wars at home in this land made them to lose it. It did chance that the King of England, for some cause best known to himself, went into France with a great army, where after many victories he did besiege a strong town and lay before it full three months without doing to the town any great damage, but rather received the hurt himself. This did so vex the king that he sought to take it in any way, either by policy or strength. To this intent he made proclamation that whosoever could deliver this town into his hand, he should have for his pains ten thousand crowns truly paid. This was proclaimed, but there was none found that would undertake it.

At length the news did come into England of this great reward that was promised. Friar Bacon hearing of it, went into France; and being admitted to the king's presence, he thus spake unto him: "Your Majesty, I am sure, hath not quite forgot your poor subject Bacon. The love that you showed to me, being last in your presence, hath drawn me for to leave my country and my studies, to do Your Majesty's service. I beseech Your Grace to command me so far as my poor art or life may do you pleasure." The king thanked him for his love, but told him that he had now

more need of arms than art, and wanted brave soldiers more than learned scholars.

Friar Bacon answered: "Your Grace saith well; but let me, under correction, tell you that art oftentimes doth those things that are impossible to armies, which I will make good in some few examples. I will speak only of things performed by art and nature, wherein shall be nothing magical. And first, by the figuration of art there may be made instruments of navigation without men to row in them, as great ships to brook the sea, only with one man to steer them; and they shall sail far more swiftly than if they were full of men. Also chariots that shall move with an unspeakable force, without any living creature to stir them. Likewise, an instrument may be made to fly withal, if one sit in the midst of the instrument and do turn an engine, by which the wings, being artificially composed, may beat air after the manner of a flying bird. By an instrument of three fingers high and three fingers broad a man may rid himself and others of all imprisonment; yea, such an instrument may easily be made whereby a man may violently draw unto him a thousand men, will they, nill they; or any other thing. By art also an instrument may be made wherewith men may walk in the bottom of the sea or rivers without bodily danger. This Alexander the Great used (as the ethick philosopher reporteth) to the end he might behold the secrets of the seas. But physical figurations are far more strange, for by that may be framed perspects* and looking-glasses, that one thing shall appear to be many, as one man shall appear to be a whole army, and one sun or moon shall seem divers. Also perspects may be so framed that things far off shall seem most nigh unto us. With one of these did Julius Caesar from the sea coasts in France mark and observe the situation of the castles in England. Bodies may also be so framed that the greatest things shall appear to be the least, the highest lowest, the most secret to be the most manifest, and in such like the contrary. Thus did Socrates perceive that the dragon which did destroy the city and country

* Perspects: telescopes.—Ed.

adjoining with his noisome breath and contagious influence did lurk in the dens between the mountains. And thus may all things that are done in cities or armies be discovered by the enemies. Again, in such wise may bodies be framed that venomous and infectious influences may be brought whither a man will. In this did Aristotle instruct Alexander; through which instruction the poison of a basilisk being lift up upon the wall of a city, the poison was conveyed into the city, to the destruction thereof. Also perspects may be made to deceive the sight, as to make a man believe that he seeth great store of riches when that there is not any. But it apperraineth to a higher power of figuration that beams should be brought and assembled by divers flexions and reflexions in any distance that we will, to burn anything that is opposite unto it, as it is witnessed by those perspects or glasses that burn before and behind. But the greatest and chiefest of all figurations and things figured is to describe the heavenly bodies, according to their length and breadth in a corporal figure, wherein they may corporally move with a daily motion. These things are worth a kingdom to a wise man. These may suffice, my royal Lord, to show what art can do; and these, with many things more as strange I am able by art to perform. Then take no thought for winning this town, for by my art you shall, ere many days be past, have your desire."

The king all this while heard him with admiration. But hearing him now, that he would undertake to win the town, he burst out in these speeches: "Most learned Bacon, do but what thou hast said, and I will give thee what thou most desirest, either wealth or honor—choose which thou wilt—and I will be as ready to perform as I have been to promise."

"Your Majesty's love is all that I seek," said the friar. "Let me have that, and I have honor enough. For wealth, I have content; the wise should seek no more. But to the purpose. Let your pioneers raise up a mount so high, or rather higher, than the wall; and then shall you see some probability of that which I have promised."

This mount in two days was raised. Then Friar Bacon went

with the king to the top of it, and did with a perspect show to him the town, as plainly as if he had been in it. At this the king did wonder, but Friar Bacon told him that he should wonder more ere next day noon; against which time, he desired him to have his whole army in readiness, for to scale the wall upon a signal given by him from the mount. This the king promised to do, and so returned to his tent full of joy that he should gain this strong town.

In the morning Friar Bacon went up to the mount and set his glasses and other instruments up. In the mean time the king ordered his army, and stood in a readiness for to give the assaults, when the signal was given, which was the waving of a flag. Ere nine of the clock Friar Bacon had burnt the state-house of the town, with other houses, only by his mathematical glasses; which made the whole town in an uproar, for none did know how it came. Whilst they were quenching of the same, Friar Bacon did wave his flag, upon which signal given, the king set upon the town, and took it with little or no resistance. Thus through the art of this learned man the king got this strong town, which he could not do with all his men without Friar Bacon's help.

»V«

MORAL TALES

The Execrable Devices
of Old Women

This (and the three following examples) are taken from the
Gesta Romanorum, a thirteenth-century collection of stories
intended for the use of preachers, to enliven their sermons
and point useful morals. It was extremely popular; many of
the tales were utilized by later writers, including Shakespeare,
in more sophisticated form. The translation is that of the
Reverend Charles Swan, revised by Wynnard Hooper (Lon-
don: George Bell, 1877).

IN THE kingdom of a certain empress there lived a knight,
who was happily espoused to a noble, chaste, and beautiful
wife. It happened that he was called upon to take a long journey,
and previous to his departure he said to the lady, "I leave you no
guard but your own discretion; I believe it to be wholly suffi-
cient." He then embarked with his attendants. She meanwhile
continued at her own mansion, in the daily practice of every
virtue. A short period had elapsed, when the urgent entreaties
of a neighbour prevailed with her to appear at a festival; where,
amongst other guests, was a youth, upon whom the excellence
and beauty of the lady made a deep impression. He became vio-
lently enamoured of her, and despatched various emissaries to
declare his passion, and win her to approve his suit. But the vir-
tuous lady received his advances with the utmost scorn. This
untoward repulse greatly disconcerted the youth, and his health
daily declined. Nevertheless he visited the lady oft, which availed
him nothing; he was still despised. It chanced that on one occasion
he went sorrowfully towards the church; and upon the way, an
old woman accosted him, who by pretended sanctity had long
obtained an undue share of reverence and regard. She demanded
the cause of the youth's apparent uneasiness. "It will nothing profit
me to tell thee," said he. "But," replied the old woman, "as long

as the sick man hides his malady from the physician he cannot be cured: discover the wound, and it is not impossible but a remedy may be found. With the aid of Heaven I will restore you to health." Thus urged, the youth made known to her his love for the lady. "Is that all?" said the beldam—"return to your home, I will find a medicine that shall presently relieve you." Confiding in her assurances, he went his way and the other hers.

It seems she possessed a little dog, which she obliged to fast for two successive days; on the third, she made bread of the flour of mustard, and placed it before the pining animal. As soon as it had tasted the bread, the pungent bitterness caused the water to spring into its eyes, and the whole of that day tears flowed copiously from them. The old woman, accompanied by her dog, posted to the house of the lady whom the young man loved; and the opinion entertained of her sanctity secured her an honourable and gracious reception. As they sat together, the lady noticed the weeping dog, and was curious to ascertain the cause. The crone told her not to inquire, for that it involved a calamity too dreadful to communicate. Such a remark, naturally enough, excited still more the curiosity of the fair questioner, and she earnestly pressed her to detail the story. This was what the old hag wanted; she said, "That little dog was my daughter—too good and excellent for this world. She was beloved by a young man, who, thrown into despair by her cruelty, perished for her love. My daughter, as a punishment for her hard-hearted conduct, was suddenly changed into the little dog respecting which you inquire." Saying these words, a few crocodile tears started into her eyes; and she continued, "Alas! how often does this mute memorial recall my lost daughter, once so beautiful and virtuous: now—oh, what is she now? degraded from the state of humanity, she exists only to pine away in wretchedness, and waste her life in tears. She can receive no comfort; and they who would administer it can but weep for her distresses, which surely are without a parallel." The lady, astonished and terrified at what she heard, secretly exclaimed—"Alas! I too am beloved; and he who loves me is in like manner at the point of death"—and then, instigated

by her fears, discovered the whole circumstance to the old woman, who immediately answered "Beautiful lady, do not disregard the anguish of this young man: look upon my unhappy daughter, and be warned in time. As she is, you may be." "Oh!" returned the credulous lady, "my good mother, counsel me; what would you have me do? Not for worlds would I become as she is." "Why, then," answered the treacherous old woman, "send directly for the youth, and give him the love he covets." The lady said, "May I entreat your holiness to fetch him: there might be some scandal circulated if another went." "My dear daughter," said she, "I suffer with you, and will presently bring him hither." She arose and returned with him; and thus the youth obtained his mistress. And so, through the old woman's means, the lady was led to adultery.

APPLICATION.

My beloved, the knight is Christ; the wife is the soul, to which God gave free will. It is invited to the feast of carnal pleasures, where a youth—that is, the vanity of the world—becomes enamoured of it. The old woman is the devil; the dog, the hope of a long life, and the presumptuous belief of God's clemency, which lead us to deceive and soothe the soul.

ꙮ Of the Cunning of the Devil, and of the Secret Judgments of God

> This apologue from the *Gesta Romanorum* has been frequently imitated in modern literatures, as by Parnell, Voltaire, and Schiller.

THERE FORMERLY lived a hermit, who in a remote cave passed night and day in the service of God. At no great distance from his cell a shepherd tended his flock. It happened that this person one day fell into a deep sleep, and in the mean time a robber, perceiving his carelessness, carried off his sheep. When the keeper awoke and discovered the theft, he began to swear in good set terms that he had lost his sheep; and where they were conveyed was totally beyond his knowledge. Now, the lord of the flock, when he heard this, was filled with rage, and commanded him to be put to death. This gave great umbrage to the hermit before mentioned. "Oh, Heaven," said he to himself, "seest thou this deed? the innocent suffers for the guilty: why permittest thou such things? If thus injustice triumph, why do I remain here? I will again enter the world, and do as other men do."

With these feelings he quitted his hermitage, and returned into the world; but God willed not that he should be lost: an angel in the form of a man was commissioned to join him. Accordingly, crossing the hermit's path, he thus accosted him—"My friend, where are you going?" "I go," said the other, "to the city before us." "I will accompany you," replied the angel; "I am a messenger from Heaven, and come to be the associate of your way." They walked on together towards the city. When they had entered, they entreated for the love of God harbourage during the night at the house of a certain knight, who received them with cheerfulness, and entertained them with much magnificence. The knight had an only son lying in the cradle, whom he exceedingly

loved. After supper, their bed-chamber was sumptuously deco-
rated; and the angel retired with the hermit to rest. But about the
middle of the night the former got up and strangled the sleeping
infant. The hermit, horror-struck at what he witnessed, said
within himself, "Never can this be an angel of God: the good
knight gave him everything that was necessary; he had but this
poor innocent, and this strange companion of mine has strangled
him." Yet he was afraid to reprove him.

In the morning both arose and went forward to another city, in
which they were honourably entertained at the house of one of
the inhabitants. This person possessed a superb golden cup which
he highly valued; and which, during the night, the angel pur-
loined. The hermit thought, "Verily, this is one of the lost angels;
our host has treated us well, and yet he has robbed him." But still
he held his peace, for his apprehension was extreme. On the
morrow they continued their journey; and as they walked they
came to a certain river, over which a bridge was thrown; they
ascended the bridge, and about mid-way a poor man met them.
"My friend," said the angel to him, "show us the way to yonder
city." The pilgrim turned, and pointed with his finger to the road
they were to take; but as he turned, the angel seized him by the
shoulders, and precipitated him into the stream below. At this the
terrors of the hermit were again aroused—"It is the devil," ex-
claimed he internally—"it is the devil, and no good angel! What
evil had the poor man done that he should be drowned?" He
would now have gladly departed alone; but was afraid to give
utterance to the thoughts of his heart. About the hour of vespers
they reached a city, in which they again sought shelter for the
night; but the master of the house to whom they applied sharply
refused it. "For the love of Heaven," said the angel, "afford us a
shelter, lest we fall a prey to the wolves and other wild beasts."
The man pointed to a sty—"That," said he, "is inhabited by
pigs; if it please you to lie there, you may—but to no other place
will I admit you." "If we can do no better," returned the angel,
"we must accept your ungracious offer." They did so; and in the
morning the angel, calling their host, said, "My friend, I give you

this cup"; and he presented to him the stolen goblet. The hermit, more and more astonished at what he saw, said to himself, "Now I am certain this is the devil. The good man who received us with all kindness he despoiled, and gives the plunder to this fellow who refused us a lodging." Turning to the angel, he exclaimed, "I will travel with you no longer. I commend you to God." "Dear friend," answered the angel, "first hear me, and then go thy way. When thou wert in thy hermitage, the owner of the flock unjustly put to death his servant. True it is he died innocently, but he had formerly done deeds for which he deserved to die. God allowed him to be slain, to enable him to escape the future consequences of those former sins of which he had not repented. But the guilty man who stole the sheep will suffer eternally, while the owner of the flock will repair, by alms and good works, that which he ignorantly committed. As for the son of the hospitable knight, whom I strangled in the cradle, know that before the boy was born he performed numerous works of charity and mercy, but afterwards grew parsimonious and covetous, in order to enrich the child, of which he was inordinately fond. This was the cause of its death; and now its distressed parent again is become a devout Christian. Then, for the cup which I purloined from him who received us so kindly, know that before the cup was made, there was not a more abstemious person in the world; but afterwards he took such pleasure in it, and drank from it so often, that he was intoxicated twice or thrice during the day. I took away the cup, and he has turned to his former sobriety. Again, I cast the pilgrim into the river; and know that he whom I drowned was a good Christian, but had he proceeded much further, he would have fallen into a mortal sin. Now he is saved, and reigns in celestial glory. Then, that I bestowed the cup upon the inhospitable citizen, know nothing is done without reason. He suffered us to occupy the swine-house, and I gave him a valuable consideration. But *he* will hereafter reign in hell. Put a guard, therefore, on thy lips, and detract not from the Almighty. For He knoweth all things." The hermit, hearing this, fell at the feet of the angel and entreated pardon. He returned to his hermitage, and became a good and pious Christian.

❦ Of the Transgressions and Wounds of the Soul

This story is from the *Gesta Romanorum*.

I N THE reign of Titus there lived a certain noble and devout
knight, who had a beautiful wife; but she dishonoured her-
self, and persisted in her dishonour. The knight, therefore, was
very sorrowful, and resolved to visit the Holy Land. In this de-
termination he said to his wife, "My beloved, I go to the Holy
Land, and leave you to the guidance of your own discretion." No
sooner had he embarked than the lady sent for a certain skilful
necromancer, whom she loved; and he dwelt with her. It happened
that, as they lay in bed, the lady observed, "If you would do one
thing for me, I might become your wife." "What is it," replied he,
"that will please you, and which I can perform for you?"

"My husband is gone to the Holy Land, and loves me little;
now, if by your art you could destroy him, all that I possess is
yours." "I acquiesce," said the clerk, "but on condition that you
marry me." To this the lady bound herself, and the necromancer
fashioned an image under the similitude and name of the knight,
and fixed it before him on the wall.

In the mean time, while the knight was passing through the
main street of Rome, a wise master met him in the way, and
observing him narrowly, said, "My friend, I have a secret to
communicate."

"Well, master, what would you please to say?"

"This day you are one of death's children, unless you follow
my advice: your wife is a harlot, and contrives your death." The
knight, hearing what was said of his spouse, put confidence in the
speaker, and said, "Good master, save my life, and I will amply
recompense you." "Willingly," answered the other, "if you will

do as I shall tell you." The knight promised, and the master took him to a bath, undressed him, and desired him to bathe. Then putting into his hand a polished mirror, said, "Look attentively upon this, and you will see wonders." He did so, and the meanwhile the master read to him from a book. "What see you?" he asked. "I see," said the knight, "a certain clerk in my house, with an image of wax which resembles me, and which he has fastened in the wall." "Look again," continued the master; "what do you perceive now?"

"He takes a bow, and places in it a sharp arrow; and now he aims at the effigy."

"As you love your life, the moment you discern the arrow flying to its mark, place yourself in the bath, and remain there until I tell you to come out."

As soon, therefore, as the arrow quitted the string, he plunged his body into the water. This done, the master said, "Raise your head and look into the mirror. What do you perceive now?" "The effigy is not struck, and the arrow is sticking by its side. The clerk appears much concerned." "Look in the mirror once more," said the master, "and observe what he does." "He now goes nearer to the image, and refixes the arrow in the string in order to strike it."

"As you value your life, do as before."

Again the knight plunged his body into the water as soon as he saw by the mirror that the clerk was bending the bow; and then, at the command of the master, resuming his inspection of the mirror, said—

"The clerk makes great lamentation, and says to my wife, 'If the third time I do not strike the effigy, I shall lose my life.' Now he approaches so near that I think he cannot miss it."

"Take care," said the master, "as soon as you see him bend the bow, immerse your body as I before told you." The knight watched attentively, and as soon as he saw the clerk draw back the bow to shoot, plunged below the water. "Rise quickly, and look into the mirror." When he had done so, he began to laugh. "My friend," said the master, "why do you laugh?" "I observe,"

answered he, "very distinctly, that the clerk has missed the effigy, and that the arrow, rebounding, has entered his bowels and destroyed him. My wife makes a hole under my bed, and there he is buried."

"Rise, then, dress yourself, and pray to God."

The knight returned sincere thanks for his life, and, having performed his pilgrimage, journeyed toward his own home. His wife met and received him with much apparent pleasure. He dissembled for a few days, and then sending for her parents, said to them, "My dear friends, hear why I have desired your presence. This woman, your daughter and my wife, has committed adultery; and, what is worse, designed to murder me." The lady denied the accusation with an oath. The knight then began to relate the whole story of the clerk's actions and end. "And," he continued, "if you do not credit this, come and see where the clerk is buried." He then led them into the bed-chamber, and dragged the body from its hiding-place. The judge was called, and sentenced her to be burnt, and her ashes to be scattered in the air. The knight soon afterwards espoused a beautiful virgin, by whom he had many children; and with whom he finished his days in peace.

APPLICATION.

My beloved, the emperor is Christ; the knight is man; and the wife, the flesh. To visit the Holy Land is by good works to attain Heaven. The wise master is a prudent confessor. The clerk is the devil, and the image represents human pride and vanity. The bath is confession; the mirror, the Sacred Writings, which ward off the arrows of sin.

This story is from the *Gesta Romanorum*.

ALEXANDER HAD an only son, called Celestinus, whom he loved with the utmost tenderness. He desired to have him well instructed, and sending for a certain philosopher, said, "Sir, instruct my son, and I will bountifully remunerate you." The philosopher acquiesced, and took the boy home with him. He diligently performed his duty; and it happened that one day, entering a meadow with his pupil, they perceived a horse lying on the ground, grievously affected with the mange. Near the animal two sheep were tied together, which busily cropped the grass that grew in abundance around them. It so chanced that the sheep were on each side of the horse, and the cord with which they were bound passed over his back and, chafing the sores, galled him exceedingly. Disturbed by this circumstance, he got up; but the cord, then loaded with the weight of the sheep, afflicted him more and more; and, filled with fury, he began to run off at a great speed, dragging along the unfortunate sheep. And in equal proportion to their resistance was the augmentation of the horse's suffering. For the cord, having worn itself into a hollow, sunk, at every struggle, yet deeper into the wound.

Adjoining the meadow was the house of a miller, toward which the horse, impelled by the anguish of his wound, galloped, and entered, with the sheep hanging as we have said. The house was then unoccupied; but there was a fire burning upon the hearth, and the quadruped, plunging and striking with his hoofs, so scattered the fire that the flame caught hold of the building, and reduced it to ashes, together with the horse and the sheep.

"Young man," said the preceptor to his pupil, "you have perceived the beginning, the middle, and the completion of this incident: make me some correct verses upon it, and show me who is responsible for the burning of the house. Unless you do this, I assure you I will punish you severely." Celestinus, during the absence of his master, applied himself diligently to study, but he was unable to execute his task. This much troubled him; and the devil met him in the likeness of a man, and said, "My son, what has made you so sorrowful?"

CELEST. Never mind; it is no use telling you.

DEVIL. You know not that; tell me, and I will help you.

CELEST. I am charged, under a heavy punishment, to make some verses about a scabby horse and two sheep, and I don't know how.

DEVIL. Young man, I am the devil in a human form, and the best poet that ever lived: care nothing about your master, but promise to serve me faithfully, and I will compose such delectable verses for you that they shall excel those of your pedagogue himself.

Celestinus gave his word to serve him faithfully if he fulfilled his engagement. The devil then produced the following verses:—

> Bound by a thong, that passed along
> A horse's mangy hide,
> Two sheep there lay, as I you say,
> One upon either side.
>
> The steed uprose, and upward goes
> Each sheep with dangling breech;
> Borne by the horse's rapid course,
> The miller's hut they reach.
>
> Scattering the fire with reckless ire,
> The rafters caught the flame;
> And bleating breed and scabby steed
> Were roasted in the same.
>
> Now had that wight, that miller hight,
> Vouchsafed his house to keep,

Ere he returned it had not burned,
Nor burned his horse and sheep.*

The boy, made happy by the present, returned home.

MASTER. My child, have you stolen your verses, or made them?

CELEST. I made them, sir.

He then read what we have given above; and the master, struck with the greatest astonishment at their uncommon beauty, exclaimed, "My dear boy, tell me if any one made these verses for you?"

CELEST. No, sir; no one did.

MASTER. Unless you tell me the truth, I will flog you till the blood run.

The lad, fearful of what might follow, declared all that had occurred, and how he had bound himself to the devil. The preceptor, grieved at the communication, induced the youth to confess himself and renounce this fearful confederacy. When this was done he became a holy man, and, after a well-spent life, gave up his soul to God.

APPLICATION.

My beloved, the king is Christ; the philosopher, any prelate; the mangy horse, a sinner covered with sins. The two sheep are two preachers bound by the cord of charity; the miller's house is the world; and the fire, detraction.

* As these are probably the only verses on record of the devil's composition (at least, so well authenticated), I cannot do less than transcribe them for the edification of the curious:—

"Nexus ovem binam, per spinam traxit equinam;
Læsus surgit equus, pendet utrumque pecus.
Ad molendinum, pondus portabat equinum,
Dispergendo focum, se cremat atque locum.
Custodes aberant singula damna ferant."

(Note by the Rev. Charles Swan.)

The Marvelous Conversion of the Blessed Hildegund, Virgin by Caesarius of Heisterbach

Caesarius of Heisterbach was born in Cologne, about 1180. He entered the Cistercian order in youth, and spent his life happily in the beautiful Rhineland abbey of Heisterbach, and there he died, about 1250. As Master of Novices and as Prior he had occasion to instruct the young in the wonders worked by ever-watchful angels. He was a natural storyteller; he must have held his charges spellbound. He set down his edifying anecdotes in his *Dialogus Miraculorum*. An edition by Joseph Strange was published in Cologne in 1851. The translation of this and the two following stories is by Morris Bishop.

THE MONK. In the town of Neuss, five miles from Cologne, lived a burgher who had a beautiful and well-beloved daughter, named Hildegund. His wife died when the girl was still in her tender years. The burgher went pilgrim to Jerusalem to make his devotions and took his daughter with him. But on his return journey the father fell ill and in Tyre departed this life. Dying, he confided the girl and all his possessions to the fidelity of his servant. But this servant ill served his master, showing no pity for the dead. Impious and avaricious, he slipped away by night and secretly took ship, abandoning the girl and exposing her to a thousand woes.

When she arose in the morning and learned that the faithless guardian had sailed away with all her father's wealth, bitterly she complained. She knew not what she should do nor whither she should turn. Ignorant of the language of the country, she began to suffer the pangs of hunger. For a year she begged at the doors of the schools of that town. Eventually she exposed her sad state to some German pilgrims and besought them, with tears, to take

pity on her. One of them, a worthy nobleman, richer than the others, consoled the poor pilgrim in her affliction, took her on his own ship, supplied her with necessaries, and brought her back to the homeland.

Now at this time a controversy arose in the church of Trier between two candidates for the bishopric, Wolmar, archdeacon of that church, and Rudolph, chief provost. Pope Lucius favored the first, Emperor Frederick promoted the second. The church of Cologne, supporting the first of the candidates, wished to send a letter to the Pope, who was then residing in Verona. But because of the machinations of the Emperor no messenger was safe. Therefore the bearer feared for his life. And taking the aforementioned girl for a youth, because of her tonsure and dress, he persuaded her by prayers and offers of money to carry the letter enclosed in a cane, and, the better to escape suspicion, advised that she should walk rather than ride.

When she got near Augsburg she chanced to meet a thief, who proposed that they join company. Thinking no ill, she agreed willingly. When they had gone a little way the thief heard the sound of pursuers. Pretending that he had to withdraw for a moment, he loaded the girl with the spoil of his robbery and hid in the bushes. To be brief, she was seized by the pursuers, brought before the court with the bag of stolen goods, and condemned to be hanged. Her protests and allegations of innocence were dismissed, on the evidence of the stolen property. So she asked the service of a priest, and this was granted. Confessing all her small misdeeds, she naïvely explained the reason for her journey and revealed all the wickedness of the thief. And to convince the priest of her truth-telling she showed him the cane containing the letter to the Pope. And she added: "If the thief should be hunted, he would be quickly found."

So at the urging of the priest the wood was encircled by men with nets and dogs. The thief was taken, and, with the girl, was brought before the court. And after that wretch had been compelled by torture to confess his crime, he said: "I have been forced unjustly to confess what I did not do; according to civil

law the person caught with the stolen property should be condemned." The girl rejoined that the spoil had been confided to her by trickery, and that she wished only to restore it to its owner. He answered: "I deny that the property was in my possession; and the testimony of a single person is of no value." At this the girl fell silent. Then the priest stood up and testified in her favor, and stoutly affirmed that she was innocent, being victimized by the man's dodges. "And," he added, "if you don't believe my words, apply the ordeal of the red-hot iron, and it will be easily proved who is innocent and who guilty." All agreed; the thief's hand was burned, but the girl's hand was unscathed. Then the thief was promptly hanged; the confessor, the girl's liberator, rejoicing, took her into his home.

But only hear! At the instigation of the devil, irked at the rescue of the maiden, a kinsman of the thief, who was enraged at the man's shameful death, kidnapped from the priest's home the innocent maiden, liberated by God's judgment. He cut down the malefactor, and hanged the girl in his place. But straightway an angel of God appeared, and supported her so that she would not feel the torturing rope; and he refreshed her with the wonderful odor of his countenance. She felt no pain, rather a sharing in utmost delights. And that night she heard so sweet a melody, so varied and joyful a symphony, that no choir, whether of voices or instruments, could be compared to it for sweetness. She asked what it might be; the angel replied: "It is the soul of your sister Agnes, being borne to heaven with this angelic concord. And in two years you will follow her to bliss."

Thus this blessed creature hung on the gallows for two days. And shepherds grazing their flocks near by were stirred to pity, and took counsel to remove the body and give it burial. And when they cut the rope the body did not fall of its own weight, as normally, but descended gradually, being upborne by the angel; and when it touched earth it stood upright. At this sight the shepherds fled in terror.

Said the angel of the Lord: "Now you are free; go where you will."

"My lord," said she, "it was my purpose to go to Verona." And in a trice she was transported to the outskirts of that city. Said the angel: "Verona is three miles away." (Now from Augsburg to Verona is reckoned a seven-days journey.)

THE NOVICE. In the case of this girl two ancient miracles seem to me to be repeated; to wit, those of Saint Benedict Abbot and of the Prophet Habakkuk. The first saw from far away the soul of his sister Scholastica penetrating the fastness of heaven in the form of a dove; while the other, the Prophet, was translated in a moment from Judea to Babylon.

THE MONK. You are quite right. And I think her deserving to hear her sister's soul, so far away, in transit to heaven with an angelic choir was no less wonderful than the awareness of Saint Severin in Cologne that the soul of Saint Martin was borne with supernal harmony to his Lord. Two other glorious graces were vouchsafed her, in that, upheld by the angel, she felt no pains from the noose, and that she foresaw her end so long in advance.

To resume, she happily fulfilled her mission in Verona. And on her return she entered the diocese of Worms; and mindful of divine mercy, she obtained, by the prayers and good works of a venerable recluse, permission from Dom Theobald, Abbot of Schoenau, to enter on a novitiate. Schoenau, taking its name (Fairmeadow) from the place, is a very attractive spot. The abbot, thinking her a young man, bade her ride behind him on his horse. When she spoke in a charming feminine voice, the abbot said to her: "Brother Joseph, hasn't your voice changed yet?" Said she: "My lord, it will never change." (Passing herself off as a youth, and having to combat the two enemies, the flesh and the devil, she had taken the name of Saint Joseph, the better to impress on her mind the virtues of him who had triumphantly trodden down powerful temptations, and the more fully to invoke his aid. Here we see fulfilled the words of Solomon: "Who can find a virtuous woman?" Nothing of this sort has ever occurred in our order; it is unexampled. It is written, again: "A woman among all these I have not found.")

Entering on her probation, she undertook the hardest tasks. She slept among the men, ate and drank with them, bared her back to them for the discipline. And though she was very serious of nature, in order not to arouse suspicion of her sex she would sometimes reveal some hint of levity among her fellow-probationers. A monk named Hermann told me that he was then a fourteen-year-old boy; and in the absence of the novice-master she pointed to her cup, and said: "Let's look in this mirror and see which of us is handsomer." And when he was gazing at their reflections, she said again: "Hermann, how do you like my face?" He replied: "It seems to me that your chin is formed like a woman's chin." Then she went out as if angry. Afterwards both of them were flogged for breaking the rule of silence.

THE NOVICE. I wonder if she experienced any temptations in our order.

THE MONK. I never heard of any temptations to her; but I have heard enough hints of her being a cause of temptation to others. When the time for her release from this world drew near she began to ail. And when owing to her great weakness she was put to bed, a certain monk standing by her side and regarding her said plainly: "This man is either a woman or the devil, for I could never look at him without temptation." This was said in jest, but it sufficiently proves how mighty is the power of nature.

She called the prior, and when she had confessed to him certain small sins, he asked her if she had ever carnally known a woman. She replied: "Never, master, have I been guilty with any woman, or man either,"—adding the last phrase on account of her sex. Then she recounted to him, in proper order, all I have told you, all her experiences, save only the fact of her sex. Said the astounded prior: "Brother, your story seems to strain credulity. How can I prove that these things are true?"

Said the girl: "Just two years ago, as I hung on the gallows, the angel of the Lord predicted my passing for today. 'I know him in whom I have believed; I have kept faith; I have finished my course; henceforth there is laid up for me a crown of righteous-

ness.' If on this day which I have foretold I do not lose the power of speech for about the length of a mass before my death, do not believe me."

She added: "When I am dead, something will be revealed which will amaze you, and you will properly give thanks therefor to divine favor."

When she had said this, on the fourth day of Holy Week, the 20th of April, in the year of our Lord 1188, toward sunset, that sanctified soul left its virginal body and ascended to meet its Master. The gong was struck; the abbot and the other brothers assembled for the post-mortem rites. And when her body was carried out to be washed, her feminine sex appeared. All were stricken with amazement at this new miracle. The news was brought to the priest who was reading the supplications. And when he learned of her sex he changed the text, and for "monk" he substituted "nun," and "sister" for "brother." Afterwards when the records were written up they appeared (since her name was unknown) as follows: "On the 20th of April died the hand-maiden of Christ in Schoenau."

A few days later the brothers, desirous of learning the name of the blessed woman, sent inquiries to the Cologne area, which she had stated to be her place of origin. A persistent search for her family was made; and by divine favor an old lady was discovered who said she was a relation, and that the girl's name was Hilde-gund.

When, a few years ago, a new oratory was consecrated in Schoenau, people poured in from several provinces for the dedication, and when they heard of the virtues of the blessed Hildegund they resorted to her tomb, especially the matrons, beseeching her holy prayers, and praising God for his wonderful works. And we, her brothers, let us join with them in thanks to our Savior, who willed these marvels to occur in our own time and in our own order, to his own glory and to our edification, and who liveth and resigneth with the Father and the Holy Spirit, *in saecula saeculorum*. Amen.

The Cleric Who Deflowered a Jewish Maiden by Caesarius of Heisterbach

This story, like the preceding one, is taken from Caesarius' *Dialogus Miraculorum*.

THE MONK. In an English city lived a girl, daughter of a Jew, and very pretty, as is often the case among that people. Now a young cleric, related to the bishop of the city and a canon of the cathedral, saw her and lusted for her; and with cajoling words he strove to persuade her to his lewd desires. Longing for her embraces and inflamed with passion, he made daily proposals for their union. Eventually she said: "I am very dear to my father, who watches me so close that I cannot come to you, nor you to me, except on that Friday night which precedes your Easter." For then the Jews are said to suffer a certain infirmity called the bloody flux, which so occupies them that they can be little concerned with other matters.

When the youth heard this, being almost out of his mind with excess of passion, he forgot his Christian religion and the Passion of his Lord. On that very night he sought out the maiden and lay with her until morning. But her Jewish father, bearing a light, entered her room before dawn, to see how she slept and if perhaps she needed warmer covering. When he saw the young man by her side he fell into a rage, and was moved to kill him. But recognizing him as a relative of the bishop, he held his hand out of fear, and cried in fury: "What are you doing here, wicked Christian? Where is your faith, your religion? You have been delivered into my hands by the just judgment of God! If I did not fear my lord bishop, I would kill you on the spot!"

The young man, frightened and begging for mercy, was thrown out of the house in the utmost confusion. On the same

day the bishop was about to celebrate the solemn service of nones, and the youth, being on duty for the week, was to read the epistle. But his conscience was so befouled that he feared to approach the sacred mysteries, or to find a substitute on such a day, or to reveal in confession his fresh and filthy sin. And when, blushing with shame, he had donned his sacred vestments and stood in his place before the bishop, the aforementioned Jew with a great swarm of Jews poured noisily into the church, to complain to the bishop about his kinsman.

When the youth saw him he well recognized his purpose. He turned pale and shook with terror. He spoke to God in his heart, saying: "Lord God, save me in this hour, and I promise thee that I shall not offend thee in aught else, but I shall make amends for this sin." And when the most merciful Creator, who hates the sin but loves man's nature, saw the man contrite, he turned the dreaded riot upon the head of the faithless. The bishop, wondering what the Jews could be seeking in the church, especially on such a day, when Christians represent their Lord's Passion, gestured to them to stand silent. They crowded toward him; but as soon as they opened their mouths to accuse the cleric, their voices were stilled, and all fell mute. The bishop, seeing the mouths of the Jews gaping at him with no words issuing forth, thought they had come only to mock the divine mysteries, and he angrily ordered that they should all be driven out of the church. After this manifestation of divine clemency, the cleric came to the prelate as soon as the service was over, confessed his guilt, and asked to do penance. The bishop marvelled at God's mercy and glorified him for the greatness of the miracle and for the repentance of his kinsman. He persuaded the youth to marry in due form the girl he had debauched, once she was renewed by the grace of baptism. As a just and pious man, he preferred that his relative should be deprived of ecclesiastical benefices, rather than that the girl should be exposed to many perils in the sinful abode of her father. The cleric, mindful of divine favor, wished to make amends to God for his sin, and was later inspired to join our order, as the girl entered a convent at his urging.

This story was often recited to me by a monk, abbot in our order. So you see how much good contrition worked in this man. It rescued an erring soul, struck the Jews dumb, and brought an infidel girl to the faith.

THE NOVICE. I see, I admire, I rejoice, observing God's bounty environing us in many ways.

How the Novice Theobald Conquered His Pride by Caesarius of Heisterbach

This is the third story translated from Caesarius' *Dialogus Miraculorum.*

THE MONK. There was once among us a monk named Theobald, something of a wastrel before his conversion, much given to wine and dice, well known for his buffooneries throughout Cologne. I have often seen him walking naked through the city's public places. At last he repented of his clownishness, and by the intercession of the clerical eminences of Cologne he was accepted by our abbot, Dom Gevard, and was received in our house as a novice. During his probation, thinking that nothing was more acceptable to God than works of humility, he asked and received permission to wash the dirty linen.

After he had done this for a few days the Tempter appeared, and wounding his heart with the arrow of pride, set him to these thoughts: "What are you doing, fool? What business is it of yours to wash out the foulnesses of your inferiors in rank?" After turning over such thoughts for a time in his spirit, he recognized that they came from the devil, who is king over all the sons of pride. And one day he washed the dirty clothes more diligently than usual, and the better to confound and check the promptings of pride, he drank the washing-water.

The devil saw this, and regarded him balefully, and attacked with all his terrors him whom he could not lay low by the spirit of pride. (All this I learned from Dom Heinrich our abbot, who said that he had had it from the man's own lips in confession.) From his foul, fetid drink he felt such griping pains in his stomach that all his inwards seemed to be bursting out. And one

night when at the call of nature he was setting out for the privy, he saw two human bodies hanging from a beam in the room. These bodies were black, their garments in rags, their faces shrouded, so that one would have thought them punished criminals. When the novice suddenly caught sight of them he was terrified almost out of his wits. He ran back to the dormitory and sat down, gasping, by the bed of Heinrich, monk and later our head cellarer. As Heinrich told me, the novice shook so, racking his breast with repeated sobs, that Heinrich marvelled at what he could have seen and endured. Heinrich urged him to go to bed, for it was cold, and the man was sitting only in his undershirt; but he would not consent. So Heinrich put part of his own blankets over this Theobald's shoulders, and let him sit there until the signal for matins.

THE NOVICE. I am amazed that a new wall, so mightily shaken, could stand firm.

THE MONK. In fact, he did not stand long. For, battered by the frequent assaults of temptation, he was finally misled and undone by a false semblance of good. At last received as a monk, he importuned the abbot for permission to visit his relatives in France, whom he had not seen for twenty years before his conversion. There he was to remain for a year in a house of our order. So he departed and returned; and then he fell into apostasy, and died outside the order. A certain wandering cleric, who was present at his death, told us that he had confessed to a secular priest, and was by him anointed and admitted to communicate; and so he died in contrition.

THE NOVICE. I learn from these importunate temptations of demons that they feared the humility of this novice more than the virginity of the monk in your last story.

In the sweet story of Saint Francis of Assisi, Brother Juniper supplies the comic relief. His simplicity amused the Saint and his companions, but he is treated by the chronicler with evident affection. *The Little Flowers of Saint Francis* was compiled in Latin some time after 1322 and soon translated into Italian. This rendering is from the book *The Little Flowers of St. Francis*, translated by Thomas Okey. It was first published in 1894, and in an Everyman's Library Edition (New York: E. P. Dutton) in 1906; it is reprinted by permission of E. P. Dutton & Co., Inc., and J. M. Dent & Sons Ltd.

I. *How Friar Juniper cut the foot off a pig only to give it to a sick man.*

FRIAR JUNIPER was one of the most chosen disciples and first companions of St. Francis. He was a man of deep humility and of great zeal and charity; and of him St. Francis said, speaking on a time with those holy companions of his, "He were a good friar that had so overcome himself and the world as Friar Juniper hath." One day, as he was visiting a sick friar at St. Mary of the Angels, all aflame with charity, he asked with great compassion, "Can I serve thee in aught?" The sick man answers, "Much comfort and great solace would it be to me if I might have a pig's foot." And Friar Juniper said, "Trust to me, for I will get one forthwith." And off he goes and snatches up a knife (I believe 'twas a kitchen knife) and goes in fervour of spirit about the wood, where certain pigs were feeding, and falling on one of them, cuts off a foot and runs away with it, leaving the pig maimed; he returns, washes and dresses and cooks this foot, and having well dished it up, carries the said foot to the sick man with much charity. And the sick friar ate thereof greedily, to the great consolation and joy of Friar Juniper, who told the story of

the assaults he had made on the pig with great glee, to rejoice the heart of the sick man.

Meanwhile the swineherd, that saw this friar cut the foot off, told over the whole story with much bitterness to his master. And he, being informed of this deed, comes to the friary and calls the friars hypocrites, thieves, false knaves, and wicked rogues, exclaiming, "Wherefore have ye cut off my pig's foot?" Hearing the great uproar he made, St. Francis and all the friars hurried along, and St. Francis made excuse for his friars, saying, with all humility, that they knew naught of the deed; and to pacify the man, promised to make amends for every wrong done to him. But for all this he was not to be appeased, but departed from the friary in great wrath, uttering many insults and threats, repeating over and over again how that they had wickedly cut off his pig's foot, and accepting neither excuses nor promises, he hastened away greatly scandalised. But St. Francis, full of prudence, bethought him the while the other friars stood all stupefied, and said in his heart, "Can Friar Juniper have done this thing out of indiscreet zeal?" So he bade call Friar Juniper secretly to him, and asked him, saying, "Hast thou cut off that pig's foot in the wood?" To whom Friar Juniper answered, right gleefully, and not as one having committed a fault, but as one that believed he had done a deed of great charity, and spake thus, "My sweet father, true it is I have cut off a foot from that said pig; and the cause thereof, my father, hear, if thou wilt, compassionately. I went out of charity to visit a certain friar that was sick"; and then he related the whole story in order, and added, "I tell thee this much, that considering the consolation this friar of ours felt, and the comfort he took from the said foot, had I cut off the feet of a hundred pigs as I did this one, I believe of a surety God would have looked on it as a good deed." Whereupon St. Francis, with righteous zeal, and with great bitterness, said, "O Friar Juniper, wherefore hast thou wrought this great scandal? Not without cause doth that man grieve, and thus rail against us; and perchance even now, as I speak, he is going about the city defaming us of evil, and good cause hath he. Wherefore I command thee,

by holy obedience, run after him until thou overtake him, and cast thyself on the ground prostrate before him and confess thy fault, and promise to make him such full amends as that he shall have no cause to complain of us: for of a surety this hath been too monstrous an offence."

Friar Juniper marvelled much at the aforesaid words, and was filled with amaze, being astonished that there should be any disturbance over such an act of charity; for these temporal things seemed to him naught, save in so far as they were charitably shared with one's neighbour. And Friar Juniper answered, "Fear not, father mine, for anon will I repay him and make him content. And wherefore should he be so troubled, seeing that this pig, whose foot I have cut off, was God's rather than his own, and a very charitable use hath been made thereof?"

And so he sets forth at a run, and cometh up with this man that was raging beyond all measure and past all patience; and he told him how, and for what cause, he had cut off the said pig's foot, and withal in such great fervour and exultation and joy, even as one that had done him a great service for which he ought to be well rewarded. But the man, boiling with anger, and overcome with fury, heaped many insults on Friar Juniper, calling him a mad fellow and a fool, a big thief, and the worst of scoundrels. But Friar Juniper cared naught for these abusive words, and marvelled within himself, for he rejoiced in being reviled, and believed that he had not heard aright; for it seemed to him matter for rejoicing, and not for spite: and he told the story anew, and fell on the man's neck and embraced him and kissed him, and told him how that this thing had been done for charity's sake alone, inviting him and entreating him to give likewise what was left of the pig; and all with such charity and simplicity and humility that the man, being come to himself, fell on the ground before him, not without many tears; and asking pardon for the wrong he had said and done to these friars, he goes and takes this pig and kills it, and having cooked it, he carries it, with much devotion and many tears, to St. Mary of the Angels, and gives it to these holy friars to eat, out of compassion for the said wrong he had done them.

And St. Francis, considering the simplicity and the patience under adversity of this said holy friar, said to his companions and to the others that stood by, "Would to God, my brethren, that I had a whole forest of such junipers!"

II. *An ensample of Friar Juniper's great power against the devil.*

That the devil was unable to endure the purity of the innocence of Friar Juniper and his deep humility appeareth in this. On a time, a man possessed with a devil, flung out of the way he was going, and, beyond his wont and with much fury, all of a sudden fled full seven miles by divers paths. And being overtaken and questioned by his kinsfolk who followed after him with bitter grief, wherefore in his flight he had taken such devious ways, he answered, "The reason is this: forasmuch as that fool Juniper was passing by that way, being unable to endure his presence, nor to encounter him, I fled through these woods." And certifying themselves of this truth, they found that Friar Juniper had passed along at that hour even as the devil had said. Wherefore St. Francis, when the possessed were brought to him that they might be healed, was wont to say, if the devils departed not straightway at his command, "An thou depart not forthwith from this creature I will bring Friar Juniper up against thee." And then the devil, fearing the presence of Friar Juniper and unable to endure the virtue and humility of St. Francis, would straightway depart.

III. *How at the instigation of the devil Friar Juniper was condemned to the gallows.*

On a time, the devil, desiring to affright Friar Juniper and to vex and trouble him, went to a most cruel tyrant named Nicholas that was then at war with the city of Viterbo, and said, "My lord, guard this your castle well, for anon a false traitor is to come hither, sent by the men of Viterbo, that he may slay you and set fire to your castle. And, in token of the truth of this, I give you these signs. He goeth about after the fashion of a poor wight, with garments all tattered and patched, and with a ragged cowl falling on his shoulders; and with him he beareth an awl where-

with he is to kill you, and he hath a flint and steel with him to set fire to this castle. And if you find I speak not sooth, deal with me as you will." At these words Nicholas was filled with amaze and grew sore afraid, because he that spake these words seemed an honest fellow. And he commanded diligent watch and ward to be kept, and that if this man, with the aforesaid tokens, came, he should be straightway brought into his presence.

Meanwhile Friar Juniper comes alone, for because of his perfection he had licence to go forth and stay alone, even as it pleased him. Now Friar Juniper happened on certain evil youths that began to mock and abuse him shamefully; and at all these things he was not troubled, but rather led them to deride him the more. And when he came up to the door of the castle, the guards seeing him thus ill favoured and in a scant habit all in rags (for he had given part thereof to the poor by the way), and seeing he had no semblance of a friar minor, and that the tokens given them were manifestly apparent, dragged him, with great fury, before this tyrant Nicholas. And being searched by his servants for hidden weapons, they found an awl in his sleeve wherewith he was wont to mend his sandals; likewise they found a flint and steel, which he carried with him to kindle fire; for his time was his own, and oft he abode in woods and desert places.

Nicholas, beholding these signs on him, in accord with the testimony of the accusing devil, commanded his servants to bind a rope about his neck, and this they did, with such great cruelty that the rope entered into his flesh; and then they put him on the rack and stretched his arms and racked his whole body without any mercy. And being asked who he was, he answered, "I am the greatest of sinners." And when asked if he had purposed to betray the castle and give it over to the men of Viterbo, he answered, "I am the greatest of traitors, and unworthy of any good thing." And asked if he purposed to kill Nicholas the tyrant with that awl and set fire to the castle, he answered that he would do even worse things and more monstrous, if God permitted. This Nicholas, maddened with rage, would suffer no more questioning of him, but, without any term or delay, condemned Friar Juniper, in

his fury, as a traitor and manslayer, to be tied to the tail of a horse and dragged along the ground to the gallows and there straight- way hanged by the neck. And Friar Juniper made no defence, but, as one that was content to suffer tribulation for love of God, was all joyous and glad.

And the sentence of the tyrant being put in execution, Friar Juniper was bound by his feet to the tail of a horse and dragged along the ground; and he complained not, nor lamented, but as a gentle lamb led to the slaughter, went with all humility. At this spectacle and swift justice all the people ran to behold him executed thus hastily and thus cruelly: and they knew him not.

But, as God willed, a good man that had seen Friar Juniper taken and thus quickly dragged to execution, runs to the house of the friars minor, and saith, "For love of God, I pray you, come quickly, for a poor wretch hath been taken and straightway condemned and led forth to die: come that at least he may give his soul into your hands; for he seemeth to me an honest fellow, and hath had no time wherein he may confess; lo, he is led forth to the gallows and seemeth to have no care for death, nor for the salvation of his soul: ah! I beseech you, deign to come quickly." The warden, that was a compassionate man, goes forthwith to provide for the salvation of his soul, and coming up to the place of execution, finds that the multitudes who have come to see were so increased that he could not pass through: and he stood and watched for an opening. And as he waited, he heard a voice in the midst of the crowd that cried, "Don't, don't, ye bad men; ye hurt my legs." At this voice a suspicion took the warden that this might be Friar Juniper, and in fervour of spirit he flung himself among them and tore aside the wrappings from the face of him; and there truly was Friar Juniper. Wherefore the compassionate warden was minded to take off his cloak to clothe Friar Juniper withal; but he, with joyous countenance and half laughing, said, "O warden, thou art fat, and it were an ill sight to see thy nakedness. I will not have it." Then the warden, with many tears, besought the hangmen and all the people for pity's sake to wait a while until he should go and entreat the tyrant for Friar Juniper,

that he might grant him pardon. The hangmen and certain by-standers consenting thereto (for they truly believed he was a kinsman), the devout and compassionate warden goes to Nicholas the tyrant, and with bitter tears saith, "My lord, I am in such great bitterness and wonderment of soul that tongue cannot tell thereof, for meseems that the greatest sin and the greatest wickedness ever wrought in the days of our forefathers is this day being done in this city: and I believe it is done in ignorance." Nicholas hears the warden patiently, and asks of him, "What is the great wrong and evil deed committed this day in our city?" The warden answers, "My lord, you have condemned one of the holiest friars in the Order of St. Francis, for whom you have singular devotion, to a cruel death, and, as I verily believe, without cause." Saith Nicholas, "Now tell me, warden, who is this? for perchance knowing him not I have committed a great wrong." Saith the warden, "He that you have doomed to death is Friar Juniper, the companion of St. Francis."

Nicholas the tyrant, stupefied, for he had heard of the fame and of the holy life of Friar Juniper, runs, astonied and all pale, together with the warden, and coming up to Friar Juniper looseth him from the tail of the horse and sets him free; then, in the presence of all the people, flings himself prostrate on the ground before Friar Juniper, and with many tears confesses his guilt, and bewails the wrong and the villainy he had done to this holy friar, and cried, "Verily I believe that the days of my evil life are numbered, since I have thus tortured the holiest of men without cause. God will appoint an end to my wicked life, and in brief time I shall die an evil death, albeit I have done this thing in ignorance." Friar Juniper freely forgave Nicholas the tyrant; but God suffered, ere a few days were passed, that this Nicholas the tyrant should end his life and die a very cruel death. And Friar Juniper departed, leaving all the people edified.

IV. *How Friar Juniper gave to the poor all he could lay hands on for love of God.*

So much pity and compassion had Friar Juniper for the poor that when he saw any one ill clad or naked, anon he would take

off his tunic, and the cowl from his cloak, and give them to poor souls such as these. Therefore the warden commanded him, by obedience, not to give away the whole of his tunic, nor any part of his habit. Now it fell out that Friar Juniper, ere a few days had passed, happened on a poor creature, well-nigh naked, who asked alms of him for love of God, to whom he said with great compassion, "Naught have I, save my tunic, to give thee; and this my superior hath laid on me, by obedience, to give to no one; nay, nor even part of my habit; but if thou wilt take it off my back, I will not gainsay thee." He spake not to deaf ears, for straightway this poor man stripped him of his tunic and went his way with it, leaving Friar Juniper naked. And when he was back at the friary, he was asked where his tunic was, and he answered, "An honest fellow took it from my back and made off with it." And the virtue of pity increasing within him, he was not content with giving away his tunic, but likewise gave books and church ornaments and cloaks, or anything he could lay hands on, to the poor. And for this reason the friars never left things lying about the friary, because Friar Juniper gave all away for love of God and in praise of Him.

V. *How Friar Juniper stripped certain little bells from the altar, and gave them away for love of God.*

Friar Juniper, being on a time in Assisi, at the Nativity of Christ, engaged in deep meditation at the altar of the friary, which was richly decked and adorned, was asked by the sacristan to guard the said altar while he went to eat. And while he was in devout meditation, a poor little woman begged alms of him for love of God: to whom Friar Juniper thus answered, "Tarry a while and I will see if I can give thee aught from this altar so rich." Now there was on that altar a hanging of gold, richly and sumptuously adorned with little silver bells of great worth. Saith Friar Juniper, "These bells are a superfluity." So he takes a knife and cuts them all from the hanging, and gives them, out of compassion, to this poor little woman.

No sooner had the sacristan eaten three or four mouthfuls than he remembered the ways of Friar Juniper, and was sore afeard

lest out of his zealous charity he might work some mischief to the rich altar he had left in his charge. And straightway he rose from the table, in much dread, and went to the church and looked to see if any of the ornaments of the altar had been removed or taken away; and lo, he beheld the hanging hacked about and the bells cut off: whereat he was beyond all measure perturbed and scandalised. And Friar Juniper, beholding him thus agitated, saith, "Be not troubled about those bells, for I have given them to a poor woman that had very great need of them, and here they were of no use, save that they made a show of worldly pomp." Hearing this, the sacristan ran straightway through the church and about the whole city, in great affliction, to see if haply he might find her. But so far from finding her, he could not even find any one that had seen her.

Returning to the friary, he took the hanging from the altar, in a great rage, and carried it to the general that was at Assisi, and said, "Father-general, I demand of you justice on Friar Juniper, who hath spoiled this hanging for me, that was the most precious thing in our sacristy; look now how he hath destroyed it and stripped off all the little silver bells, and he saith he hath given them away to a poor woman." The general answered, "Friar Juniper hath not done this, rather hath thy folly done it, for thou oughtest by this time to know his ways well; and I say unto thee, I marvel that he hath not given away all the rest; but none the less will I correct him for this fault."

And having called all the friars together in Chapter, he bade call Friar Juniper, and in the presence of the whole house rebuked him very harshly because of the aforesaid little bells; and he waxed so furious in his wrath, that by raising his voice so high he grew quite hoarse. Friar Juniper heeded those words little or naught, for he rejoiced in contumely and when he was well abased; but returning good for evil, he began to think only how he might find a remedy for his general's hoarseness. So having endured the general's scolding, Friar Juniper goes to the city and orders a good dish of porridge and butter; and a good part of the night being spent, he goes and lights a candle and comes back with this mess of porridge and takes it to the general's cell and

knocks. The general opens to him, and, beholding him with a lighted candle in one hand and the dish of porridge in the other, asks softly, "What is this?" Friar Juniper answered, "My father, to-day, when you chid me for my faults, I perceived that your voice was growing hoarse, and, as I ween, from over-fatigue; therefore I bethought me of a remedy, and I had this porridge made for thee; pray eat thereof, for I tell thee it will ease thy chest and throat." Said the general, "What hour is this for thee to go disturbing folk?" Friar Juniper answered, "Look now, for thee 'tis made; prithee make no more ado, but eat thereof, for 'twill do thee much good." And the general, angry at the late hour and at his importunity, bade him begone, for at such an hour he had no desire to eat, and called him a base fellow and a caitiff. Friar Juniper, seeing that neither prayer nor coaxing was of any avail, spake thus, "My father, since thou wilt not eat of this porridge that was made for thee, at least do me this favour: hold the candle for me, and I will eat it." And the pious and devout general, bearing in mind Friar Juniper's compassion and simplicity, and knowing that all this was done by him out of devotion, answered, "Look now, since thou wilt have it so, let us eat, thou and I, together." And both ate of this dish of porridge, because of his importunate charity. And much more were they refreshed by their devotion than by the food.

VI. How Friar Juniper abased himself to the glory of God.

On a time Friar Juniper, desiring truly to abase himself, stripped him of all save his breeches; and having made a bundle of his habit, placed his clothes on his head, and entering Viterbo, went to the market-place to be derided. And standing there, the children and youths of the city, deeming him bereft of his senses, reviled him sorely, casting much mire at him, and pelting him with stones. Hither and thither they rushed him, with many mocking words; and thus persecuted and scorned, he remained for the greater part of the day: then he went to the friary. And when the friars beheld him they were full of wrath, most of all for that he had come through the whole city with his bundle on his head; and they rebuked him very severely, uttering great

threats. And one said, "Let us cast him into prison." And another said, "Let us hang him." And the others said, "We cannot inflict too great a punishment for so evil an example as this friar hath made of himself this day and of all the Order." And Friar Juniper, right glad, answered with great humility, "Ye say well, for I am worthy of all these pains and many more."

VII. How Friar Juniper, to abase himself, played at see-saw.

On a time as Friar Juniper was journeying to Rome, where the fame of his holiness was already noised abroad, many Romans, of their great devotion, went out to meet him; and Friar Juniper, beholding so many people coming, imagined how he might turn their devotion into sport and mockery. Now there were two children playing at see-saw, to wit, they had placed one log of wood across another, and each of them sat at his end of the log and see-sawed up and down. Away goes Friar Juniper and takes off one of these children from the log, and mounting thereon begins to play see-saw. Meanwhile the people came up and marvelled to see Friar Juniper see-sawing, yet, with great devotion, they greeted him and waited for him to end the game of see-saw, in order to accompany him honourably as far as the friary. And Friar Juniper heeded little their greetings, their reverence, and their waiting, but held very diligently to his see-sawing. And waiting thus a long space, certain of them began to weary thereof, and said, "What a blockhead!" Others, knowing his ways, waxed in greater devotion. Nevertheless all departed and left Friar Juniper on his see-saw. And when they were all gone, Friar Juniper was left wholly comforted, because he saw that certain of them had mocked at him. He then set forth and entered Rome, and with all meekness and humility came to the house of the friars minor.

VIII. How Friar Juniper once cooked enough food to last the friars a fortnight.

Friar Juniper, being on a time left alone in a small friary, inasmuch as all the friars, for a certain reasonable cause, had to go

out from the friary, the warden saith to him, "Friar Juniper, all we have to go abroad; look to it, therefore, that when we return thou have some dish ready cooked for the refreshment of the friars." Friar Juniper answers, "Right gladly, leave it to me!"

And all the friars being gone forth, as hath been told, Friar Juniper saith, "What unprofitable care is this, for one friar to be lost in the kitchen and far away from all prayer! Certes, if I am left here to cook, this time will I cook so much that all the friars, and even more, shall have enough to eat for a fortnight." And so he goes very diligently to the city and begs several great cooking pots and pans, and procures fresh meat and salt, fowls and eggs and pot herbs, and begs much firewood, and puts everything on the fire, to wit, the fowls with their feathers on, and eggs in their shells, and all the other things one after the other.

When the friars came home, one that was ware of Friar Juniper's simplicity entered the kitchen and beheld many great pots and pans on a raging fire. And he sat him down and looked on with wonderment and said no word, but watched with what great diligence Friar Juniper went about his cooking. Now the fire was very fierce, and since he could not get very close to his pots to skim them, he took a wooden board and bound it closely to his body with his cord, and then leapt from one pot to another, so that it was a joy to behold.

Thinking over these things, with great delight, this friar comes from the kitchen and seeks the other friars, and saith, "Friar Juniper is making a wedding feast, I can tell you!" But the friars took this for a jest. And Friar Juniper lifted his pots from the fire and bade ring the bell for supper. And the friars, having taken their places at table, Friar Juniper comes into the refectory, all ruddy with his toil and the heat of the fire, with that meal of his, and saith to the friars, "Eat well, and then let us all to prayers; and let no one have any care about cooking for days to come, because I have cooked so much to-day that I shall have enough for more than a fortnight." And he served up this hotch-potch to the friars at table, and there is no hog in the whole of Rome hungry enough to have eaten thereof. Friar Juniper, to push his

wares, cries up his cooking, but seeing that the other friars eat naught thereof, saith, "Now look you, fowls such as these are comforting to the brain, and this mess will keep the body moist, for 'tis right good."

And while the friars were lost in wonderment and devotion at the simplicity and devotion of Friar Juniper, lo, the warden, angry at such folly and at the waste of so much good food, rebuked Friar Juniper very harshly. Then Friar Juniper dropped straightway on his knees before the warden and humbly confessed his fault to him and to all the friars, saying, "I am the worst of men: such a one committed such a crime, and therefore his eyes were plucked out, but I was more worthy thereof than he: such a one was hanged for his sins, but I deserve it far more for my wicked deeds: and now have I wasted so much of God's bounty and of the good things of the Order." And thus he departed, all sorrowing, and all that day was not seen of any friar. And then the warden said, "My dearest friars, I would that every day this friar should spoil, even as he hath now, as many more of our good things, if we had them, solely for our edification; for he hath done this thing out of his great simplicity and charity."

IX. *Of the grief that Friar Juniper felt at the death of his companion, Friar Amazialbene.*

Friar Juniper had a companion friar that he dearly loved, whose name was Amazialbene. And truly had this friar the virtue of highest patience and obedience; for if he were beaten the whole day long never did he utter one single word of lamentation or complaint. Often was he sent to friaries where the whole community was ill to get on with, and from whom he suffered much persecution; and this he endured very patiently and without murmuring. He, at the bidding of Friar Juniper, was wont to laugh and to weep. Now, as it pleased God, this Friar Amazialbene died in the highest repute; and Friar Juniper, hearing of his death, felt such great sadness of spirit as he never in his life had felt for the loss of any material thing. And he showed forth outwardly the great bitterness that was within him, and said,

"Woe is me! poor wretch! now no good thing is left to me, and all the world is out of joint at the death of my sweet and most beloved brother Amazialbene. Were it not that I should have no peace with the other friars, I would go to his grave and take away his head, and with the skull I would make me two bowls: and from one I would ever eat for devout memory of him; and from the other would I drink whenever I were athirst or had desire to drink."

»VI«

MERRY TALES AND

SALTY FICTIONS

ᔰ Of the Churl
Who Won Paradise

This is a *fabliau*, like *The Dapple-Gray Palfrey*. The trans-
lation, by Isabel Butler, is taken from her *Tales from the Old
French* (Boston: Houghton Mifflin, 1910).

WE FIND in writing a wondrous adventure that of old befell
a churl. He died of a Friday morning, and it so chanced,
neither angel nor devil came thither, and at the hour of his death
when the soul departed out of his body, he found none to ask
aught of him or to lay any command upon him. Know ye that
full glad was that soul for he was sore afraid. And now as he
looked to the right towards Heaven, he saw Saint Michael the
Archangel who was bearing a soul in great joy; forthright he set
out after the angel, and followed him so long, meseemeth, that he
came into Paradise.

Saint Peter who kept the gate received the soul borne by the
angel, and after he had so done, turned back towards the en-
trance. There he found the soul all alone, and asked him who had
brought him thither: "For herein none hath lodging and if he
have it not by judgment. Moreover, by Saint Alain, we have little
love for churls, for into this place the vile may not enter." "Yet
greater churl than you yourself is there none, fair Sir Peter," saith
the soul, "for you were ever harder than a stone; and by the holy
Paternoster God did folly when he made you his apostle, little
honour shall be his thereby, in that three times you denied your
Lord. Full little was your faith when thrice you denied him, and
though you be of his fellowship, Paradise is not for you. Go
forth, and that straightway, ye disloyal soul, but I am true and of
good faith, and bliss is rightfully mine."

Strangely shamed was Saint Peter; quickly he turned away, and
as he went, he met Saint Thomas, to whom he told all his

misadventure word for word, and all his wrath and bitterness. Then saith Saint Thomas: "I myself will go to this churl; here he shall not abide, and it please God." So he goeth into the square to the countryman. "Churl," quoth the apostle, "this dwelling belongeth of right to us and to the martyrs and confessors; wherein have you done such righteousness that you think to abide in it? Here you cannot stay, for this is the hostel of the true-hearted." "Thomas, Thomas, like unto a man of law ye are over quick to make answer; yet are not you he who, as is well known, spake with the apostles when they had seen the Lord after his resurrection? Then you made oath that never would you believe it and if you felt not his wounds with your hands; false and unbelieving were ye." Then Saint Thomas hung his head, and yielded him in the dispute; and thereafter he went to Saint Paul and told him of his discomfiture. "By my head," quoth Saint Paul, "I will go thither, and try if he will argue."

Meantime, the soul who feareth not destruction taketh his delight down in Paradise. "Soul," quoth Saint Paul, "who brought thee hither, and wherein have you done such righteousness that the gate should be opened to you? Get you gone out of Paradise, you false churl." "How is this, Don Paul of the bald pate, are you now so wrathful who erst was so fell a tyrant? Never will there be another so cruel; Saint Stephen paid dear for it when you had him stoned to death. Well know I the story of your life; through you many a brave man died, but in the end God gave you a good big blow. Have we not had to pay for the bargain and the buffet? Ha, what a divine and what a saint! Do ye think that I know you not?" Then had Saint Paul great sorrow.

Swiftly he went thence, and met Saint Thomas who was taking counsel with Saint Peter, and privately he told him of the churl who had so vanquished him: "Rightfully hath he won Paradise of me, and I grant it to him." Then all three went to bring complaint to God. Fairly Saint Peter told him of the churl who had spoken shame of them: "By his tongue hath he silenced us, and I myself was so abashed that never again will I speak thereof." Then spoke

Our Lord: "I will go thither, for I myself would hear this new thing."

He cometh to the soul and bespeaketh him, and asked how it chanced that he had come there without leave: "For herein without consent hath no soul, whether of man or woman, ever entered. My apostles you have slandered and scorned and outraged, yet none the less you think to abide here!" "Lord," saith the churl, "if judgment be accorded me, my right to dwell here is as good as theirs: for never did I deny you, or doubt you, nor did any man ever come to his death through me, but all these things have they done, and yet are now in Paradise. While I lived on earth my life was just and upright; I gave of my bread to the poor, I harboured them morning and evening, I warmed them at my fire, and saw that they lacked not for shirt or hose; I kept them even till death, and bore them to holy church: and now I know not if I did wisely. Furthermore, I made true confession, and received your body with due rites; and we are told that to the man who so dies God forgiveth his sins. Well know you if I speak the truth. I entered in and was not denied, and now I am here, why go hence? Were it so, you would gainsay your word, for surely you have declared that whoso entereth here goeth not out again; and you would never lie because of me." "Churl," saith the Lord, "I grant it. You have made good your case against Paradise, and have won it by debate. You were brought up in a good school; ready of tongue are you, and know right well how to turn a tale."

The countryman saith in proverb that many a man who hath sought wrong hath won it by argument; wit hath falsified justice, and falsity hath conquered nature; wrong goeth before and right falleth behind. Wit is mightier than force.

❧ A Dean and a Magician
by Juan Manuel

Prince Juan Manuel (1282–1347) was nephew and cousin of Spanish kings. His storybook is titled *Count Lucanor*, after one of the interlocutors. The conduct of the stories is invariable: the Count, in a dilemma, asks advice of his friend and counselor, Patronio, and is treated to an exemplary tale. The translation, by Dr. James York, is dated 1868; it was published by Pickering and Chatto, London, in 1888, as *Fifty Pleasant Stories of Patronio*.

ONE DAY Count Lucanor was conversing with Patronio, whose advice he sought under the following circumstances. "Patronio," said he, "a man came to me and begged I would assist him, knowing I was able to do so, promising to serve me in return, at any time, either for the promotion of my interest or honour. I rendered him all the assistance in my power, when, before his trouble was removed (although he believed it to be so), a circumstance happened in which I knew he could render me assistance, which I begged him to do; but he made me some excuse. Since then another case has arisen where he could have been of service to me, but again, as before, he has excused himself, and in every instance when I have needed his help he has always declined assisting me under some plea or other. Now his difficulties are not yet removed, nor can they be without my assistance. I, therefore, pray you, having so much confidence in your judgment, to advise me how to act under such circumstances."

"Count Lucanor," said Patronio, "in order that you may know how to act in such a case, it is desirable that you should hear what happened to a Dean of Santiago, with Don Illán, who was a great magician, and dwelt in Toledo."

The Count begged he would narrate it.

"My lord," said Patronio, "there was a Dean of Santiago who had a great desire to be initiated in the art of necromancy; and, hearing that Don Illán of Toledo knew more of this art than any other person in that country, came to Toledo with a view of studying under him. On the day of his arrival he proceeded to the house of Don Illán, whom he found reading in a retired chamber, and who received him very graciously, desiring him not to inform him of the motive of his visit until he had first partaken of his repast, which was found excellent, and consisted of every delicacy that could be desired.

"Now, when the repast was concluded, the dean took the magician aside and told him the motive of his visit, urging him very earnestly to instruct him in the art in which he was so great an adept, and which he, the dean, desired so anxiously to be made acquainted with.

"When Don Illán told him that he was a dean and, consequently, a man of great influence, and that he would attain a high position, saying, at the same time, that men, generally speaking, when they reach an elevated position and attain the objects of their ambition, forget easily what others have previously done for them, as also all past obligations and those from whom they received them—failing generally in the performance of their former promises, the dean assured him such should not be the case with him; saying, no matter to what eminence he might attain, he would not fail to do everything in his power to help his former friends, and the magician in particular.

"In this way they conversed until supper-time approached; and now, the covenant between them being completed, Don Illán said to the dean, that, in teaching him the art he desired to learn, it would be necessary for them to retire to some distant apartment, and, taking him by the hand, led him to a chamber. As they were quitting the dining-room, he called his housekeeper, desiring her to procure some partridges for their supper that night, but not to cook them until she had his special commands. Having said this, he sought the dean and conducted him to the entrance of a beautifully carved stone staircase, by which they descended a

considerable distance, appearing as if they had passed under the river Tagus, and, arriving at the bottom of the steps, they found a suite of rooms and a very elegant chamber, where were arranged the books and instruments of study; and, having here seated themselves, they were debating which should be the first books to read, when two men entered by the door and gave the dean a letter which had been sent to him by his uncle the archbishop, informing him that he was dangerously ill, and that if he wished to see him alive it would be requisite for him to come immediately. The dean was much moved by this news—partly on account of the illness of his uncle, but more through the fear of being obliged to abandon his favourite study, just commenced— so he wrote a respectful letter to his uncle the archbishop, which he sent by the same messengers. At the end of four days, other men arrived on foot bringing fresh letters to the dean, informing him that the archbishop was dead, and that all those interested in the welfare of the Church were desirous that he should succeed to his late uncle's dignity, telling him, at the same time, it was quite unnecessary for him to inconvenience himself by returning immediately, as his nomination would be better secured were he not present in the church. At the end of seven or eight days, two squires arrived, very richly dressed and accoutred, who, after kissing his hand, delivered to him the letters informing him that he had been appointed archbishop.

"When Don Illán heard this he told him he was much pleased that this good news had arrived during his stay in his house; and, as God had been so gracious to him, begged that the deanery now vacant might be given to his son.

"The archbishop elect replied, that he hoped Don Illán would allow him to name to the vacancy his own brother, saying, at the same time, that he would present him with some office in his own church with which his son would be contented, inviting, at the same time, both father and son to accompany him to Santiago.

"To this they consented; and all three departed for the city, where they were received with much honour. After they had resided there some time, there arrived one day messengers from

the pope bearing letters naming the former dean Bishop of To-
losa, permitting him at the same time to name whom he pleased to
succeed him in his vacant see.

"When Don Illán heard this he reminded him of his promise,
urging him to confer the appointment on his son. But the arch-
bishop again desired that he would allow him to name one of his
paternal uncles to succeed him. Don Illán replied, that, although
he felt he was unjustly treated, still, relying on the future accom-
plishment of his promise, he should let it be. The archbishop
thanked him, again renewed his promise of future services, and,
inviting Don Illán and his son to accompany him, they all set out
for Tolosa, where they were well received by the counts and
great men of the country.

"They had resided there about two years when messengers
again came from the pope with letters in which he announced to
the archbishop that he had named him cardinal, allowing him, as
before, to name his successor.

"On this occasion Don Illán went to him, and again urging that
many vacancies had taken place, to none of which he had named
his son, so that now he could plead no excuse, and he hoped the
cardinal would confer this last dignity on his son. But once more
the cardinal requested Don Illán would forgive his having be-
stowed the vacant see on one of his maternal uncles; saying he
was a very good old man, and proposing they should now depart
for Rome, where undoubtedly he would do for them all they
could desire. Don Illán complained very much; nevertheless, he
consented to accompany the cardinal to Rome. On their arrival
they were very well received by the other cardinals and the
entire court, and they lived there a long time. Don Illán daily
importuned the cardinal to confer some appointment on his son,
but he always found some excuse for not doing so.

"While they were yet at Rome, the pope died, and all the
cardinals assembled in conclave elected our cardinal pope.

"Then Don Illán came to him, saying, 'You have now no
excuse to offer for not fulfilling the promises you have hitherto
made me.'

"But the new pope told him not to importune him so much, as there was still time to think of him and his son.

"Don Illán now began to complain in earnest. 'You have,' said he, 'made me very many promises, not one of which you have performed.' He then recalled to his mind how earnestly he had pledged his word at their first interview to do all he could to help him, and never as yet had he done anything. 'I have no longer any faith in your words,' said Don Illán, 'nor do I now expect anything from you.'

"These expressions very much angered the pope, who replied, tartly, 'If I am again annoyed in this manner I will have you thrown into prison as a heretic and a sorcerer, for I know well that in Toledo, where you lived, you had no other means of support but by practising the art of necromancy.'

"When Don Illán saw how ill the pope had requited him for what he had done, he prepared to depart, the pope refusing to grant him wherewith to support himself on the road. 'Then,' said he to the pope, 'since I have nothing to eat, I must needs fall back upon the partridges I ordered for to-night's supper.' He then called out to his housekeeper, and ordered her to cook the birds for his supper.

"No sooner had he spoken, than the dean found himself again in Toledo, still Dean of Santiago, as on his arrival, but so overwhelmed with shame that he knew not what to say.

" 'How fortunate is it,' said Don Illán to him, 'that I have thus proved the intrinsic value of your promises in prosperity; for, as it is, I should have considered it a great misfortune had I allowed you to partake of the partridges.'

"And you, Count Lucanor, will now see how you ought to act towards the man, who, desiring your assistance, is so ungrateful. Risk not too much on the chance of your services being repaid at some future time, or you may anticipate the reward Don Illán received from the dean."

The Count found this to be very good advice, acted upon it, and was benefited.

And Don Juan, thinking this to be a very good example, had it written in this book and composed these verses, which say as follows:—

> Who pays thy kindness with ungratefulness,
> The more he has to give, he'll give the less.

✤ King Ben Abit and Queen Romaquía by Juan Manuel

This story, like the preceding one, is taken from the collection titled *Count Lucanor*.

THE COUNT conversed with Patronio one day in the following manner:—"There is a man," said he, "who has begged me frequently to assist him, and, whenever I have done so, he has always given me to understand how grateful he feels. Lately, he has again called upon me for aid, but I find if I do not do as he requires, he becomes angry, and does not fail to give me to understand, by his manner, that he has forgotten all his previous obligations. Now, as you are a man of good understanding, I beg you advise me how I should act towards this man."

"Count Lucanor," said Patronio, "it appears to me that what has occurred to you with this man resembles much that which happened to the King Ben Abit, of Seville, with the Queen Romaquía, his wife."

The Count begged him to recount what that was.

"My lord," said Patronio, "the King Abit, of Seville, was married to Romaquía, and he loved her better than anything in the world. She was a very virtuous woman, and the Moors recount many of her good acts. But in one thing she did not display much wisdom; this was, that she generally had some caprice or other which the king was always willing to gratify.

"One day, being in Cordova during the month of February, there happened to be (which was very unusual) a very heavy fall of snow. When Romaquía saw this she began to weep. The king, seeing her so afflicted, desired to know the cause of her grief.

" 'I weep,' said she, 'because I am not permitted to live in a country where we sometimes see snow.'

"The king, anxious to gratify her, ordered almond trees to be

planted on all the mountains surrounding Cordova, for, it being a very warm climate, snow is seldom or never seen there. But now, once a year, and that in the month of February, the almond trees came forth in full blossom, which, from their whiteness, made it appear as if there had been a fall of snow on the mountains, and was a source of great delight to the queen for a time.

"On another occasion, Romaquía being in her apartment, which overlooked the river, saw a woman without shoes or stockings kneading mud on the banks of the river for the purpose of making bricks. When Romaquía saw this she began to cry, which the king observing, begged to know the cause of her grief.

"She replied, 'It is because I am not free to do as I please; I cannot do as yonder woman is doing.'

"Then the king, in order to gratify her, ordered a lake at Cordova to be filled with rose-water in place of ordinary water; and, to produce mud, he had this filled with sugar, powdered cinnamon, and ginger, beautiful stones, amber, musk, and as many other fragrant spices and perfumes as could be procured; and, in place of straws, he ordered to be placed ready small sugar canes. Now when this lake was full of such mud, as you may imagine, the king informed Romaquía that now she might take off her shoes and stockings and enjoy herself by making as many bricks as she pleased.

"Another day, taking a fancy for something not immediately procurable, she began weeping as before. The king again entreated to know the cause of her grief.

" 'How can I refrain from tears,' she said, 'when you never do anything to please me?'

"The king, seeing that so much had been done to please and gratify her caprices, and feeling now at his wit's end, exclaimed, in Arabic, '*Ehu alenahac aten*,' which means, 'Not even the day of the mud.' That is to say, that, although all the rest had been forgotten, she might at least have remembered the mud he had prepared to humour her.

"And you, Count Lucanor, if you see, after having done so

much for this man, that he is ungrateful, and forgets all previous obligations because you are not disposed to do more, I would now advise you to have nothing more to do with him, for he might act in a manner injurious to you.

"But, above all things, I counsel you never to forget a previous obligation, although the person who was once your friend, and conferred it, is no longer disposed to do all you may require."

And the Count thought this very good advice, and, acting upon it, found the results favourable.

And Don Juan, considering it a very good example, caused it to be written in this book, and composed the following lines, which say:—

> Waste not your kindness on one
> Who heeds not the good you have done.

This story, and the following one, are taken from *Il Novellino*, or *Cento Novelle Antiche*. This collection of popular tales, written down in the late thirteenth century, is the first (or perhaps second) book of Italian stories, and is the oldest (or almost the oldest) example of Italian literary prose. Crude though the anecdotes are in structure and style, they preserve some of the qualities of everlasting humor. The translation is by Morris Bishop. Of several editions, most reliance has been placed on that edited by Guido Biagi (Florence, 1880).

IN ALEXANDRIA, the one in the Levant—for there are twelve Alexandrias which Alexander founded in the March before he died—well, in that Alexandria there are streets where the Saracens set up their cook-shops. And men seek out these streets to get fine foods and delicate, just as with us a man seeks out the location of the best cloths. One Monday a Saracen cook named Fabratto was standing in his shop and a poor Saracen came to his kitchen with a piece of bread in his hand. He had no money to buy the cook's wares; he held his bread over the pot to soak up the vapor that issued forth. When the bread was well suffused with the sweet smell of the cooking meat, he took a great bite and devoured it all.

Now Fabratto had done little trade that morning. He was in ill humor, thinking his luck was out. He seized the poor Saracen, and said: "Pay me for what you have taken of my property!"

Said the poor man: "I have taken none of your wares except steam."

"Then pay me for what you have taken!"

A dreadful dispute followed. And as the question at issue was strange and unprecedented, it reached the ears of the Sultan. To settle the novel problem he summoned the wisest Saracens to meet in counsel. He propounded the question. The wise men

began to argue and subtilize. Some maintained that the vapor did not belong to the cook; they produced many fine arguments. The steam escaping from a cooking-pot cannot return; it has no useful substance or property; the poor man need not pay. Others held that the vapor was still conjoined to the meat and under its seignory; the effluvium was engendered by the meat's essential property and it emerged therefrom; and the cook had the right to sell his skills; and whoever profits thereby must, according to custom, pay. But since the substance of steam is rare, the beneficiary need pay only rarely.

Many opinions were voiced. Finally a wise man laid down this judgment: "Since the cook sells the products of his skills and others are wont to buy them, do thou, O just Lord, decree that he be properly paid, according to his desire. If he is accustomed to receive hard money for the useful properties of his meats, now that he has sold vapor do thou, Sire, ring a coin, and rule that the payment be properly made by the sound issuing from that coin."

Thus judged the Sultan, and the decision was carried out.

This story, like the preceding one, is from *Il Novellino*. It was often retold by later writers, noteworthily, Chaucer. The translation is by Morris Bishop.

THERE WAS once a rich man and he had a very beautiful wife. And this man was mad about her, and he was very jealous. Now it pleased God that this man should be afflicted by a malady of the eyes, whereby he was stricken blind and could not tell the light from the dark. Now this man would not leave his wife's side; rather he kept her so close that she could not take a step away, and this through his fear that she would deceive him.

Well, it chanced that a fellow-townsman fell in love with the lady, and he saw no means of speaking to her, because the husband was forever at her side. And he showed the lady by signs and gestures that he was dying of love for her. The lady, seeing how he was enamored of her, was sorry for him. She said to him by signs: "You see how I am fixed! This man never leaves me!" Thus the good man did not know what to do or say, and he thought he would go crazy with all the signs and signals. He could find no other way of encountering the lady.

But the lady, seeing the state and actions of the gentleman, was filled with pity, and she thought of ways to aid him. She had a long tube of cane made, and she put it to the gentleman's ear, and thus she talked to him, to keep her husband from overhearing. She said to the gentleman: "I am very grieved for your sake; and I have thought of a way to oblige you. Go into our garden, and climb up into a certain pear tree loaded with very fine pears. And wait for me there, and I will come up to you."

The good man went straightway to the garden, climbed the

pear tree, and awaited the lady. Soon afterward she entered the garden, being desirous of contenting the good man. And she said to her husband, who was forever by her side: "How I should like to have some of those pears on the tree! How good they look!"

"Call someone to pick them for you," said her husband.

"I'll pick them myself!" said the lady. "Otherwise they would give me no pleasure."

Then the lady began to climb the tree, and the husband stood at the foot while she mounted up; and he embraced the trunk so that no one could climb up after. Then the lady got up in the tree where her friend was waiting, and the two enjoyed great solace; and the whole tree shook so that some pears fell down on the husband's back. He said: "What are you doing, woman? Why don't you come down? You are shaking down all the pears!"

She said: "I wanted the pears from a certain branch; I couldn't get at them otherwise."

Now you must know that our Lord God and Saint Peter observed all this. And Saint Peter said to our Lord God: "Don't you see the trick that lady is playing on her husband? Alas! Command that the husband gain his sight, so that he may see what his wife is doing!" And the Lord God said: "I tell you, Peter, that as soon as he gains his sight the lady will find some explanation or excuse. And so I will that he shall regain his sight; and you will hear what she will find to say."

Then the husband's eyes were opened, and he looked up and saw what the lady was doing. He said to her: "What are you doing with that man? This is no honor for you or for me; it is woman's treachery!"

And the lady promptly answered: "If I had not done what I did with this man, you would never have seen the light!" When the husband heard this he was satisfied.

Thus you see what women's fidelity is, and how readily they can find excuses.

❧ Fra Cipolla
by Giovanni Boccaccio

This is an example of Boccaccio's humorous anti-clerical-
ism. The translation, from *The Decameron*, is by John Payne
(London: privately printed, 1895).

ⒺACH OF the company being now quit of his story, Dioneo
perceived that it rested with him to tell; whereupon, with-
out awaiting more formal commandment, he began on this wise:
"Charming ladies, albeit I am privileged to speak of that which
most liketh me, I purpose not to-day to depart from the matter
whereof you have all very aptly spoken; but, ensuing in your
footsteps, I mean to show you how cunningly a friar of the order
of Saint Anthony, by name Fra Cipolla, contrived with a sudden
shift to extricate himself from a snare which had been set for him
by two young men; nor should it irk you if, for the complete
telling of the story, I enlarge somewhat in speaking, an you con-
sider the sun, which is yet amiddleward the sky.

Certaldo, as you may belike have heard, is a burgh of Val
d'Elsa situate in our county, which, small though it be, was once
inhabited by gentlemen and men of substance; and thither, for
that he found good pasture there, one of the friars of the order of
St. Anthony was long used to resort once a year, to get in the
alms bestowed by simpletons upon him and his brethren. His
name was Fra Cipolla and he was gladly seen there, no less, belike,
for his name's sake* than for other reasons, seeing that these parts
produce onions that are famous throughout all Tuscany. This Fra
Cipolla was little of person, red-haired and merry of countenance,
the jolliest rascal in the world, and to boot, for all he was no

* *Cipolla* means onion.

scholar, he was so fine a talker and so ready of wit that those who knew him not would not only have esteemed him a great rhetorician, but had avouched him to be Tully himself or may be Quintilian; and he was gossip or friend or well-wisher* to well nigh every one in the country.

One August among others he betook himself thither according to his wont, and on a Sunday morning, all the goodmen and goodwives of the villages around being come to hear mass at the parish church, he came forward, whenas it seemed to him time, and said, "Gentlemen and ladies, it is, as you know, your usance to send every year to the poor of our lord Baron St. Anthony of your corn and of your oats, this little and that much, according to his means and his devoutness, to the intent that the blessed St. Anthony may keep watch over your beeves and asses and swine and sheep; and beside this, you use to pay, especially such of you as are inscribed into our company, that small due which is payable once a year. To collect these I have been sent by my superior, to wit, my lord abbot; wherefore, with the blessing of God, you shall, after none,† whenas you hear the bells ring, come hither without the church, where I will make preachment to you after the wonted fashion and you shall kiss the cross; moreover, for that I know you all to be great devotees of our lord St. Anthony, I will, as an especial favor, show you a very holy and goodly relic, which I myself brought aforetime from the holy lands beyond seas; and that is one of the Angel Gabriel's feathers, which remained in the Virgin Mary's chamber, whenas he came to announce to her in Nazareth." This said, he broke off and went on with his mass.

Now, when he said this, there were in the church, among many others, two roguish young fellows, hight one Giovanni del Bragoniera and the other Biagio Pizzini, who, after laughing with one another awhile over Fra Cipolla's relic, took counsel together, for all they were great friends and cronies of his, to play him some

* The term "well-wisher" (*benivogliente*), when understood in relation to a woman, is generally equivalent (at least with the older Italian writers) to "lover" (translator's note). † None: about 3:00 P.M.—Ed.

trick in the matter of the feather in question. Accordingly, having learned that he was to dine that morning with a friend of his in the burgh, they went down into the street, as soon as they knew him to be at table, and betook themselves to the inn where he had alighted, purposing that Biagio should hold his servant in parley, whilst Giovanni should search his baggage for the feather aforesaid, whatever it might be, and carry it off, to see what he should say to the people of the matter.

Fra Cipolla had a servant, whom some called Guccio Balena,* others Guccio Imbratta† and yet others Guccio Porco‡ and who was such a scurvy knave that Lippo Topo§ never wrought his like, inasmuch as his master used oftentimes to jest of him with his cronies and say, "My servant hath in him nine defaults, such that, were one of them in Solomon or Aristotle or Seneca, it would suffice to mar all their worth, all their wit and all their sanctity. Consider, then, what a man he must be, who hath all nine of them and in whom there is neither worth nor wit nor sanctity." Being questioned whiles what were these nine defaults and having put them into doggerel rhyme, he would answer, "I will tell you. He's a liar, a sloven, a slugabed; disobedient, neglectful, ill bred; o'erweening, foul-spoken, a dunderhead; beside which he hath divers other peccadilloes, whereof it booteth not to speak. But what is most laughable of all his fashions is that, wherever he goeth, he is still for taking a wife and hiring a house; for, having a big black greasy beard, himseemeth he is so exceeding handsome and agreeable that he conceiteth himself all the women who see him fall in love with him, and if you let him alone, he would run after them all till he collapsed. Sooth to say, he is of great assistance to me, for that none can ever seek to speak with me so secretly but he must needs hear his share; and if it chance that I be questioned of aught, he is so fearful, lest I should not know how to answer, that he straightway answereth for me both Ay and No, as he judgeth sortable."

* I.e., whale. † I.e., dirt. ‡ I.e., hog.
§ A painter of Boccaccio's time.

Now Fra Cipolla, in leaving him at the inn, had bidden him look well that none touched his gear, and more particularly his saddle-bags, for that therein were the sacred things. But Guccio, who was fonder of the kitchen than the nightingale of the green boughs, especially if he scented some serving-wench there, and who had seen in that of the inn a gross fat cookmaid, undersized and ill-made, with a pair of paps that showed like two manure-baskets and a face like a cadger's, all sweaty, greasy and smoky, leaving Fra Cipolla's chamber and all his gear to care for themselves, swooped down upon the kitchen, even as the vulture swoopeth upon carrion, and seating himself by the fire, for all it was August, entered into discourse with the wench in question, whose name was Nuta, telling her that he was by rights a gentleman and had more than nine millions of florins, beside that which he had to give others, which was rather more than less, and that he could do and say God only knew what. Moreover, without regard to his bonnet, whereon was grease enough to have seasoned the caldron of Altopascio,* and his doublet all torn and pieced and enamelled with filth about the collar and under the armpits, with more spots and patches of divers colors than ever had Turkey or India stuffs, and his shoes all broken and hose unsewn, he told her, as he had been the Sieur de Châtillon, that he meant to clothe her and trick her out anew and deliver her from the wretchedness of abiding with others, and bring her to hope of better fortune, if without any great wealth in possession, and many other things, which, for all he delivered them very earnestly, all turned to wind and came to nought, as did most of his enterprises.

The two young men, accordingly, found Guccio busy about Nuta, whereat they were well pleased, for that it spared them half their pains, and entering Fra Cipolla's chamber, which they found open, the first thing that came under their examination was the saddle-bags wherein was the feather. In these they found, envel-

* Said by the commentators to have been an abbey where they made cheese-soup for all comers twice a week; hence "the caldron of Altopascio" became a proverb (translator's note).

oped in a great taffetas wrapper, a little casket and opening this
latter, discovered therein a parrot's tail-feather, which they con-
cluded must be that which the friar had promised to show the
people of Certaldo. And certes he might lightly cause it to be
believed in those days, for that the refinements of Egypt had not
yet made their way save into a small part of Tuscany, as they
have since done in very great abundance, to the undoing of all
Italy; and wherever they may have been some little known, in
those parts they were well nigh altogether unknown of the
inhabitants; nay, the rude honesty of the ancients yet enduring
there, not only had they never set eyes on a parrot, but were far
from having ever heard tell of such a bird. The young men, then,
rejoiced at finding the feather, laid hands on it and not to leave
the casket empty, filled it with some coals they saw in a corner of
the room and shut it again. Then, putting all things in order as
they had found them, they made off in high glee with the feather,
without having been seen, and began to await what Fra Cipolla
should say, when he found the coals in place thereof.

The simple men and women who were in the church, hearing
that they were to see the Angel Gabriel's feather after none,
returned home, as soon as mass was over, and neighbor telling it
to neighbor and gossip to gossip, no sooner had they all dined
than so many men and women flocked to the burgh that it would
scarce hold them, all looking eagerly to see the aforesaid feather.
Fra Cipolla, having well dined and after slept awhile, arose a little
after none and hearing of the great multitude of country folk
come to see the feather, sent to bid Guccio Imbratta come thither
with the bells and bring his saddle-bags. Guccio, tearing himself
with difficulty away from the kitchen and Nuta, betook himself
with the things required to the appointed place, whither coming,
out of breath, for that the water he had drunken had made his
belly swell amain, he repaired, by his master's commandment, to
the church door and fell to ringing the bells lustily.

When all the people were assembled there, Fra Cipolla, without
observing that aught of his had been meddled with, began his
preachment and said many words anent his affairs; after which,

thinking to come to the showing of the Angel Gabriel's feather, he first recited the Confiteor* with the utmost solemnity and let kindle a pair of flambeaux; then, pulling off his bonnet, he delicately unfolded the taffetas wrapper and brought out the casket. Having first pronounced certain ejaculations in praise and commendation of the Angel Gabriel and of his relic, he opened the casket and seeing it full of coals, suspected not Guccio Balena of having played him this trick, for that he knew him not to be man enough; nor did he curse him for having ill kept watch lest others should do it, but silently cursed himself for having committed to him the care of his gear, knowing him, as he did, to be negligent, disobedient, careless and forgetful.

Nevertheless, without changing color, he raised his eyes and hands to heaven and said, so as to be heard of all, "O God, praised be still Thy puissance!" Then, shutting the casket and turning to the people, "Gentlemen and ladies," quoth he, "you must know that, whilst I was yet very young, I was despatched by my superior to those parts where the sun riseth and it was expressly commanded me that I should seek till I found the Privileges of Porcellana, which, though they cost nothing to seal, are much more useful to others than to us. On this errand I set out from Venice and passed through Borgo de' Greci, whence, riding through the kingdom of Algarve and Baldacca, I came to Parione, and from there, not without thirst, I came after awhile into Sardinia. But what booteth it to set out to you in detail all the lands explored by me? Passing the straits of San Giorgio, I came into Truffia† and Buffia,‡ countries much inhabited and with great populations, and thence into the land of Menzogna,§ where I found great plenty of our brethren and of friars of other religious orders, who all went about those parts, shunning unease for the love of God, recking little of others' travail, whenas they saw their own advantage to ensue, and spending none other money than such as was uncoined.|| Thence I passed into the land

* Confiteor: confession of sins.—Ed. † I.e., Nonsense-land.
‡ I.e., Land of Tricks or Cozenage. § I.e., Falsehood, Lie-land.
|| I.e., paying their way with fine words, instead of coin.

of the Abruzzi, where the men and women go in clogs over the mountains, clothing the swine in their own guts,* and a little farther I found folk who carried bread on sticks and wine in bags. From this I came to the Mountains of the Bachi, where all the waters run down hill; and in brief, I made my way so far inward that I won at last even to India Pastinaca,† where I swear to you, by the habit I wear on my back, that I saw hedge-bills‡ fly, a thing incredible to whoso hath not seen it. But of this Maso del Saggio will confirm me, whom I found there a great merchant, cracking walnuts and selling the shells by retail.

"Being unable to find that which I went seeking, for that thence one goeth thither by water, I turned back and arrived in those holy countries, where, in summer-years, cold bread is worth four farthings a loaf and the hot goeth for nothing. There I found the venerable father my lord Blamemenot Anitpleaseyou, the very worshipful Patriarch of Jerusalem, who, for reverence of the habit I have still worn of my lord Baron St. Anthony, would have me sell all the holy relics that he had about him and which were so many that, an I sought to recount them all to you, I should not come to an end thereof in several miles. However, not to leave you disconsolate, I will tell you some thereof. First, he showed me the finger of the Holy Ghost, as whole and sound as ever it was, and the forelock of the seraph that appeared to St. Francis and one of the nails of the Cherubim and one of the ribs of the Verbum Caro§ Get-thee-to-the-windows and some of the vestments of the Holy Catholic Faith and divers rays of the star that appeared to the Three Wise Men in the East and a vial of the sweat of St. Michael, whenas he fought with the devil, and the jawbone of the death of St. Lazarus and others. And for that I made him a free gift of the Steeps of Monte Morello in the

* I.e., making sausages of them.

† *Bachi:* drones or maggots. *Pastinaca* means "parsnip" and is a meaningless addition of Fra Cipolla's fashion.

‡ A play of words upon the primary meaning (winged things) of the word *pennate,* hedge-bills, or pruning-hooks.

§ I.e., the Word [made] flesh. "Get-thee-to-the-windows" is only a patter tag (translator's note).

vernacular and of some chapters of the Caprezio, which he had long gone seeking, he made me a sharer in his holy relics and gave me one of the teeth of the Holy Rood and somewhat of the sound of the bells of Solomon's Temple in a vial and the feather of the Angel Gabriel, whereof I have already bespoken you, and one of the pattens of St. Gherardo da Villa Magna, which not long since at Florence I gave to Gherardo di Bonsi, who hath a particular devotion for that saint; and he gave me also of the coals wherewith the most blessed martyr St. Lawrence was roasted; all which things I devoutly brought home with me and yet have. True it is that my superior hath never suffered me to show them till such time as he should be certified if they were the very things or not. But now that, by certain miracles performed by them and by letters received from the patriarch, he hath been made certain of this, he hath granted me leave to show them; and I, fearing to trust them to others, still carry them with me.

"Now I carry the Angel Gabriel's feather, so it may not be marred, in one casket, and the coals wherewith St. Lawrence was roasted in another, the which are so like one to other, that it hath often happened to me to take one for the other, and so hath it betided me at this present, for that, thinking to bring hither the casket wherein was the feather, I have brought that wherein are the coals. The which I hold not to have been an error; nay, meseemeth certain that it was God's will and that He Himself placed the casket with the coals in my hands, especially now I mind me that the feast of St. Lawrence is but two days hence; wherefore God, willing that, by showing you the coals wherewith he was roasted, I should rekindle in your hearts the devotion it behoveth you have for him, caused me take, not the feather, as I purposed, but the blessed coals extinguished by the sweat of that most holy body. So, O my blessed children, put off your bonnets and draw near devoutly to behold them; but first I would have you know that whoso is scored with these coals, in the form of the sign of the cross, may rest assured, for the whole year to come, that fire shall not touch him but he shall feel it."

Having thus spoken, he opened the casket, chanting the while a

canticle in praise of St. Lawrence, and showed the coals, which after the simple multitude had awhile beheld with reverent admiration, they all crowded about Fra Cipolla and making him better offerings than they were used, besought him to touch them withal. Accordingly, taking the coals in hand, he fell to making the biggest crosses for which he could find room upon their white smocks and doublets and upon the veils of the women, avouching that how much soever the coals diminished in making these crosses, they after grew again in the casket, as he had many a time proved. On this wise he crossed all the people of Certaldo, to his no small profit, and thus, by his ready wit and presence of mind, he baffled those who, by taking the feather from him, had thought to baffle him and who, being present at his preachment and hearing the rare shift employed by him and from how far he had taken it and with what words, had so laughed that they thought to have cracked their jaws. Then, after the common folk had departed, they went up to him and with all the mirth in the world discovered to him that which they had done and after restored him his feather, which next year stood him in as good stead as the coals had done that day.

❧ A Father's Wise Counsel
by Franco Sacchetti

Franco Sacchetti, a Florentine, lived from about 1335 to 1400. In his later years he amused himself by setting down, with admirable realism and humor, a host of current tales and anecdotes, under the title *Trecentonovelle*. This sample, and the four following, appear in several modern Italian editions, notably one published by Bompiani (Milan, 1946) and one by Rizzoli (Milan, 1957). They are translated by Morris Bishop.

NOT LONG since there was in Siena a rich citizen with only one son, a lad of twenty. As his death neared, he gave his son much good advice, and in especial these three capital counsels. The first was, not to frequent anyone to the point of boring him; the second was, that if he had bought something and could sell at a profit, to do so, and not begrudge the purchaser any further profit; and the third, that when he should come to marriage, to pick a girl from near by, and if he couldn't find one near by, rather to seek one in his own province than from far away. The son took these counsels to heart. And the father died.

This young man had long been in relations with one of the Forteguerras. This gentleman had always lived beyond his means, and he had several daughters to dispose of. His parents were constantly complaining of his spendthrift ways, without result.

One day Forteguerra had prepared a fine dinner for the young man and other friends. His parents objected violently, saying: "What is the matter with you, idiot? Are you trying to outdo that rich young man and stage banquets, when you have daughters to provide for?"

They shouted him down, until in despair he went home and retrieved all the food in the kitchen. He took an onion, and put it on the table laid out for the meal, and gave orders that if the

young man came to dine, to tell him to eat the onion—that was all there was—and that he, Forteguerra, was not dining at home.

When the dinner hour came the youth arrived. Entering the hall, he asked the maid for his host. She replied that he was not there, he was dining out; but he had left for his guest, if he should turn up, the onion—that was all there was. The young man was reminded by this dainty of his father's first counsel, and recognized that he had observed it very ill. He took the onion, went home, tied it up with a string and hung it from the ceiling above his customary seat at table.

Shortly after this he had a chance to sell for ninety florins a riding-horse for which, a few months earlier, he had paid fifty. He refused the offer, holding out for a hundred florins. And one night the horse developed a colic and died. Thinking this over, the young man realized that he had not heeded his father's second counsel; he cut off the horse's tail and hung it from the ceiling beside the onion.

It happened then that, being in the mood to marry, he could find no bride to his fancy in his neighborhood nor in all Siena. He cast about in various towns, and finally came to Pisa. There he fell in with a notary who had been in business in Siena, and whom he had known as a friend of his father's. The notary greeted him very warmly and asked what affairs brought him to Pisa. The young man told him that he was looking about for a pretty wife, but he hadn't found any to his liking in all Siena.

The notary said: "If that's the way of it, God has certainly sent you here. You're a lucky dog! I know a young girl, one of the Lanfranchi, the prettiest girl you ever saw! I should be overjoyed to promote such a match."

The young man liked the idea, and was impatient to meet her. Matters were arranged; after he saw her, he had the marriage contract drawn up. It was settled that she should accompany him to Siena for the ceremony. Now the notary was a creature of the Lanfranchi, and the girl was no better than she should be, and had had affairs with certain young men of Pisa, and so she had never been able to marry. Hence the notary attempted to get her off

her parents' hands and pin her on the Siena youth. Arrangements were made for a lady's maid—or perhaps a procuress—a light woman of the neighborhood, named Monna Bartolommea, who often went off on wild parties with the lady. And a travel-party was organized, including a young man, one of those who had often made love to the lady. So all of them went off with the betrothed pair toward Siena, where preparations were made to receive them.

On the road, the displaced gallant felt as if he were on the way to the gallows, as he thought the lady would be married in a foreign city, and he would have to return to Pisa without her. And so deep was his distress and his sighing that the groom noticed both him and her; for as the proverb well says, you can't hide love or a cough. So, with his eyes opened, he became suspicious. He learned who the young gentleman was, and realized that the notary had deceived and betrayed him. So, on arriving at Staggia, he slyly said that he wanted to dine betimes, because he planned to leave early in the morning for Siena, to make the necessary preparations. He said this at such a moment that the gallant would overhear it.

The bedrooms of the inn were all in a line. The groom had one, the bride and her maid another, and in the next were the gallant and another man, who had also heard the Sienese gentleman's intention, and had made a deal with the maid for the morning hours. Thus they went to bed. And in the morning, about an hour before dawn, the groom got up to go to Siena, as he had announced. He went downstairs, mounted his horse, and rode about four bow-shots toward Siena. Then he turned about and returned very quietly to the inn. Tying his horse to a ring, he ascended the stairs. At the door of the lady's room he stood silently on watch. He could hear that the young man was inside. Pushing the door, which was ajar, he entered, and softly approached the chest at the bed's head, looking for some possession of the man in bed. And by chance he found there his under-breeches. The occupants of the bed either kept silence out of fear or they heard nothing at all. So the good man put the breeches

under his arm, descended the stairs, mounted his horse, and was away to Siena. And when he got home he hung the breeches from the ceiling beside the onion and the horse's tail.

When the lady and her lover got up in the morning at Staggia, the gallant, not finding his underbreeches, mounted his horse without them, and proceeded with the party to Siena. When they reached the house where the wedding was to be held, they dismounted. All assembled for a lunch, under the three objects hanging from the ceiling. The bridegroom was asked what these dependent objects signified. He replied: "I'll tell you; and I ask the attention of all. My father died a little while ago, and he bequeathed me three bits of advice. The first was this [and he told the story]. And so I took the onion and hung it up there. And his second counsel I disobeyed, and when my horse died I cut off his tail and hung it up. And the third counsel was to take a wife from my own neighborhood. And far from that, I went all the way to Pisa and picked out this girl, thinking she would be what unwed maidens are. And on our journey that young man sitting there went to bed with her in the inn. And I slipped into their room, found his underbreeches, and brought them along, and hung them from my ceiling. And if you don't believe me, look for them—he hasn't got them on." And that was the fact. "And so, when lunch is over, take care of that lady, for not only will I never sleep with her, but I intend never to see her again. And as for the notary who advised the match and drew up the marriage contract, tell him to use it for book-linings."

So that was the way of it. The bridal party went glumly home, and the lady, in time, found a number of mates, and so did the groom.

❧ The Rustic Ambassadors
by Franco Sacchetti

For a note on the author see the preceding selection.

WHEN BISHOP GUIDO ruled in Arezzo, the Communes of the Casentino appointed two ambassadors to make certain pleas to him. They were informed of what they were to tell the Bishop; and late one evening they were ordered to be on their way next morning. So they went to their homes and packed their saddle-bags, and in the morning they started off on their journey.

After they had gone a few miles, one said to the other: "Do you have our mission well fixed in mind?"

The other said he couldn't remember it.

And the first: "But I was depending on you!"

"And I on you!"

They looked at each other, exclaiming: "This is a fine business! What are we going to do?"

Said the first: "Look here; we'll be stopping at the inn for lunch soon, and we'll go off by ourselves and meditate, and certainly we will call it to mind."

"That's right."

And riding along and pondering, they arrived, at about 9:00 A.M., at the inn where they were to lunch. Going over and over the matter until they were ready to sit down at table, they could not recall a word of their charge.

At lunch a very fine wine was set before them. The ambassadors, who were much more retentive of wine than of their commission, began to punish the bottle. They drank and redrank, toasted and retoasted, till when they had finished lunch, far from recalling their mission, they had no idea where they were, and so

went off to sleep. After a good nap, they woke up with a hangover. Said one to the other:

"Now do you remember what we were supposed to do?"

"No more than you do! What are we going to do? And say?"

"Let's stay here for the rest of the day. And tonight—you know that one thinks more clearly at night—we are bound to remember it."

They agreed on that, and remained there the rest of the day, frequently seeking inspiration in the bottle. Their dinner was more liquid than solid. When it was over, they could hardly communicate with each other. They went to bed, and all night they snored like pigs.

In the morning they got up. The first said: "Now what will we do?"

"I'll be damned!" said the second. "Since all last night I couldn't remember anything, I don't think I ever will."

"By the Book, we're in fine shape! I don't know how it is, whether it was that wine or something else, but I never slept so sound, without waking a minute, as I did last night in this inn."

"What the devil!" said the other. "Let's climb on our horses and get going. Perhaps on the way we'll still remember."

So they set off. From time to time one would say to the other: "Do you remember?" "Not me!" "Me neither!"

Thus they arrived in Arezzo, and went to the inn. They took a private room and sat with their heads in their hands, thinking. But they couldn't remember a thing. Finally one of them, almost desperate, said: "Well, let's go. May God help us."

"And what shall we say, if we don't know what to say?"

"Well, we can't leave things in this state."

So they made the plunge, and went to see the Bishop. Arriving before him, they made deep reverences, without broaching any matter. The Bishop, who was sharp enough, rose from his seat, approached them, and took their hands, saying: "Welcome, my sons! What news do you bring?"

The first looked at the second, and said: "You tell him."

"No, you tell him."

Silence. Then said the first: "Lord Bishop, we were sent to your lordship as ambassadors by your servants in the Casentino; and we who were picked out are just everyday fellows, and they gave us our commission in the evening in a great hurry, and somehow either they couldn't tell us straight or we couldn't understand them properly. We earnestly beg you to accept the humble homage of those Communes and their people, and may those who sent us perish by the sword, and we too who came here."

The wise Bishop put his hands on their shoulders and said: "Now go and tell my sons that I always intend to do all I can for their welfare. And so that henceforth they may not be put to the expense of sending ambassadors, let them, whenever they want anything, write to me; and I shall reply by letter."

Then they took their leave and departed. And on the road one said to the other: "Let's make sure the same thing doesn't happen to us as on our journey here."

"What do we have to bear in mind?"

"Just this—we will have to tell what we proposed and what answer we got. If our people in the Casentino should know how we forgot our charge, and if we should appear before them as so forgetful, they would never send us out again as ambassadors or give us any other job."

The other man was slyer. He said: "Leave it to me. I will say that after we delivered our ambassadorial message to the Bishop, he graciously offered to be always concerned, in everything, for our welfare; and of his great love he added that, to save expense, whenever we should need him we should write him a letter, for our peace and repose, and omit the embassies."

"Well thought and spoken!" said the other. "Let us get going, in order to reach that wine as soon as possible."

Spurring on, they arrived at the inn. A boy came out to hold their stirrups. They did not ask for the host, nor what was for lunch; their first word to ask how the wine was.

"Better than ever!" said the boy.

Thus they fortified themselves the second time no worse than

the first. And since many tipplers had gathered from the countryside to sample that wine, before they left the level of drink sank so far that the barrel was rolled away. The ambassadors, grieving thereat, went on their way. They presented themselves to the man who had dispatched them, remembering the lie agreed upon better than the truth of the first instance, and said that before the Bishop they had made a splendid harangue, giving the impression that one had been Tully and the other Quintilian. They were much commended, and thenceforth they had many fine jobs, most often as treasurers and comptrollers.

A note on the author appears at the head of a preceding story.

THERE WAS a gentleman in Florence, one of the Bardi family, very short of stature. He had had little or no practice in the use of arms, and even very little in horsemanship. He was elected Mayor of Padua; and having accepted, he began to collect the martial harness suitable for such an office. And needing a helmet with crest, he took counsel of his relations, to find what he ought to do about it. The relations met together and concluded thus: "He is very slight and undersized; and so it seems to us that we should do the contrary of ladies' practice; for if they are too tiny they add inches under their feet; and we shall raise him up and exalt him on top of his head."

They found a crest representing half a bear, rampant, with his claws defiantly outthrust, and bearing an inscription reading: "Trifle not with the bear; he bites!" So this crest he obtained, and all his gear. And when the time came, the cavalier left Florence, with great dignity, to assume his office.

Passing through Bologna, he displayed his magnificence. Then he proceeded to Ferrara, and there made a greater show, feeling that he was on the verge of entering on his high office. He had brought out his robes and helmet and the great bear-crest. And crossing the Piazza del Marchese, he found many soldiers of the Marchese in the piazza. And as he was passing among them a German knight, seeing the bear-crest, started up from his seat and began to shout arrogantly in his language, saying: "Who is this fellow wearing my crest?" And he ordered his squire to bring his

horse and armor, since he intended to fight the usurper of his crest and to brand him as a traitor.

This German knight was a very doughty fellow, big like a giant falcon. His name was Schindegger.* Some bystanders, German and Italian, seeing his fury, gathered round to calm him down, without effect. Two of them, at his behest, went to the Florentine's inn to caution him to abandon that bear-crest, or he would have to fight Messer Schindegger, who alone had right to the crest. The Florentine, ill versed in such matters, replied that as for him he had not come to Ferrara to fight, but just to pass through on his way to assume the mayoralty of Padua, and that he regarded everyone as his friend and brother, and that was all there was to it.

When the envoys returned to Messer Schindegger with this reply, he was already fully armed and making a mighty uproar and commanding that his charger be brought. The envoys begged him to be patient; they would make another effort for understanding. They returned to the inn and said to the Florentine: "We have done the best we could, but the German knight is in such a fury that he is fully armed, and now, we think, he is already mounted."

The Cavaliere de' Bardi said: "He can arm himself all he pleases, but I am no fighting man, and I don't intend to do battle." And after much parleying he finally said: "All right; put the matter on a money basis, and talk no more of honor. If he is willing for me to continue on my way, as I came into town, I will set off immediately. If he means that I shouldn't wear his crest, I swear on all the Holy Gospels that it is mine. I got it in Florence from Luchino the painter, and it cost me five florins. If he wants it, let him send me five florins, and take the crest."

The envoys returned therewith to Messer Schindegger. When he heard their report he called a servant, and had him give them five ducats. And he said to the servant: "Go with them and get the

* Schindegger suggests Italian *scindere*, to split.—Ed.

crest." And so they did. They delivered the five florins, and the Florentine took them and handed over the crest. And the envoys brought it, covered with a cloak, to Messer Schindegger, who acted as if he had conquered a city. And the Mayor, without his crest for the entrance into Padua, had a search made through all Ferrara for a helm he could wear instead of the bear-crest. By good luck he found in a painter's atelier a crest of a half-monkey, dressed in yellow, with a sword in his hand. And when he had obtained this covertly, one of his staff said to him: "You have certainly had a bit of luck! Take the sword out of the monkey's hand, and put a red pick-axe there, and there are your arms!"

The Mayor liked the idea, and so it was done. It cost altogether about a florin. And the scraping and repainting cost him another; and in all his equipment these become his arms forthwith. Thus he had three florins left; and the German had his bear.

However, if he had followed the precedent of another in a similar case, perhaps he would have done even better. That man had a crest of a horse's head, and a German informed him that the crest was his own, and that the usurper must get rid of it or fight. And the man said: "What is the crest that the valiant gentleman bears?"

"A horse's head," said the German.

"Well, mine is a mare's head; there is no conflict." This satisfied the German; and thus was avoided the battle, for which the man had no taste at all.

✨ Sacchetti and the Astrologer
by Franco Sacchetti

See the note under *A Father's Wise Counsel*, our first selection from Sacchetti.

A FEW YEARS AGO, happening to be in Genoa, I found myself in the Merchants' Square with a group of clever fellows from all over. Among them were Messer Giovanni dell' Agnello, exiled from Pisa, and some of his relatives, and a number of Florentines banished from their city, and some Lucchesi banned from Lucca, and Sienese refugees from Siena. There were even a few Genoese. We fell into talk on such subjects as exiles often vainly discuss—that is, the news, and lies, and hopes for the future. And from that we came to astrology. On this theme an ex-Pisan named Fazio talked very brilliantly, saying that by the stars he could tell in what year any outcast from home was destined to return there, and insisting that he could see all this prophetically. I took the opposite side, saying that neither he nor anyone else could be assured of the future. He countered, mocking me with all the airs of Ptolemy or King Alfonso of Castile, as if all that was destined to happen was laid out before his eyes, and as if I could not even see the present.

So I said to him: "Fazio, you are the greatest of astrologasters. But now answer me truly in the face of this gathering: which is easier to know, things past or things to come?"

"Obviously," said Fazio, "one remembers readily the things he has seen; but things to come are not to be learned so easily."

"All right," said I. "Now let's see how you know past things, which are so easy. Tell me what you did a year ago today."

Fazio meditated. I went on: "Now tell me what you did six months ago today." And he cudgeled his brains.

"Well, make it easier. What was the weather like three months ago today?"

Trying to think, he gazed about with rolling eyes. Said I: "You needn't look for help. Where were you two months ago at this hour?"

He became more and more confused. I plucked at his cloak and said: "Stand still, and look at me. What ship came to harbor a month ago? And what ship sailed?"

He stood as if stupefied. I went on: "What are you staring at? Tell me, two weeks ago today did you eat at home or somewhere else?"

"Wait a minute," he said.

"Why wait? I don't want to wait. What did you do a week ago at this hour?"

"Give me time to think," said he.

"Why give time to someone who knows the future? What did you eat four days ago today?"

"All right; I'll tell you—"

"Well, why don't you tell me?"

"You're in such a hurry!"

"What do you mean, hurry?" said I. "Tell me now, now: what did you eat yesterday morning? Why don't you tell me?"

But he fell totally silent. Seeing how confused he was, I took hold of his cloak and said: "I'll bet you ten to one that you don't know if you're awake or asleep."

"By the Book!" he answered. "I'd be glad if I didn't know I'm awake!"

"I tell you you don't know, and you could never prove it."

"What do you mean? Don't I know I'm awake?"

"So it seems to you," said I. "And so it seems to a man asleep."

"You have too many sophisms in your head," said the Pisan.

"Sophisms indeed! I am telling simple, natural truths. But you are chasing will-o'-the-wisps. Let me ask you something else. Did you ever eat medlars?"

"Of course. Thousands of times."

"Good! How many pits has the medlar?"

"I don't know," he said. "I never noticed."

"If you don't know that, such an obvious thing, how will you ever know the secrets of the firmament? Let me go on: how many years have you lived in your house?"

"I've been there six and a half years."

"How often do you go up and down stairs in a day?"

"Sometimes four times. Or six; or eight."

"Now tell me, how many steps in your staircase?"

"I surrender!" said the Pisan. And I: "You are quite right that I have won the argument, and that you and many other stargazers with your wild fads and crotchets want to astrologize and foretell fate; and you are all poorer than grindstones—though I have always heard people say that if they could foretell the future they would be rich. Now see what a good fortune-teller you are, and behold your wealth!"

And it certainly is true that all those who go moonraking, spending their nights on the roof, like cats, have their eyes so fixed on the sky that they lose hold on earth, and they're always stony broke.

So that's how I confounded Fazio of Pisa with my novel reasoning. And when some worthy gentlemen asked me if I had found in some book the arguments with which I had conquered Fazio, I said yes; I had found them in a book I always carry with me, called the Book of Common Sense. And that pleased them mightily.

❧ The Blind Man of Orvieto
by Franco Sacchetti

This is the last of five examples from Sacchetti.

THERE WAS a barber in Orvieto named Cola, who lost his sight when about thirty. As he was a poor man who could no longer ply his trade, or any other, he was forced to beg for alms. It was his practice to take his stand every day before the door of the chief church of Orvieto, at least until mid-morning. There, for God's love, he received so much charity from most of the faithful that before long he had a hundred florins stored up. He kept these hidden in a little bag under his rags.

The money kept coming in, more than he had ever made with razor and scissors. And one morning, when he thought the church was totally empty, it occurred to him to go behind the door and hide the purse with the hundred florins under a loose tile of the flooring, which he had previously noticed. He put his idea into effect, thinking there was no one in the church to see him. But by chance a cheesemonger named Juccio had remained in adoration of Saint John Chrysostom—which means Saint Goldmouth. And while adoring, he observed Cola scratching away, but he did not know why. So he waited till Cola left, and went to the place behind the door and noticed a tile a little out of alinement. And he took his knife and levered it up, and saw the purse. Immediately he grabbed it, and replaced the tile just as it was before. He took the money home, with the firm intention never to show it to anyone.

Now it happened that before three days had passed, the blind man longed to know whether his hoard was secure. So he picked

his time, and visited the spot where he had hidden his treasure. When he lifted the tile and felt in vain for the purse he nearly swooned. But still he replaced the tile carefully and went home very sadly. Meditating how at one swoop he had lost the wealth accumulated over so long a time, he had one of those bright ideas that come often to the blind.

Next morning he called his nine-year-old son, and said: "Come, take me to the church." The boy prepared to obey. But before starting, the father took him into his room, and said: "Come here, my son. You will accompany me to church; and don't leave me. You will sit nearby at the portal, and you will watch carefully all the men and women who pass; and you will take note if anyone who passes looks at me more attentively than the others, and who laughs, or makes any gesture toward me. And remember well who it is. Can you do that?"

"Yes," said the boy.

After these instructions, the blind man and his son went to the church, and the beggar took his usual post. The boy, obedient to his father's orders, spent the whole morning on the watch. And he noticed that Juccio, passing by, fixed his gaze on the blind man and smiled. When the two returned home for lunch, as soon as they were indoors the father asked: "My son, did you see anything, according to my instructions?"

"Father, I saw just one who stared at you and laughed."

"And who was that?"

"I don't know his name, but I know well that he is a cheese-monger, and he has a shop near the Minorite Brothers."

Said the father: "Could you take me to his shop and tell me if you see him?"

The boy said he could. And delaying not a moment, the father said: "Take me there. And if you see him, tell me. And when I talk to him, you go aside and wait for me."

The boy guided his father to the cheese shop, and so informed him, and led him in. When the blind man heard the shopkeeper talk with the buyers, he recognized him as Juccio, whom he had

known before he was stricken blind. He said to Juccio that he wanted a little private talk with him. Juccio, though suspicious, took him into a back room, saying: "Cola, what good news?"

Said Cola: "Brother, I have come to you in trust and love. As you know, I lost my sight long since; and being in poverty with a large family, I have been forced to live on charity. And by God's grace and the kindness of you and other citizens, I have saved up two hundred florins. And of these florins I have a hundred available in a safe place, and the other hundred I have given to some relatives to keep for me; and I am to have them back in a week. Therefore, if you would see fit to take these two hundred florins and invest them as you please, to support me and my children, I should be very happy; because there is no one in this city whom I can trust more fully. And I don't want any papers signed; I want nothing to be said and nothing to be known. So I beg you most earnestly that, whatever use you make of the money, never repeat anything of what I have told you. For you realize that if it were known that I have this money, all the almsgiving would stop."

Juccio, hearing this and imagining that he could cast his net for another hundred florins, overwhelmed Cola with kind words and assurances of secrecy, and said that he must think it over, but for Cola to come back next day and he would give him his answer. The blind man left; and Juccio, as soon as he could manage, went back to the church with the purse, and replaced it beneath the tile from under which he had taken it. He had tumbled to the fact that the hundred florins which Cola claimed to have available were the same florins that he, Juccio, was now replacing under the tile, so that he wouldn't lose the other hundred. Cola, on his part, presumed that when Juccio said to his proposal, "I'll tell you tomorrow," it was clear that in order to get the second hundred Juccio would return the first hundred before giving an answer. So Cola went that same day to the church, and, taking precautions not to be observed, raised the tile and found the purse under it. He hid it on his person and replaced the tile, taking no great care about it. Then he went home and slept well.

Next morning he paid his call. Juccio, seeing him, ran to meet him, exclaiming: "Where are you going, my dear Cola?"

"I'm coming to see you."

They entered the private room, and Juccio said: "The great confidence you show me obliges me to do what you ask. Get hold of the two hundred florins. Within a week I will make an investment in salt meat and caciocavallo cheese, and I expect to make enough profit to pay you a good share."

"God bless you!" said Cola. "Now I'll go and fetch the hundred florins, and perhaps also the other lot, and I'll bring them to you. And afterwards do the best you can with them."

"Good-bye," said Juccio. "And come back soon, because I'm ready to make that investment. Messer Comes, the Count, is collecting a big body of troops for the Church, and it is expected that they will make their headquarters here; and the soldiers are very fond of salt meat and cheese. So go and get the money; I think I can turn a nice profit both for you and me."

Cola left, but not in the state of mind that Juccio supposed, for the blind man was now blinding him who could see.

Next day Cola, with a very gloomy face, paid his call on Juccio. Juccio, beaming, came to meet him, with "A very good day to you, Cola."

"I wish it were a good day, or even just an ordinary day."

"What do you mean by that?"

"It is a very bad day for me. I don't find my hundred florins where I put them. They've been stolen! And of my several relatives who were taking care of the other hundred for me, one says he hasn't got them, and some say worse. So I grieve to say, all I can give you is a handshake."

Said Juccio: "My cursèd bad luck! Where I thought I was going to make money I will lose a hundred florins or more! And the worst is that I have already made the deal! If the man who sold me the goods insists that the bargain go through, I don't know what to pay him with!"

Said Cola: "I'm sorry indeed for you, but I am much more sorry for myself. I'm in such a state that I can hardly endure it. I

will have to start all over making a new capital. But if God grants that I ever possess anything again, I won't put it in any hiding-place or entrust or lend it to anyone, even were he my father!"

When Juccio heard this, he wondered if he might not regain the hundred that seemed to have been lost. Said he: "Those hundred florins your relatives have—if you could get them back and give them to me, I would do my best to raise the other hundred, so we could close the salt-meat deal. And if this could be managed, you might find yourself before long with two hundred in your pocket."

"My dear Juccio," said the blind man, "if I wanted to come into the open about the hundred florins in my relatives' hands, I would go to law, and I would win. But I don't want to reveal this, because I would lose all my alms, as you must know. Therefore I write them off as lost, unless God inspires my kin to return the money. So you can't hope for anything from me, since Fortune has thus disposed. All that remains to me is to recognize your good will and your desire to enrich me. I will pretend to myself that I have received the money, that I have in pocket two hundred florins, just as if you had turned it over. And after all, you are no worse off than before. One thing I will do. I will have a friend of mine cast a spell, to see if by chance he can discover the thief. And if it should turn out properly, I'll be seeing you again. Good-bye; I don't want to delay a moment."

Said Juccio: "Go ahead. Do what you can to get your money back. And if you find out and need anything, you know where I live. Cheer up as much as possible; and good-bye."

Thus finished the investment in salt meat and cheese. And the blind man succeeded in doubling his store, to his great comfort. He would say: "By Santa Lucia, Juccio was blinder than I!" And that was true enough, for he had taken Juccio on his hook, using a hundred florins for bait.

The Reeve's Tale
by Geoffrey Chaucer

Geoffrey Chaucer (about 1340 to 1400) certainly needs no
introduction, and will get none. This story, told by the Reeve
(an overseer, or supervisor), is one of the Canterbury Tales.
It is a variation on a French *fabliau*. This prose modernization
is by Morris Bishop. It is based chiefly on the Globe Edition,
edited by Alfred W. Pollard, and first published by Mac-
millan, London, in 1898.

AT TRUMPINGTON, not far from Cambridge, there runs
a brook, with a bridge over it. By this brook stands a mill;
and there lived for many a day a miller, proud and gay as a pea-
cock. He could pipe, and fish, mend nets, make cups, wrestle, and
shoot. He wore a long dirk at his belt, and flaunted a sharp sword,
and in his pouch he carried a dainty dagger. "Touch me not!"
proclaimed his bearing. He had even a little Sheffield whittling-
knife in his hose. His face was round, his nose was pug, his skull
bare as an ape's. He was the bully of the markets. No one dared
lay a hand on him, or he would have sworn instant vengeance. He
was also a thief of corn and meal, a trickster always ready to steal.
His name was Simpkin, commonly called High-and-Mighty
Simpkin.

He had a wife of gentle blood. Her father was the village
parson; he had dowered her with many brass utensils to tempt
Simpkin to the match. She had been brought up in a nunnery; for
as Simpkin was wont to say, he would have no wife save one
gently bred and a maid, to preserve his estate and yeoman's rank.
She was as proud and pert as a magpie. It was a fair sight to see
the two of them. On holy days he would go before her, with his
tippet about his head; and she followed after in a red gown, to
match his hose. No man dared address her otherwise than as

"Madame"; and no one walking by the way dared jest or trifle with her, lest he be slain by Simpkin's dirk, knife, or bodkin. For jealous folk are ever dangerous; at least they make their wives behave. And though, as a priest's offspring, her reputation was somewhat besmirched, she was as disagreeable as ditch-water, and full of scorn and disdain. She thought that ladies should defer to her, because of her family and her convent education.

The two had a daughter, twenty years of age; and they had no more progeny except a baby a half year old, a lusty lad. The girl was stout and sturdy, with snub nose and glassy gray eyes, and broad buttocks and round, high breasts. But to do her justice, her hair was very lovely.

Her parson grandfather, finding her fair, proposed to make her heir to his buildings and beasts. He had so far vetoed her marriage; he wanted her to make a great match, entering into some ancient family, for the wealth of Holy Church should be spent on those of churchly lineage. Therefore he would honor his own holy blood, even though he should devour Holy Church's wealth.

This miller assuredly took a great toll of all the wheat and malt of the region. He had as one of his clients a great college, called the Cambridge Soler-Hall,* which had its grain and malt ground by the miller. And it happened once that the college steward fell ill; in fact, it was feared he might die. And therefore the miller stole grain and meal a hundred times more than before. Previously he had stolen only courteously, but now he was a thief outrageously. Thereat the Warden grumbled and scolded, but the miller cared no whit. He shouted to heaven, swearing to his honesty.

Now there were two young students living in this Hall. They were an unruly and frolicsome pair. And for the fun of it they asked the Warden to give them leave for a brief absence, to go to the mill and watch the grinding of their grain. They boldly offered to forfeit their necks that the miller would not steal half a

* Soler-Hall: Clare College and King's strive for the honor of identification with it.—Ed.

peck, by sleight or force. And at last the Warden gave them leave. One was named John, the other Alan. They both came from a town named Strother, far in the north, I cannot say exactly where.*

This Alan made ready his gear, and put the sack of wheat on the horse. And John joined him, each carrying sword and buckler. John knew the way; he needed no guide. At the mill he set down the wheat-sack, and Alan called the miller: "All hail, Simon! I' faith, how does your fair daughter and your wife?"

"Welcome, Alan, by my life!" quoth Simpkin. "And John also. How now? What do you here?"

"Simon," quoth John, "by God, if needs must, then it must be. If a man have no lackey, he must serve himself, or else he is a fool; so the clerks say. Our steward, I think he won't last long—all the teeth in his head are loose. And therefore I have come, with Alan, to grind our corn and bring it home again. I pray you, speed us hence, as well as you may."

"It shall be done," said Simpkin, "by my faith. And what will you be doing while the work goes forward?"

"By God, I'll stand right by the hopper," said John, "and see how the corn goes in. For by my father's kin, I have never seen how the hopper wags to and fro."

"And will you so, John?" said Alan. "Then I shall stand below, by my crown, and see how the flour falls down into the trough. That shall be my sport; for John, i' faith, I am no more a miller than you."

The miller smiled at their simplicity, and thought: "They are doing this just as a trick. They think no one can fool them. But by my thrift, I'll pull the wool over their eyes, for all the tricks in their philosophy! The more sly shifts they try, the more will I steal when the time comes! Instead of flour, I'll give them bran. 'The greatest clerks are not the wisest men,' as the mare said to the wolf; and I count all their art not worth a straw."

* In fact, in the West Riding of Yorkshire, where their dialect, as rendered by Chaucer, persists.—Ed.

When he saw his chance, he slipped out the door, and looked up and down till he saw the students' horse, tied behind the mill under an arbor. He stepped up to the horse and pulled off his bridle. And the horse, when loosed, set off toward the fen, where the wild mares run free, whinnying "we-hee!" through thick and thin.

The miller, without a word, finished his task, and joked with the students, till the corn was fairly ground. And when the flour was sacked and tied, John goes out and finds his horse is gone. He began to cry: "Haro!" and "Wellaway! Our horse is lost, Alan, by God's bones, look lively, come out, man, at once! Alas, our Warden has lost his palfrey!" And Alan abandoned all, both flour and corn; his supervision was all forgotten. "What! Which way has he gone?" he began to cry.

The wife came running in, saying: "Alas! Your horse is off to the fen to the wild mares, as fast as he can go! A curse on the fool who tied him so, who should have fastened him properly!"

"Alas," quoth John, "Alan, by Christ's pains, put down your sword, as I will do mine. I am as nimble as a deer, God knows. By God's heart he shan't escape us both. Why didn't you put the nag in the barn? Bad cess to you, Alan, you're a fool!"

The simple students, Alan and John, ran fast toward the fen. And when the miller saw that they had gone he took half a bushel of their flour and bade his wife knead it into a cake. He said: "I think these clerks were well scared! But a miller can trim a clerk's beard, for all his art! Now let them go their way. Look at them run! Yes, let the children play. They won't catch him easily, by my crown!"

The simple clerks ran up and down, shouting: "Hold, hold! Stand, stand! Whoa! Watch out behind! You whistle to him, and I'll block his retreat!" But in spite of all they could not capture their steed, so fast he ran, until nightfall, when they caught him in a ditch. Weary and wet, like cattle in the rain, returned simple John, and Alan with him.

"Alas the day that I was born!" said John. "Now everyone will

mock and laugh at us. Our corn is stolen; men will call us fools, the Warden and our fellow-students and the miller most of all! Ah, wellaway!" Thus he grieved on the way to the mill, leading his charger.

They found the miller sitting by the fire. It was night, and they could go no farther. The boys begged the miller for a night's lodging, and they would pay their penny. Said the miller: "If there be any room, such as it may be, you shall have your share. My house is small, but you are great scholars; by argument you can turn twenty feet into a mile. Let me see now if these quarters will suffice, or see if you can enlarge them by your book-learning!"

"Now, Simon," said John, "by Saint Cuthbert, you're always a joker; you give us a fair answer. I have heard that a man has two choices: to take things as they come, or bring his solution with him. But especially, dear host, I pray you to get us some meat and drink; make us good cheer, and we will truly pay our scot. You can't lure a hawk with an empty hand; so here is our silver."

The miller sent his daughter into the village for ale and bread, and roasted a goose, and tied the students' horse so that he could not get loose. And in his own chamber he set up a bed well spread with sheets and coverlets, no more than ten or twelve feet from his own. His daughter had a bed of her own near by, in the same room. There was no alternative—no other sleeping quarters in the house. So they supped and talked cheerily, and drank strong ale, and about midnight went to rest.

Well had the miller varnished his head; his face turns pale, not red, with drink. He hiccoughs and talks through his nose, as if he were hoarse with a bad cold. So he goes to bed, his wife beside him. She was as light and frisky as a jay; she had wet her whistle to good purpose. The cradle was set at the bed's foot, so that the babe could be rocked and nursed. And when the jug was drained dry, the daughter went anon to bed, and so did Alan and John; they needed no sleeping-potion. The miller had so soundly downed his ale that he snorted like a horse; nor did he put any

muffler on his rear. His wife joined in the chorus; one could hear her snoring two furlongs off. And the girl snored too, *par compagnie.*

Alan the clerk, hearing this melody, poked John, and said: "Are you asleep? Did you ever hear such music? What an evening compline they sing! May wildfire consume them! Who ever heard such a strange symphony? This ending puts the lid on it; I shan't get a wink of sleep tonight. But no matter; all shall be for the best. For as I hope to thrive, I will lay that girl, if I can. For law accords us some compensation; you see, John, there is a law prescribing that if a man is injured in one point, he may recoup himself in another. Our corn is stolen, to be frank. There's no denying that. And we have had a very bad day of it. And since I see no amends coming, I shall establish some easement of my losses. By God's soul, I'll have nothing less!"

John answered: "Alan, be careful! The miller is a dangerous man, and if he should wake he might do us an injury." Said Alan: "I don't care a damn for him!" And up he rose, and crept in by the girl. She lay on her back, fast asleep, until he was beside her. Before she could realize what was happening, it was too late for her to cry out; and to put it briefly, the two were made one. Now play, Alan! I would speak of John.

John lay still while a man might go a furlong or two; and how he suffered! "Alas," he muttered, "this is a wicked jest! This makes a monkey of me! My comrade gets some return for his misfortunes; he is holding tight the miller's daughter. He has taken his chance, and won; and I lie in my bed like a sack of chaff! And when this tale is told, I shall look a fool, a milksop. I shall get up, and risk it! 'No pluck, no luck,' says the proverb." Then up he rose and went softly to the cradle, picked it up, and transported it to the foot of his own bed.

Soon after this the wife stopped snoring, awoke, and went out to piss. Returning, she missed the cradle, groped here and there, but found it not. "Alas!" she said, "I had almost gone astray. I had almost gone to the students' bed! Bless me, that would have been a bad business!"

She felt around until she touched the cradle, groped further and found the bed, without suspicion, for the cradle stood by it. She crept confidently in beside the clerk and lay still, to catch a little sleep. But John was up and at her, laying on with a will. It was long since she had had so merry a time. Hard and deep he pricked, as if he were mad.

And so the students took their pleasure until the third cock crowed. Dawn was near; Alan grew weary, for he had labored well all night. He said: "Farewell, Malin, my dear. The day is at hand; I may linger no more. But always, wherever I may go, I am your devoted clerk, as I may come to bliss."

"My dear lover," said she, "go, farewell. But before you leave, I will tell you something. When you return home by way of the mill, at the entry of the back door you will find a half-bushel cake, made of your own flour, which I helped my father to steal. Dear lover, God save and keep you!" With that she almost began to weep.

Alan arose, and thought: "Before dawn I will creep in by my comrade." He felt the cradle with his hand. "By God," he thought, "I have gone wrong! My head is dizzy with my night's labors; no wonder I lose my way. I know well by the cradle that I have gone astray. Here lies the miller by his wife." So with a curse he goes to the miller's bed. He thought he was rejoining friend John, but he crept in by the miller, pinched his neck, and said softly; "Wake up, John, you pig-head, by Christ's soul. Listen to a noble story. For by Saint James, I have three times taken the miller's daughter flat on her back, while you, you coward, have been lying there trembling!"

"Have you so, false scoundrel!" cried the miller. "False traitor! False clerk! By God's dignity, you shall die! Who dares to make so bold as to disgrace my daughter, come of such high lineage?" He took Alan by the Adam's apple, choked him grievously, and with his fist smote him on the nose, breaking his nose and mouth. Down ran a bloody stream; they wallowed on the floor like two pigs in a poke. Up they got, and down they went again; until the miller tripped on a floor-tile and fell down backward on his wife,

who knew nothing of all this silly battle, for she had fallen asleep with John the clerk, who had lain awake all night. At the fall she started up, crying: "Help, holy cross of Bromeholm! *In manus tuas!* Lord, to thee I call! Wake up, Simon, the fiend has attacked us! My heart is broken, help, I am undone! One is on my belly, one on my head! Help, Simpkin! These false clerks are fighting!"

John started up as fast as he could, and felt along the wall, looking for some weapon. She sprang up also, and knowing the disposition better than John, she promptly found a staff. And by a glimmer of light (for the moon shone in at a gap) she saw the two combatants. But she could not tell who was who; and seeing something white presumed it was the student's nightcap. She drew near, and thinking that she would hit Alan squarely, smote the miller on his bare skull. Down he goes, crying: "Haro! I die!"

The students beat him well and let him lie. They make ready, take their horse and their flour, and go their way. At the mill they take also their cake, well baked with half a bushel of their flour.

Thus was the proud miller well beaten. He got no fee for grinding the wheat, and paid for Alan's and John's supper, and got only a beating. His wife was laid, his daughter too. Lo, how a cheating miller is rewarded! Well goes the proverb: "He that doeth evil can expect no good; the cheater shall himself be cheated."

And may God, who sits high in majesty, save all this company, great and small!